HOLLOW

WHO PUT BELLA IN THE WYCH-ELM?

BARRY N RAINSFORD

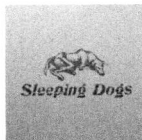

Sleeping Dogs

Though based on the discovery of the skeleton in a tree in Hagley wood in spring of 1943, this book is a work of fiction. Despite access to the police files of the enquiry, for the most part names, characters, places, and incidents are products of the author's imagination or have been used fictitiously. The actions and motives of historic individuals presented in the story are fictitious. Beyond those individuals, resemblance to actual persons, living or dead, events or locales is entirely coincidental.

Published by *Sleeping Dogs*

Paperback ISBN: 978-1-0686335-2-2

e-Book ISBN:978-1-0686335-3-9

Cover design Spiffing Publishing Ltd.

For my Family

and for Bella, whoever she may be

FOREWORD
WHO PUT BELLA IN THE WYCH-ELM?

The following is a fictional story based on real events. The actions and personalities of characters in this novel are in no way meant to represent the actions, motives, or personal qualities of those real-life characters who appear in it.

My novel is based on the true story of what has come to be known as the 1943 Hagley Wood murder. The case, though closed, remains unsolved. Since 2009, the original police and pathology files have been stored in the Worcester Hive archive and I am grateful to its staff for the access they provided to this material during my research.

The work is situated in the values and ideas of its era. Values and ideas that today are seen to be what they always were - prejudiced and culturally located. However, I find it necessary to present them as they were at that time and as they are documented in the interviews and police reports. Without this, it is impossible for modern readers to fully understand the issues that beset the considerable efforts made by investigators to solve this horrific murder or to immerse oneself into the period.

HOLLOW

WINTER 1941

She plunges into darkness; arms flailing, legs kicking.

Helpless.

Throat aflame, heart racing to its last beat.

She gulps for air, jaw slack.

A high-pitched ringing fills her ears. Her temples throb, separating her from everything but the guttural bark from her own throat, her compressed larynx now but a voiceless reed.

Legs twitch, arms spasm. Her body falls, trapping her spirit as she breathes her last. There will be no more. Soon she will black out, spin into the endless void that rises to claim her.

She slumps like a puppet, feels the cold earth on her knees. Only the scarf, tight around her neck, holds her from the ground. The edge of her vision darkens; a purple-tinged blackness spirals towards its centre.

She summons what is left of her.

She finds him. Holds him with her gaze, knows he cannot look away. They are bound, entwined as lovers might be.

She curses him.

He knows. Even without hearing her words. She sees the fear awaken in his eyes.

She has power. It cannot be escaped. He knows this. It is why he has to end her.

She will come for him. He knows this too. She will reach out from the grave and reel him to her.

There will be a reckoning.

1

18TH APRIL, 1943: MORNING

It is not how he imagined.

He'd buried bodies before. Too many. Shallow graves torn from the hard earth. Then there had been no shovels - sticks, jagged stones, and his own bare hands had sufficed. And always driven by urgency. Hiding remains in the earth before the rot set in. The stench. Wild dogs and wolves. The creatures that scurry across the white clay of the Basque country. Creatures seeking whatever flesh it might lay teeth and claws upon.

If it is possible to get used to such things, then he's an expert. An old hand.

But here, it is not how he imagined.

No sense of urgency, no pressing tension, no sense of work to be done. No one hurries. No one moves with swiftness or the certainty of action he feels such matters require. No-one directing. No-one anxious for tasks to be completed. No-one concerned with chasing what was surely their objective: the securing of the dead body of the woman found in the tree.

What strikes DC Alec Porter as he stands at the edge of the clearing is the ordinariness of it all. The huddled groups. Men, shirt-sleeved, standing in clumps. The murmuring of voices. They could just as easily be stood outside the saloon bar of the village pub savouring a spring evening of drinking. Enjoying the warmth. Talk of the football, the cricket. Bradman's chances at the Oval that coming summer.

He has to admit to finding himself disappointed, expecting something more...visceral.

But he is here.

Two years filling in forms, taking statements, recording the minutiae of crime. His biggest investigation is over a year ago: a break-in at a local factory and the theft of several bales of parachute silk. Thus far, duties as a Detective Constable in the Bromsgrove area have been an unending diet of bicycle thefts and poaching.

This is different. A corpse. A victim. A murder.

He gazes at the open expanse of scrub and tufted grass that extends some thirty yards or so towards a large elm tree, its branches like horns.

Woods. A clearing.

He pauses, feels his palms grow steadily sweaty. His mind starts a check list of sensations. Notes a sudden increase in heart rate, pulse quickening. His breathing shifts, each intake shallower than the one before. He tries breathing deeply, but finds he can't. His stomach churns - a sensation like the sudden fall when traversing a humped back bridge at speed. Things are changing, and not in a good way - the sense of a cold hand grasping his heart, his groin. A growing panic. The realisation he has to concentrate harder on each breath.

He senses beads of sweat forming under his collar, goose pimples on his arms. His legs quiver, muscles tensing uncontrollably. Somewhere in the background is a sound, a distant buzzing, like flies...No, angrier, like wasps. Some part of him detecting it...locking onto it before he's actually heard it. Before he's actually designated what it is.

Engines.

Woods. Trees. A clearing.

His mind flicks the images. A quickening slideshow; *hot skies; high sun; dark shadows.*

The sound forms into consciousness, the unmistakable hum of approaching aircraft. His stomach lurches, ice-cold. The taste of metal fills his mouth as he feels the sudden desire to drop and flatten himself against the earth.

The ground swims. He feels his legs shuddering, bladder tightening.

The sound of the engines is closer now, a sound resolving to a high-pitched whine. Primeval. A sound hard-wired into his brain. *The mind never forgets*, they'd told him. The doctors. *Shell shock. The stukas. The sound of fighter-bomber engines under stress. The sound of fighter bombers about to attack.*

He gazes ahead. A world hazy, greying out, fading, shapes harder to define. He screws his hands into balls, before raising his now shaking arms upwards, hands rubbing at eyes, desperate to clear them, focus his mind. He screws them closed. *Focus.*

He lowers his arms, stomach churning. Holds shaking hands in front of his crotch, fearful his bladder is about to empty itself.

'Porter! Porter!'

His name. Opening his eyes, he looks up; vision still blurred. An outline of grey, the rain-coated shape of Detective Inspector Dafydd Williams beckoning him. 'Over here,' Williams calls.

With an effort of will, Porter moves his hands to his side, clenched fists digging nails into his palms.

Take control.

The doctors had warned him of this. The nightmares. The visions. The trauma. Your physical wounds heal, but your mind has scars too. They'd given him coping strategies. A check list helping him sift fact from fiction, real from imagined. Real. Not real. Real Life or Nightmare. Find the difference. See what's real. This was in his head, a panic triggered by the sound of the aircraft. *It was not real; this was not an attack. He was home. Worcestershire countryside.*

3

'Come on, man. What are you waiting for?' William's voice calls through the mist of grey.

Closing his eyes, holding his breath and pushing back the visions, Porter takes three steps forward. The thrumming of the aircraft engines overhead shudders the ground, drowning out the voices screaming in his mind. *He could do this! He could-*

A hand grabs his shoulder, spinning him round. 'Look out, sir!'

Only the firmness of the grip halts the urge to dive to the sanctity of the ground.

Turning, wrenching at the hand clasping his shoulder, he opens his eyes. The arm that swims into focus, holding him upright, is wrapped in the uniform of a Special Constable. With his free hand, the officer at the end of the arm points to the ground. 'Nearly a nasty fall there, sir. Rabbit holes everywhere.'

Porter looks down, sees the dark hole of a burrow hidden among the tufts.

'Did my own ankle twice already, sir,' the elderly Special says, releasing his hold. 'Pesky buggers.'

'What? Yes. Erhm… thanks,' Porter hears his voice reply. Looking up, he watches the planes pass over, the noise of their engines fading. *Hurricanes. RAF fighter-bombers. Ours.*

Williams approaches, gazing upwards. A hand shades his eyes, lips muttering something about *the bloody row.*

Shifting his feet, Porter finds stable ground. He breathes deep. Unclenches fists and locks knees, the latter an action pushing him upright. Williams gestures towards the rapidly disappearing Hurricanes. 'Glad they're ours. Must put the fear of God into Jerry, hearing that lot coming at you!'

'Yes, sir,' Porter's voice agrees.

Williams nods, flicking his head in the direction of the Special who'd grabbed Porter. 'You've met Special Constable Willetts, then. It was his boy found the body, at least him and his mates. Bit of poaching, eh, Bert?'

'Wouldn't know about that, sir,' Willetts answers.

4

'Don't worry, Bert. Secret's safe with me, eh?' Williams confides, tapping the side of his nose. Not for the first time, Porter notices how pale his DI's hands are. His face too. Like parchment. He'd heard there was an illness, a sickness. No-one seemed to know the details, other than it had been sufficient to have retired him in the early thirties only for the war to have made his recall essential. Manpower. Even in growing warmth of Spring the elderly DI seems cold, preferring his ever-present raincoat to a jacket. The off-white trench coat covers him almost neck to toe, belted loosely around his body it dwarfs him.

Williams turns, breaking Porter's train of thought. 'Anyroad, young Willetts and the other boys were out here yesterday afternoon. One of them climbed the tree and found her.' The Brummie patois of *'anyroad'* sounds strained amid the DI's pronounced Welsh accent. The tone is some distance from the singsong of the valleys, more guttural, the urban south. Cardiff, Porter thinks he'd once heard. Whatever the origin, it was harsh on the ear.

'Her?' Porter asks.

'The dead woman. Least, seems it's a woman. Not much left, you see. A few strips of what looks like silk on the skeleton. Most likely the remains of a dress or blouse. We'll know better once we get it - *her* - out.'

'A skeleton?'

'Been there for years by the look of her.'

Porter looks around the clearing, understanding the lack of urgency. A murder, maybe. But not a good one. 'Is the police doctor here?' he asks.

'What, at this time of day?' Williams shakes his head, guffawing. 'Hardly, boy. DS James and I have been waiting around most of the morning as it is. Far as we can see, there's no need for either of us to be here, let alone both of us. Headquarters, though. Procedure.' He kicks the turf with the tip of a boot. 'All medical staff are needed at the hospitals, what with the raid the other night. Anyroad, what's a doctor going to do here?' He shrugs, though whether at the vagaries of procedure or the sadness of the victim's internment Porter can't guess. 'Willetts here alerted the local station, and their man came out first thing. Their bobby confirmed what the boy had told them. His sergeant sent for CID.' He shrugs once more, cheeks puffing out at the memory. 'And a right bloody game we had getting up there, I can tell you!' He flicks a hand in the direction of the tree, the ladder pushed against its trunk. At the same time, he begins using his other hand to brush at dust and shards of tree bark that he suddenly recalls remain stuck to the front of his raincoat. His effort merely swirls the debris, creates the image of a blue-grey cloud, dark at its centre, paler at the edge. It appears bruise-like against the cream of his trench coat. 'Anyroad, we've had a poke about whilst we've been waiting,' he says with finality, rubbing his hands together and wrinkling his mouth in annoyance at the stain.

'Nothing to identify her?' Porter asks.

'Not after all this time.'

'No idea who she might be?'

Williams looking up, scoffs. 'There's the worst of it. Given where we are... Well, she's more than likely a bloody gypsy, isn't she? It's a favourite place of theirs, you see. They camp here at various times of the year, don't they, Albert?'

Willetts nods.

'The tree's special to them, see. A Wych-elm. Magical apparently.' Williams guffaws once more. 'Scared the bejesus out those boys, I bet, finding her stuffed in there. What with all the stories. The legends and the like.'

'Legends?' Porter asks, puzzled.

'Evil spells, curses... that sort of stuff.'

Porter considers what he's told. 'So, she might be a Romany.'

'Who knows? But given the silk remnants...Oh, and these-,' the DI pushes a finger towards his own mouth. He tugs at his bottom lip, lowering it to tap a nicotine-stained finger against the bottom row of yellowed teeth. He leans into Porter '-Bloody awful, see. All jagged and nasty.'

'Might make her easier to trace,' Porter responds. 'Dental records.'

Williams allows his lip to flop back into place. 'You'd think so.' He sighs in contemplation of the point before shrugging it off. 'Anyroad, we've got you here, DC Porter because…well…to be honest, I don't intend spending the next few weeks chasing round after bloody gypsies…or searching for dental records and the like.' He stands back, taking a pipe from his coat pocket. He slides a finger along the stem, examining the bowl. 'Mysterious death or not, no matter what the papers might say tonight, this whole thing looks pretty straightforward to me.' He slips a finger inside the pipe's bowl, rubbing at the residue. 'So, I'm delegating this to you, DC Porter. It's most likely a bit of a paper chase, but on the plus side, it'll give you something to get your teeth into, bright lad like yourself.'

He pauses, finger finding an unyielding burr of ash that requires harder rubbing to remove, a spot demanding a little more of his attention. 'What you do is…You get yourself over to records, missing persons and the like - though god knows how far you'll have to go back. Years by the look of her. Maybe then you should contact the local council, see if you can track down who's been camping here the past few years. Frankly, I doubt you'll get much.' He upends the bowl, finger tapping hard against its side, dumping the remnants of ash to the floor. 'If she's a *gypo*, she'll have been put in that tree for good reason - though none we could fathom, of course. One of their blooming weird practices no doubt. And, even if you can find them, that lot will tell you next to nothing about who or why. Close ranks, you see. Tight knit and tight-lipped. Can't trust a bloody thing they tell you at the best of times. Asking about dead gypsies in trees …?' He jabs the stem of the pipe towards Porter. 'Still, be good for you. A young DC like yourself. A step up. Better than chasing stolen bicycles across the county, eh?'

'Yes, sir.' Porter nods. It was true. Skeleton or not.

Williams pats him on the arm, letting his hand rest there a moment. 'Good man. Any problems you talk with Detective Sergeant James over there.' He inclines his head towards the elm where DS James is busy directing the erection of a second ladder against the tree, its branches thwarting the attempt of two workmen in finding secure placement.

Williams turns back to Porter, leans close once more, dropping his voice to a fatherly murmur. To Porter's ears the intended intimacy only lends greater discord to the guttural tone. 'No expectations, Porter, lad. Don't worry if you can't come up with anything. Just give it a go. You write it up nicely for us. Keep Detective Superintendent Knight over at headquarters happy. Put that college education of yours to use.' He drops his arm. 'Don't worry about the press. I'll have a word with the local rag. Give them the bones of it.' He turns to leave, stopping midway, his expression breaking into a smirk of self-satisfaction. 'Bones of it. Get it?' He shakes his head before walking off, chuckling to himself.

'What do you think, Constable?' Porter asks.

'Well, he's an ass isn't he, sir.' Willetts responds.

'I meant the body.'

'Oh…sorry, sir … It's just … I mean …'

Porter smiles. 'Don't worry. He is something of an ass, isn't he?'

Willetts's face sinks in relief. 'Thank you, sir.'

'But an ass who's given us a job to do.'

'Us, sir?'

'Us.' Porter nods. 'Stands to reason that I'll need a man like yourself. Someone with decent local knowledge. That's of course if you want it. Probably not that much of a posting but I dare say it's a bit of a change from all the other stuff for yourself too.'

'Yes sir. Thank you, sir.'

Feeling more than a little uncomfortable, Porter holds up a hand. The Special's' use of *sir* to someone of his DC rank is unnecessary, but clearly a mannerism. It's something of a throwback, old school and old ideas. Deferential. He ponders on making a point of it, but stops short. There are things people still cling to. Reminders of who they once were, the life they had, what they hold close. Amidst his own uncertainties, who was he to question such matters. 'Don't thank me yet, Willetts. We might be biting off more than we can chew. There's a reason the Inspector wants rid of this.'

'The gypsies?'

'The gypsies.' Porter grimaces. 'Plus, it's hardly pressing, is it?'

A step up from chasing stolen bicycles, Williams had said. But not much.

'*Gypos*,' Willetts mutters before spitting, rubbing the yellow-white phlegm into the grass with the toe of a highly polished boot.

The Special was a tall man. Lean rather than muscular. His face had a gauntness, the greyness of a life spent in hard physical work. A factory. A production line. Porter notes the pronounced limp, one leg permanently stiff. *The Great War. Shrapnel.* He knew all about the effect of a wound like that. Not just on the body. The months of recuperation. The sense of your life changing in ways you'd never thought. He knew little of the man but enough of the type, the circumstance, to guess he'd been called into service as a Special when the able bodied constables had all been conscripted. Like Porter himself, he carried within him the sense of being an imposter. The left over bit of a jigsaw that didn't fit.

Porter hears his name being called, this time with a Brummie twang. Turning in the direction of the tree, he watches DS Harry James approach. From a few paces away the overweight DS blows out his cheeks as herald of his arrival. 'Porter. DI Williams gave you the news then?'

'My assignment to the case, sir?' Porter asks.

'The case. Yes, of course the case.' The flattened vowels of his Brummie accent ooze disapproval. Physically, he reminds Porter of a stump. Despite three years of rationing, his body remained as wide as it was tall, thick neck disappearing into a worn collar. A collar whose only purpose appears to be in acting as the marker of where body ends and chin began. James takes a handkerchief from a pocket, and mops his brow, the fabric as grey and worn as his collar. 'Assignment.' James rolls the world around his mouth, tasting it. 'Is that the same as *given*?' he asks.

'Yes, Sergeant.'

James smiles. 'Simple word, *given*. Not like your *assignment*. But a good word all the same. You know, to the point.'

'Sir.'

James thrusts the handkerchief back into the pocket, tutting. 'So how do you plan to proceed, *Detective*?'

'Examine the victim,' Porter offers.

'And what would you be hoping to find by doing that?'

'Clues.'

'Clues?'

'Evidence.'

'I know what a clue is. I know it's evidence. It's a skeleton. It's been in there years. What sort of evidence?'

'I won't know till I've had a look, Sergeant. Maybe I should get an expert to help.'

'An *expert*? What? A lumberjack?'

'A doctor. Forensics.'

The acting DS turns to Willetts, eyes widening in mock incredulity. Willetts's face is impassive.

'Like in America,' Porter continues. 'The FBI. They use specialised doctors who can tell them things about a corpse. How they died. When they died. The means of their death.'

James, returning his attention to Porter, holds up a hand. 'I know what forensics is. The FBI, eh? And just where would you be finding one of these *forensic* doctors over here?'

'There's a professor at Birmingham University. Chap called Webster. He started a few months ago. It's work financed by the Home Office.'

James puffs out his chest. 'And how would you know all of this?'

'I read about it.'

'Oh, you *read about it*.' He looks once more at Willetts, seeking shared scepticism. The Special's face remains inscrutable.

'Yes. In a magazine,' Porter responds. He stands waiting for the sarcastic response. The set text of James's scathing commentary on DC Alec Porter and his *reading* had become a constant theme of his evaluation of Porter. He knew James thought him an upstart. A too clever a young man with an education. He knew James as someone who took satisfaction in beating down a subordinate, especially one who in James's eyes thought themselves smarter than the rest of the force. Porter didn't blame him entirely. Like himself, he'd been left to oversee a pointless investigation whilst the real war is fought elsewhere.

The rebuke doesn't come. James already seeming to have tired of the conversation. Instead he settles for a simple homily, one accompanied by a contemptuous wave of his hand. 'Look, frankly, I don't care who you get in. Could be Doctor *bloody* Frankenstein for all I care. Just find out how she died, when it happened, who she is. Was.'

'Yes, Sergeant.'

'And get it done quickly. Couple of days tops, and then I want that report on my desk.'

'Sergeant.'

Satisfied, James inflates his cheeks and stomps away.

'Don't say it,' Porter says, sensing Willetts is poised to comment on the DS and their exchange. Willetts looks to the ground, suppressing a smile. Porter turns back to the scene, tired eyes surveying the clearing. The crime scene. *His* crime scene. 'What do you think?'

'Clues seems a good place to start, sir.'

Porter smiles. 'Dumb, eh?'

Willetts looks up, raising an eyebrow. 'Dumb or not, it's true, isn't it, sir? I mean, we need some sort of clue as to who she was, where she came from, before we can even begin to think about how she got here. I mean, a *tree*? It's not right, is it? Not *normal*.'

Porter shifts his gaze to the elm.

The council workers had jammed a second ladder into the tangle of branches. They stand to the side, seemingly debating how to extract the body. Next to them, a uniformed constable, hands on hips, oversees proceedings. Two other officers stand close by, one of them yawning and stretching out his arms. Further on, the ambulance crew sit with their backs against a tree. Two women, eyes closed, watery sunlight filtering through branches to lie across their faces as they doze. Everyone worked two shifts. A day job, and then as ARP wardens or bomb spotters at night. If it wasn't that, then it was clearing rubble from the raids. Searching for the missing. Exhuming the dead.

'If you don't mind me asking, sir. Who's this professor you mentioned?' Willetts asks.

Porter looks back to Willetts. 'He's setting up what he calls a pathology laboratory. He's got an office down by the Victoria Law Courts in Birmingham.'

'And he'll do what, sir?'

'Examine the scene. Look at the body. Examine the surroundings. See if there's anything that might explain who she was or how she got here.'

'That might not be so easy,' Willets comments.

Porter agrees. That day alone at least a dozen people would have trampled through the scene. And that was after the boys who'd stumbled across the gruesome find. What had they disturbed? What clues had been lost or spoiled since then?

And, of course, the body looked to have been lodged in the tree for some time - maybe years. In between it being stuffed in there and its discovery, how many others would have visited the site unwittingly destroying evidence? At least the fact that she'd lain undiscovered for so long indicated that no one had been in the tree itself.

Preserving what remained until Webster could be summoned was his priority.

He looks around. DI Williams is with the local reporters at the edge of the pathway. DS James is standing near him, chatting with a photographer. Porter watches James detach himself and sidle up to his superior, no doubt anxious to be included in the story.

'Albert,' Porter calls.

'Sir?'

He points towards where Williams and James stood. 'When he's finished with DI Williams, get that photographer over there, would you?'

'Sir.' Willetts set off, walking over to the man in the blue suit, waving an arm as he nears. The photographer is busy screwing a bulb into the flash-pan of his camera.

Clues. Evidence. He'd read the articles during his time in Spain - American *True Crime* magazines that some of the Yanks brought over with them. The FBI was using new technology to solve crimes and find criminals. Short of reading material, he'd devoured the magazines, reading most of the articles again and again.

Willetts returns with the photographer - early twenties, thin, pale as a ghost, wheezy of breath. *Tuberculosis. A2: Unfit for duty.*

'I want you to take some pictures.'

'Righto. Where do you want to stand?' The young man whips up his camera and angles it in front of his face. 'By the tree would be good.'

'Not of me. Of the scene.'

The photographer lowers the camera to his waist. 'The scene? Like a postcard?'

'No. Well, yes. One or two long shots. But lots of close-ups. The tree. The branches. The corpse.'

The photographer nods towards the ladders. 'Up there?'

'Yes. Is that a problem?'

'Well, tricky…But, nah, I can get you those.'

'Good. I want lots. Have you seen those *True-Crime* magazines?' The photographer nods. 'Then like those. As many as you can of everything around here, especially what's in the tree.'

The photographer picks up his camera-bag and rucksack. 'Be fun.'

'It's a crime scene, son,' Willetts states. 'Someone died.'

'Interesting, I mean,' the boy says sheepishly.

'Get it done. Get the pictures to the station as soon as you can,' Porter tells him.

The young man walks over to the council workers, both now busy sawing off the outer limbs of the elm in their efforts to better fix the ladders in place and extract the body.

'Albert, you'd better get over there as well. Tell them to leave her where she is. And the branches, too. I'll contact Webster, see if I can get him to come out here.'

Willetts hesitates. 'Sir, I hope you don't mind me saying this, but, well…bit like the Detective Sergeant said…she'll most likely turn out to be a gypsy.' He grimaces. 'They have their ways. Strange ways…I don't mean like magic and stuff. That's all bollocks, if you don't mind me saying so, sir. I mean dealing with things in their own community…You perhaps don't know them, sir. They won't take kindly to us interfering.'

Willetts had a point. The woman would most likely turn out to be a gypsy, an outsider. A tribe within a tribe, in a country fighting for its very existence. Who would care? Few before the war; even fewer now. Not DI Williams, not Acting DS Harry James. Not even the local paper. Everyone was living under the shadow of invasion, haunted night after night by the bombing of their homes, their communities, their lives. They woke each morning to find the world and its certainties disappearing in front of their eyes. Who would fret over a long-dead woman from a world within a world, a community that wanted nothing to do with what lay outside its own?

Williams's insinuation. James's instruction. Willetts's advice.

It was clear as day. There was little in the way of appetite for anything other than the most routine of investigations.

He finds himself in agreement, aligned with everything they'd said. Except, that is, for some deeper sense he finds somewhere in his mind. Some remnant of whatever it was had led him to quit a life of academia to volunteer to fight in Spain. Some spark in the ash of Spain, the fires of the orange grove, that had stubbornly refused to burn.

He looks across the clearing to the elm.

It stands shadowed in the gloom of surrounding trees and bushes. Shadowed even on a spring morning as bright as this one. It was, so he'd been told, a place of myth and legend. A dark place. A lonely place. A place of nightmares.

He finds himself tightening his lips. He knows about nightmares, the dark.

He shivers as if a grave has been walked on.

19TH APRIL 1943: NIGHT

He feels it before he sees it. A shiver. A shadow blocking out the sun. An ice-cold chill where a moment before had been warmth.

The day had been good. Wandering into the thick grove of orange trees, the sweet scent of fruit heavy in the air – deep cloying tones of citrus. The sun was high; a heat penetrating deep into the bone.

Laughter. Voices.

The buzzing of flies. Wasps. A banshee howl.

The shadows close in, shrouding the clearing where they walk. Voices raised - urgent, clamouring. He runs. There is no elegance, no athleticism. He skitters, careers, stumbles, and falls, urging his legs to move, seeking shelter though none exists. There are no hollows, no boulders, no ditches. He is exposed.

Not daring to look back, not daring to look up, he plunges forward, changing direction, legs suddenly windmilling beneath him. Lifted. Turned sideways, head over heels. A blast of solid air catches him, punches him, flicking him across the open ground. He spins once, twice, a third time and hits the dry earth, breath torn from his body.

He lies on his stomach, trying to breathe. The blast has sucked away the air. He gulps, lungs burning, eyes bulging. Coughing. Choking.

It comes as a rush. A dam bursting.

Air.

He drinks it in, tasting the dust, gagging on its gritty texture.

Retching. Alive.

His choking bursts the bubble of silence wrapping him, ears now assaulted by a deafening rumble.

Thunder. Rain.

Rain falling on dry rock and hard soil. Rain pattering back and legs.

Rain? He could still feel the hot sun high above him. How can there be rain?

He opens an eye, turning his head so one cheek is pressed hard to the dusty floor.

Sand – it was raining sand. And soil. Wood. Fruit. Blood.

Blood rain. A shower of it, soaking his clothes, wetting his hair.

He catches sight of the orange trees, broken, twisted, blackened.

There are bodies.

New notes play on the air – screams, shouts, pleas.

He tries to turn, to better see what is happening – what has happened – but agonising pain lances up his spine. Screaming, he falls still. The warmth of his own blood oozing over his back; hot pokers jabbing his flesh. His spine.

He opens his lips. Tries to shout.

Nothing.

He has to tell them what was happening. Warn them.

They were being bombed.

He was here. He was hurt. He was alive.

His lips form words, sure that he screams them, but he hears only the banshee wail of the bombs raining down.

Screwing his eyes shut, he presses himself into the earth, its resistance pushing back, pushing him away, lifting him up – an offering to the darkness edging ever closer. He feels a warmth on his groin, a wetness. Eyes scrunch tighter; his lips move murmuring a silent prayer.

'Alec! Alec!'

Someone calling his name.

His name.

He opens his eyes.

'Alec, it's okay. It's okay!' a voice reassures. Soft. Urging. She cradles him; her flesh enveloping him, warm like the sun. He feels the silk of her slip against his chest. Feels her hands, slick with his own sweat under her palms where she embraces him. The scent of her - ripe, honeyed.

'Was it the dream again?' she asks. 'You were back there, weren't you?'

He holds her fast, unwilling to let go. He has no words, his mind seeks only confirmation of the truth of where he is, what she said.

The sheets... The wardrobe. The dressing table.

He lifts his head. He slips from her grasp, levering his body up against the bedstead, the metal cool against the back of his head. He sits, cupping his face in his hands. He lets them hold him there a moment before sweeping them across his face, mopping the sweat up and over his scalp. He lowers a hand, touches his chin. Feels the stubble.

Real. Safe.

2

'I see what you mean,' James Webster calls out. Below him, footing the ladder, Willetts nods. Webster, taking a freshly sharpened pencil from the top pocket of his Harris Tweed jacket, reaches towards the eyeless sockets of the skull.

It was just as Willetts' boy described. Tatters of rotting flesh dangle from the frontal bone; tufts of light-brown hair cling to patches of scalp; protruding teeth, jagged and crooked. The remnants of what appear to be a scarf lie around the neck, a piece of silk-like fabric covering the top of the shoulders. The rest of the body is hidden, wedged deep into the hollow of the tree.

Webster, using the pencil, levers the jaws apart, carefully teasing out a loose ball of material. He holds it draped over the pencil, moving it closer for better inspection. It was taffeta and had quite obviously been forced into the throat.

He drops the silken cloth into a large brown envelope, securing that packet in turn inside a canvas haversack that hangs from his shoulder. Returning to his examination, he once more uses the pencil in turning the skull from side to side.

'No signs of any contusions,' he calls out.

'So, she wasn't battered to death?' Porter replies from the foot of the ladder, notebook in one hand, pencil stub in the other. He scribbles a note. A spidery scrawl joining the other jottings he'd made over the past ten minutes or so. A list of isolated facts.

'I wouldn't go that far.' Webster calls down, accent nasal, high Edinburgh. 'There are many ways to beat someone to death without crushing the skull. Breaking the ribs, splintered bones stabbing vital organs; crushing the spleen; punching the throat; choking them.' He pauses a beat, a checkpoint in his listing. 'But at this stage I'd say we're looking at something else. I'll know more once we've got her out. It is *her*, by the way.' He tilts the skull upwards. 'Hmmm. Tracheal bones appear damaged. Maybe asphyxiation…' he mutters. He turns the skull, examining the neck of the skeleton. 'It could well be strangulation,' he calls down. 'But the damage could just as well have been caused by scavenging creatures, or even possibly as she was shoved into the tree.'

Unsteadily, Porter ascends a second ladder that rests to the side of the one occupied by Webster. His view of the corpse is limited, but he wants to see the location for himself. It will enable him to speak with credibility about the corpse. A bonus of the climb is in it enabling him to talk to Webster with a degree of confidentiality

'Anything?' Porter asks as he reaches the crown of branches, fingers gripping tight to the rungs.

Webster halts his examination, head turning to face him. 'Such as?'

'I'm not sure.'

Webster grunts. 'Detective, I prefer to talk of what I *am* sure of. Supposition, guesswork…that's the stuff of amateur detectives. *Miss Marple, Agatha Christie*, cheap fiction. No time for it. Distracting. Diverting. Worse, misleading.' He returns to his examination. 'I've spent too many wasted hours chasing others' suppositions and guesswork. Wait. Be sure. That's the maxim of my work.'

The rebuke suited Webster's bearing. Imposing had come to Porter's mind on the professor's arrival at the scene. The Scot was large and balding. His Edinburgh accent offered an educated, aloof, slightly airy tone barely modified by a particular manner of speaking; the clipped utterances of one not to be trifled with, a man with no time for small talk. The monocle jammed in one eye reminds Porter of his old Cambridge lecturers. He has the bearing of an academic, but Porter knows his reputation is one of the enthusiastic advocate of the hands on forensic examination of a corpse. Examinations enabling medical investigators to detail much of what had happened to the victim both pre- and post-mortem. Hoover's newly created FBI - the so-called *G-Men* - had identified killers from the evidence acquired by just such techniques.

More in hope than expectation, he'd rung the Professor the previous evening and had been both surprised and grateful when he'd agreed to assist. Even more grateful for his rapid appearance at the crime scene that morning.

'Any idea how long she's been here?' Porter asks, hoping a specific question might find an approving response.

Webster doesn't look up. 'A year, maybe a little longer. Not more than two.'

'So sometime between spring or summer 1941 and 1942.'

Webster removes loose twigs from the skeleton's shoulder. Plucking at the bone, he holds a thread to the light. He furrows his brow, monocle pushing against the rim of his eye socket. 'I'd say so. I'll have more precise information once we've got her to the lab. Once more, Detective, you're asking for guesswork and supposition, and I won't be drawn on it. We must wait. Be sure.'

He returns to tilting the skull this way and that, teasing at threads trapped on the collar bone, prodding the remains of the scalp. Porter watches him work. Fascinated by the rhythm and delicacy of the examination. Webster's hands move to the top of the skeleton's arm closest to him. 'A long time to be out here,' Porter says. 'A long time to be missing.'

'The War,' Webster responds, nose wrinkling.

'The war,' Porter echoes. 'Lot of folks go missing. Hard for relatives to keep up. Families separated by conscription, bombings, evacuation. Buildings falling, leaving ruins of where people lived. So much rubble to pick through in the bigger towns. It's easy to think someone's been killed in a raid, not realising they've gone missing. Or been taken.' He knew the stories. Young women abducted by men, their kidnapping, rape, and eventual murder lost in the chaos of bombing raids. The impossibility of keeping track of corpses, the wounded, the missing.

He decides to fish. 'They think she's a gypsy.'

'They?'

'Local officers. Is there any way to tell?'

Webster stops his examination. He looks up. 'Ha! Thought you were an educated man, Detective. Just what is you expect might tell me that? A third eye? Webbed feet?' He laughs, the sound a short bark. 'Her golden earrings no doubt fell out when her flesh rotted.' He shakes his head. A humourless smile is turned to Porter. 'It's a skeleton, Detective. She could be a gypsy or a duchess. I will not indulge in supposition.'

'No, I meant—'

'She's got bloody awful teeth if that's any sign.' Webster interrupts, pointing his pencil at the skeleton's jaw. 'Get her profile on the wires and her dentist will recognise her right away. And the taffeta stuffed down her throat - bright and shiny. That's a gypsy material, isn't it?'

Porter, keen to avoid demonstrating stereotyping or prejudice, seeks recovery. 'Possibly. But as you say, there's a war on. Real silk's difficult to get hold of. I'm told that even fine ladies use synthetics these days.'

Webster waves his pencil in Porter's direction. 'Ah, you're thinking now. Make a detective of you yet, lad.'

Was he being patronised or praised? He had no way of knowing. He takes the latter. 'Maybe there's a label in the dress. Might tell us where she bought it from…if she's local. The manufacturer might recognise the pattern of the material.'

Webster places the pencil in the top pocket of his jacket, patting it securely into place. 'All things are possible if one can simply develop the capacity to see what is available.'

The professor begins taking off his tweed jacket. He tosses it to Willetts. 'Catch!' he shouts, sending Willetts scrambling to retrieve the garment. Webster rolls up his shirt-sleeves. 'Time for us to get her out, don't you think?'

'Us?' Porter asks.

'Well, it appears that we're *Johnny-on-the-Spot*, so yes. Come on, grab a shoulder.'

'My back—'

'My dear fellow, look at her. She's all bones. She won't be heavy. Just be careful not to pull too hard under the skull. We want her out, not decapitated.'

Realising there is no argument to be made, Porter reaches under the skull. The bone is rough against his hands, like scales. Closing his eyes, he pushes down into the hollow, seeking her shoulder, the sharp shoots of shorter branches catching against his skin. Arriving at what he thinks to be her shoulders, he seeks to grasp the skeleton. Remnants of silky fabric slip under his touch, making purchase difficult. The collar bone pokes at him. It feels jutted under his grip. His mind flashes images of a young woman, a woman once smooth and sensual now rendered coarse and brittle.

'Ready?' Webster announces. 'One, two, three—'

They pull up, a soft tug revealing arms, elbows, wrist, a hand. A second pull sees her clear to the waist; a third effort exposes the skeleton to the knees.

Webster calls to the workers below. 'Get that stretcher over here. We're going to lower the body down. Take the strain,' he tells Porter. 'And try not to grab her too hard.'

With a final pull, the corpse is clear, Webster scooping his arm under her knees.

Slowly, he leans back, pulling her towards him. Then, with her corpse held slightly to the side of his upper body, he descends the ladder using his knees to brace himself.

Porter notices how gentle he is. A parent carrying a sleeping child; a lover swooned in a partner's arms. Near the bottom of the ladder, he holds her out to willing hands. 'Careful! Gently! Don't grab at her.' Under his guidance, she is laid on the stretcher. 'Put a blanket over her!' he barks.

Above, Porter stares into the hollow.

'Anything?' Webster shouts up.

'Nothing.'

'Nothing? Are you certain?'

'Absolutely. See for yourself.'

Webster once more ascends the elm. Inserting his monocle, the Professor of Forensics scours the deserted nest where she'd lain. 'Curious,' he mutters after a moment of silent consideration.

'How so?' Porter asks. 'Were you expecting something?'

'A hand. The right one to be precise. It's missing. I noticed it as I carried her down the ladder. A first albeit cursory look, indicates it was amputated.'

Porter stares across the hollow. 'I don't understand.'

Webster pauses and looks up. 'Detective, whoever put her in here cut off her hand. And apparently, they took it with them.'

3

The news was full of the previous night's raid. A large one, the biggest for weeks targeting the north of Birmingham. There had been smaller raids on Coventry and London had been hit badly again. The discovery of a long dead corpse in a wood outside the small village of Hagley merited little in the way of coverage, let alone headlines. Even the fact it had been found inside the hollow of a tree aroused little more than passing interest.

The article relating the discovery was tucked away on page five of the local paper. DI Williams featured in a short official quote, but they hadn't found sufficient interest to include any of the photographs they'd taken of the DI or of the location. Newsprint was a scarce resource, and *The Birmingham Post* wasn't about to waste it on something of such limited interest. *Gypsies.* Slipped into the article was an appeal for anyone with information regarding the possible identity of the body to contact the authorities.

Porter pulls the broadsheet pages together, neatly folding the paper in half before placing it back on the parlour table. He'd little experience of a major criminal investigation, let alone a murder enquiry. Thus far the only advice he'd been given consisted of Williams leaving a note warning him that in the wake of his press appeal he should be prepared for *'a flood of letters and calls, busy-bodies and lunatics all claiming to know who the body is'*. At best, Williams had cautioned, only one of them might know who she was, and none would know how she got there. He'd ended with a reminder that *'gypos'* would *'no way get in contact'*.

Sitting at the table, Porter buries his head in his hands, massaging his temples. His back aches from the afternoon's exertions in removing the body from the tree. He'd taken his prescribed painkillers but not the full dose. He wants his mind clear.

Webster had overseen the body's removal to his lab at the university. He'd told Porter his first action would be to circulate dental records across the region. Then, if that failed to get a response, later in the week he'd circulate them more widely. The full autopsy would be completed within a few days, with an inquest the following week. He was aware of the difficulties in predicting such matters. A bad air-raid would require medical timescales stretching to accommodate a fresh influx of bodies. War was no respecter of the needs of bureaucracy, and certainly not the demands of a years old murder investigation.

Porter had instigated a search of the area around the tree. By nightfall it extended to about an acre of land. A young Special - a serving soldier home on sick leave who'd previously been a constable - had been roped in by Willetts. He'd been left at the scene overnight to protect the site from ghoulish sightseers or the dim possibility of the return of those who'd placed the body there. Knowing the stories and legends as well as anyone, the man had been far from pleased.

The search would begin again at first light, but with only Willetts and the part-time use of two other officers, it would take at least until the end of the week to complete.

The body had been there a while - anywhere between a year

to two years Webster had said. *How much had the undergrowth spread in that time? What had the weather been like? How had the ground altered? What about animal activity?* They were looking for a number of things; her hand, her shoes that were nowhere to be seen, possibly a handbag, and then anything else that might yield some insight as to her identity or to her fate.

A shriek of childlike joy stops his thoughts. The sound of Tommy splashing in the kitchen sink along with Rachel's playful protestations as she fought to wash him ready for bed. The sound is accompanied by the gruff chuckles of her ex-father-in-law, his comments of Tommy being *'just like his dad at that age.'*

The door opens and Rachel stands there; Tommy held tight against her body, legs wrapped around her waist. Tommy giggles as his granddad extends an arm from behind Rachel to tickle him, the boy squirming with delight, wriggling under the tickle.

'Hey, hey! Steady on, cowboy,' Rachel calls out. 'Time for bed. Let's not get so excited we can't sleep.'

'Story!' Tommy yells, punching his hand high in the air, sending it whistling past her ear, the near miss causing a further explosion of giggles.

'Okay, Okay. But a quiet one. No cowboys or space-men.'

'Rabbits!' Tommy shouts.

'Okay, rabbits it is. But just a quick one. Mommy and Alec are going out tonight, and mommy needs to finish getting ready. Get her make-up on.'

'Mommy's beautiful!'

'Well thank you, kind sir!' She buries a kiss on his cheek, causing him to shriek out. She looks to Alec, her face a plea for re-assurance. 'I'll be ten minutes, darling.'

Porter nods. She smiles, at the same time shooting a glance between Porter and her father-in-law. She leaves the room, both men listening to the exaggerated thump of her feet on the stairs as she ascends them chattering away to her son.

Arthur Morris picks up the newspaper. He settles into the

armchair occupying one corner of the room. He unfolds the paper, flapping it fully open, eyes examining the creases.

'I had a quick look earlier, Arthur. Hope you don't mind. Case I'm working on is in there. Just wanted to see how it's being reported.'

Arthur Morris sniffs. 'Case, eh? More bicycles, is it?'

'Murder.'

Arthur raises an eyebrow. 'Murder? Bit of a step-up.'

'It's an old case. Body's a year or so old.'

Arthur's brow ceases its furrowing, enlightenment occurring. 'Ah. They sent for you for this one then, did they? A skeleton.'

Porter shrugs. He didn't want to get into this. 'Sort of.'

'Sort of? I'd have thought that education of yours was just what they needed. History, wasn't it? Finding a use for you. Using your talents. Clearly the army can't.'

'No, that's right.'

'Your back,' Arthur puts in.

'The shrapnel,' Porter corrects him.

'Yes, the shrapnel. How's the back now?'

'Not too bad. Comes and goes'.

Arthur's brow raises itself once more. 'That right? Comes and goes.' He looks back to his newspaper.

'How's the factory?'

Buried in the newspaper, Arthur fails to look up. 'Can't say. Carless talk and all that.'

'Busy though,' Porter persists.

Arthur looks up, fixes Porter with his eyes. 'Enough. Keeping our lads at the front supplied. Helping win the war. Every time I feel tired or unwell, I think of him. Think of our Jack, what he did. What he suffered. His sacrifice. It makes me feel ashamed not to get in there and do my bit. Working there, it's like I'm doing my part. It's what Jack would have wanted. Feels like I'm honouring him. Honouring all of them that aren't coming back.'

Rachel comes into the room, hesitating in the doorway. 'You two okay?'

27

Porter stands, plucking his jacket from the back of one of the chairs. 'Fine.'

Arthur nods, turning the page of his paper. 'Just fine, luv. Talking about the war. Boys at the front. All those sacrifices they're making for us.'

She glances to Porter.

'Off somewhere nice?' Arthur enquires.

Rachel sighs, fixing a smile. 'Pictures.'

'Pictures. Lovely.' Pause. A beat. 'You have a good time.'

Rachel takes her coat off a peg on the back of the door. She walks over, leaning across to kiss Arthur on the forehead. 'Tommy ought to be okay. He's gone down well despite all the bath-time excitement.'

'Don't you worry. I'll take good care of my grandson.'

Rachel pauses, checking the contents of her handbag. She picks up the cardboard box containing her gas-mask. 'Did Alec tell you about his case?'

'The dead body? Yes.'

'What do you think?'

Arthur Morris shakes his head. Snorts. 'Old bodies. Picking over what's left of the dead. What they've left behind.' He looks down at his newspaper. 'He should do well.'

19TH APRIL 1943: EVENING

He watches them.

Shadows. Silhouettes. Purple-blue sky smudged with dark cloud.

Sees a light approaching. Distant at first, but with each passing second looming larger, sweeping towards where they lay.

Close-up: a battered wooden box, hand on a plunger. A sharp downwards push. The darkness illuminated by a red-white ball of fire.

Quickly, they scamper across the rocks where land meets sky. Blue-grey outlines, shapes of men against the horizon. Scrubland. Blooms of red. A surging of helmeted pursuers firing wildly into the night. A shot rings out. A man falls.

His comrade hesitates.

'You promised,' the fallen man calls out.

'Adios' the other replies, levelling his pistol and firing twice into the recumbent figure.

He runs off before the pursuing soldiers reach the corpse. They kick it in frustration. Turning and firing into a darkness that descends to blackout.

Porter stirs in his seat, back aching.

Rachel had insisted on *For Whom the Bell Tolls*. Gary Cooper was a favourite, and he knew she loved Ingrid Bergman, she of the dark brooding eyes and accented, sultry tones. He'd read the book when it was first published. Hemingway. A novel set in the Spanish Civil War, written by a man who'd been there. It held obvious appeal for someone like himself, one of its victims. The ending, where Jordan lies wounded, trapped and awaiting his death, has particular resonance. But of course, Robert Jordan never pissed himself. Gary Cooper would never beg God for release.

'Okay?' Rachel murmurs, squeezing his hand.

Yes,' he whispers.

She squeezes tighter, snuggling into him.

They sit a few rows from the rear stalls, the cinema half-empty. Despite only the dim possibility of a raid that night, there would still be ARP wardens and fire-spotters required to be on duty. Others had no doubt simply preferred to keep close to shelters. For some, the chance to spend a night at home without the threat of a raid brought a semblance of normality amid the chaos of war.

Escape from the war in a cinema was impossible.

The newsreels shown as part of each night's programme detailed the suffering at home and elsewhere. That night it had been a documentary feature reminding audiences of the sacrifices already made. *The Battle of Britain; Dunkirk; Tobruk; Pearl Harbour*. Clips shown to sobs and muffled gasps. Silver images played to jeering insults hurled at Hitler, the Nazis, and the Japanese. That Pearl Harbour figured so prominently demonstrated civilian suffering was not confined to this island in its stand for freedom. *The Blitz*, now in its second year, was to be seen - according to those in charge of propaganda - in context. *We are not alone. Suffering is shared with other nations. American fathers, American mothers, American sweethearts. Unlike the Nazis and Japanese, our cause is not one of aggrandisement or naked nationalism - it is a just cause. A noble and honourable fight that must be won. We do not stand alone. We will prevail.*

During its showing, he'd turned his head, scanning faces illuminated in the glow of the screen. How many here had suffered the death of a loved one? The loss of a home? The loss of a way of life? Old certainties blasted apart as if they too had been struck by incendiaries.

He thought of Arthur Morris sat at home, grandson sleeping above him. His world shaken, overturned. His son was dead. His daughter-in-law, the mother of his only grandchild, finding comfort in the arms of a man he believed to be a coward. *Unfit in every sense of the word* was but one comment he'd overheard Arthur make to a neighbour.

Maybe.

He knew his limits, his capabilities. He was no-one's idea of a hero. He knew few who were. What defined a hero? Actions or motive? A sense of knowing what you were doing, of what was placed at risk? What the sacrifice you were called to make might be? Whatever their propaganda value, wars were not won by heroes. The legacy of the hero was all too often simply the manner of their end, a rallying call for those who followed in their wake

He'd known good men in Spain. Good people. Brave. Enduring. Stoic. He'd sacrificed his education, a career, but many had given much more. There were debts owed in that fight he could never repay, sacrifices he could never forget. Such things had consequences for those who survived, torches to be carried into the darkness, the battles against those who preyed on the helpless and vulnerable. Wounded and feted in his Spanish hospital, on his return he'd found only apathy and misunderstanding. Even now with the War, few wished reminders of their own isolationism, the bravery and sacrifice smade in Spain.

He thinks of the body in the tree. What had warranted her sacrifice? What laws of man or God had she so offended that deemed only internment in a hollow tree to be sufficient penance?

And what of the tree itself? A tree of worship. A tree, so some held, of a magical nature. He sees it in his mind's eye, branches spiking up. A Devil tree. Hollow. A thing that appeared not as it was.

Hollow. Empty. A void, like himself.

19TH APRIL 1943: NIGHT

'But did you enjoy it?' she asks.

Porter examines the pavement ahead; the lack of street lighting during blackout means the walk from bus terminus to home is difficult to negotiate without turning a foot in a pothole, a heel being snapped. 'Yes. It was good,' he replies with little conviction.

She clings tight to his arm, fearful of her best heels, allows his lack of enthusiasm to pass her by. 'Was it like that?'

He looks down at her. She walks tight against him, arms wrapped around his arm, head close to his shoulder. 'How do you mean?' he asks.

'The people. The things they did. Their lives.'

He thinks of those he'd known in Spain. 'They were like you and me. Ordinary. Ordinary people trying to lead their lives as best they could. Finding they're the ones called on to fight. That they're the ones called to make the sacrifice to protect that ordinariness.'

She leaves a pause. 'Did it bring back bad memories?'

'No. Nothing I can't cope with. Nothing worse than facing Arthur and the rest.'

She looks up. 'You have to ignore him. He doesn't really mean it.'

'Mean what? Mean what he says? Of course he does!' he scoffs. 'He hates me, at least hates what he sees in me. I'm here safe, and his son's dead. And he doesn't see why it's like that. None of them do.'

'It's not your fault. It's your back. The shrapnel.'

'Which none of them can see.' He knows the looks, lives with them every day. After three years of the war he's still struggling to get past the compulsion to explain to each new person he met - every shop assistant, bus conductor, tram driver, or passer-by - that according to the military doctors he was incapacitated: *A2, unfit for active duties*. 'What they see is an apparently fully fit man who's not in uniform.'

'But you have the diagnosis from the doctors, the A2 certificate from the army medical board,' she reminds, as she does every time he talked of some new encounter - a stranger spitting at him in the street, a confrontation with a grieving mother.

'What? You think I should walk round with it stuck on my chest?'

'I'm not saying that. You know I'm not.'

'Then what are you saying?'

'That it's not your fault. You're not fit for war.'

'Great. Sounds so much better when you put it like that.'

'Alec, I'm sorry... you know what I mean.'

'Yes. Of course I do.'

They walk in silence, she snuggling back against him. In the distance, the now familiar sounds: the thump of bombs; the drone of engines; the dull pop of anti-aircraft guns.

'Birmingham,' he judges.

'Poor devils,' she says.

Birmingham had been having it hard for two years now.

Aircraft factories, tanks, guns, transport. It was a hot spot for air raids. A honeypot for the Luftwaffe: the Austin at Longbridge; BSA arms factories in Small Heath; Fisher and Ludlow's wings for Lancaster's and Spitfires; GEC in Witton; SU Carburettors; Rover. Most of them cramped into what the planners termed a conurbation - Birmingham and the Black Country. Tonight, he judges it to be to the south-east of the city, most likely the massive BSA armaments factory. Perhaps even beyond that too A raid stretching out to the north-west and the long line of supply factories daisy-chained across the region.

For too long it had been much closer. Longbridge.

Longbridge was a massive industrial complex. He knew from ARP briefings that the scale of the enterprise there was huge. It built fighters; Hurricanes flown out from a nearby airfield. It built bombers - Lancasters and Sterlings - their carcasses transported by road to the bigger airfields at Elmdon or Castle Bromwich ready for final assembly and take-off. As well as completed aircraft, they built fuselages for Horsa Gliders and Bristol Beaufighters. They manufactured Mercury and Pegasus aircraft engines. Made thousands and thousands of military vehicles. Close to the main site, a host of smaller factories produced components such as the suspension units for tanks.

It was a massive military target, one set in the heart of the pre-war workers' estates that surrounded it. Thousands of homes clustered around factories that prior to the war had provided security, a way of life.

They were hit hard and often.

And all just a few short miles from where they walked.

He felt a familiar tremor rising. *Not now. Not now.*

'At least it's not us tonight,' she says.

'Yes.'

She shudders. 'It's awful to think of it like that. But I can't help it.'

'It's okay. It's natural.'

'Is it? I feel such a coward.'

'You're no coward,' he reassures.

'How do you know?'

'I just do. I know cowards. You're not a coward.'

Rachel returns to silence; their footsteps cut against the distant soundtrack of the raid. He feels the breath escape from her. The whisper of a sigh. 'Sometimes…when the bombs fall so close…when they overshoot or whatever…or to get away from the flak guns they drop them here instead, I just want to roll myself into a ball.' She clutches his arm. 'I screamed one night… when it first started. I screamed and screamed…Not a movie scream, I mean a real scream, like that painting in that book you showed me. My hands were clutched to the side of my head. I could feel the vibrations of my screams…the tremors in my throat…. But no-one heard. I couldn't even hear myself. The noise of the bombs was so loud it drowned out the world.'

'I know. I know.'

She stops suddenly, turning to face him, blocking his path. 'It must have been awful. What you went through. The orange grove. That's what I mean when I say it's not your fault. You've already done more than most.' She hugs him tight. 'Oh, Alec, my love! You don't need to prove anything to anyone.'

He stands still, holding her whilst she squeezes him tight. His arms settle - resting, not holding - on her hips. 'We'll see. We'll see,' he says to the empty horizon, wishing he too could drown out the world.

4

The Wolseley pulls up with a lurch, Willetts yanking the handbrake and switching off the engine, which putters and splutters for a few seconds before dying. The poor quality of petrol allocated to official vehicles was taking its toll.

Willetts climbs out, looking across at Porter who stands waiting at the edge of the pavement. 'Sorry sir,' Willetts offers, arm waving across the vehicle in apology at the allotted car.

'Not a problem,' Porter responds. 'The war.'

'The war,' Willetts echoes.

'Let's get in and have a look-see,' Porter says with as much enthusiasm as he can muster. Willetts makes to come round to open the passenger door, but Porter holds up a hand to halt him. 'Not quite a cripple. And certainly not elevated enough to expect being waited on.'

'Sir. I didn't mean to imply...'

Smiling, Porter shakes his head. 'It's okay. Took me a while to get used to it. I still wake up some mornings and look in the mirror and forget my...circumstance.'

Both men get in. The leather upholstery is worn, the covering

35

of the front seats flecked and battered whilst the broken springs mean the seats sag under the weight of both men. Willetts tells him the vehicle's been in service since 1937 with no hope of replacement until after the war.

'Okay,' Porter says tapping the dashboard and forcing a smile. 'Not as bad as I'd thought.'

He'd spent the best part of the morning persuading James of the necessity of a car being allocated to the enquiry. James had been reluctant, arguing the case was primarily a paper exercise and that such precious resources were needed elsewhere. Porter had argued the necessity of getting to Birmingham to meet Webster, at the same time reminding the DS of his own assertions about the traveller connection. If they located those travellers it would require a car to catch up with them. James had relented, agreeing they could have the use of one for a few days. The transport he'd assigned them had been sitting unused for some time, not quite a wreck, but certainly a vehicle in need of attention.

'Where to then, sir?'

'The woods first, then on to Brum.'

'Righto.' Willetts cranks the engine into life. It turns over several times before firing. With a grinding of gears, they stutter away from the station, taking the main road to Hagley.

On arrival at the woods, they realise just how quickly it has become a source of local interest. Despite low-key reporting, word of the discovery had spread. Children with time off school because of the raids, along with elderly local villagers are gathered at the end of the footpath commentating on the search. There's much speculation as to who the corpse might be, alongside ghoulish conjectures as to the state of the body. The four boys who'd made the initial discovery now found their adventure taking on a near mythic status amidst schoolmates.

'At least it takes their minds off the raids and the rationing,' Porter offers as they pass through the crowd.

'Bogey men and magic!' Willetts scowls. 'More time than sense, the lot of them!'

'Do you think any of them have any idea who she is?'

Willetts shakes his head. 'Doubt it. No-one's come forward as yet.' He jerks a thumb over his shoulder. 'I'll get someone to talk to this lot, but I doubt they'll find anything beyond most folk thinking her being a *gypo*.'

They arrive in the clearing to find two Special Constables walking back and forth. Every few paces one either bends over or pokes the undergrowth with a stick stripped from the trees. Willetts nods. 'I got these two to volunteer for an extra shift, sir. They sort of owed me.'

'Good work, Albert. Good work.'

The tree itself stands at the centre. Apart from a few bushes, little else grows in either direction for thirty yards. It is the edge of this clearing that the Specials are searching. From there on there is a ring of bushes and smaller trees - poplars and larch for the most part - that merge into the rest of the wood. The worn single track offers the only access.

Porter looks back and forth from the edge of the clearing to the tree. Fanciful or not, it is as if the rest of the wood kept a wary distance from the wych-elm.

He looks up at the sky, shading his eyes from the sun. He realises that what ought be a space dappled in Spring sunshine, remains dark and shadowed.

Lowering his hand, he looks to the centre; the wych-elm and its fearsome crown of spiked branches. It is a fairy-tale tree: A *Brothers Grimm* myth of a tree. He understands the draw of it; the power of the stories and legends attaching to it. Being here, seeing it in the flesh, gives credibility to the myths that have grown around it; the power bestowed on it by those who knew of its presence.

He feels an involuntary shiver, goose-pimples erupting on his arms. Shrugging them aside, he calls to the nearest Special. 'Anything?'

37

The constable looks up, acknowledging the question. He walks over, the better to make a report. He's stocky with a ruddy, weather-beaten face, undoubtedly a local farm worker. He holds up what appears to be a pair of crumpled shoes, gesturing with his head towards the bushes to his left. 'We found these over there. Under one of the bushes. Looked like they'd been buried, but something had part dug them up. Probably a badger.'

Porter takes the shoes. He holds them away from his body, twirling them round. 'What do you think?' he asks.

Willetts narrows his eyes, an action emphasising the deep wrinkles that line his brow. The shoes are covered in dirt, muddy streaks across the toes. 'Must be hers. Who else would come out here and bury shoes?'

Porter agrees. 'Who would kill someone and bury her shoes?'

'*Gypos*,' the farmer states flatly, a judgement accompanied by his spitting a ball of phlegm onto the grass.

'I take it you're not a fan, constable.'

'I've worked this land for thirty years. Sweat and blood. And some tears. My boy's out in Africa.' He shakes his head, spitting again. '*Gypos*. They just take. They set up camp wherever they want. Do whatever they want. No laws for them. They don't pay no taxes. They don't have allegiance to no one but themselves.' He shakes his head, this time resisting spitting for emphasis. 'I tell you; there's some things old Adolf's got right. Thieves. Vagabonds. I've no time for 'em. Them or their curses or their charms.'

Porter exhales. There was no point in offering a rebuttal. The man had his views, and like many wasn't about to be shaken from them - certainly not by someone like Porter. A college boy. A man unfit to do his duty.

The other officer stepped forward. He holds out a hand, un-cupping the palm. 'There's this too. Underneath the shoes.'

He holds up a gold ring.

'A wedding ring?'

The officer passes it to Porter, who takes it between thumb

and index finger, turning it from side to side. He raises it to eye level for closer scrutiny. Willetts wrinkles his brow once more. 'Could be,' Willets states. 'Not an expensive one, I'd say, but too good for just decoration.'

'You say you found it with the shoes?' Porter asks.

'Yeah.'

Porter tightens his lips. 'Who kills someone then buries her shoes and wedding ring?'

'No self-respecting *gypo's* going to pass up a ring like that,' the first Special suggests.

Porter raises his eyebrows in consideration. 'Possibly not.'

'Unless it was cursed,' the Special says before spitting once more.

'So, it's not robbery then,' Willetts suggests.

'So, what, then?' the second Special asks.

'Passion.' Porter responds.

'Passion?' Willetts repeats.

Porter half-shrugs. 'Love. Sex. Hatred.'

They stare at the band of gold held between them, the centre of their circle. 'Betrayal.' The first Constable states, breaking the silence.

'Why do you say that?' Porter asks.

'Who else would kill a woman and bury her wedding ring?'

Porter furrows his brow in puzzlement. 'Who?'

'Her husband,' the constable spits. 'Her betrayed husband.'

20TH APRIL 1943: MORNING

The Dutchman was late. It was no surprise. It had been his manner, his nature from the start. Annoying, but considering the man's usefulness something that could be accommodated.

Making a last scan of the meadow, *The Great Fellaini* finds himself checking the flattened grass where vehicles and trailers enter and exit, his gaze travelling over the tents and caravans and the line of vehicles and generators to the big top, the centre of their winter quarters.

Though he'd played no part in the decision - like much of circus life it was down to a matter of tradition - he was pleased with the location. The meadow was large, the stream running along the bottom offering a ready supply of fresh water for animals and staff alike. In addition, despite its relative isolation, it was close to major roads with easy transport from Birmingham to the north and the smaller towns and villages of Bromsgrove to the south. They had access to shops and suppliers. It was a good place to winter, a place they returned to each year after summer travels across the Midlands and the North-west.

Being arable farmland there was plenty of fodder for horses and camels. The farmer who owned the land took a good rent from their presence so made certain there was a plentiful supply of butchered cattle unfit for human consumption for the big cats. Even at this early hour he hears them stirring in their cages. Maybe it was the smell of warm Spring air, a reminder of their grassland home. Like them, he too yearns for home, but there remained much to be accomplished before he could indulge such ideas.

Turning, he plunges his hands into the bowl of talcum powder that is perched on a stand next to his equipment. Rubbing them together, he pauses every now and then, rotating and inspecting palms and fingers, ensuring sufficient coverage.

Satisfied, he stands back.

He counts a beat, before leaping up onto the pommel horse. With casual ease he raises his legs up above his head, holding the handstand position for a moment whilst mentally preparing himself for the next series of movements. With a rotation of his hips, he simultaneously lowers his legs whilst slowly swivelling them out to the side, finally coming to rest, legs extended in front of him. Muscles straining with the effort, he holds the pose for a few seconds before embarking on a rapid sequence of spins, twists, and swivels. The momentum takes him through a series of balances and manoeuvres that work arms, legs, abdomen, and shoulders, before a clean dismount leaves him standing parallel to the equipment almost on the very spot where he'd started.

The sound of clapping causes him to turn. The Dutchman approached, hands slowly applauding in appreciation. 'Bravo! Bravo! A wonderful display!'

Fellaini picks up a towel, wiping hands and rubbing his muscular forearms. 'You're late.'

The Dutchman shrugs. 'You know how it is,' he offers.

Fellaini pauses, looks directly into the face of the man for a second or two before continuing his drying. 'No, I don't know how it is. I know that you are late.'

The Dutchman ignores the rebuke. Instead, patting its suede cover, he indicates the pommel horse. 'Well, you've kept yourself busy.'

'My training isn't the issue here. This is what I do. This is my work.'

'And I admire you for it. There's no way you'd get me on this thing, let alone on that bloody trapeze of yours doing those damned tricks you do.'

'Like most things, it's a matter of practice and training. Dedication.'

'Ah, dedication. Yes, I see your wider point. Something you feel is lacking in myself.'

Fellaini snorts dismissal of the point. 'I am not interested in your shortcomings. Except, of course, where they interfere with our work.'

'My lateness.'

'Your lateness is tiresome. It has not yet approached a level to threaten our work.'

'It won't'

Fellaini pauses before tossing the towel over his shoulder. He tugs the loose end around the back of his neck, forming a scarf that he drapes across his chest. He pats it into place, deciding to let the matter drift. 'You've seen the newspapers?'

The Dutchman nods.

'And?'

The Dutchman raises his eyebrows in contemplation. 'Nothing.'

'Nothing?'

The Dutchman produces a silver cigarette case. Extracting a cigarette from the tape holding it in position, he snaps the case shut, tapping the cigarette on the lid. 'It poses no threat.'

Fellaini rubs a hand down an arm, flexes the muscles. 'You seem confident.'

'At the time-'

Fellaini fixes him with a glare. 'At the time you screwed up. You and Dronkers and the Englishman.'

'That's-'

'Something they paid for.'

The Dutchman lights the cigarette, inhales deeply. 'Dronkers was a liability. I told you that. A liability. He panicked, as did the Englishman. I was the only one who kept his head.'

'Ah, yes, your arcane solution. Your plan.' Fellaini turns, beckoning the Dutchman to follow across the temporary compound of the circus. They pass between rows of dirty white canvas tents, their heavy flaps fluttering in the breeze. Further on, metal barred cages form a narrower alleyway. In one, a disinterested lion raises its head at their passing but makes no real effort to move to the bars. In the near distance a camel bellows, ponies whinny.

'It has kept us safe these past eighteen months,' the Dutchman states.

'Until now. Now it threatens to expose us.'

'Expose us? Expose us how?' The Dutchman responds whilst scuttling to keep up with Fellaini's stride. 'The authorities have little time for something as...trifling as this. A dead woman. Little more than a skeleton. She's unidentified.' He hesitates. 'I spoke with the locals. Had word from one of my contacts in the police.'

Fellaini stops, wheels to face him. The Dutchman holds his

hands up in front of his chest. 'Don't worry. I was careful,' he reports. 'They believe she's some sort of gypsy. A waif caught out in a storm. Some say she's a prostitute killed by a client. They're dumfounded, as Dronkers thought they would be. They have nothing.' He steps back a pace, enumerating on his fingers. 'A gypsy girl, a prostitute, a poor unfortunate raped and murdered whilst sheltering in the woods. They haven't a clue because there are so many possibilities. It is as I said at the time. Should they find her - as they now have - they'll spend years trying to identify her. We made sure of that.'

'What about the intelligence services? Their SIS?'

'SIS? What interest would they have in her now? It's two years ago. They may not even make the connection. Besides, surely such matters long ago lost any value. It serves them nothing for things to be stirred up. If you think about it, they've more cause to be concerned about her being identified than we do.'

Fellaini closes the distance to stand face to face with him. 'Do I have to spell it out for you? If they find out who she really was. What she knew. Who she knew. What she had. These men are not stupid.' He advances closer to the now startled Dutchman. Fellaini's eyes are dark, cold, offering no clue as to his intention.

The Dutchman steps back, out of the corner of one eye conscious of a tiger occupying the cage he finds himself two paces closer to. He is torn between turning to look where the beast is or facing Fellaini's belligerence. He speaks fast, eyes rolling to the side, every nerve on alert. 'What will they find? She's a gypsy girl. As far as they are concerned, she has no country. She has no relatives. She has no friends. No-one will come forward to claim her.' The tiger looks up, now conscious that something is happening, aware of the newly acquired tang of sweat in the air, the sharp acrid odour of fear in its nostrils. Fellaini advances, forcing the Dutchman to mirror his movement one pace closer to the tiger's cage. The Dutchman twitches. He speaks quickly. 'There is no one left to speak for her. You know that. We made certain of it. As for the rest...They're dead. What can they say? We're safe.'

'We still have no idea what she told them.'

'If they knew anything they would have acted at the time. We're safe.'

Fellaini steps back, half-turning away. He clasps the ends of the towel hanging either side of his neck. 'There's still much about the whole thing that bothers me.'

A grateful Dutchman steps away from the bars of the cage, glancing back as he increases the distance between himself and the enclosure. The great cat lowers its head, disinterested in whatever might now follow. 'Why? We got away with it. The work has gone on, possibly better than before. The latest blueprints our man procured are incredible in their detail. Soon they too will be in Berlin, shaping the war.'

He runs a hand down the sleeves of his suit, the other back across his hair. He composes himself, finds his best smile of assurance. 'For the past eighteen months we have done more for the war effort of the Reich than Berlin could ever have expected. Do not mourn the loss of the gypsy. The High Command will not. What was done is done. You will be a hero.' He ventures a step closer, clasping a hand on Fellaini's shoulder and looking him in the eye. 'When the war is over, you will be feted for what you have achieved here. Honoured. No-one will care about a dead gypsy. Especially one without a name.'

5

The building is massive. Birmingham Victoria Law Court stands as an intimidating chunk of Victorian grandeur, a statement of intent writ large in red-brick and gothic arches. It was why Webster's Pathology offices came as a surprise. Enquiries of several passers-by had elicited little in the way of finding them until a magistrate's clerk, on his way to meet solicitors, was able to lead them to an unnamed doorway in Newton Street in a building opposite the court. A doorway leading into a vestibule tiled in an uninviting shade of dark-green. Inside, a metal caged lift shaft ran to the higher floors whilst a narrow staircase led down to the offices of Professor James Webster Head of the newly created *Home Office West Midlands Forensic Science Laboratory*.

'Come in, come in. Do come in,' Webster welcomed at the doorway.

The room was tiny - squat ceilinged and cramped even though containing only a desk, two chairs, and several dull-grey metal filing cabinets. A glass block panel in the alcove ceiling above the far wall provided the room's only natural light. It

45

came from street level, an arrangement leaving the office itself shrouded in gloom. The clatter of shoes sounds through the space as pedestrians made their way across the panel, unaware of what lurked beneath their feet.

'Find yourselves a chair. Just move any of the stuff that's in the way. Still finding a home for it,' Webster informs cheerily. He reaches across to relieve Willetts of a stack of folders the constable has removed from a chair. The Special nods gratefully, having stood holding them for a few moments whilst considering resting places that might not precipitate an avalanche of paper. 'Been here a few months now and still haven't got round to sorting things out. Manpower. Very scarce commodity these days,' Webster observes, shuffling round the desk.

'The war,' Willetts says.

'The war. Yes. Still, we can't complain. It's a just cause. A good war. One we need to fight.'

'One we need to win,' Willetts rejoins.

'Yes, of course,' Webster nods. 'Winning. Goes without saying.'

Finding a patch of floor, Webster places the folders down. Job completed he sits, jamming himself into an old captain's chair with a scalloped back whose spindles creak ominously under his weight. He waves an arm in front of him, a gesture taking in the surroundings. 'What do you make of it all?'

Porter sits on a high-backed chair scavenged from somewhere, most likely the remnant of a dining set ushered into new service. He looks around at shelves piled high with folders. In the gaps, scientific instruments are jammed into any vacant space, instruments that look as if they too have been retrieved from a museum to find renewed service. Equipment is short. The mantra of greater need. 'It's not as I imagined,' Porter observes.

Webster leans back; hands clasped behind his head. 'Oh, I grant it's long way from America and their G-Men - but it's a start. Can't get anywhere without a start, eh?'

Porter nods. His contact with pathology or what was now called forensics, was limited. He'd read of the developments in America. He knew things were changing, the growing application of technology and science to crime scenes leading to ways of finding evidence beyond that obvious to the naked eye. Microscopic fragments. Hair. Skin. Blood. Webster was right. A start was better than what they had; doctors who, between delivering babies or administering potions for colds, established cause of death for local police.

'It all takes time Detective,' Webster reaffirms.

Willetts sits in a corner, cap on lap. His chair has been dragged through from the corridor outside. He sits, one leg stretched to the right, his favoured posture for easing the discomfort Porter knew troubled him more than he let on. The Special found his attention drawn to a series of handwritten charts and data concerning decomposition. He shakes his head, pointing at the diagrams and labels. 'I don't understand any of this.'

Webster sits forward, a teacher by inclination as much vocation, an audience was not easily passed by. 'Not many do, Constable. Not even those who run the police. It astonishes me that we've had fingerprinting since the start of the century - you know of course that the Galton-Henry method was the brainchild of the then Commissioner at Scotland Yard - but now lag far behind the French and Americans. At least, lagged behind the French at the start of the war. God knows what's happened to Locard and his work under the Occupation.'

'Locard?'

'Edmund Locard. Head of the world's first crime investigation laboratory. He was based in Lyon. Amazing man. Amazing. A real-life Sherlock Holmes. Handwriting, blood work, dust as well as fibre analysis.' Webster sighs in wonderment. 'Amazing fellow. But his genius was his *Principals of Exchange* written, oh… ten years ago. He believes that if there is contact between two objects then there will be what he terms *an exchange*. The criminal cannot avoid leaving something at the scene of the crime, be it fingerprints, hair, fibres, saliva and all manner of things like that. And in turn, during this exchange, the criminal cannot avoid taking something similar away from the scene. All the police must do is find it, collect it, and identify it. Then they have them. There's your criminal. Irrefutable proof. Science, you see. Science. *Bang to rights* as you might say.'

'What? From dust? Isn't dust just...dust?' Willetts asks, disbelief evident in his voice.

'Oh, goodness, no. Dust varies from place to place, house to house. Even room to room.'

Willetts shakes his head at the wonder of it all. Science fiction.

Webster sits back, waving his arms expansively. 'But even Locard is following work that goes back way beyond him. The Chinese were writing books on it as long ago as the mid-1200s. The Italian *Foirtunatus Fidelis* wrote about all this during the *Renaissance*. The *Renaissance*!' Webster pauses. 'There was a case not so far from here of a miller convicted of the rape and murder of a young woman. They identified him from the wheat husk powder found on the body of his victim. And that was a hundred years ago! But it's the FBI leading the way now. They opened a *National Crime Laboratory* ten years ago. Cutting edge. Lie detectors and gunshot analysis. They've evolved systems of fingerprint analysis that's taken Locard's work to even finer detail.'

'And you can do this stuff?' Porter asks.

Webster smiles. He sits back, hands held open in weary acknowledgement of their current surroundings. 'Alas, we're limited by resources.'

'The war,' Willetts puts in.

'The war,' Webster completes the mantra.

'So, what can we do?' Porter enquires.

Webster sits forward, rummages through the papers on his desk, before pulling out a manila folder. He tugs a monocle from the top pocket of his jacket, adjusting it into his eye socket. He flicks the folder open, consulting a typewritten sheet. 'Well, we've looked at your body. I worked with my colleague, John Lund - he's what we call a forensic biologist. There was little in the way of flesh on the actual skeleton - but you saw that for yourself. However, we did find a small amount of hair attached to what flesh there was on parts of the skull. From this we can be sure that her hair had neither been dyed nor permanently waved as is the practice among many women these days, or so I'm told. It suggests she was either poor and couldn't afford such treatments or that she lived in a community where it was simply not fashionable to do so.' He looks up, shrugging shoulders at the mystery and foolishness of the ways of women and fashion. He returns to his notes. 'We know she was suffocated. The bones in the neck - the *hyoid* - are shattered. All in line with strangulation. The taffeta stuck in her mouth was thus either for show or a gag applied to keep her from screaming prior to the killer gripping her throat.'

Porter scribbles in his notebook.

'The hand was severed post-mortem.' He taps the sheet of paper. 'Tricky one this, as the corpse is so old, but I'm certain that is the case. It's a clean cut, you see.' He makes a downward motion with the edge of his hand. 'Chopped, not bitten, or snapped, or torn by wild animals.'

'So, she wasn't tortured?'

Webster wrinkles his nose. 'At least not by having her hand removed. As for anything else...hard to tell. The bones are intact - ribs and such. Little sign of a beating in that sense, but, with so little flesh and so much time elapsed, that's about all we can say with any degree of certainty.'

'Okay. What else?'

'Given the difficulty we had in getting her out, she was undoubtedly placed in the tree feet first prior to *rigor* setting in. If *rigor* had been present in any form, it would have been impossible to fit her into that hollow so close to the crown. That means she was either alive when she was put there, or much more likely, given the problems of trying to force someone in whilst they were alive, she was killed close by. The area around the tree or somewhere near to it. In short, we can safely assume the wood is also the murder scene as well as the place where the body was disposed of.'

'I can't imagine anyone would have climbed up and got in there voluntarily,' Porter states. 'Is there anything else?'

Webster, adjusting his monocle, looks once more at the sheet. 'Well, as I said, female, mid-thirties. Short, just above five feet or so. Very poor teeth. Shocking. If nothing else, she ought to be identifiable by dental records. Overlapping front incisors, a very distorted tooth at the bottom.' He gazes at Porter and the scribbling Willetts. 'Maybe not quite unique, but certainly sufficient for a dentist to recognise. And she had dental treatment some short time prior to her death - a tooth extracted or maybe knocked out.'

Willetts scowls, 'Don't know of gypsies using dentists. Too pricey.'

Webster taps the sheet, 'And she'd had a child.'

Porter sits forward. 'A child? Are you sure?'

'Detective… May I call you Porter?' Porter nods. 'Porter. I may be a scientist in a laboratory rather than a practicing GP, but I remember basic anatomy. This woman had a child. Whether the child lived, what its sex was, or what its age, I cannot say. But she had given birth. The state of the pelvic bones.' Webster illustrates his point with a series of hand movements, 'The pubic bones expand during birth, you see. The pelvic bones pushed wider. After the birth they don't quite return to their original shape. A question of measurements. Her height, size, and the width of her pelvic bones. This woman had a child. Lund and I are agreed. Straightforward.'

'But there's no way of telling when she had it?'

'Afraid not. Given her age it could have been anywhere from her late teens to her early thirties. My own opinion is later, a birth in her teens would have led to significantly greater changes to the pelvic bones, and women's bones finish growing by eighteen. For a more specific dating of the childbirth, you'd need a specialist, a gynaecologist.'

Porter writes the Professor's words down, as too does Willetts, though the Special noticeably pauses at the hurdle of *gynaecologist.*

Porter taps the pencil against his lips, considering the implications. 'So, a child.' He pauses a beat. 'Someone who would know she was gone. She would be missed. A relative. A friend. Depending on the child's age at the time, someone would have been left to look after it. Possibly even the child itself. Young. Left alone. Mother not returning.'

Willetts bites his bottom lip. 'Or the child is dead too.'

Porter agrees. 'Yes. There's that too.' He indicates for Willetts to pass him the paper bag he'd brought along. 'We found these earlier today,' he says, unwrapping the package, revealing the silk shoes and gold ring. 'They were buried in the ground at the edge of the undergrowth, close to where the body was found.'

Webster takes them, lays them out on the desk. He selects a shoe, picks it up, squints inside, adjusting his monocle. 'Hmm, some sort of marking inside the tongue. It could be the manufacturer. With luck, they'll have lists of stockists and suppliers who could tell us where she bought them. I'll cut one of them out and get it looked at under a microscope. At the very least it gives us her shoe size, which will help confirm our ideas about her overall frame.' He places the shoe on the desk, next taking up the ring. He turns it in his fingers. 'Gold. Inexpensive. No inscription.' He screws his face in thought. 'Could be a wedding ring or just for decoration. Buried, you say?'

'Yes. With the shoes.'

'Rules out theft then.'

'That's what we thought.'

Webster places the ring inside a plain envelope and drops it onto the desk. 'So, she could have been married. That fact might

51

give us a father for the child. As you suggest, Porter, someone who would have known she was missing. Someone who can identify her. Someone who would have notified the authorities that she was missing.'

'Unless he was the one who done her,' Willetts observes.

'Good point, Constable. Good point.' Webster shuffles the autopsy file he'd read from. 'Well, at least we're beginning to compile a picture of her at the time of her death. Not just her shape and size and distinguishing features. We now have shoes and a ring. From these, we have some indication as to her life beyond the physical evidence: marriage, a child, a family. In addition, we have sufficient materials still attached to the body or found at the scene to get a good idea as to what she may have been wearing at the time of her death. Enough for a useful description. We can get posters circulated. Post offices, dentists. Be enough for local forces to have a look through their missing persons lists.'

Willetts sighs.

'What is it?' Porter asks.

'If you don't mind my saying, sir?'

Porter nods for Willetts to go ahead.

'That won't be so easy. Since the war, there's hundreds on them lists now. Especially places like around Birmingham. So many raids, so many families just...well...gone. And, what with all the movement; all the children evacuated out here, families evacuated, families re-housed, men gone off to war, women in the Land Army. Well, it's hard for people to keep track of their neighbours. And as for the police...short-staffed, volunteers rather than experienced men...' He lets the words trail off, observations pouring a heavy dose of reality into the room.

'The war,' Porter states.

'The war,' Webster responds dully.

'Having said all that,' Porter concludes, 'we can at least begin with the missing persons records of our own force. See if we can find a match for what you've given us, Professor. We might hit lucky.'

'And the dentists and GPs,' Webster adds. 'The state of her teeth. The fact she's had a child. There'll be medical records if nothing else. War or not, no-one can just disappear. Not without leaving something. Some impression of who they were.'

'Unless she's a gypsy,' Willetts scowls. 'Bloody *gypos*.'

20TH APRIL, 1943: LATE AFTERNOON

She held him, cradles him against her body, her breasts cool and yielding against his head. He opens his eyes, takes in the scene. The sun, low in the late afternoon sky, patterning the walls with the stencil of the net curtains. Shadows play on the ceiling, dance across the glass shaded lightbulb. Waves that flit across patches of yellow-brown stain where the damp has intruded. He feels her heart beating slow and measured, his own pounding hard against his chest slowing to match it. They lie like this for a moment, his understanding of real and nightmare re-balancing.

'Was it the dream?' she asks.

He feels the metallic taste in his mouth, the yawning emptiness in the pit of his stomach. The familiar aftermath of a fear that had woken him screaming into the afternoon heat of the room. He holds her, his words trapped somewhere inside, eyes scouting the space. *The sheets. The bedstead. The wardrobe. The dressing table.*

She shifts, a hand reaching across, smoothing the side of his face. 'It's okay,' she says. It's the voice she uses with Tommy. 'It's okay, Alec. You're here with me. You're safe. Safe.'

He pushes upright, pillows yielding beneath his back, the familiar ache of his spine, a pain more reassuring than her words. He senses the polished smoothness of his scars as they rub against the starched cotton of the pillowcase. Gently, he moves her hand away. Reaching for his cigarettes, he lights one, draws the smoke greedily into his lungs.

'It was the dream again, wasn't it?' she pursues.

'Did I shout?' he asks.

She hesitates. A pause. A stumble. 'It's okay. There's no one here. Arthur's taken Tommy to the allotment. Remember?'

He nods. Remembering making love, fast and urgent before drifting into sleep. Before the nightmare had come to claim him.

'It's getting better,' she murmurs.

Her reassurances are part of her. Her unerring sense of finding joy amidst despair. Light in the dark. She'd had plenty to hone it on over the past four years. 'Yes,' he says, more to blunt her enquiries than out of any agreement with her diagnosis. 'It's getting better.'

Stubbing the cigarette in the ashtray, he swings his legs off the bed. She reaches towards him, but he slips away, her arm dragging across his flank as he sits on the side of the bed. He is aware of her shifting on the mattress, half-turning towards him, knowing her gaze would be drawn to the scars on his back; the starfish of red, tissue worn smooth and shiny against the milk-white of his flesh. 'It was a good idea,' she offers. 'Coming to bed,' she clarifies in response to his lack of reaction. 'So hard to get time to ourselves these days. What with Arthur and Tommy.'

Porter looks ahead, still re-balancing: *net-laced curtains, sash-window, the garden beyond*. The afternoon sun was fading. It was April. Spring. Growth. Re-birth.

'I'm glad, anyway,' she states.

She climbs out of bed, smoothing the silk slip over her hips as she crosses the narrow gap to the marble-topped washstand. She stands gazing out of the window, eyes distant as she pours water from a pitcher into a matching porcelain bowl. When the bowl's almost full, she places the pitcher down, plunging a towelling cloth into the cool water. Wringing it out, folding it, she washes hands, face, neck, before moving to her thighs and cleaning away all trace of their love-making.

He watches her for a moment before sitting forward.

Tensing his body, he stands. At each gradient of his rise he waits for the tug of pain that accompanies any stretching of the muscles in his back. Grimacing, he stands away from the bed, lowering himself until he lies on the carpet parallel to the bedstead. Clasping both hands behind his neck, he begins a series of sit-ups, each one a shudder of muscle and tendon.

She dries herself. 'Should you be doing that?' she asks through her reflection in the mirror.

Porter grunts. 'I'm fine.'

'It's just…' her voice trails away.

He stops. Despite himself, he begins glowering at her. 'I'm not an invalid,' he snaps.

She looks down. A hesitation. A tell. She picks up underwear from the end of the bed. 'I know. I meant…'

'I know what you meant. I don't care what it says on my forms. I'm not an invalid.'

'Alec, you need to…'

'What, Rachel? What is it I *need* to do?'

She sighs. 'Let go. What happened… people understand. You need to forgive yourself.'

He stands. Picks up his vest from the chair and pulls on his trousers. The braces hang in slack loops at his side. 'There's nothing to forgive.'

She slides a dress over her head, covering her face, creating a moment. 'You know what I mean. I can't say it like you. I don't have your gift for words. You were hurt. Badly hurt. Your back.' She sighs. 'It's not your fault that you're not fit enough. You did your bit.' She looks at him, eyes appealing for calm, for help. 'You went off to Spain when everyone else sat at home. You've nothing to prove.'

He picks up his shirt, one hand smoothing out the creases. 'What about your father-in-law?'

She groans. 'Oh, for goodness' sake. Arthur's…Arthur. You know what he's like. How he thinks. He can't understand…' She halts, biting her bottom lip.

'Understand what?' He pulls the shirt over his head, muscles pulling, scar tissue stretching, the ache burning. 'Why I'm here?'

She shakes her head. He was twisting her words, her intentions. 'No.'

'Why Jack's not here?'

'Alec, don't,' she appeals.

Undaunted he persists, uncertain even within himself as to his intended victim. 'That's it, isn't it? Why I'm here and Jack's not? Why I'm here, fucking his dead son's wife?'

'Alec, please…That's not fair.'

'And what about Tommy?' he demands.

'Tommy loves you.'

He buttons his trousers. 'Tommy doesn't understand. But he will. One day.' He hitches the braces over his shoulders, snaps them into place. 'And what's he going to say to me then? What do I say when he asks me why I'm here and his dad isn't?'

She feels her composure crumbling. She turns away. 'He doesn't remember his dad. His dad died before he was born.'

'You know what I mean,' he retorts.

She sits on the upholstered stool that fronts the dressing table with its triptych mirror. Picking up a silver-plated hairbrush, she begins brushing her hair. He watches the steady rise and fall of her brushing. 'I'm sorry,' he murmurs.

She pauses; brush caught mid stroke. Placing the brush on the dresser, she adjusts one of the mirror's panels to look at him through its reflection. 'I know,' she says. 'I know.'

He moves to the small walnut wardrobe, part of her wedding trousseau. He picks out his ARP uniform, the heavy serge trench-coat, and the satchel containing his gas-mask. He drops them onto the bed.

Rachel adjusts her hair with her hands, nestling and patting it into shape. A silence is in the room. She stands and looks at the rumpled bed. 'I'd better make it before Arthur gets back,' she says.

Porter lifts his clothing from the eiderdown, draping them instead over the high-backed bedside chair.

'What time will you be back?' she asks, tugging sheets and cover into place.

'Late. If there's a raid like the one last Thursday, it could be the morning.'

'And you've a shift at the station tomorrow.'

Alec Porter: ex-Cambridge undergraduate dropout; ex-International Brigade Volunteer; invalid, unfit for military duty; ARP Warden; acting Detective Constable; lover; surrogate father. How many guises could a mind contain without each falling into the other? Sometimes it was only the change of uniform that told him who he was that day.

He simply nods. 'It's a late one though. I'll get some sleep before it starts.' He snorts. 'Black market and bloody blackout violations. It's hardly *the Public Enemy*.'

'People are pulling together. It's good there's so little crime.'

She was right. Much of what passed for crime would have registered low on police business before the war. There were still opportunist crimes - the burglary of bombed property being top among them - but the decision to re-classify such crime as looting had succeeded in banishing much of that. Looters could in theory be shot on the spot. More realistically, it made the crime unpatriotic, and even criminals appeared to have some sense of patriotism these days.

She crosses the room. It was tight, cramped, full of furniture intended for a home that had never come to pass. Jack Morris was dead, her husband of but a few weeks killed in the opening salvoes of the war in France. She left pregnant with a houseful of furniture. She'd no home or family. Jack's father, Arthur, had taken her and her new-born child in. For Arthur, his dead son is a hero, his widow and child all that's left of him. It was easy to see why Arthur resented anything that came between himself and that legacy, and at present that something was Porter. A man wounded in Spain and declared unfit for military service. A man who slept safe at home in the bed of his dead son's wife whilst others, like his Jack, died.

Rachel puts her arms round him, leans her face against his chest. 'What you do is essential. I'm proud of you. Proud of what you do.'

He holds her to him, stroking her hair. 'Rachel, there's a war on. I'm only a police officer because there's no place for me in the fighting units. Worse than that, I'm a police officer with a chunk of Spanish metal in his back. A piece of shrapnel that every time it moves the doctor's say might paralyse me forever. Even when I get handed what looks like a big case, like this skeleton in the tree, no-one trusts me with anything beyond a few enquiries. Paperwork. Ticking boxes. *College boy*, James calls me.'

She looks up, pushing her head away to see him the better. 'It's because you're educated. He's jealous. As for the rest, those doctors don't know everything. The last one said it was possible that in a few years there'd be advances in surgery. That they'd be able to remove it. Make you whole again.'

He notes but let pass her choice of words. The idea of becoming whole. The implication that for now he is less than that. 'Doctors,' he snorts. 'I've had my fill of doctors. A few years? The war will have to be over for that to happen.'

'Good,' she says. 'I've had my fill of war.'

6

The knock at the door disturbs his thoughts, his reverie. Porter looks up as Willetts opens the door and pokes his head round. 'The next ones' here, sir.'

Porter pushes aside a cup and saucer, slopping remnants of cold tea. He re-arranges his note pad and pencil for the tenth time that morning. He sits waiting, adjusting the knot of his tie.

The entire morning has been spent in Hagley police station interviewing anyone who might have some idea as to the identity of the dead woman. Thus far he'd spoken with the bank manager, the grocer and his assistants, the vicar, and two farmers who took on migrant workers during the harvest. So far, he'd drawn a blank in everything but a deeper understanding of community politics. At the same time he'd amassed an impressive array of insider rumour and gossip about a variety of villagers. As yet, he'd learned nothing to indicate the identity of the woman in the tree, nor found new avenues for his enquiry.

The premise he and Webster had agreed was a simple one. Webster and his man Lund, plus enthusiastic under-graduate students would work to identify the source of the remnants of

59

retrieved clothing and footwear. Whilst awaiting their findings, Porter was to check the possibilities of a local missing person. Such enquiries, to Willetts' evident satisfaction, had meant putting off attempts to contact those traveller communities who may have passed through the area during what Webster thought to be the relevant period of roughly eighteen months previously - around the autumn of 1941.

Porter looks at his notepad. *Elaine Craddock*, barmaid at *the Gypsy's Tent*, the public house closest to Hagley Woods and thus the building nearest the scene of the discovery of the body.

The door opens wider, allowing both Willetts and the interviewee to enter. Elaine Craddock is in her mid-thirties, short dark red-blonde hair with what the movie magazines were these days calling a generous figure. She wore a fashionable two piece comprising a tight fitting pencil skirt and blouson jacket. It was a choice calculated to emphasise wide hips, narrow waist, and what was clearly a good figure. The collar of a white blouse pokes from the top of the jacket, on the lapel of which is a silver brooch in the shape of a star. Her make-up is understated rather than the mask of rouge and lipstick he'd anticipated of a woman in her mid-thirties who'd been a barmaid for almost fifteen years. Her lips are full and plump, the bright red lipstick enhancing a generous mouth. Her eyes are narrow, more slits than ovals, with deep sockets and hooded eyelids. Her face is slim, with her eyes it is almost snake-like. She is not a beautiful woman, not even a conventionally pretty one, but it struck him she was a woman who looked life straight in the eye, and life would be the one that flinched. He thinks Jean Harlow more than Jean Arthur.

'Thank you Willetts,' he says. Willetts closes the door, Porter certain he catches a look of disdain on the Special's face as he withdrew. 'Take a seat Miss Craddock.'

'Thank you, Inspector. S'kind of you, must say.' The voice, straining for RP, is betrayed by vowel sounds lapsing towards

Black Country. She crosses her legs, brown nylon stockings ending in black high heels.

'I suppose you know why we've asked to see you today?'

'The body. The one in the tree, God bless her.'

'That's correct.'

She inclines her head in a gesture of regret. 'Poor soul. I'm not religious myself Inspector but you have to think, don't you? Oh, don't get me wrong, I'm a god-fearing Christian like most folk round here. I just don't find the need to get to church that much.' She screws up her face. 'All that praying. But that's no way for anyone to be left, y'know, stuffed inside a tree. I hope she's getting a decent burial.'

'I'm certain that when the time comes the authorities will see she's properly taken care of. And it's Detective Constable, not Inspector.'

'Oh, Sorry.'

He waves a hand in dismissal of the need of any apology.

She opens her bag, taking out a cigarette. She places it in her mouth, sitting forward expectantly as Porter, taking the hint, leans across and lights it. She sits back, exhaling. Porter returns to outlining his interest. 'The reason we've asked you here is that I'm particularly interested in your knowledge of the area. You work in the *Gypsies' Tent* don't you? Just across the road from Hagley Wood?'

'Yes. Yes, I do.'

'You've worked there for some time.'

Elaine tilts her head in calculation, 'Five years. Since before the war.'

'So, you'd know all of the barmaids who were there during that time.'

She smiles. It is wide and open. 'That'd be quite a few. There's some regular staff like me. Most of the rest, it's seasonal, especially since the war.' She drags on her cigarette.

'We're interested in a couple of women who worked there in late Forty-one, maybe early Forty-two. I'm led to believe they both at different times just upped and left. Didn't come in for work one day and were never seen again. I understand there were rumours about them.'

She wrinkles her brow, sucks deep on the cigarette before exhaling. The smoke sits like early morning mist over the desk. 'Well, to be honest, Inspector, in our trade it happens quite a bit. You know, staff just not turning in. After a few shifts of them not turning up, well, you just get on. Advertise for replacements.'

'Seems a little odd. Doesn't anyone look into why?'

She drew on her cigarette once more, adding yet another layer to the veil of smoke that lies across the space between them. 'Oh, there could be so many reasons. Often it's a husband or boyfriend who goes off the idea of them working there - you know, they get a bit jealous. Some of the girls get fed up with being pawed by the customers, especially them soldiers down from Malvern or those Yanks over at Wolverley. Some girls get evacuated, bombed out. And of course, some might very well be dead, what with all the bombings and that. If we chased around looking for them, well, it'd be a full-time job. It's always been like that. Just that the war makes it more frequent.'

'What about names? I'm told there was a young woman worked there in 1941. A Dutch woman, someone said. Went missing.'

'Dutch you say?' She shakes her head, 'Only foreign woman I worked with was a woman called Annie. Oh, sorry, Anna. Can't say if she was Dutch or where she came from. Can't say I can properly recall her surname either. One of those long, funny ones. Lots of zeds and w's stuff. You know. A *wiki* or something like that. No need for me to know it really. Not as if I'd be writing to her asking her over for tea.' She smiles at the thought. 'Anyway, I think she'd left the area before then. Think it was before the Yanks. You know Pearl Harbour and all that malarkey. That was the Christmas, wasn't it? 1941?'

'Yes. Sort of. But you say you were friends with her?'

'Wouldn't say friends. Friendly. But that's different. Friendly to lots of people me. It's the job.'

'But she just stopped working there. No reason. No goodbyes?' he persists.

'Like I said. The war. It happens.'

He jots on his notepad, Elaine watching him. 'You're not from round here, are you?' she states more than asks.

'Me? No.'

'Thought not. The accent. Posh.'

He stops writing. 'Posh?' he asks.

'Yeah, posh. You know, educated.'

He smiles, returning to his note pad.

'You not been called up?' she enquires.

'No.'

'Fit looking man like you?' She stubs her cigarette out in the glass ashtray. 'You look like you could handle yourself.'

'I'm unfit.'

'Unfit? Blimey, you want to see some of 'em comes in the pub. If you're unfit well...Blimey. You look a damn site fitter than my Barry, and he's out in Tobruk with Monty and the Eighth.'

'I was wounded. A2. My back.'

'Shame.' She watches him write. 'You with someone?'

'Yes.'

'Shame.'

He stops writing. 'So, no...gossip? No stories about girls who left around that time?'

'Gossip? Ooh I've got lots of gossip. Goes with the job. People confide in barmaids, you see. We get to hear all their troubles and woes, especially the fellas. Especially about their wives or girlfriends. Make your hair curl some of the stuff I get told.' She smiles, before becoming serious, looking him in the eyes. 'But no, nothing about those particular girls.'

'I see. You're certain?'

She fishes for another cigarette from her bag. 'Pretty much. Mind you, there was some scandal about one of the women round that time finding herself up the duff. You know, pregnant. She left suddenly.' She pauses in extracting her cigarette. She wrinkles her nose. 'But that would have to be early '42.'

'Early Forty-two? You're sure it was then, not earlier?'

'Well, it would have to be. They said it was a Yank that was the father. One of them lot over here early, you know, one of them involved in preparing things out at Wolverley. You know, that big hospital they've built there for the Yanks. They didn't get here till early Forty-two.'

She pauses, cigarette in mouth, waiting. Porter realising his cue, leans across and lights it. 'Do you remember anything more about her? A name, an address, a description?'

She drew in the smoke, tilting her head to what she'd clearly been told was an appropriate movie star pose. She exhales a cloud of smoke. 'She was dark haired. Pretty girl. Quite short, too. Never smiled much. Kept herself to herself.' She smiles. 'Though clearly not with everyone.'

'Anything you can recall about her - or any other missing women - would be useful. We believe the body in the tree was there no longer than 18 months, but it could have been as little as a year. That could put your pregnant barmaid as a possibility.'

Elaine frowns, engages in the struggle to capture further details, 'Susan... Susie, something like that. She was only there a few weeks, maybe a month or so.'

'And she just left?'

'Like I say, it's the war.'

'Yes, the war.'

'What about anything else around then?'

'What do you mean?'

'Stories. You said you heard lots of gossip. That husbands and boyfriends talk to you. What about women around the area other than the staff? Did you hear anything about a missing woman? Maybe an abandoned child?'

She shakes her head. 'Gosh. No, not that I can recall. It's a small community, farmers mostly. Soldiers and GIs lately. And the gypsies, of course.'

'The Travellers? Do they come in the pub?'

'All the time when they're in the area. Their markets and fairs each year. Regular as clockwork. That and their festivals, their *ceremonies*.' She shudders. 'Fair gives me the creeps.'

'Why is that?'

'Not Christian, is it? Like I said, I'm no churchgoer, but I still believe in a proper Christian God and Jesus. That lot…they worship trees and stuff. Some nights, when they're there in the woods, you hear stuff. Strange goings on. Singing. Dancing.'

'Isn't that just normal. I mean, if it's a festival or a feast. You'd expect singing and dancing.'

'You wouldn't say that if you heard it. I won't go near the place. There's many live around there won't. Especially that tree.'

'The tree?'

'The wych-elm where they found her.'

'Why would that be?'

'It's one of their places. They say it's haunted. Full of spirits and demons. The pub too. There're parts of the pub none of us girls go in alone. Ghosts. Witchcraft and magic.'

'Magic?'

'You know, Black Magic. Ceremonies. Curses. They believe in all that, don't they? The gypsies. I hadn't used to…but I've seen things, heard things…in the pub…around the wood.'

'Things?'

'Cries. Doors slamming late at night.' She shivers again. 'Unbelievable cold in the passages. Unnatural. The cellar as well.'

'How often are they there? In the woods?'

'Two or three times a year. Around the autumn, they have this big gathering. God knows what they do there. Locals say they build big fires and dance around that tree where she was found. Like I said, witchcraft. Black magic and curses. I don't know, and don't want to.'

He thinks back to how he'd felt standing in the clearing. All too easy to believe. Myths, legends. Stories to scare the kids with. He pulls his mind back to the interview. 'And do the women come to the pub?'

She draws on the cigarette, exhaling as she shakes her head. 'No, just the men. The landlord's not bothered. He likes the money they bring. But a lot of the locals won't come in the pub whilst they're there. The women stay at the camp. Only time you see them is when they're out on the streets selling their charms, that lucky heather and all that. Lovely dresses some of them. beautiful designs. And the material. All gold threads and taffeta.'

'Taffeta?'

'It's a sort of silk but cheaper.' She grinds the remains of her cigarette into the ashtray. 'They make lovely scarves and shawls and dresses out of it. I bought one once, gorgeous, not like anything you get in the shops. And their shoes, beautiful silk shoes.'

As her ash splutters burning embers across the ashtray and onto the desk he sees fires and charms, swirling silks and gold. Sees the easy connections between the evidence they had and the beliefs of Williams, James, and Willetts as to who she was, why she'd been killed and left in a hollow tree.

Maybe it was true. *Occam's Razor*. The idea that sometimes the obvious answer is just that, the answer, plain and clear. A woman murdered for who she was. Murdered for what others thought she was.

He watches the embers of the cigarette turn grey, their fire dying.

In the end all he sees is a woman terrified for her life.

7

21ST APRIL, 1943: LATE EVENING

The balding head of Harry James bobs up and down, each dip reflecting the light from the green metal shade of the lamp fixed to his desk. His bobbing motion is accompanied by a series of plosive grunts and sighs as he works his way down the pages of Porter's report of the first three days of his enquiry.

'Humph!' he snorts, reaching the bottom of the final page. He turns it face down onto the previous pages, tapping the pile into shape before flipping it over. Carefully, he re-attaches the paper clip and lays the document on his desk.

He sits, gazing at Porter's work, studying the sheaf of loosely held pages.

As far as he can tell, the report is disappointingly textbook. A catalogue of actions taken, witnesses interviewed, a preliminary medical report, and men deployed. It ends with a summary of what has been found and how the investigation is to proceed.

He dislikes Porter. As far as Harry James is concerned the man's a *conchie*, a coward working his ticket to avoid the draft. Worse than that, a college boy who thinks himself better than the rest. Whilst James had always been forced to work hard for the little that came his way, he sees Porter as having had it easy. The man was going to sit through the war whilst the rest did all the fighting. If he had his way men like Porter would have been sent to the frontline. If they still wouldn't fight he'd have them shot as deserters, like they did in *the Great War*. As it is, all that it's in his power to do is to see to it that wherever possible the man's life is made a misery. The shitty details, the shitty shifts. And, of course, whenever possible, that words were put in the ears of colleagues and superiors alike lamenting Porter's lack of talent, his poor attitude, and the fact that above all else he was a coward: *what can you expect, the man's a bloody conchie!*

From the report, the investigation is following the path Williams has outlined. Straightforward. Open and shut. The victim had been dead for well over a year. A gypsy. The chances of finding out anything about her from her own kind - even who she was - is limited; the chance of finding her killer even less likely. A paper chase.

He turns off the reading lamp, leaving his office to walk down the corridor to that of his DI. He knocks and enters. Williams sits behind his desk, paperwork piled high, loading a pipe with tobacco. 'Harry,' Williams greets his Acting Detective Sergeant. 'Come in. You're working late.'

James crosses the room to stand in front of the desk. Williams inclines his head in the direction of the report held in James' hand, 'What's on your mind?'

James places the report on the desk, taking the chair opposite. 'Report from Porter, sir. The body in the tree enquiry.'

'Ah, yes.' Williams says. He continues attending to his pipe with little apparent interest in the document. 'How's he getting on?'

James nods in the direction of the report. 'The report's pretty standard fare, sir. A preliminary medical report and confirmation of a cause of death. He's listed interviews with some of the locals who might have some idea as to who she is. Apparently that professor of his...erhm, Webster, seems he's sent off some fabric and shoes found at the scene for identification. He's circulating local dentists. You'll remember her teeth were pretty messed up. Apparently, this Webster character seems to think anyone who'd treated her would know her in a shot.'

Williams picks up a box of Swan Vesta matches, strikes one, and begins to ignite the tamped tobacco bedded in the bowl of the pipe. With tobacco scarce and the price so high, a fresh bowl is a thing to be savoured, and he finds himself resenting James' intrusion on the moment. 'Good stuff. Good,' he mutters.

'Yes, sir.'

Williams gets the pipe smouldering, drawing hard to stoke it, cheeks puffing rhythmically. His DS sits expectant. He's little choice but to humour him. 'But?' he prompts between puffs.

'Well, sir, it's difficult...criticising a fellow officer, especially such a novice.'

'Oh,' *Puff.* 'Come now.' *Puff.* 'Part of the job.' *Puff.* 'Part of your job, Harry. He's a lot to learn. Nothing wrong with a bit of healthy criticism.'

'If you say so, sir.'

Williams flicks the match in the air, dousing it, dropping it into an ashtray. 'I do. I do. So, come on, out with it. What is it that's troubling you?'

'Doesn't need a trained eye to see this one isn't going anywhere, sir. My opinion; she's a gypsy. Killed a year ago. More than likely by another gypsy. The chances of bringing in a killer nigh on impossible.'

'You're certain it's gypsies, eh?'

'Quite sure, sir. So, I can't see why Porter's using up time and resources on what we all know is a bloody wild goose chase - if you pardon the expression. Trying to find shoemakers. Dress makers. Be bloody candle stick-makers next. He's using a car, as well! There's talk in the station he's booked petrol for a round trip out to Wolverley. Going out to the big Yank hospital over there.'

'Wolverley? Why on earth's he going out there?'

'Exactly, sir. Some story about a GI and some pregnant bar-maid.'

'He has a lead?'

James screws his face. 'Gossip. *Tittle-tattle*. If you want my opinion, he's dragging this out to get off other duties.' He sits forward. 'You must know that he doesn't really belong here, sir. The rest of the men...Well, they find him a bit...distant. Bit of a loner. They don't like him.'

Williams puffs on his pipe. 'He's a rum one, that's for sure. Clever lad, though. Very clever. University, you know. Scholarship boy.'

'Yes, sir. I heard.'

'Cambridge. He had some bad luck. Out in Spain.'

'Yes, sir.'

Williams holds the pipe out, jabbing it in the direction of his Acting DS. 'Mustn't judge, you know, Harry. Appearances being deceptive and such like. Mustn't judge. Keep an open mind.'

'I try to, sir.'

Williams sits back, mollified, point made, leadership established. 'Having said that, we don't want folk not pulling their weight. Bad for morale.'

'It is, sir,' James concurs.

Williams sucks on his pipe. 'Tell you what. We'll give him the week.' He waves the pipe around airily. 'Let him get off to Malvern or wherever it is these Yanks are. Let him chase the dentist and these shoes. And be sure you get him to find some of those gypsies. Things like that, dealing with that sort, bound to put him off, he'll soon want done with it all. And, you never know, he might even get something from them about who this woman might be. Doubt it, but at least we'll have given it a shot. Looks good at HQ. Boxes ticked and all that. *I's* dotted. *T's* crossed.' He sits back, satisfied. 'Once he's done that, get him to tidy up the file and close the investigation: *killing by person or person's unknown*. You know the drill.' He snorts. 'You never know, maybe after all this lot's over, after the war, we might get a break with it. Beat the Hun and we'll all have a bit more time to spare to chase down gypsies and fairy tales.'

21ST APRIL, 1943: NIGHT

They came just before eleven. He'd sat on the roof of the observation post on Monument Hill for over 3 hours before they arrived. *Heinkels* he thought, maybe *Dorniers.* Hard to tell from this distance. Difficult to judge shape or engine noise. Occasionally one is caught in the searchlight beams. Then the sky blossoms with the plume of *ack-ack* as the anti-aircraft barrage chases it across the night.

He saw a few hits, a yellow-grey plume replaced by a redder ball of fire. At such moments he can trace an aircraft's path by the line of flames. Follow as its pilot tacked first one way then another attempting to shake off the hungry guns. In two cases he was certain the line of flames dipped diagonally towards the ground. He'd followed one right down, watched it turn into a fireball before crashing into the city, a pall of smoke rising to mark its end. He logged it as *KILL* on the ARP form.

Afterwards, he'd scanned the sky with his binoculars for some five minutes looking for parachutes that might drift his way. There'd been none. He wondered if any of the crew got out. Imagined them imprisoned in the burning fuselage, a canvas and plywood coffin of fire. Enemy or not, it was no way to die.

Having dropped their bomb load, the wave of bombers had moved on, circling to pass closer to the Beacon where he looks out across the Birmingham conurbation. He listened as engines whining and screaming, they sought the altitude to escape the flak. *Dorniers.*

With their disappearance, the searchlights had doused and the guns ceased. Apart from the fires studded across the landscape everything returned to black. It was hard to believe he was overlooking a major industrialised city. With the blackout it appears emptier than any desert.

He squats pulling the collar of his greatcoat down, unbuttoning the tunic despite regulations requiring it be buttoned at all times. Late April and the weather was changing for the better, the nights warmer. Farmers were busy. Driving around the country lanes he'd watched them sowing crops in fields, the weather at last showing signs of sustained sun. The Land Girls were out too. He'd seen them through gaps in the hedgerows as they'd sped along in the old Wolseley that Willetts was somehow managing to keep going.

Awaiting results from the posters Webster had circulated to dentists or for replies to his own enquiries to clothing suppliers and manufacturers, they'd spent the best part of the day calling in on the larger farms in the area. They'd spoken with farmers and Land Girls, hoping someone might remember a worker or colleague who'd gone missing in the previous eighteen months.

They'd run up against the same responses he'd had from Elaine Craddock. There were simply too many transients. *Land Girls* coming and going every month, their associated paperwork missing or delayed or never arriving at all. Who's to tell if she'd been one of them? Young women were criss-crossing the country daily - some eager and willing, some resentful and under compulsion. Some running away, disappearing to no doubt re-surface after the war.

The war, y'know they'd all said.

The war he'd duly responded.

On their return to the station, Williams' message had been waiting.

Keep it simple. A week, then get the paperwork straight. Case unsolved: person or persons unknown; on-going investigation. When the war's over and things get straight again, the authority records will get completed. Maybe then we'll know. Maybe then we'll find out who she was.

Fat chance.

War or no war, he knew that once the week was up there'd be little chance of anyone bothering with the case again. Once the immediate paperwork was straight, she'd be filed away and confined to records: *Unidentified female. Strangled. Probably gypsy. Case unsolved; person or persons unknown.*

And he wanted to solve this case.

He'd told Rachel just that before starting his ARP shift. She'd urged him to take it easy - the fire watches, the travelling around the area, the effort he was putting in. *Your back. You know you're not right. The doctors' told you to be careful. The stress. It's not good for you. You're making yourself ill. Just do what your bosses say, sort out the paperwork. Let it go.*

It wasn't that simple. That's what he'd told her.

'It's not that simple.'

'Why?'

'I can't explain it,' he'd floundered. He'd sat in the kitchen, shirt out, braces loose, busying himself brushing his boots. Rachel making tea. 'She deserves more,' he'd told her.

'Deserves more? Who?'

'Bella,' he'd responded without thinking.

'*Bella?*' Rachel had sounded out the name. 'Who's *Bella?*'

He'd hesitated. Brush poised mid-air. Tentative. 'The woman in the tree.'

She'd sought understanding. 'So, you've found out who she is?'

He'd returned to polishing, brush skimming back and forth across the toe-cap. 'No. I just...call her that.'

She'd stared at him. 'Sorry?'

He'd shrugged, pinned, part resentful, part embarrassment. 'I can't go around thinking of her as *that woman in the tree* or *the victim.* She needed a name. Something.'

'Bella?'

He'd nodded. 'Bella.'

'Why Bella?'

He'd bent down, scooping more polish onto a cloth, smearing it around the sides and heel. He'd looked up. Rachel had stopped her work to stare at him. 'I was looking at the records of gypsy names, people who'd been arrested,' he'd explained. 'Names of the women we've been given to follow up on - *Bella Tonks, Bella Leur, Bella Beeg*. Most of the women are called Isabella or Arabella or Annabella. So,...Bella.'

'So, she's a gypsy?'

'Looks that way,' he'd shrugged.

She'd sighed, 'That means you'll be off chasing gypsy caravans around the country.'

He'd frowned. 'Maybe. We're hoping local forces can go through their records. Tell us where they've been. Help us track their movements over the past year or two.'

'And in the meantime?'

'We're following up other ideas. She may be more local. Maybe a *Land Girl* over from Brum, or an evacuee - she had a child.'

'What, and she just goes missing and no-one notices?'

'It happens. We're going back over missing persons details for the past 18 months.'

'Who'd want to kill her?'

'Maybe she was just unlucky. A stranger, someone local, another evacuee. Maybe a GI or soldier from the bases.'

'Or maybe her gypsy husband or boyfriend.'

'Maybe.'

'Whoever it is, is it worth it? What with the raids and the ARP duties and you off chasing after this killer, I don't get to see you at all. When you do get home, you just fall asleep. It's not good for you, Alec. Nor for me or Tommy.'

'It's my job, Rachel. I'm a police officer. It's what I do.'

'This is more than your job. This desire to find answers. Answers that in all probability aren't going to be found. I don't understand, Alec. You're not well. Emotionally it's got to be tough. Your nightmares are back again. And this case, it's becoming...well, it's like an obsession. And naming her. Like you knew her.' She'd shaken her head in exasperation and incomprehension.

He'd stopped brushing. Lowered the boot he'd been working on. 'This is my job, Rachel. It's what I do. What I can do. You know how I feel about everything; the war, living here with your father-in-law. This is a chance to do something…I don't know… meaningful, worthwhile.' He'd put the boot down, holding her gaze. 'There's been a crime. A murder. Maybe it was two years ago, it's still a crime. A woman's dead. She deserves someone to find out why, someone to bring her killer to justice. At the very least she deserves to have people know her name.'

'There's others could look. Others who could go chasing after gypsies.'

'Rachel, no-one is interested. No-one. Williams, James… they're decent coppers, but at the moment, they don't really care. It's paperwork to them. A file to be closed. This matters. Matters to me.' He'd shaken his head. 'Maybe it's Spain. Maybe that no-one thinks it can be done. That I've been given it only because everyone else thinks it's not worth their time. A losing battle. But she had a child, Rachel. A child. She could have been you. Out there, alone, the middle of a war. Terrified of what life held for her and for her child. And someone killed her. Someone took her by the throat, looked her in her terrified eyes, and choked the life from her. Then, they chopped off her hand before shoving her still warm body inside a tree in the middle of those dark woods. They left her there to rot. Not even the comfort of a proper grave. A proper burial.'

'Mommy!' They'd both turned to find Tommy standing in the doorway, sobbing.

Rachel had rushed across, scooping the alarmed child into her arms. 'There, there,' she'd soothed. 'It's okay, Alec was telling mommy a story about witches. It's okay. It's like one of those stories from your books. Witches and magic and little children.' She'd hugged Tommy to her, rotating him on her waist back and forth in reassurance. 'It's just a story. Don't worry, they all live happily ever after in the end don't they, Alec?'

He'd picked up his boots and stood.

He'd walked over, reaching down a hand to ruffle the sobbing Tommy's hair. He'd smiled at the little boy, seeking to re-assure both Tommy and his mother of their certainty of happy endings, even though he himself was no longer sure of the possibility of such a thing anymore.

8

The GI at the barrier eyed Porter with suspicion. His eyes moving from Porter and Willetts' papers to their faces and back again. His attention particularly drawn to the car, its engine sputtering and shuddering on tick-over.

'So, you're like, the FBI or somethin'?' he asks.

'Something like that, yes.'

'You from Scotland Yard?'

'Not quite. We're here to see the base commander. Colonel Wyatt.'

The MP raises a hand to his helmet, nudging it upwards from his forehead. 'He ain't here right now.' He takes a moment considering his options, his face beneath the white helmet branded *MP* fixed with concentration. 'I'll send you to the adjutant's office, Captain Tolvey,' he decides. With that he turns and whistles over one of the soldiers from the hut. 'O'Hara. Take these guys to Captain Tolvey,' he instructs.

'Bloody Yanks!' Willetts mutters, winding up the driver's window whilst the junior MP receives instruction. 'Think they own the bloody place.'

77

'Well, here they do,' Porter states. 'At least for the foreseeable future. Until the war finishes.'

'The war,' Willetts grumbles. 'Almost as bad as having the bloody *Gerries* occupying us. Gum and coffee and their bloody nylons. Sick of 'em.'

A fresh-faced GI jumps on the running board. 'Straight ahead and then second right,' he instructs through the window as the red and white chevron striped barrier is raised. 'Shit! This is one beat up motor!' he comments as they pull away.

They drive along roads lain out in a logical north/south and east/west grid. As they drive, Porter becomes aware of just how huge an enterprise the base is. Camp Wolverley had opened the previous winter in the grounds of Lea Castle. Fitted out by an advance party of American pioneers, it had been erected in mere months to serve as a hospital base for the 52nd battalion and US aircrew. Beyond that, little was known of it.

The young MP guided them past block after block of single storey buildings. Signs attached to the sides of them indicated they were offices, research laboratories, and operating theatres. Further on were row upon rows of Nissen huts. When asked, the MP tells them they're accommodation for military guards and medical staff.

The MP signals Willetts to stop outside a newly built block, leaving them to wait whilst he enters. Willetts turns off the engine, which splutters and shudders to its familiar standstill some five seconds after.

'Impressive, eh?' Porter asks of Willetts as he gets out to stand by the car.

Willetts climbs out, leaning against the bonnet. He stretches each leg in turn, rubbing at his knees before rolling a cigarette. 'Not as much as that,' he responds, indicating with a nod the walls of Lea Castle.

Porter ceases the back exercises he'd been going through and follows Willetts' gaze. The castle, despite its ruined walls, remained imposing. 'Fair point,' he acknowledges.

'Stands as long as that and I'll be impressed.' Willetts grimaces, rotating a knee. 'Bloody Yanks!'

The MP re-appears, snapping out a salute. 'Captain Tolvey will see you now, sir.'

They follow the MP into an outer office where a female civilian secretary is busy typing. Willetts indicates a chair near to the secretary's desk. 'I'll wait here if that's okay with you, sir. My leg,' he adds.

'Fine,' Porter says before following the MP along a freshly painted corridor to a door marked *Captain Tolvey: Adjutant*. The MP opens the door and Porter enters.

Tolvey rises from his desk to greet him. 'Hey there, pleased to meet you,' he says whilst quickly glancing down to his desk, checking a handwritten note. 'Inspector Porter,' he adds.

Porter shakes Tolvey's hand. 'It's Detective Constable Porter, I'm afraid.'

Tolvey was, like most Americans of Porter's experience, tall, well-built, and of an easy disposition. All broad smiles and a *good to know you* nature. His hair was longer than the style of the average British soldier, swept back and brilliantined. The uniform is of a noticeably lighter material than the British serge, sharper in design. He understood Willetts' jibe about the GIs: *oversexed, overpaid, and over here.*

'Oh, sorry. Detective Constable Porter.' He indicates a seat. 'So, how can I help? One of our boys been painting the town a little too wildly? Or is it another complaint about our carefree Yankee sexual mores?' he smiles, revealing two rows of gleaming white teeth.

'Nothing like that. It's about a murder, actually.'

'Seesh! A murder. Wow!' Tolvey sits upright, manner snapping to business-like. 'Hey, listen, Detective, I'm sorry if I came across a little jokey. It's just that we've been getting complaints almost every other day about raucous behaviour and pregnant daughters. Almost weekly visits from you guys about some angry boyfriend or husband.' He sweeps a hand through his hair even though there isn't a single one out of place. 'How can we help?' He picks up a pencil, drawing a pad of writing paper closer.

Porter takes out his notebook. 'That's what I'm here to find out.'

'Sorry?'

'We're trying to establish the identity of the victim.'

'You think it's a GI? I've not had word of anyone missing roll-call, though it's a little more hit and miss in a hospital camp like this.' He reaches a hand for the phone. 'We don't run on the strict military lines of a barracks.'

'No, sir, it's not a soldier. It's a woman.'

Tolvey pauses, receiver in hand. 'A woman. A nurse?'

'No. In fact, we don't believe the victim is from the base. She's more than likely a civilian. There's evidence she's more than likely a traveller.'

Tolvey struggles to make sense of what he's hearing. He lowers the receiver to its cradle. 'A gypsy?' He considers the idea for a moment. 'Detective, I have to tell you I don't quite see where we fit into all this.'

'Let me explain. A few days ago, we found a body. A female, dead for over a year, possibly 18 months. A place called Hagley Woods a few miles from here.'

'A year you say?'

Porter nods. 'That's something we're trying to establish. A year, possibly more. We think 18 months or so at the outside.'

'Well, let me stop you right there, Detective. We weren't here a year ago. Most of us arrived six months ago, around Fall. Sorry, that's your autumn.' He shakes his head. Porter wonders if it is at the strangeness of the language or his puzzlement at the time-scale. 'I don't see how this brings you here,' Tolvey clarifies.

'In our investigation we came across the story of a young woman who went missing around the time of the possible murder of our victim. A *Land Girl*, we think. She was originally from the Kidderminster area, so quite close to here. She was pregnant. Story is the father was a GI, one of your advance party over here preparing the base.'

Tolvey deliberates the idea for a moment. 'I can assure you… Detective, there's very little chance of that. Do the Maths. Eighteen months ago, we weren't even in this war. It took Pearl Harbour, December Forty-one, to get us here. Earliest any of our guys were here would have been February of Forty-two. That's what? Just over a year ago.'

'I understand that. But it's possible we might be a little out with our dating of the murder. Our facilities for establishing such things are basic. Our medical expert suggests it's no more than eighteen months, but it could conceivably be as little as a year.'

Tolvey smiles. 'I think conceive is the moot point, Detective. If you think it's a GI, then your guy would have to have wooed this woman and knocked her up pretty damn quick to get to killing her a year ago.'

'But it is feasible. As you've said, some of your men were here from late Christmas Forty-one/Forty-two. She could have been killed as little as a year ago - say April Forty-two. It could be she met a GI here in Malvern whilst visiting friends or family - Kidderminster's not that far. Discovering she's pregnant, she arranges to meet the father close to where she was then working, near Hagley.'

Tolvey sits back, twirls the pencil in his hands. 'Okay. Say it is possible. Just what is it you expect from us?'

'A list of personnel who were here from late Forty-one to mid Forty-two.'

Tolvey nods, but not in agreement, rather in appreciation of what such a request requires. 'That's something I'll have to clear with my superiors. Of course, they'll want an official request from your government or military command before they'll consider it.'

Porter frowns, rubs his chin. 'I don't know about your set up, but things like that take time here. British bureaucracy. I was wondering that as I'm already here, if there wasn't some possibility of…speeding things up.'

Tolvey shakes his head, a faint smile doing little to ameliorate his decision. 'Sorry, Detective. I'd like to help - hands across the water and all that - but we have rules too. My ass would be straight out of here if I went against protocols. Get your superiors to write to Colonel Wyatt and I'll see it gets to him as soon as he gets back.'

'No chance of a quick look? Just to eliminate it as a possibility?'

'Detective, we have many patients here. Guys who've been through a lot. Not just their physical wounds, their minds. What we call battle fatigue. They need time, and they need rest. What they don't need is British police running around the wards asking questions about a woman who, by your own admission, died long before most of them were even in this country.' He begins rising to his feet. 'So, I'm certain you can see why it's out of the question. Put in a request and we'll do our best to help. It's the best I can do.'

Tolvey stands, offering a hand. Porter, taking his cue, stands too. 'Pretty impressive facility you have here,' he says.

Tolvey walks him to the door, opening it. 'State of the art. Nothing but the very best for our guys.' He pauses waiting for Porter to go through. 'I hope you don't mind me saying this, but I'm surprised you're not at the front yourself. I was under the impression all you police were either too old for the army or unfit.'

'I have an injury. My back. A piece of shrapnel lodged there.'

'Oh. Too bad.'

'Yes. Too bad.'

'Pity I can't get one of our guys to look at it. We've developed some radical surgery practices here. Maybe after the war. Hey, come to think of it, if you're having trouble with dating the age of this corpse of yours maybe we can help out. We have some pretty fine labs here. Top people too.'

'Thanks. I think we've got that part of the investigation covered, but I'll be sure to mention it to our Professor Webster. See what he says.'

'Sure. Keep it in mind. Here to help. We're allies, after all.'

'Thank you, I will.'

Back at reception, Tolvey nods at the MP and leaves.

Willetts bids farewell to the secretary he's been talking with and the three men walk to the car. A few moments later they've dropped off the MP, left the camp, and are driving back to Bromsgrove.

They'd sat in silence for a mile or so before Willetts broached the subject. 'Useful visit, sir?'

Porter, who'd been absent-mindedly fiddling with his notebook since they'd left the camp, slams a hand against the dashboard. 'Bureaucracy. We'll be tied up in bloody paperwork for weeks. By the time we get anything we'll have been shut down. Case closed.' He turns, stares out the side window, contemplating the arcane mechanics of military protocol.

Willetts sighs. 'Not too promising then. Pity. Suppose they have their reasons.'

'They're concerned about the morale of their patients.'

'Pity.' Willetts drove on, attention fastened on the road ahead, the ever-present danger of potholes and bomb craters that litter the roads around the conurbation. 'That secretary was nice. Linda. Local girl. Really friendly. Got quite upset when I told her why we were there. Seems she had a friend went missing a few months back. Very upset she was. Still wonders what happened to her.'

'It's an awful thing.'

Willetts continues staring at the road ahead but allows a smile to play across his face. 'She was so upset, she decided she ought to help out. She thought you might have problems with getting anything from the Yanks. Seems they tend to be a little uncooperative on account of all the paternity suits against their boys. She thought that was a scandal too. Anyway, she decided it would be an act of justice if she short-cut the system, so to speak. Hands across the ocean and all that.' He reaches a hand into the inside pocket of his greatcoat, pulling out a sheet of paper. As he holds it up, Porter can see it is a list of handwritten names. Willetts gestures for him to take it. 'American personnel working in the area from January Forty-one to June Forty-two,' he states. 'Twelve names. An advance party. Seems, according to Linda, that most of them are still there. The third name from the top is the most interesting.'

Porter takes the proffered list, scanning the names, stopping at the third entry. 'Staff-Sergeant Bukowski. Why him?'

'Well, according to Linda, it seems Staff-Sergeant Bukowski came over here early in Forty-one, around Christmas time. Even before Pearl Harbour the yanks were offering all sorts of practical support short of sending actual combat troops. Seems that some in their high command were keen to be of help. They most likely knew they'd get pulled into it. They wanted to be prepared. The setting up of a military hospital was part of it. Of course, once the Yanks came into the real war, they took over the whole thing for themselves. Anyroad, after all the work was completed, this Sergeant Bukowski and the rest were kept on. Helped supervise things, acting as sort of liaison with the locals.'

'And?'

'According to Linda, this Bukowski took the whole liaison thing a bit too far. Bit of a man for the ladies, she says. One thing led to another, and one day a few months ago things got a little out of hand. He's a patient there now. Seems he went a bit *doolally*. Attacked a nurse he was seeing. Almost killed her. Strangled her, so they say. They say she's lucky to be alive.'

23RD APRIL 1943: EARLY HOURS

Porter squats in the corner of the structure. Four hours into a fire-watch with nothing out of what now passes for the ordinary to log. Some hours ago they'd launched barrage balloons over the Leyland factory, but they'd long since been taken back down.

He closes the cardboard covered exercise book, lying it onto the sandbags that form one side of the ARP placement. He tugs over his haversack, pulling the canvas flap open and burrowing into it. He extracts a thermos flask and the brown paper bag of sandwiches Rachel has prepared for him. Opening the package, he feels rather than sees the grease staining the paper. Squinting, he lifts it towards his face. Even in such poor light he can make out the dark blotch of oil. He missed butter.

He lifts a corner of the sandwich. Meat paste.

He lets the top slice drop back and takes a bite, slowly moving bread and paste around in his mouth, testing rather than savouring the taste. Screwing his face, he drops the sandwich back in the bag. Pouring a drink, he swills the hot tea in his mouth, a gargle dispersing the taste of potted meat.

He stands. *Porter's War*, he scoffs to himself, staring up into a pitch-black sky.

The ARP position sits atop the Lickey's Monument. The sandbagged battlements of the Monument are part the evocation of a medieval fort in miniature erected at the start of the century. A plaque by the steps indicate it to be a tribute to the generosity of the Cadbury family. A gift bequeathing these acres of hilltop to the community that served their factory. It was to be a place of recreation, a spot where workers might commune with nature.

The location afforded a spectacular view across the Birmingham Basin. From here he could see Kidderminster to the West, Lichfield to the North, and Coventry to the East. To the South, the land is flat to the horizon; Bromsgrove, the Malverns, Worcester. The South was of little interest to the Luftwaffe. Their interest focused on the heavily industrialised conurbation to the North. Whenever there was a raid, it was a grandstand seat to the horrors of what the Allied High Command euphemistically termed carpet-bombing. On some nights he thought the entire city burned.

He scans the Basin. Not tonight.

He slips off his helmet, placing it on the crenelated battlement. He thinks about what Rachel had said the previous night, how she'd had enough of war. They all had. For her, it had taken away the man she'd married, the father of her child, and the future she'd planned for. Loss was a subject most people could talk about. Everyone you met had a story to tell: the loss of a husband, a wife, a mother, a father, a daughter, a son.

Spain had been an adventure. Souls linked by burning righteousness, belief in the new world they would build. They'd gathered there, *The International Brigade*, a coming together of race, religion, and nationalities. The flowering youth of Europe and of America, men and women united in opposition to a great and terrifying evil.

He'd quit his university course. How could he sit in lecture rooms when men and women like himself were dying for those ideas and truths he was merely reading about in books? The undergraduate debates of college bars had grown tiresome. More than that, they'd sickened him. His decision to go to Spain had been spur of the moment, but in reality it had been brewing ever since his arrival at university. He was the Scholarship Boy. His home, his life, everything about him different to most of those there; he was an interloper, one never allowed to forget it. In the end his decision to leave for Spain had been forced upon him by his own assertions, his own self-righteousness, his own sense of himself as outsider and rebel in their world. After all, how could he maintain credibility, continue to espouse liberalising ideas, when across the channel lay the chance to prove to himself and to others that his wasn't empty rhetoric?

The reality of Spain dispelled all ideas of romance. At first, there had been welcoming rallies. The generosity of the Catalan people and the Brigade's youth and passion had created the sense of immersion in the great sweep of history. It had taken one action - the slaughter of his platoon in the orange grove - to disabuse him of any notion of the glory of war. His one-time under fire had not only finished his war, crippling him, but had left him with lingering doubts, questions of himself that he feared to confront.

He'd lain in the clearing of the orange grove bleeding out, unable to move. Staked out on the baking earth, he'd cried, prayed to a god he'd never believed in to save him.

When he thought of Spain, he could never see it as Rachel did, some act of romantic heroism. He'd tasted the bitter salt of his own tears, choked on the fiery bile of his vomit. Felt the hot sensation of his own piss as he'd lain on the rocky ground, splayed out like a frog on a dissecting table, wetting himself like a baby.

If he'd discovered one thing in Spain, it was the certainty that he was no hero. Worse, he now knew himself to be a coward.

9

24TH APRIL, 1943: MORNING

Major Francis Pidgeon busied himself, meticulously picking flecks of hair from the sleeve of his uniform. Time after time, he's told his wife about letting the damned dogs on the furniture. The result of him draping his best uniform jacket on the back of the kitchen chair during breakfast that morning were these bloody stubborn hairs.

A knock at the door is followed by the appearance of his adjutant. 'Dogs, sir?' Captain Solomon enquires on entry.

'Dogs,' Pidgeon confirms. Slipping his blouson jacket on, he buttons it. 'Confounded things!' he snaps, shrugging shoulders into the best fit he can find and tugging the waistband into position.

Solomon stands in mute agreement. Over the past three years he's learned it better to roll with the Major's punches rather than intervene with words of comfort over whatever irritation might be troubling him on any particular day. Dog hairs, Germans, Americans; if the mood took him, they were all the same to Pidgeon.

Satisfied with his work, Pidgeon sits at the desk, stretching

88

his arms in a final inspection. Turning to Solomon, he holds out an expectant hand for the clipboard his adjutant carries. It is a resume of the previous night's intelligence. 'So, David, what have we got today?'

Solomon passes the clipboard. 'Pretty much the usual, sir. Raids over the Midlands. Seems they're targeting the tank and armoured vehicle facilities.'

'Poor blighters,' Pidgeon tuts. 'They've had it bad of late. Anything else?'

'Routine intelligence, really. The usual stuff. There've been a couple of arrests near Liverpool - some foreign nationals the local police found a little too close to the docks. The local intelligence boys are interrogating them. If there's anything they'll pass it to Section 2.'

Pidgeon skims the list of signals, nodding in satisfaction. He proffers the clipboard back to Solomon. 'What about operations?'

Solomon holds the clipboard loosely at his side. 'All of our active agents have checked in as per their schedules. Operations around Lyons and Peenemunde are progressing as planned. The rest is pretty much as usual.'

Pidgeon strokes the ends of his moustache. He'd run Section D since its inception. *Special Intelligence Services,* or SIS, was part of the *Joint Intelligence Committee* overseeing intelligence operations. Section D controlled the recruitment, training, and active operational matters of a small group of highly trained agents. Agents charged with running espionage and sabotage operations in enemy occupied territory. It carried a heavy casualty rate. Operatives in France, Belgium, and the Low Countries had a life expectancy of six weeks.

Pidgeon himself was a career soldier. A textbook path from Sandhurst to tours of duty in the Far East and India. Tall and elegant in the manner of the cavalry officers his father and grandfather had once been, he regarded himself as a man of action. In reality, he'd seen little of it apart from breaking up quarrels amongst fellow officers in the Mess and the odd bar fight between men in his command and the locals wherever they were stationed.

Solomon hesitates. 'There is just one other matter, sir.'

'And that is?'

'The morning paper.'

'The papers? Don't tell me we're reduced to the *London Times* for our intelligence?' Pidgeon scoffs.

'There's a story. It might be of interest. It seems to have been picked up from one of the local papers in the Midlands.'

Pidgeon sat back. 'Well, let's have it. I'm all ears, Captain.'

'It appears that the local police close to Bromsgrove - that's a small town on the southern outskirts of Birmingham - discovered a corpse.'

'Well, that's hardly front-page stuff even for up there,' Pidgeon observes. 'The pounding they've been taking of late. There must be thousands of them.'

'This one's unusual, sir.'

'Unusual? How?'

'The body was found stuffed in the hollow of a tree.'

The Major raises an eyebrow. 'Bloody hell! That is unusual.'

'It seems the body had been there for some time. Maybe a year. Possibly eighteen months. The report says the skeleton is that of a young woman.'

'Ye gods! Poor wretch. How did she get there?'

'As yet, no one actually knows for certain. There's speculation it's the work of gypsies. One report has some of her limbs having been removed. The press up there spoke to locals who seem to think it's part of some sort of ritual. Either that or one of their gypsy trials.'

'Bloody gypsies!' Pidgeon snorts. He smooths his moustache back into place, then looks to his adjutant. 'Fascinating as this is, David, I'm still uncertain why you think its worthy of our attention.'

Solomon took a beat, knowing he was coming to his key point, wary of Pidgeon's reaction once he'd shared his thinking.

'Something nagged at me. I rang one of our contacts up there. Got them to make a few discrete enquiries. The skeleton is certainly that of a young woman. The theory amongst the local police is that if she's not a gypsy, then it's most likely she was the victim of a rapist. That she's some unfortunate sheltering in the woods during a bombing raid who stumbled on someone who attacked and killed her. Maybe even a woman who'd made an assignation with a GI.'

'So, they don't know who she is?'

'Not yet. All they know for certain is that it is a woman. Probably a young woman.'

'Poor devil.' Pidgeon says. He shuffles in his chair, a tick making clear his anxiety for whatever point was being made to be reached. 'But I'm still unclear why you think it's of any interest to ourselves. To SIS.'

'Well, if the timing is as they say - some eighteen months to a year previous - then it's in the right place and time for her to be *Tarpeia*.'

Pidgeon sits forward, the motion a sudden jerk. '*Tarpeia*. Is it possible? After all this time?'

'Possible? Yes. Likely?' Solomon shakes his head as a measure of his lack of any definitive answer. 'Currently, we have insufficient information to be certain of anything one way or the other. Should it be her…Well, it would explain a great deal about what really happened. The loose ends we could never tie up.'

Pidgeon stares into the distance, lost in thought. 'I thought this had all gone away.'

'We all did. But I think that may have been wishful thinking. There was always the possibility of it returning. Unfinished business. The Dutchman, for one.'

Pidgeon nods. 'The Dutchman.'

He sits back. *Tarpeia*. He'd scratched at the thing for so long it had come to be a part of him; scabbed over but always liable to erupt. 'I thought Dronkers was the end of it. What do you suggest?'

Solomon shrugs. 'For the moment, we do nothing beyond a watching brief. We use our man up there to keep a close eye on what's happening. It may be nothing. It may even turn out that it's not her at all.'

'But if it is?'

'Then we need to ensure that this time there are no loose ends. That nothing emerges as to who she was. If it does, it could cost us the war, everything.'

25TH APRIL, 1943: EARLY AFTERNOON

They sat considering their options.

Webster sighs, adjusting his monocle. He reads the message once more.

Porter sits tapping a pencil against the side of his notepad, eyes dwelling on the glass blocks above, the passage of pedestrians patterning the fall of light into the room. Willetts sniffs loudly whilst wrestling with the task of finding comfort on the chair he'd yet again been forced to drag in from the corridor.

'Six pairs,' Webster says, lowering the message, finger rapping against the sheet of paper with a dull snap.

'Six,' Porter repeats.

'And that's it?' Webster enquires, frustration evident in the brusqueness of his tone.

'At present.'

'A market trader in Dudley,' Willetts offers. 'We're trying to trace him. I've rung up the local Chamber of Commerce, but they're a bit short-staffed at present. The war.'

'The war,' Porter echoes.

Webster shakes his head. 'So, we can account for all of the pairs of these crepe shoes apart from the six pairs in Dudley?' he asks.

Porter nods. 'The manufacturers keep records of the shops and retailers they sell them to. The shops keep records of the pairs they've sold. Even in the war they have to keep records for their stock. The only ones we can't trace are the six sold to a market trader in Dudley in September forty-one. A trader who's not been seen for some time. He may have been called up. killed in a raid. Simply just moved on.'

'And if we find him?' Webster asks.

Willetts scratches his head. 'Well, I doubt we'll get much further than that. Those blokes don't keep records. Hand to mouth. They pick stuff up where they can, move it on quickly. They don't keep books like shops. Some of them play the Black Market an' all.'

'So, what do we know?'

Porter consults his notes. 'They were made in Northampton, or so the label in the ones we found says. *Silesby Shoes*. They made them from Spring 1939 to summer 1942. Most of them went to local stores. Some went to a couple of the big stores in London. Six pairs to Dudley.'

'The ones you can't trace.'

'Yes.'

Webster considers the matter. 'So, she was local, or at least lived or shopped in the area.'

Porter nods. 'Looks that way. Dudley's less than ten miles from where she was found.'

'Seven,' Willetts corrects.

'Seven,' Porter concedes.

The tick of the wood framed clock above the door seems to mock the lengthening span of silence. If nothing else, the silence highlights the lack of any other leads. Webster leans back in his chair, the creak of polished wood snapping the stillness. 'Well, what about this GI?'

'Bukowski,' Porter looks to Willetts, who consulting his notes, nods.

'What do we know about him?' Webster asks.

Porter dragging a hand through his hair, is aware of the twinge growing in his back. He sits a little more upright, face creasing at the effort. 'Precious little. We acquired our intelligence by less than conventional means.' He looks to Willetts who wrinkles his brow. 'At least not by any means where we might challenge the Yanks.'

'So why did this commander…'

'Tolvey.'

'Tolvey…not mention this when you met him? What are they concealing?'

Porter raises his shoulders, a motion making the pain bite more sharply. He shifts position. 'Possibly nothing. He isn't the commander, that's a Colonel Wyatt who was off somewhere. Maybe he was simply uncertain how far he should go with co-operation. It might just be a matter of protocol.'

'Protocol?'

'Bukowski's one of their own. They're reluctant to believe anything the locals might say - seems there's friction between the GIs and the town. Their inclination is to not co-operate. Then again, it might be they're just not prepared to give up one of their own to civil authorities.'

'But surely,' Webster says, 'if this man's committed acts of violence of similar brutality against other women, there's every reason for us to talk to him. Surely they can't be willing to shield a possible murderer?'

Porter sighs. 'Again, what we have is hearsay. It's all down to channels. I've put in a request to military command in Whitehall to see if they can find some lever for us to get an interview with him. Army to army. It could take a while. The difficulty is we're not supposed to know anything about this Bukowski. The liaison I spoke with at High Command thinks it makes it look as though we're spying on our allies.'

'And the young woman he assaulted? What about her account?'

Porter flicks open his notebook. He'd spent part of the morning talking with the officers who'd been out to Wolverley to investigate the attack on Rose Collins. Neither of the two constables had left any doubt as to how they saw the event.

'When the officers investigating the attack spoke with Bukowski he was adamant she was the one who wanted sex. He says she was *drunk and out of control.* All he will admit to is,-' he looks down at his notes '*acting unlike a gentleman by taking advantage of her inebriated condition.*'

'What about the strangulation? The marks on her throat?'

'He says she wanted him to do it. What they call-' Porter skims his notes for the precise term.

'*Erotic asphyxiation,*' Webster states.

Porter looks up. 'Yes. How do you know?'

Webster pulls the monocle from his pocket, cleaning it on his handkerchief. 'There's the notion that such practices brings on a hallucinogenic state – heightens the arousal, the pleasure. There have been examples since the 1700s. Seems it was first noticed at public hangings. Male prisoner's necks that failed to break. They hung there, asphyxiating. Accounts tell us they often got an erection - some reports even have them ejaculating. There are famous incidents of people dying whilst having sex at the same time as being asphyxiated.' He holds up a hand, enumerating with his fingers. 'The writer Mottcaux, the composer Kotzwara, and most famously, Kichizo Ishida whose lover - the beautiful Sada Abe - *post mortem* cut off his penis and testicles and carried them around in her handbag for days.' He places the monocle into his eye socket, tucking the handkerchief back into his top pocket. 'That was Tokyo, oh, about twelve years ago. Most famous Japanese homicide investigation ever, which, to answer your question, is how I am aware of the practice.'

Willetts sits open mouthed. 'A handbag?'

'Now you're sounding like Lady Bracknell!' Webster chimes. 'A handbag!' He repeats in what he intends to be a feminine upper-class tone of shock. Willetts laughs, as much at Webster's effort at impersonation as at the realisation of his own comment being the foundation for the joke.

Webster continues chuckling whilst Willetts repeats the

mimicry himself. 'A handbag!' the Special shouts out, collapsing into guffaws.

Porter smiles. Maybe levity was what was required to leaven the mood of frustration, but it still felt as if they were swearing in church. 'Whatever the matter,' he says as the laughter abates, 'the fact is that Rose Collins won't press charges. More to the point, her mother will do all she can to prevent us from pursuing the case. The scandal. The shame. The doubt.'

'Public morality. No smoke, eh?' Webster states.

'Sadly so. The officers involved say they've been told – unofficially - Bukowski is undergoing some kind of therapy. Appears the Yanks are keen to send him home as soon as they can. Anxious to avoid further enquiry. You know, worried about the impact on troop morale or community relations that a trial would bring. It seems our own military agree. They're Allies. We need them. Good will. Monty and Eisenhower are scrapping over control of the campaigns. Last thing they want is a sex scandal souring things.'

'So where does that leave us?'

'We'll persist with our attempts to talk with Bukowski, but to be honest I'm not even certain he's the one we want.'

'Because?' Webster asks.

'If we believe Rose's account of the attack, it means the motive for Bukowski's assault was rape. Sex. He didn't kill her. He didn't try to hide her body. He didn't cut off her hand.'

Webster holds up a hand. 'I see all that, but I still don't understand your reasoning for excluding what is a decent possibility for the man being our killer. The location's right. The timing. A violent assault. One involving a woman's attempted strangulation. Let's be honest, currently it's the only possibility we do have.'

'The man's an engineer, not a combat soldier. He's not used to death or killing. More than that, there's no evidence how he and our victim might have met. Rose Collins was a nurse filling in a shift at Wolverley. He met her there. Until we know who our victim is we have no idea as to what she did, where she went, or how or who she might have met. Hagley is a relatively long way from Wolverley.'

'Seven miles,' Willetts affirms.

'So, where does that leave us?' Webster asks once more.

'Where we've always been. Where we started. Finding out who she is. Our only hard evidence takes us back to our spiv from Dudley.'

The clock ticked forward. Willetts flicks his notebook. 'What about the rest of the clothing we recovered, sir? The cardigan, the blouse and skirt?' he asks.

Webster shakes his head. 'Nothing. The labels have been cut out.'

'Cut out?'

'Removed. Gone. Not there.' Webster sits back. 'Most odd. We have remnants of her dress and underwear. The most complete items are the metal stays from her corset. So, given that fact, it's more than a little odd that whilst we have some of the material from the places where we would expect to find a label, they're just not there. They've been cut off.'

'Everything?'

'That's the oddest thing about it. Every last one. Whoever killed her intended to leave nothing that might help discover who she was.' He sits forward, hands intertwining on the desktop. 'Maybe that tells us something in itself. The killer felt it important to make it difficult to trace her. If they were so keen to keep us at a distance from her life and those who might know her, then doesn't it suggest our killer was involved in her life? Deeply involved? That we no longer consider her murder as the act of a stranger or someone peripheral in her life. The killer was desperate to keep any later investigation at arm's length. They were protecting themselves, their own identity.'

'It's possible,' Porter agrees.

Willetts nods. 'Either that or she was a spy.'

Webster turns to face the Special. 'A spy?'

Willetts shrugs. 'That's what they do. When they're parachuted into enemy territory. They have the labels taken out of their clothing so nothing can give them away.'

'And you know this because?'

Willetts furrows his brow, at the same time narrowing his eyes and wrinkling his nose. 'I talk to people. Some of the blokes down the pub. One of them does something over at Malvern. That radar station, or whatever it is they call it. Boffins,' he spits his mistrust of the word. 'They work with spies, or at least with whatever bit of the military that controls all that.'

Porter furrows his own brow, his expression one of uncertainty. 'SIS. Spies. I don't know. It all sounds a bit…'

'Like a penny fiction,' Webster puts in.

'Yes,' Porter concurs. 'I mean, if she was a spy, wouldn't our government be looking for her? They'd have circulated something about her, even if they didn't actually tell us she was a spy. They'd be trying to find her. They'd be all over our investigation by now.'

'And what would she be spying on round here?' Webster observes. 'One of our own?'

Willetts shrugs. 'Maybe she wasn't one of ours.'

'What?' Porter asks.

Willetts looks from Porter to Webster. The Special offers a twitch of the shoulders. 'Maybe she was a Nazi.'

'A German?' Porter mulls the idea over.

'There's a lot of stuff round there. Longbridge. Malvern,' Willetts adds in support of his idea.

Porter deliberates the point. There was merit in it. He'd read Home Office circulars sent to police forces close to military facilities telling them to be on the lookout for newly arrived groups of strangers. Only last week a cell of German sympathisers had been picked up in Liverpool spying on the dock facilities. 'There's just one thing about that,' he finally responds.

'Which is?' Willetts asks.

'If she was a Nazi, then who killed her and put her in the tree? And why? Surely our chaps would want to interrogate her. Find out what her mission was. What she was sent to do. Why would SIS kill her and stuff her body in a tree?'

'Why indeed,' Webster agrees. 'It's a good point. A point that, for me, rules her out as a Nazi spy. She wouldn't have ended up like that if she'd been a spy caught by our chaps.'

Willetts shrugs, unconvinced. 'Spies. They do things. Secret things.'

Porter sympathised. Willetts' local knowledge and contacts had proven invaluable, but it was clear he was trying hard to be a part of the investigation beyond that of chauffeur. Maybe too hard. 'It's an interesting idea,' Porter grants him, 'but we have to stick to hard evidence rather than run off on some wild goose chase searching for spies.'

'I agree,' Webster states, waving a hand across the files and papers spread across his desk. 'We have a range of evidence. Concrete evidence. Facts that have to be followed-up.'

Porter stands and begins picking up the pile of folders closest to him. 'We'll take some of this with us. The quicker we get through it, the sooner we'll have a better idea who she is, who we're looking for.'

Willetts stands and he too begins shuffling together a sheaf of papers. As he does so he exchanges a look with Porter. 'Not quite what you were expecting, eh sir?' he suggests, a finger tapping the files held loosely in his hands. 'This Detective lark.'

'No. You're right. It's not.'

Willetts shuffles the folders into place. 'Spies, sir,' he cautions. 'You mark my words. Spies.'

25TH APRIL, 1943: LATE AFTERNOON

Arriving back at the station, Willetts brings the car to a halt close to the front entrance. Alighting, Porter, turns to shut the passenger door, eyes falling on the pile of manila folders taking up most of the Wolseley's rear bench seat. Willetts half-turns, following Porter's gaze. 'More paper, sir.'

'More paper,' Porter repeats. They'd taken the files from Webster's office, adding to them the bundles of missing person's files they'd collected from several South Birmingham police stations on the journey back. A desk sergeant had told them that someone at the council said that currently there were more than 3,000 young woman missing in Birmingham and its surrounding area.

'Dealing with the authorities now, sir. Eight or nine local councils. Then there's the parish councils, the ARP, the hospitals. Not to mention the charities. They all need to keep records. Like that sergeant said, hundreds, maybe thousands.'

'I feel buried under it.'

'Better than chasing stolen bicycles, though, eh sir?'

Porter smiles. 'Not that much difference at present.' He stands upright, stretching out his back, thinking of the long days ahead sifting through these records.

Just then, the duty officer emerges from the station and walks to their car. 'Excuse me sir,' the Special says, hand snapping to a salute that takes Porter by surprise.

He returns it sloppily, cursing his ineptitude. The Special is a burly man. Late fifties, black hair cut short at the sides military style. Porter knows him to be a figure of authority with the locals, the reputation of a man not to be trifled with despite the fact that he, like Willetts, walks with a pronounced limp. A retired Sergeant, he'd been brought back to ensure the station was run according to strict pre-war guidelines. He also knows the man to be a hero, pulling three young members of a family from a burning building in the early weeks of the Blitz. Although he'd no official standing beyond that of Special, the regular officers treated him with deference.

'What is it, Gosling?'

'There's some old grannie in reception wants to see you,'

Gosling states in clipped tone whilst hooking a thumb over his shoulder in the direction of the station door.

'Me?' Porter looks back into the car and the stack of files. 'I'm busy with this enquiry at present. What's it in connection with? A stolen bicycle?'

'Not quite, sir. She says she can tell you who your body in the tree is.'

10

25TH APRIL, 1943: LATE AFTERNOON

The woman sitting in the cramped entrance of Hagley police station is not at all what he'd anticipated. She is admittedly slight of body, shocking white hair held in a tight bun that correlates with Gosling's description of *'some old grannie'*. However, as he walks towards her, she looks up, a sharp movement exposing a small round face, almost translucent skin, and the most startlingly blue eyes. Even at this distance her eyes bore into his own as she awaits his approach, bolt upright on the scuffed wooden bench.

Next to her lies a long black cloak. Alongside that is a wicker basket and a gaudily patterned carpetbag, its leather handles worn and fraying. She herself wears a pale blue shawl pulled loosely around small shoulders. Her manner of dress is Edwardian in styling; a long dress of taffeta or silk covered in elaborate patterns of blues, greens, and gold. It echoes a time before *the Great War*, a woman of substance and style though now somewhat faded. In her lap is a leather-bound notebook in which she scribbles with surprisingly quick, darting movements of her hand.

As he drew close, she snaps the book shut, standing up ready to greet him. The hand reaching out to meet him is adorned with bangles and rings. Taken by surprise at the suddenness of the movement, he hesitates in taking it. She half-smiles, delighted by the effect on him of such a simple gesture.

Standing closer, he takes in the intricate design of the necklace that hangs around her neck. A brooch on lapel of the dress is equally ornate and unexpected. He thinks it a beetle or insect of some kind. It is spun in silver, long horns or antennae pointing towards her throat, around which a band of black ribbon is held in place by a similar, smaller insect spun from the same precious metal.

When she speaks, her voice is clear, unmistakably public school, 'Detective Inspector.'

'Detective Constable, ma'am,' he corrects.

'Constable?' She raises a finger to her lips in thought. 'Oh, I was rather hoping to speak directly with the officer in charge of the investigation of the poor woman whose body was found in the tree.'

'That would be myself, ma'am.'

She re-appraises him. Her tone fails to conceal her evident disappointment. 'Oh. I see. I rather expected a more senior officer.'

Porter half-smiles, 'I'm afraid I'm it. There's myself and Special Constable Willetts,' he says, indicating Willetts who at that moment is making his way into the station.

She taps an index finger against her lips. She seems to reconsider her approach in the light of these new options that are presenting themselves. Finally, she relents, a shrug of acceptance. 'Oh well, I suppose if that's the case, you'll have to do.'

'Erhm. Thank you, Mrs. …'

She bends down, scooping up her cloak and bags from the wooden bench. 'It's Miss.' Turning back to face him, she waves a hand dismissively in the air. 'Actually, if we must stick to the niceties of convention, it's Professor. And you are Detective…?'

'Porter. Detective Constable Porter, ma'am.'

She nods, as if in acceptance he'd finally got a question right. 'Excellent. I'm Professor Margaret Murray. Please lead the way to your office.'

In the back room that presently passed for the CID office, she circles like a sparrow hawk seeking out prey. Her bright eyes scan the space, take in the books, the photographs, the tired and worn fittings and furniture before finally settling herself on the wooden chair opposite Porter's desk. Once more, he has the inescapable sense there is a test being conducted. A test to which he is neither privy to its subject or whether he might pass.

He sits, picking up a pencil and opening his notepad. 'Well, Professor, I understand from Constable Gosling that you claim to know the identity of our body.'

Professor Murray busied herself deep in her carpetbag, barely glancing up. 'That's correct, Detective Porter. And it is Margaret. You may call me Margaret.'

'Perhaps, if you don't mind, I'll stay with Professor Murray.'

She looks up, the object of her search for the moment forgotten. 'Very well. It would seem you're a man of convention, Detective Porter. The uniform. I suppose.'

'Sorry?'

She inclines her head in his general direction. 'The uniform. It imposes a certain conformity on those who wear it. Even if, like yourself, there's no obvious uniform to speak of.'

Porter sits back, laying the pencil on the desktop. 'Ah, I see.'

'Do you, Detective?'

'I believe so. You believe all policemen follow *the book*. By *the letter*. The uniform makes us unimaginative.'

She shakes her head. 'Bless my soul, Detective Porter. You've clearly not yourself come up the ranks then. What's an intelligent young man like yourself doing here when there's all that adventure out there? I'm certain our country must have better use for a man like yourself than chasing lost bicycles and kittens.'

He looks down to his notebook. 'Disability.'

'Disability?' She wrinkles her brow. Considers him anew.

'Shrapnel. In my back,' he feels compelled to clarify.

'France?'

'Spain.'

Her expression is one of understanding. 'A volunteer. *International Brigade.* How very glamorous. An idealist. You must be a grammar schoolboy, then.'

'Scholarship. Oxford.'

'Oh, you'll do just fine. A policeman of learning. Just the sort of open mind I was hoping for.'

'Open mind?'

She busies herself with the bag again, finally producing the leather-bound notebook she'd previously been writing in. 'Someone prepared to believe there are forces beyond the mundane at work in our world if we only have the wit to look for them.'

'Forces ?'

'Forces. Spiritual energies.'

'I'm not sure I understand. You said you know the identity of the victim.'

'I believe I do. All of the evidence points to it. I just need a little more detail from you.' She takes out a pencil, opening her journal.

Porter's head inclines in puzzlement. 'Detail?'

'The position of the body. Where the hand was found.'

'The hand?'

'The missing hand.'

Porter leans forward. 'How do you know about the hand?' he asks.

'It is always missing.'

'Always?'

'Previous cases.'

'Previous cases?'

'Detective Porter, we're not going to make much progress if

your sole contribution to this conversation is merely to repeat everything I say. I came here for answers, not to have some parroting of my words.'

'Professor Murray, you have the better of me. I need clarification as to what it is that you're here to tell me. Am I right in thinking that you not only know the identity of this woman, but that she is one of a number of victims?'

'*Victim.* Such a loaded word, don't you think? Perhaps *target*, *quarry*, possibly…*object*. Yes, *object*. It dehumanises the whole thing, which of course is how they're seen.'

'They?'

'Witches, Detective Porter. Witches.'

'Witches…Sorry, Professor, I know I'm repeating what you just said but…witches?'

'Well, that's the common term. Of course, I don't believe any of this, but they do.'

'They?'

'The covens. The worshippers.'

'Professor Murray, with all due respect…witches, covens.'

'Oh, don't feel bad about your scepticism, Detective. Long ago I myself shared some of your misgivings, but there is no doubt those who follow this path do indeed believe in the power of the dark arts. Magic.'

'Professor, do you know who this woman is?'

'If you mean her name, well of course not, that would be preposterous. That's police work.'

'But you told the officer at the desk that you knew who she is.'

'Yes. I do. A witch. She was a witch. And, if the signs are to be believed, a most powerful one indeed!'

26TH APRIL, 1943: MORNING

'Pardon my saying so, sir, but she sounds a bit *doolally* if you ask me. Witches?' Willetts shakes his head. 'Never heard such a thing.'

'Can't argue with you there, Willetts. I feel the same way.' Porter says, casting his mind over the previous afternoon's meeting. 'But she believes it. Absolutely. And she's certainly not crazy. Eccentric, maybe. But crazy? No. She's as sane as you or I.'

'Women of that age, sir,' Willetts puts in confidentially.

It is Porter's turn to shake his head. 'She isn't senile, quite the reverse. Mind as sharp as a knife. Brilliant woman too.' He picks up his notebook, turning to the page where he'd made his notes. 'I spoke with Professor Webster. He rang some of his contacts in London. It seems our Professor Murray was regarded by her academic contemporaries as one of the most brilliant and accomplished women of her time. A true academic in every sense of the word. Brought up in India, brilliant scholar at Cambridge. She was Professor of Egyptology for decades at University College. Seems she got into all this witches stuff around the time of *the Great War.* She's written books on it. Webster says her ideas upset her academic colleagues, quite a falling out. Seems they thought she was bringing them into disrepute. From what he could gather, she believes witchcraft is part of a pagan religion that's been persecuted by Christianity for hundreds of years. It demonised them. Her argument is that witches and witchcraft are victims of Christian propaganda.'

'Propaganda? What, like that Haw-Haw bloke?'

'Something. Webster says it was her persistence in pursuing her ideas that finally cost Murray her job. Seems the scandal and sensationalism her ideas attracted was frowned on by her employers. She was forcibly retired. Since then, she's been writing pamphlets and touring the country giving lectures. A woman of eighty. Amazing.'

'So, she's saying that our woman's a witch?' Willetts asks.

'According to Murray. She tells me there are facts about the death and the way she was disposed of - her corpse in the tree for a start - that have been written about for hundreds of years.

She says it's a common way of how believers dealt with those of their own who broke coven rules.'

'So, not only was she a witch, but she was killed by other witches,' Willetts says, clarifying his understanding of what Porter is telling him.

'Something like that.'

Willetts sighs. 'Madness.'

'I know,' Porter replies, sympathising with the Special's struggle for comprehension.

'These similarities?' Willetts asks.

Porter finds the relevant page of his notepad. 'The severing of the hand. The body being placed in the hollow of a wych-elm tree.'

Willetts screws his face. 'Coincidence?'

'Yes, no doubt. But unusual that she should know of the severed hand. It's hardly commonplace in a murder.'

Willetts confines himself to a non-committal shrug of the shoulders.

'Murray says that's how the tree got its name. Wych-elm. Seems the crown of the tree lends itself to imprisoning the souls of dead witches,' Porter adds.

'What did Professor Webster say?' Willetts asks, seeking a rational view of the ideas he's hearing from the young Detective.

Porter closes the notepad, tossing it onto the desk. He stretches, a sudden pain compelling him to reach a hand round to ease the ache in his back. 'Much the same as ourselves. She's undoubtedly a brilliant woman. Bit of an eccentric. But the idea that Bella was the victim of a coven...preposterous was his verdict.'

'Bella?'

Porter ceases massaging his back. 'Oh, yes. I call her Bella. The dead woman.'

'I see.' Willetts looks quizzically at Porter. Clearly, he did not.

'A bit easier to think of her with a name rather than *the dead woman*. What with all this evidence of possible links to gypsies and witches. Lots of Clarabellas and Belladonnas among them. It's a common name. Belladonna's also a plant widely used in spells and herbal remedies. It seemed…appropriate.'

Willetts murmurs. 'Bella it is then.'

'Anyway, Webster wants to meet her. Professor Murray, that is. She's staying at the *Gypsy's Tent*. Opposite the woods.'

'She's keen then.'

'She wants to see the tree. Like I said, she tours the country giving talks on pagan religions and witchcraft. Quite popular so Webster tells me.'

Willetts wonders at the naivety of so many. 'Some people. Believe anything. I've seen them at the music hall, the Hippodrome. Magicians and them that say they can talk to the spirits of the dead. Con men.' He stops short, thinks for a moment. 'Could this be a stunt? Publicity? Get her name in the papers. Tricksters, taking in the gullible. If I had my way,-'

'Maybe they just have open minds on things we can't explain,' Porter suggests.

'That's as maybe,' Willetts concedes, 'But I'm with the Professor - Webster I mean, not her. Stick to the facts. Evidence. Things you can see. Proof.'

There was a pause, both acknowledging the topic had run its course. Pulling back to the essence of their work - reports, routines, procedure - Porter wearily eyes the stack of folders Willetts and Gosling have ferried in from the car. 'Talking of which, anything from Dudley?'

'Not a thing.'

Porter picks up a sheet of paper from the pile of evidence they'd been compiling. 'What about the dentists? Anyone been in contact?'

'Not as yet. Early days though, sir,' Willetts encourages.

Porter tosses the sheet onto the pile. 'Yet Webster was convinced that her dental profile is so distinct that any dentist who'd worked on her would recognise it straight away.'

'Maybe she was foreign.'

'Back to your spies?' he chuckles.

'There's as much evidence for that as there is witches,' Willetts offers defensively.

'Sorry. You're right.' Porter shuffles the sheets into a folder, closing the flap and patting his hand on it. 'I'll make the call and arrange for Webster to meet with her. Perhaps after that we can put an end to some of this wild goose chase stuff once and for all.' He waves the ever-growing folder in his hand. 'Then we can get back to focusing on the facts.'

'I'll get the car, sir.'

Porter picks up the phone, dials, and waits for the connection. He stares at the file: each day fatter, each day harder to close. Despite that fact, all they have is speculation. Gypsies, angry GI's, a murderous stranger. Willetts with his spies and secret agents. Murray and her theories of witches and black magic. Looked at objectively, each possibility fitted parts of the evidence, but none left them closer to a solution, none of them made a whole.

Speculation.

Maybe they did in fact require a little magic.

26TH APRIL, 1943: EARLY EVENING

Sitting in the bay window of *the Gypsy's Tent*, Margaret Murray gazes out across the gravelled car park to the winding A456 that forms the twisting link between Hagley and the outskirts of Birmingham. Beyond that lies an open field, and in the near distance the hunched silhouette of Hagley Wood.

It was early evening, dusk, what little sun there had been is rapidly fading. A pale light silvers the room, persuading the ageing Professor of Egyptology and witchcraft to an involuntary tremor which she ascribes to the encroaching chill of evening.

Tugging her shawl more tightly around her, she fishes deep in her carpet bag, exchanging her battered, leather-bound notebook for the newspaper article which some days earlier she'd cut from *the Times*. Retrieving it, she no more than glances at the article. There is no need, she knows it by heart. A short piece, a few paragraphs concerning the discovery of woman's body in a hollow tree in the Midlands.

She places the clipping on the table and rises to stand looking out towards the woods.

What has drawn her here? *Curiosity*? Certainly, the part of her teased by the story. *Academic interest*? That too. A professor whose latter career concerned researching and writing on pagan worship is obviously intrigued at such a discovery. *The publicity*? Oh, yes, she had to admit to that too.

She smiles at her own conceit. She was *'someone'*, a celebrity. Her work may not have gained favour with her peers in academia, but she'd stumbled into popularity with the wider general public, an audience who found her work intriguing, racy. The controversy surrounding her ideas bestowed a cachet, an illicit attraction making her not only a best seller, but a speaker in demand on the town hall lecture circuit.

Satisfying as these public appearances are, she wants more; the acceptance of her peers. Credibility. What she's discovered of this case suggests the hallmarks of a coven trial. Here at last is the possibility of proof, proof that such beliefs and practices continued to this day. Beliefs with a liturgy that the Christian faith had for centuries fought to expunge. If the police could be persuaded to look openly at her theory, a theory based on her own detailed research, then others too would have to take what she said seriously. The publicity attached to such an investigation would inevitably attach itself to her life's work. The public would see that what they thought of as witchcraft was in fact their own ancestral religion, a religion denied to them by the political power of imposed Christian doctrine.

Though she remains uncertain what the young Detective Constable will do with the evidence she'd presented, his call to arrange a meeting encouraged her. Maybe this Porter is made of sterner stuff.

Porter. *A carrier of baggage.* Maybe he is as driven as she is. That he has his own demons, she is certain.

She turns her thoughts to the woods and shivers. In the fading twilight it looms dark, cold, impenetrable. On her return from the police station yesterday evening she'd walked through it. Walked to the very spot. The tree itself.

Despite the ravages to the branches caused by extracting the body, it had been all she'd hoped. A Wych-elm, a wrinkled crone of a tree, named for its shock of suckers supposedly calling to mind a witch's spiky hair. She'd stood for some time, unable to tear her gaze away. What had she done, this woman, this *creature*, to have her soul so darkly imprisoned?

The crunch of tyres on gravel alerts her to the arrival of Porter and Webster. She watches the two exchange words with their driver, the elderly policeman she'd seen the previous day. Watches as they make their way to the main door of the public house where a well briefed landlord awaits them.

The introductions are made by Porter; Murray extending a hand, Webster accepting it with a slight bow. They sit at one of the larger tables close to the window, Murray facing the two.

The initial pleasantries are suitably observed. Enquiries about accommodation, the tribulations of journeying around war time England, observations on the blight of the war on the academic work of universities. Eventually Webster takes out his monocle, polishing it with a handkerchief as he brings the conversation round to the point of the meeting. 'Detective Porter tells me you have some thoughts as to the possible motive for the killing of our young woman,' he says.

Murray inclines her head, 'From what I read before arriving here and from what I gleaned from my conversations with Detective Porter yesterday, then yes, I believe that I possess a narrative as good as any of those you have been considering. Probably better than most.'

Webster nods, placing the polished monocle in his right eye socket. He sits forward, hands on his knees, bracing them there, a short sigh preceding his words. 'If I may be frank, Professor Murray, I need you to understand-'

'Margaret.'

He pauses. Nods, half-smiles. 'Margaret. Fascinated as I am by what I know of your work, your writings, I must tell you that I fall very firmly into the camp of the sceptic. The unbeliever. In my field of physical science, I deal with facts, evidence. Theories tested with rigour. Veracity established beyond all doubt.'

She smiles, raising an eyebrow. 'Beyond all doubt, Professor?' A small, almost imperceptible, shake of her head. 'What a dull world you must inhabit.'

Webster sits back, his tone abruptly serious. 'A world of certainties.'

She shakes her head once more. 'Certainties. My, my. To be so sure.' She sighs. 'I almost envy you such conviction. It must be very reassuring. And what of belief? Of the spiritual? If not in God, then of those things that men pursue despite what all of your evidence might tell them to be the impossibilities of success? Like this war. All of the rational evidence, your *certainties*, point to the overwhelming victory of the Nazis. Yet still we fight. Still, we resist. Still, we win.'

'Hope is different to witchcraft.'

'Is it? What is hope if not belief, a blind faith in forces beyond your physics?' She turns to Porter, 'What do you say, Detective Porter?'

Porter pauses in retrieving a notebook from his jacket pocket. 'Erhm...Like Professor Webster, I'm a sceptic.'

'And yet you went off to Spain. What drove you then? Faith? Belief? These are powerful forces, Detective Porter.' She looks him hard in the eyes, pinning him. 'You've felt them. I see it.'

Porter looks to his notebook. 'Maybe we ought to focus on the matter at hand.'

'But that's part of it,' she persists. 'Her death, was all about beliefs.'

Porter raises a pencil, concentrating. 'So, what is it you think happened?'

She begins what has become a pitch, an explanation honed over countless recitations. 'Witches exist. Here in Britain today. There is no doubt of that. I have met them. Spoken with them of their beliefs and worships. They are essentially a loving, peaceful group. Misunderstood, persecuted, they understandably keep themselves hidden. They worship nature and find in that worship a contact with the life forces of the world most of us have lost. The wind, the seasons, the sun, the moon. All have a part to play in the cycle of our lives, but we've long since lost touch with such senses, our connection. Or, more precisely, they were taken from us.'

'This is the Christian persecution you talk about,' Webster breaks in.

'Yes. For centuries Christianity fought to establish itself. It did so by destroying all religions that predated it. Christianity has the idea that it is the only faith, the only true way, and in that name it has persecuted all that believe differently. We think of Christianity as a loving religion, but even our own Anglicanism has roots in the most savage tooth and claw fight for survival, let alone acceptance. It's well documented; the ravages of the inquisition, the forced conversions of the Spanish conquest of South America, the Crusades, the witch hunts of the Puritans. Even the Protestant butcheries of Catholics here in our own country. Christianity demonised all who believed in different gods, different ways of seeing the world. For early Christians, what we call Paganism was a world view that threatened their own.' She relaxes into her story, savouring the expressions on the faces of the men sitting opposite 'Paganism is a belief in which as much power rests with women as it does with men. That was what they sought to destroy. Women who had equality. Women with power and veneration in a religion valuing them as equals. Such things were an anathema to the misogyny of the Christian Church! Little wonder such women were seen as a threat to be hunted down. To be tortured and eradicated!'

Webster shakes his head. 'So, you're saying our victim was quite literally the victim of a witch hunt?'

'No. I'm merely offering background to the fact that such women - the ones you now so narrow-mindedly call witches - exist today. They are nothing like the Christian propaganda of the *Grimm Fairy Tales*. They're not hags, or crones. They're not crippled up wretches eating children whilst cursing those who cause them misery.' She looks from Webster to Porter and back again, the sweep of her gaze fixing the two. 'So, when I tell you that this woman was a witch, I want you to understand what that means. They are real. Flesh and blood, not the bogeymen we frighten children with. I want you to see how this explains not only why she was killed, but it also the manner of her killing and of her subsequent mutilation and entombment.'

Webster fiddles with his monocle cord, adjusting the eyepiece in the socket. Porter jots quickly in his notebook. 'Witchcraft,' Webster mutters. 'Black magic,' he scoffs.

Murray pulls her journal from the carpetbag, flicking it open at the place she wants. She takes from there a few pages clearly torn from a book. 'I did some research. This wood has long been associated with magic. Local legends have it as a meeting place for witches.' She passes a page with an old engraving of a tree to Webster, who glances at it before passing it to Porter. 'Trees such as the wych-elm have long associations as places of what the layman might term *magic* for witches. It would be the perfect place for a coven to meet. For her trial to have taken place.'

Porter looks up from studying the engraving. 'Trial?'

'Yes. Trial. You see, you are mistaken. We are not talking about a savage murder. You are not seeing the work of a madman, nor are you seeing some other worldly demon. Her death, her entombment, would have been the judgement of a trial based on a system of belief and lore as old as that which is practised in our own courts every day. Older. In their eyes, her trial had a legitimacy as solid as our own. She would have been tried, judged, and punished as befitted her crimes.' She surveys the silenced men. 'To be imprisoned in such a way suggests she was a powerful witch. A most powerful one. It's an ancient tradition that the spirit of a dead witch, especially one as potent as our poor soul must have been, can only be prevented from returning to cause harm by being imprisoned in the hollow of a tree. It traps her, you see, neutralises her power. Her killers would have good reason to have wanted to protect themselves from her dead spirit.'

She plunges a hand into her bag once more. She takes out another frayed book which she turns to a marked page. 'And there's the hand of course. The missing hand.' She thrusts the book towards Webster, who takes it from her. 'How did I know the hand was missing? It's the sign of a black magic execution. It's linked with *The Hand of Glory*.'

'Professor…Margaret…now you really are losing me. *The Hand of Glory*? What's that?' Webster asks, irritation creeping into his manner.

She leans forward, tapping the open page in the book held in Webster's hand. 'The *Hand of Glory* is obtained at the dead of night. It is cut from the body of an executed criminal hanging from the gibbet or gallows. The hand possesses a powerful magic used to protect its owner from evil spirits. Some beliefs ascribe other powers to it such as the ability to reveal where a witch's treasure is buried.'

Webster passes the book to Porter. 'This gets ever more unbelievable,' he judges.

'Maybe for someone such as yourself, Professor. But we're dealing with the minds of those who killed this poor soul, not yours. Surely it's about what *they* believe. *Their* motive. What do you say Detective?'

'It's certainly an explanation.'

Webster snorts at Porter's naivety. 'There are many

explanations for the missing hand. Much more likely an animal took it.'

'What animal would climb a tree such as that?' Porter muses. 'And her arms were underneath her body when we found her. What animal would root down below her other bones to retrieve a hand?'

'For goodness' sake, Porter!'

Porter passes the book back to Murray. 'And you said yourself, Professor, that it was severed cleanly. Not gnawed.'

Murray snaps the book shut triumphantly. 'There you are.'

'I still don't see,-' Webster begins.

'That's my point,' Murray interrupts, 'You don't see.' She turns from Webster to Porter, fixing him with her stare. 'You have your men hunt around, Detective Porter. You'll find the hand close by. Buried. Like the tradition. You mark my words.'

Webster stands. 'I think I've heard enough of this.' He inclines his head towards Murray. 'If you don't mind, Professor, I have work to be done. Evidence to examine. Real evidence.' He turns in leaving. 'It's been... interesting to meet you and to listen to your ideas.'

Porter stands too, gathering his notebook. 'Professor Murray, I'm sorry,-'

She raises a hand, hushing him. 'No need, Detective Porter. I'm used to such reactions. It's a hard thing to digest, especially when it challenges all you believe in. He's a man of science, your professor. A good man, no doubt, but a man of science. He lacks belief in anything outside of that.'

Porter tucks his notebook away. 'This is new for all of us. All I can say is that I'll look into what you've told us.' He inclines his head in the direction of the woods. 'First thing tomorrow morning I'll have the men look again for the missing hand.'

She too stands, turning so the two of them are facing the window. The woods fill their view of the world, a sulking outline against the ever-darkening dusk of the sky. 'Thank you, Detective Porter. It'll be close by.' She pauses; her mind caught on the image of the tree. 'Detective Porter.... Please keep your mind open. Belladonna would want it so.'

'What?' Porter turns to face her; his face draining of colour.

'Keep your mind open. It's all she asks.'

'No, not that. You called her...' Porter's mind reeled.

'Belladonna? Why, of course. We have to call her something other than *the victim* or *the skeleton*, don't you think? Though no doubt your professor there with his test tubes and his forensics would find it anathema to do so. After all, it's not a fact. Not provable by evidence. But it is liable to reasonable human powers of deduction. A traditional witch's name – *Bella*. *Belladonna*. Certainly, round here and the Black Country. Like the plant.'

'Bella,' Porter repeats stiffly.

'Yes. Bella.' She looks at him with concern, places a hand on his arm. 'Are you alright, Detective? Is it your wound?'

Porter shakes his head. 'No, I'm fine.'

'My, you look pale. Does that name mean something to you? Bella?'

Porter stares towards the woods. 'No. It means nothing. Nothing at all.

11

27TH APRIL, 1943: MORNING

Acting Detective Sergeant Harry James arranges the objects on his desk, Montgomery planning a campaign. A battle plan. The layout just so. Everything in place, each piece serving the objectives of its master's design.

He sits back, admiring. *Just right. Just so.*

The knock on his door is right on time. 'Come,' he instructs.

The door opens, and Porter walks in. 'You wanted to see me, sir?'

'Yes. Yes, I did. Do.' James picks up a folder, flicking it open, busying himself with examining a page clipped inside. He lets Porter stand expectant. 'We've had a complaint.'

'A complaint?'

'Yes. A serious complaint.'

'A serious complaint? About myself?' Porter clarifies.

'Precisely. About you, Detective Constable Porter.' He has a way of making Porter's rank seem undesirable, an ill-fitting description, something unpleasant in the mouth. A joke told in poor taste.

'A complaint from whom, sir?' Porter asks.

119

'From whom? Whom, eh?' James shakes his head, irritated at the grammatical exactitude. He slaps the folder onto the desk. 'From the Ministry,' he spits, 'That's *whom*.'

'The Ministry? The Home Office?'

'No, not the Home Office. The War Office.'

'I don't understand,' Porter states.

James points a finger at him. 'No, I'm sure you don't. You seem to have upset some very important and very busy people, Detective Porter. Men contributing a great deal to our war effort. The fighters.'

'In what way have I caused them to make a complaint?'

James opens the folder with his free hand. 'This bloody investigation of yours.'

'I don't see,-'

'That is it Porter, that is precisely the issue here. You don't see. You don't see the bigger picture. The war. The idea that we're all fighting for one thing. Except you, of course. You who seems to think you can bugger off on your own wild goose chase and to hell with the rest of us!'

'Sir,' Porter protests. 'For the past few days I've done nothing but pursue enquiries into the death of the woman discovered in Hagley wood. The investigation that you and DI Williams assigned me to.'

'And, for some reason known only to yourself, that took you to Wolverley?' James asks.

'Yes sir.'

James pauses, awaits clarification that isn't forthcoming. Nonplussed by the lack of explanation, he presses on. 'What the hell were you doing over there? That's an active base. An active base of our allies. Men who are doing the fighting.'

'We were following a lead sir. It was in my report a few days ago.'

'I know what was in your report.' James taps the desk, the folder. 'I read your report. I want to know just what was so important that you had to go charging over there upsetting our allies. Men wounded in action defending this country.'

'Well, sir, as you've read the report, you'll be more than aware we'd solid information from one of our interviewees. She informed us a barmaid at *the Gypsy's Tent* had left in a rather sudden and mysterious manner. She informed us this barmaid had been seeing a man from the base around the time we believe our victim was murdered. She's one of the young women we can't trace. At the time the rumour was she might have been pregnant by one of the GIs. It seemed logical to interview someone at the base about it. At the very least to eliminate them from the enquiry.'

'Enquiry? Enquiry? Don't you *enquiry* me, Porter. Why can't you get it into your head that this is a bloody paper exercise! You are not Sherlock *bloody* Holmes! You're a novice DC looking to tidy up the paperwork. See some gypsies. Tick the boxes. Get it closed. Not get up the noses of the Yanks!'

'So, the Americans complained?'

James stares at Porter, a mix of wonderment and exasperation at the DC's naivety. 'Of course they bloody well complained! Being harassed by some trumped up bobby is not what they came here for. They complained to our boys in Whitehall - the bloody War Office, Porter. The War Office! People who have a damn sight more on their plates than some dead gypsy! They've been on to us.' He takes a handkerchief from a trouser pocket, mops his brow. 'I can tell you for nothing that DI Williams is far from happy with all this hoo-hah. Far from happy. Looks bad, very bad. Reflects on all of us. Like I said, you need to learn how to be a team player.'

'It was a valid lead, sir. *Dotting I's and crossing T's* is just what DI Williams told me to do when he gave me the enquiry. Wouldn't we all look a bit foolish if we didn't follow something up that later turned out to have some importance?'

James stuffs the greying cloth back into his pocket. 'I can

assure you, Porter, that DI Williams did not have in mind the pestering of our allies.'

'I hardly feel we pestered them, sir. We found a decent line of enquiry. One of their men - a Sergeant Bukowski - assaulted a nurse. The local police followed it up. Interviewed Bukowski but, to be frank, did a pretty poor job of it. All they seem to have done is frighten the victim into not pressing charges. There was evidence of attempted murder, strangulation. It seemed a decent lead. A connection.'

James blows out his cheeks. 'Decent lead! So, you're not only harassing fighting men, allies of this country, you're criticising the work of experienced officers who decided that there were no grounds for further investigation.' He taps the folder with his fingers. 'Remind me, Detective Constable. How long have you been doing this? You wouldn't know a decent lead if you fell over it. You say yourself you've got nothing. All you've done is waste time and piss off the Yanks! There's a strict hands off from Whitehall on this. Stay away from the Yanks! Are we clear?'

'The officer we spoke with - Tolvey - seemed happy enough with the situation.'

'Oh yes, I'm sure he *seemed happy*. So *happy* that he got his commander to get straight on the phone to the War Office to get you to stop.'

'But why? I don't see the problem.'

'Why?' James voice rises in despair. 'Because the last thing they need is having to take time out from the war, from treating their wounded, to answer questions from a wet behind the ears DC about what is more than likely a gypsy murder.'

'With respect-'

'Don't come with your fancy *with respect*! You're not at Oxford now!' James sits forward, hand thumping the desk, traces of spittle flecking the corner of his mouth. Stray dark specks appear on the cover of the folder. 'In this game you have to earn respect, and frankly I've seen nothing from you to make me grant you any. I'm telling you for the last time,

Porter: *Get all of this fantasy G-Men stuff out of your head*! By the good grace of DI Williams, you've got a few days left to tick some boxes and get this put away for good. For *good*, Porter. Forget your crazy ideas, you, and your mad professor. Get it into your head that this isn't some Fancy-Dan murder. You are not *Sherlock-bloody-Holmes* after some Al Capone criminal genius. You're a copper. A Bobby. And, in my opinion, not a very effective one. From now on you do what you've been asked to do. I don't want to hear of you upsetting anyone else. Are we clear?'

'Yes, sir. Clear.'

James slumps back, fishing for the handkerchief once more. 'Now get out and spend the few days you've got left getting everything straightened out. Gypsies. Missing persons. That's it.' He flicks a hand in the direction of the door, terminating the meeting.

Porter steps into the corridor, makes his way to his own office, a cramped space at the end of the corridor previously functioning as storage for filing.

Time would soon be up. Whatever happened in the next few days, whatever he managed to find, he knew there would be little lingering interest in Bella or her fate. The pressures of the war, the fate of the nation, the future of democracy - who would really have time let alone interest in pursuing the fate of Bella or those responsible for her murder?

He rakes his hand across the papers littering the desk. Still nothing on the dental work. Nothing on the shoes. Missing persons; nothing. Land Girl deserters; nothing. The only likely possibilities were Bukowski, him or another of the GIs at Wolverley, or the gypsies. He'd ruled out Bukowski, but now the Yanks wouldn't co-operate with him talking with any of the other troops there. Only the gypsies were left.

His hand comes to rest on the folder he'd taken to *the Gypsy's Tent*. Of course, there was Murray and her notions of witchcraft and pagan ceremonies, but Webster and Willetts would think him even more delusional and misguided in considering such a theory than James did regarding the GIs at Wolverley.

He rifles through the file, finding the notes he'd made on Murray's idea, the pages torn from her books that she'd given him. Mad as it appeared, it did offer insight into aspects of the case that all of the other theories failed to address - the missing hand; the manner of entombment; the gold ring left behind. What rapist, murderer, or thief would bother with any of these things? What murderer would sever a hand; what rapist climb a tree to deposit his victim; what thief leave behind so valuable an object as the ring? Mad as it seemed, Murray's theory was the only one to resolve each of those enigmas.

He lets the sheets fall back onto the desk, realising the craziness of what he's thinking. There had to be something else, something more...rational. Something to explain why she was brutally murdered and so callously disposed of.

Everything came back to one simple piece of evidence. The one simple fact the investigation hung on: who was she?

27TH APRIL, 1943: LATE MORNING

Fellaini sits on the bench seat of his caravan. He's never thought of himself as being particularly tall - though he knows he stood a few inches over what is considered the average. But even after two years with the circus he still finds the accommodation cramped, pinched. He shifts position, tucking his legs so they are parallel to the bench, the outside of his left knee pressing against the cushioned seat. He pulls the documents he is reading to a similar angle on the fold down table, the better to continue studying them.

The blueprints of the factory and production lines were good. Given the shortage of decent paper and ink, maybe the best that could be done. The Dutchman's source had once more proven himself exceptional. From the first, the intelligence he'd provided had been good, but for the past eighteen months it has been incomparable. He knew Canaris and even Goering himself to be enthralled by the quality and quantity of the intelligence procured by his cell. As well as details of the factory layout there were hand scrawled notes regarding the storage of raw materials, the exact nature of each of the production lines, and the dates of proposed shipments. With such intelligence the bombing raids could be co-ordinated to maximum effect. Soon these plans, like others before, would exploit the traditional circus network to be shipped to Ireland, then Spain, and from there to Berlin. Within the month, Luftwaffe raids would focus on the very buildings whose details he held in front of him.

Once the war was won, such intelligence would lead to untold honours. He closes his eyes, drinks in the moment. He sees torches, banners; his father and mother at the front of the crowded hall, his brother and sister too, all of them waving and cheering. Only then would they would hear of all he had done, only then would they learn of his part in the victory of the Fatherland.

He opens his eyes, releasing the moment. Distraction was an enemy. Such thoughts had to be controlled. Like his cover as a trapeze artist, one slip, one stray thought at a crucial time, and he would plunge to the ground.

Discipline.

Such thoughts led to fresh consideration of the Dutchman: specifically, his foolhardiness regarding the woman. He'd known straightaway the man's thinking had been clouded, the whole plan smacking of the irrational. They'd panicked. But, by the time he'd understood just what they'd done, it would have been far more dangerous to have intervened than to leave things alone. For much of the past 18 months, he'd been able to forget the whole matter. Pushing it to the back of his mind, convincing himself everything would play out just as the Dutchman insisted it would.

But now she'd been discovered.

'Tree Murder Riddle' the local paper proclaimed. Even in the

midst of war such a strange occurrence had pushed its way up the daily news agenda. *The Daily Mirror* and even *The London Times* had at one point picked up on the story, though each had allocated merely a few paragraphs buried deep inside their edition.

The prevailing theory was of ritualistic murder. Certainly the comments from the local police suggested gypsies were the major, if not sole line of enquiry. It was the path of curses and mysterious ritual the Dutchman had always suggested would be the one followed if her body was ever discovered.

The press had little interest in gypsies other than in their allotted role as a source of mysticism. Though it added a certain *frisson*, the news played to stereotypes deeply embedded in the culture and thinking of both the investigators and public alike. It led to dead-ends, disinterest and the eventual filing away of the whole affair. Already, with the past few days' news of battles in the Far East and Libya, both the local and national media had moved on. The Dutchman was right; her power to destroy them had been contained. Nullified.

He rolls up the blueprint, tucking it inside the hollow trapeze bar and tapping the end cap back in place. He holds it up, checking for anomalies that might raise suspicion at the port. Satisfied, he lays the bar on the bench before squeezing himself out of the confines of the table and its fixed seating.

He is a cautious man. He has no time for those with over confidence. In his experience, such men became complacent, and in this line of work complacency got you caught. Got you killed. However, despite his natural caution, he is beginning to allow himself to see some light at the end of what he'd once feared might prove to be a very dark tunnel. Everything was settling back into place. Within the week these latest plans would be on their way to Berlin. Circus equipment, shipped from neutral country to neutral country as if the war does not exist. The Dutchman had assured him that by then the enquiry into the body in the tree would have come to its anticipated end. A gypsy. A nobody.

Picking up the trapeze bar, he leaves his caravan.

Outside, the site is gearing up for the afternoon show, acts running through daily routines. He passes gymnasts in the midst of warm-ups, animals being exercised, clowns preparing props. Noise, clamour, colour. Above, the sun is warm, already burning away the low morning cloud with its promise of a clear Spring afternoon.

Walking towards the Big Top, he raises a hand in greeting of everyone he passes. He is accepted. One of them. *The Great Fellaini*, star of the Big Top.

The original idea had seemed foolhardy. To embed an agent in a circus, free to travel the country, unhindered, unsuspected. Even for a man like himself, a gifted athlete, a one time Olympic hopeful, it had appeared improbable. But he was a quick learner and had trained hard. For two years he'd been the perfect spy, hiding in plain sight. Thomas Lehrer, *The Great Fellaini*, an Abwehr officer using the unfettered movement of performers and equipment to send their gathered intelligence home to Berlin.

And he had recruited well, combing Berlin's list of potential collaborators, seeking the perfect conduit. Finding one in the Dutchman, followed by the man's key contacts. Finally had come the biggest coup of all, the agent whose intelligence was shaping the war.

He twists the bar in his hands, its steely smoothness reassuring in his grip. He would secure it in the rigging where that afternoon he would perform as the man they believed him to be. If all went well, within the year the cheers of the crowds for *the Great Fellaini* would become the triumphant roar of his true peers - the officers of the *Abwehr*, the colleagues of Oberleutnant Wilhelm Lehrer hailing his achievements in sabotaging the allied war machine.

He enters the Big Top, its huge canvas flap already opened to the cooling breeze. He moves to the centre of the ring, the nets and rigging high above his head. Looking up he tugs the rope ladder, bracing for the climb.

Reaching the platform, he allows himself one last moment before setting his mind to his practice routine.

The events of the past few days have proved a timely reminder that the dead woman must remain as she was: nameless, faceless, a mystery lest the knowledge of who she was - what she was - led the police to the Dutchman, and through him to Lehrer himself. Though her secret had died with her, her connection to the Dutchman might yet threaten their wider ambition.

Most troubling of all was that after delivering this set of plans, the Dutchman has now reported the disappearance of their provider, his deepest asset. They knew him to be a nervous man. At the time, his part in the gypsy's death had unsettled him. The Dutchman now convinced that this present disappearance has been provoked by the discovery of her body rather than any intervention by the authorities. That he would re-surface once things quietened down. Lehrer himself was not so sure. It had been a good run. Maybe it was one best ended with this current material. In a few weeks they would move North of the city. In a few months it would be Liverpool and the North-West. Maybe it was time to plan a return home.

The separation of the members of the cell had ensured survival. Should one member fall, there was no possibility of linking one to another. With the gypsy's death, followed by those of the others in there cell, the only link to Lehrer's own identity was the Dutchman. Should things unravel further, the police enquiry come too close, then the Dutchman was as expendable as she had been, maybe more so. If her power, great as it was, had been unable to save her, then what chance would there be for the Dutchman, a man of more earthly powers and persuasion?

27TH APRIL, 1943: NIGHT

The music was loud, raucous. Porter stepped out of the main dance floor area and headed for the toilets. *Why had he let himself be talked into this?*

It was his night off from fire-watch, and Rachel had insisted they go out. She was worried at his mood of late, what she called his *introspection*. A night out at the *Mecca* dancing and relaxing was, she insisted, what he needed if he wasn't to burn himself out with obsession over *'this Bella thing'*. It hadn't been so much a suggestion as an ultimatum. She'd arranged it all with Sheila and her new boyfriend, Eric.

Eric. Eric Morrison. *Spiv. Wide-boy. Black marketeer.*

Every town and village had one. A sharp operator who could get the un-gettable, find the un-findable, provide the unattainable. All of course at premium profit for Eric himself. Part hero, part thief, men like Eric Morrison operated on the margins of criminality. They were polarising figures, favoured by some whilst generating outrage among others for what they saw as their under-mining of the war effort, their lack of patriotism. The difference in the public's mind between spiv and black marketeer was crucial. The spiv specialised in getting around rationing, handling goods of dubious origin. They could find you clothes, make-up, nylons, foodstuffs, cigarettes, alcohol. The black marketeer on the other hand, was a criminal figure operating at a higher level, often dealing in hi-jacked merchandise and items diverted from the war effort.

Eric Morrison, Spiv or black marketeer, appeared to have no qualms about a night out with a Detective Constable. In fact, as Eric himself intimated over their first drink earlier in the evening, some of the local force were amongst his best customers. Many of those that weren't were, for a small consideration, willing to turn a blind eye.

'Supply and demand, Alec. Supply and demand,' he'd stated in a broad Brummie accent figuring high on Porter's list of reasons to dislike the man. Top of it was his chosen line of work, run close by an attitude in which Eric views himself as heroic entrepreneur rather petty crook; an immoral man feeding insatiable human greed. 'It's just the way it is, Alec. The public want these things and if they can afford them, then I don't see why they shouldn't have them. I mean, the stuff's out there. Why should it all go to the *la-di-dah* lot in London? The *toffs*? The way I see it, I'm in the morale business. Raising spirits in dark times. Keeping the public happy. Reminding them what we're fighting for.'

He'd snapped open a silver cigarette case, offering Alec, Rachel, and Sheila American cigarettes before producing a matching silver lighter. That too was reason enough for Alec to despise him. Conspicuous consumption. Flaunting possessions and wealth as if they somehow defined his place in the pecking order. His *zoot suit* summed him up: pin-striped flamboyance finished with a silk tie of ostentation.

Porter had downed his pint, ordering another round. Morrison pulling a bulging wallet from his inside pocket. 'Put your money away, Alec. This one's on me.'

Porter had declined with a brush of the hand. Morrison persisting, putting his own hand on Porter's arm whilst thrusting a five-pound note at the barman, whom he seemed to know personally. 'Keep 'em coming Charlie! Let me know when that runs out,' he'd told the man.

Porter had been about to insist rather more forcefully but catching a glower from Rachel he'd let it go. 'Can't have our boys in uniform paying, can we?' Morrison had stated, joyfully flapping his wallet in the air. 'Not when I'm doing so well. Got to look after our heroes, eh Rach?'

Morrison had distributed the drinks, raising his own glass, and proposing a toast. 'To our heroes.'

'Our heroes!' Sheila had chorused loudly.

Soon after Porter's return they'd found themselves a table, a good one thanks no doubt to the power of Eric's money and profile. The band was taking a break from playing. Rachel and Sheila falling into conversation about nylons and make-up. It left Porter to listen to Morrison's theories on economics and market forces. The future for Britain after either victory or defeat.

'Stands to reason, don't it? America. That's who's going to do best out of all this. Whether we beat them Nazis or they beat us, the whole *shebang's* going to be flattened by bombs and artillery. Where's the only place going to have the means to re-build Europe after all this? The Yanks. That's where my contacts are. Look to the future. Back the winners.'

'I suppose so,' Porter concedes. It was a salient point. He'd heard it expressed by others in journals and newspaper articles. *Communism, Socialism, Labour, Conservative, Fascist, Democrat, Christian, Jew, warmongers, pacifists*. All had their ideas of the coming *New World Order*. The war seemed like the end of things rather than the defence of old ways or old ideas. The certainties were gone. Spain had taught him that.

'Suppose nothing,' Morrison insists. 'It's a fact. They're already preparing for it over there. They ain't got no bombs landing. No bombers over New York or Chicago are there? They're going to have a clear run at it. Whoever wins, there's blokes over there going to clean up. And I'm making damn sure I'm in on the ground floor.' He stubs out his cigarette. Sips his beer. 'You're a copper, Alec. I know you think I'm some kind of spiv, but it ain't so. It ain't. I got contacts. Ambition. I'm a businessman. My old man started with a stall in the Bull Ring, that's where I learned me trade. Buying and selling. You want something, I can get it for you. You just got to know where to look, who's up for the deal. Most of the time I get it off the Yanks.'

Porter sits silent. Morrison pauses, appraising him.

'You're an educated man Alec. Rachel says you were at Oxford and everything. That right?'

Porter nods. 'Cambridge. Yeah. Yes I was.'

'And you gave it all up. Just left? Walked away.' Morrison shakes his head. 'I don't get it.'

'It was complicated.'

Morrison, pulling out his cigarette case, takes out another cigarette and lights it. 'Stupid, more like, if you don't mind me saying so.'

Porter takes a drink of beer. 'You wouldn't be the first.'

Morrison leans closer. 'But it's worked out okay for you. Your wound. You've got yourself a decent number, young Detective in a nice area. Got yourself a cracker in Rachel, there.' He pushes his head closer to Porter's. 'However this business finishes, you could find yourself set nicely. Contacts, Alec, it's all about contacts. I could use a man like yourself. Educated. Well placed.'

'I'm not sure I follow you,' Porter replies, shifting his own head a little further away.

Morrison follows Porter's movement. Leans in tight. His voice low. 'Look, Alec, a man like you, an educated man with a little ambition and a free ticket out of the fighting, well… Let's say you're in a position to do people favours. Important people. Grateful people. Things those people will remember when this war's all over. Be in your debt so to speak. Owe you. Whatever happens, I know that a man like yourself, a man with responsibilities - you know, Rachel and her boy - well, it comes expensive. A little extra money, a few nice things every now and again. It could make life all the sweeter.'

'Is this some sort of bribe?'

Morrison sits back, laughing. 'Come on, Alec. Bribe? What do you think I am? Some kind of crook? It's more in the way of a job offer for the future. An incentive scheme, you might say. You wouldn't be the only one. Your DS James is a good friend to the local business community. A very good friend.'

'I think you've got me wrong, Eric.'

'Ooohh I love this!' Sheila coos, jumping up as the returning band break into a Lindy Hop, a dance GIs had brought over with them that was sweeping the cities where they were stationed. 'Come on Eric, let's dance!'

The brass section begin to find a tight groove, blasting out the main riff in tight unison. The drummer and double bass player fly into it like men possessed. The singer moves towards the microphone. Eric smiles at Alec. 'Women, eh?' Stubbing out his cigarette, he gets to his feet.

'Come on Rachel!' Sheila calls, waving her free arm in Rachel's direction.

She looks at Alec. 'Can't. Alec's back.'

Shelia shrugs, 'Sorry, forgot!' she calls before returning her attention to dragging a reluctant Eric towards the dance floor.

Eric smiles, nodding at Alec. 'Like I said, lucky.'

Rachel half-turns in her chair, leaning in close, her arms entwining around Porter's own. 'Isn't this great?' she says, lifting her face close to his ear.

'Great.' The noise of the band mean they have to raise their voices to hear what they're saying to each other.

'You getting on okay with Eric?' she asks, her tone making it more a hopeful request rather than a question.

'He's a shit. A crook,' Porter pissed on her parade.

'I know he's a little... shady. He's just trying to do his best. Sheila likes him.'

'Sheila likes his money.'

'That's unfair, Alec,' Rachel admonishes, her body pulling slightly away.

'Sorry. He just makes me angry. I find myself wanting to punch him in the face.'

'You're tired,' she says. 'You need to try to relax more. This case of yours.'

'Not now,' he states.

Rachel sips at Alec's drink. 'She's been dead a long time. Maybe it's just the way it is. You can't fight fate. You can't live among the dead. There's too many. What about the living? What about us?'

'It's us I'm fighting for. The world we want to live in. The sort of world you want Tommy to grow up in. I'm not fighting fate. I'm fighting the indifference of men like Harry James. Fighting the incompetence of some of the others. Rose Collins, a young woman too scared to shout rape; Bella murdered and no one seems to care. Just what is it we're fighting for? If there's no justice for the Rose Collins's or the Bella's of this world, then just what is it we have that's so worth fighting for? What is it that's worth so many dying for? Men like your Jack. Is it all so that men like Eric Morrison can make a bob or two? Is that it?' He sighs, shakes his head. 'There's got to be more. Got to be.'

She pulls away, staring at him, her face open and concerned. 'There's you and me and Tommy. Isn't that enough?'

He smiles, squeezing her arm. She holds her distance for a beat before accepting the gesture as a yes and snuggling back into him.

He sits, gazing across the dance floor, the crazed movement of the dancers, his thoughts lost in the frenzied whirl. The question Rachel had asked of him filled his thinking. *Why wasn't it enough?*

12

28TH APRIL, 1943: MORNING

Porter sits at his desk, head in hands, trying to clear his mind of the thoughts spinning inside. He needs order but finds only chaos, each thought bouncing of the next like dodgems at the fair. Eric Morrison swam there, as did Rachel and Tommy. Somewhere deep below, floated Bella, Margaret Murray, gypsy camps. There were mystical ceremonies, emotionally damaged GIs, and James Webster. There were skeletons, severed hands, silk shoes, and wych-elm trees.

It didn't help that his head ached from too much beer - a solution that had singularly failed to numb him to Morrison's unctuous manner. There was also the matter of a back grumbling its incessant pain and restricting his movements even more than usual. Order. He needed order. Needed focus. Needed a place to start.

Willetts' head appears around the door. 'We've had word from Lichfield, sir. They've got a gypsy camp set up there a day or so ago. They're regulars every spring. Seems they tend to stick to the same sites at the same time of year. One of the local

Bobbies over there reckons it's the same caravan that uses Hagley each autumn. They meet up there for their festivals.'

Porter rises, the confines of the room requiring he shuffle his seat back and to the side to extricate himself. 'We'd better get ourselves over. Have a chat.' He reaches for his notebook, grimacing at the stab of pain from his back.

'Blimey. You alright, sir? You look proper pale.'

'Back,' Porter states by way of explanation. He felt no inclination to mention his night out with Eric Morrison, though if DS James was as good a friend to local businessmen as Morrison suggested, it wouldn't be long before news of Porter's night out with a black marketeer was common knowledge.

'You want to be careful. Professor Webster told me it could go at any time. It'd leave you helpless.'

'Thanks for the concern. I think I know my limits.'

'That's as maybe, but you don't want to be pushing it. You've been putting a lot of hours into this one,' Willetts chides.

Porter takes his mackintosh from a peg behind the door, 'Yes, well, it would be good to see it yielding something then, wouldn't it?'

'All in good time, sir.'

'The one thing we don't have is time,' Porter snaps. 'This time next week I'll be back following up lonely old ladies' sightings of paratroopers and you'll be looking for stolen bicycles.' He struggles to pull the coat on; one arm in, one fighting for access against the will of the muscles in his back.

Willetts, stepping forward, helpfully tugs it onto Porter's shoulders. 'Have you spoken to the Professor today, sir?'

Porter fought the urge to wave him away, 'Thanks. Murray or Webster?'

'Webster. With the greatest of respect to you and the lady, sir, you know I've little time for Professor Murray's fancifulness.'

Porter smiles, shrugging the coat into place on his shoulders and tugging down its sleeves. 'Not today. Last we spoke there was still nothing from the dental records. He's not been able to add anything to what we already know.'

Willetts nods. 'We've had a few more letters this morning.'

Porter grimaces. Each day a flood of letters arrived at the station or to local newspapers who, having steamed them open and scrutinised them for any scoop, passed them on. For the most part they were wild speculation on the crime and its victim.

An ill-considered interview by Professor Murray in the local paper had resulted in the reporting of her assertions. A fresh spike in the story bringing in yet more letters and claims of knowing who the body was. Murray was something of a celebrity, one not above using her status to promote an upcoming lecture tour. Taken up by other papers in the region, the news had generated its own special pile of correspondence regarding myths and legends. What Willetts dubbed the *doolally* brigade. Each required not only time to be read and considered, but to be followed up. The idea of interviewing everyone named in the letters, those who suspicious neighbours thought might be members of covens, filled neither officer with enthusiasm. Some suggested names of individuals missing after air-raids. Others contented themselves in offering prayers for the victim.

Porter sighs. 'Bring them with us. I'll read them on the drive.'

28TH APRIL, 1943: LATE MORNING

The drive to the gypsy camp proved uneventful. There was little civilian traffic on the roads, less still around the town of Lichfield itself other than the odd convoy of troops or support trucks moving in and out of the barracks located to the southwest of the town. Having consulted with the local bobby, they found the camp in woods close to the village of Hopwas.

Uncertain of the Wolseley's ability to cope with pitted mud and grass tracks, Willetts parks the car in a sandy lay-by at the edge of the woods. The two then make their way on foot across an open field towards a circle of brightly painted caravans.

A group of young children stop their play to stand staring as Porter and Willetts drew nearer. Soon they are joined by a stout woman in a grey dress and greying apron, sleeves rolled up. In her arms she clutches a basket of washing. She says something, and a moment later three men appear from behind a nearby caravan. One of them holds a length of rope Porter supposes he'd been using whilst tending the horses they could hear whinnying close by. The two others hold lengths of wood whose purpose, other than intimidation, he fails to discern.

'Careful,' Willetts cautions.

'Hello there! Morning!' Porter calls to the man with the rope who has taken pole position as leader of the trio.

The man spits fulsomely to the side.

Porter and Willetts halt a few feet from him. Porter stares at the gob of phlegm that clings to the blades of grass. 'I'm Detective Constable Porter. This is Special Constable Willetts.'

The man stares at the two officers in silence.

'We'd like to have a word with you about a matter we're hoping you can help us with. An enquiry about a missing person.'

'No-one missing here,' the man states flatly. His voice is reedy, pitched somewhere between southern Irish and Northumbrian. It was more English spoken with an accent than a dialect. Some of the words were run together, forcing Porter to work hard to make out just what is being said.

'The person we're hoping to identify is a woman who probably went missing over a year ago. Possibly eighteen months or so,' Porter continues, unabashed.

'No-one missing here,' the man repeats a little slower, a little more directly. He glares at Porter, holding his gaze for a moment before turning to walk away.

'We found her body in a wych-elm,' Porter shouts after him. 'In Hagley Wood.'

The man turns towards them, this time he stands closer. He states the same words, this time he sounds each one with equal emphasis, head pushed forward. 'No-one – missing - here.' He holds the rope tightly. The two other men step up either side of him, clubs held ready.

'Michael!' A woman emerges from the caravan nearest to them. She's dressed in a blue top, taffeta, like silk. Her skirt is full, a deeper blue, almost black. She wears a bright patterned headscarf, tied at the side. It is a knot as much flourish as it is a functional means of holding her hair in place. Where it seeps through, the hair is jet black, and falls in waves across her face. Her skin is light olive in tone; her eyes green; mouth full and wide. Her features are snake-like in the shape and position of eyes, nose, and mouth. She reminds Porter of Thedra Bara or Palo Negri, silent movie stars of his youth.

She steps away from the caravan, moves to the man she'd called Michael and touches his arm. She whispers something Porter is unable to catch. The man hesitates before turning and walking away, gathering the others with him. The three withdraw around the caravan from where they'd come. Porter notices the children too have disappeared, as has the older woman.

The woman beckons Porter and Willetts to follow her, leading them to a grouping of metal-framed chairs centred on a campfire. A blackened kettle stands to one side of dully glowing embers. She sits, indicating for Porter and Willetts to do the same. With all three seated, she leans forward. Taking a metal rod, she stirs the coals to life before placing the kettle on top of a now glowing fire.

'Tea?' she asks.

Porter notices her voice is throaty, husky. Foreign. 'Please,' he replies.

Willetts shakes his head, 'Not for me.'

The woman smiles at his evident discomfort. 'Do you think it poisoned or merely charmed?'

Willetts shuffles. 'Not thirsty, that's all.'

The woman shrugs. 'You have had a long drive.'

'Bromsgrove,' Porter confirms.

She gets up, crouching on her haunches before the fire. She busies herself spooning black tea into an enamel pot. Porter tries to figure out her age but is confounded. Late twenties, thirties, possibly even early forties. Her skin is smooth, arms brown, hair silken. 'You must excuse Michael,' she says, finishing putting tea in the pot. 'He is suspicious of strangers. Particularly those in uniform. The *polis*. Too often such people treat us badly.'

'I understand.'

She fixes him with her eyes. 'Do you? Perhaps. If you have been sworn at wherever you go. Beaten and abused, or like our cousins in France and Germany, imprisoned, tortured, or murdered simply because of your way of life. Then maybe you understand.' She shrugs, 'For now I accept the words that make you feel polite, respectable. The civilities of your small-talk.'

Uncertain, Porter decides to move to the purpose of the visit. 'You intervened when we mentioned the body in the tree.'

She lifts the kettle from the fire, pours a stream of boiling water into the tall pot. 'Curiosity, Detective. Bodies in trees. Such things have sway in our culture. I'm certain you discovered this yourself before coming here.'

'Imprisoning the spirit.'

'See, you know of the myths.'

'Like the *Hand of Glory*.'

She sits back. An expression crosses her face, cloud over landscape. 'The *Hand of Glory* is not gypsy myth.'

'No. That's correct. I understand it's pagan. Witchcraft.'

She nods. 'Yet you come here. Tell me, do you seek Romany or witches? Or do you see us both the same?'

Porter shakes his head. 'I understand you camp in Hagley Wood each autumn. A festival.'

She pokes at the coals, inclines her head in acknowledgment. 'We meet. The men trade horses. Race. We meet with friends, distant relatives. Like you with your family at Christmas.'

She passes a cup to Porter, pouring into it some of the dark brew. He nods his thanks. 'You meet near a tree,' he states. 'The tree where the body was found. An ancient wych-elm. A tree that's important to you.'

'It is a place we know. We are…comfortable there.'

'You worship it,' Willetts puts in.

The woman looks at him. 'Worship?' She smiles. 'Only like you might with your Christmas tree. It unites us. Brings us together in celebration of who we are. We sit and talk of the year gone by. We tell the old stories. We eat. We drink and we laugh. Like your Christmas.'

'The woman we found was placed in that tree. The crown of the wych-elm. She would have been there for around eighteen months. That means she could have been placed there in November 1941, around the time of one of your meetings. She was certainly there during your meeting there last year.'

She raises her cup. 'Such a terrible thing.' She drinks, eyes closed, cup held in both hands.

'You know nothing of this?'

Her eyes remain closed. 'Nothing.'

Willetts leans in, 'She was one of your…'

She opens her eyes. '*Kind*?' she asks, face twisting towards him, half-smiling.

Willetts' mouth opens and closes. Porter intervenes, 'Family. Friends. None of them have gone missing during this period?'

She turns to Porter. 'No-one. It is as Michael told you. We are a close community. We keep to ourselves. Where would we go for help? What would we seek from your… *kind*?'

'She was strangled.'

'It is of little significance. Stabbed. Beaten. Strangled.' She drinks more of the tea, this time one hand passes over the cup wafting the aroma towards her. 'Tell me, why do you think she was gypsy?'

'Her clothes. She wore a taffeta blouse, a material much like your own.' He indicates the woman's scarf and blouse. 'She had a scarf too. It was wrapped around her neck. Her mouth had been stuffed with taffeta. Her body had been... desecrated after her death.'

'The *Hand of Glory*,' she says.

'The *Hand of Glory*,' Porter confirms.

'My people - my *kind* - are Romany. Not witches. This *Hand of Glory* is a story, a tale to frighten children and the weak of mind. Taffeta we buy at your markets. Ladies from all over buy it. None of these things say only *Romany*. They say only *woman*.'

'But the place is special to you? Hagley and the tree,' Willetts persists.

'It is a place. We go there. Many people go there. Who found the woman in this tree?'

'Children.'

'Children? See, many people. Do you question all the children? Do you follow children around the country with your questions? No. Just gypsy.'

'You oversimplify.'

'What is this... *oversimplify*?'

'You make it seem... ridiculous.'

'Maybe it is. You seek gypsy because gypsy is easy. You point fingers and many people believe it is so. Like Hitler.'

'That's just too much,' Willetts puts in, standing up. 'What are you saying?'

'That you look to find somebody to blame for this terrible thing. You think gypsy, and now you see only gypsy. You cannot see what else is there because all you see is gypsy. You think if you blame gypsy it will be finished. The bad things will go away. The bad dreams will end for you. Is not so?'

Porter stands. The woman remains squatting. He leans forward, placing his cup on the ground by the fire. 'Thank you for your time and the tea. Whatever you think, we're just doing our job. Following up leads. Seeking answers to the questions we have. Today it brings us here. To you and your family. Your community.'

She looks up, eyes, searching his face. 'Perhaps you ask wrong people,' she suggests.

'Perhaps.'

Her eyes fix him more fully. 'Perhaps you ask wrong questions.'

28TH APRIL, 1943: LATE AFTERNOON

The drive back from Lichfield is solemn. Porter sits in the passenger seat deep in thought. Willetts drives in silence, attention fixed on the road ahead. All road signs have been removed as preparation for harrying the enemy after any invasion. Despite some knowledge of the area, Willetts is busy scanning first the map and then the road in quick succession to ensure he navigates the route back to Bromsgrove.

Porter stirs uneasily in his seat. His back aches, a two-hour journey back to Bromsgrove following hard on the outward drive to Lichfield is taking its toll. More than any physical discomfort is his realisation that the gypsy woman had hit a nerve. What she said resonated with him, tugged at him. *Not so much the wrong people as the wrong questions.* Why did he think there was truth in this? What were the questions they weren't asking? What were the ones he was failing to think of? What was it Conan Doyle said: *Once you eliminate the impossible then whatever remains, no matter how improbable, must be the truth.* What did that mean for Bella?

Was it possible she was the victim of a gypsy ritual killing or a domestic murder? *Yes.* He'd found nothing at the camp to eliminate those motives. Were there other possibilities? *Yes.* She could be the victim of an angry GI such as Bukowski or an opportunist rapist. She might be Margaret Murray's sacrificed black magic coven member or even the victim of Willetts' Mata Hari-*esque* spy-ring. Ten days into the enquiry and they'd eliminated nothing from their original theories, no matter how outlandish some of those were. There was physical evidence in the shoes and the gold ring, but it had led them nowhere. Nor had the search of dental records.

Williams and James had been clear. The gypsy line of enquiry was the only one they wanted pursued. It was what they would have done themselves if they'd thought the case worthy of their time. Yet to Porter it was clearer than ever that to pursue merely the gypsy line of enquiry was short-sighted and foolish. Other possibilities remained. What was it that Murray had said to him? *As long as the mind is open to contemplate them.*

What were they missing? What were the questions he needed to ask?

He squirms in the seat.

'You alright, sir?' Willetts asks without taking his eyes from the road.

'Back,' Porter answers.

Willetts glances across. 'Such a long way for so little.'

'All part of it.'

'Oh, those letters are on the back seat,' Willetts reminds him.

Porter turns in his seat, a twisting movement sending splinters of pain up the right side of his body. A small plosion of breath is forced out. Grimacing, he manages to retrieve the small stack of envelopes and turn back. He places the stack on his lap, taking a moment to regain composure. His breathing steadies and he begins to flick through the correspondence.

Seven envelopes varying in thickness, handwriting, and point of origin. It is the thicker of the envelopes that catches his attention. He looks at the address. The writing is a small carefully formed script - a woman's hand he thinks. A bluish-white envelope, pre-war, postmarked from the Coventry area. It was addressed simply to THE OFFICER IN CHARGE OF THE BODY IN THE TREE INVESTIGATION followed by the police station address in smaller curved script.

He smells the envelope. Fragranced, but subtle. Old stock from before the war, a time when such things mattered, a time to think such trifles important.

He opens it, withdrawing three sheets of paper of a colour matching that of the envelope. Each sheet is covered with the same small close cursive script as the address. He scans the pages, finding the word '*Anna*' signed at the bottom.

He turns to the start of the letter.

'*Dear sir,*

I write to you because I know something of the identity of the woman found in the tree in Hagley Wood and that of one of the men who, if not directly involved in her killing, was responsible for assisting in placing her in the tree.

She was a Dutchwoman who arrived illegally in England early in 1941. She was related to a Dutchman who I have been led to believe was part of a spy-ring in the south Birmingham area providing intelligence about munitions factories to help with the bombing raids.

I am not certain whether she was actively involved in this work or not but my understanding is that she fell out with these men and was murdered to keep her from speaking out and betraying them.

One of the men, an English officer, is known to me. He is a good man, but a weak one, and a man I believe to have been misguided. I have not seen him for some months now but I know him to be truly sorry for his involvement in this tragic event and in assisting enemies of this country.

He is haunted by terrible dreams and visions of what was done to this woman. When last I saw him he woke screaming from a terrible nightmare of her speaking to him from the tree. It was then that he broke down and confessed all that he had done; the hiding of the body and the lives he had put at risk by his spying.

I know he feared for his life and to have convinced me that my own life too would be at threat should others become aware that his identity and knowledge of his role might become known. He fears the men his betrayal has tied him to.

I have heard nothing from him since late last year. I do not know if even now he may be dead and the men responsible –a Dutchman and another, a German who he told me parachuted into the country in 1941- may be gone.

Please, I am not strong enough to speak out. Find him for me. He told me he was now calling himself Claverley.

Anna

Porter read it through twice more, before reading it aloud to Willetts.

'What do you think? Porter asks as he finishes.

Willetts stares ahead. 'Damned if I know what to think.'

'Your first reaction.'

'She's *doolally.*' He flicks a glance at Porter. 'Like Professor Murray. A little too much imagination.'

'A hysterical female?'

'If you like. A bit like them old ladies who ring us up convinced they've seen paratroopers landing at the bottom of their garden. Not so much mad as...'

'Lonely?'

'Reading too many spy books.'

Porter grunts. 'But didn't you say yourself you thought Bella might be a spy?'

Willetts face crumples into a frown, 'A spy's one thing. But this is a bit too much.'

'Might explain the labels torn from her clothes. Like you said. And, if she was killed by her own, it would explain why she wasn't taken prisoner and interrogated.'

'I understand that, sir. But it all just sounds too...fantastic. All that stuff about a Dutchman and a German and a British officer involved. Parachutists. False identities. It's Alfred Hitchcock, isn't it? You know, *The 39 Steps* or *Saboteur*. Fiction.'

'Hmm,' Porter, murmurs, folding the sheets of paper and slipping them back inside the envelope. 'So, we ignore it?'

Willetts considers the question. 'Seems sensible. Especially after what DS James said.'

'Yes. DS James. I'm certain he'd ignore it. File it away.' Porter looks out of the window as the road speeds by. The landscape a blur, one thing merging into another. The faster you went, the less it was possible to make out one building from another, to make sense of anything you were looking at. It was the same with their enquiry. They were on a timetable imposed by Williams and James because to them it was simple. They looked for just one thing, saw only one thing: *all you see is gypsy.* He needed to slow things down, find time to think it through.

'So, sir. What are we to do?'

Porter turns to face the road ahead. The light is fading. The lights on oncoming vehicles coming on, the masked blackout cross of their headlights smearing across the grime of their own windscreen. 'I'm going to give DS James what he wants. A nice typed up report of our meeting with the gypsies. Their denial of any knowledge of our mystery corpse or her identity. Then I'm going to find a way to follow-up on this Claverley or whoever he is. See if I can uncover something concrete about him. There must be records. Names. Addresses. Some link.'

Willetts ponders the statement. 'Anything I can do to help, sir, just ask.'

Porter half-turns in his seat. 'Thanks, Albert. That's very good of you, but I can't countenance you getting involved in what I'm planning. It's quite possible it will get me nowhere. More than likely it'll get me disciplined.'

Willetts stares at the darkening road ahead. 'Our Tommy still has nightmares about what they found in that tree. He wakes up at night seeing those eyes staring at him from inside it. If we can sort this out, show him there's a reason - that it's not witches and demons - then I reckon he'll sleep all the better.'

Porter grunts. 'It will take longer than the few days we've got left,' he states.

He stares out of the window, the blur of the scenery rushing past. His mind chews over an idea that has been forming since the day James had presented him with his deadline. It was a plan. A germ of how he might find the answers he sought. Answers to questions he was certain James would never allow him to pursue.

13

MAY 3RD, 1943: MORNING

Porter walks along the gravelled footpath that leads from the main road towards a row of cottages. It is hot, his back is aching, and the walk from the police station tiring.

He looks up at a sky clear and blue without a hint of cloud. He draws a hand across his brow, mopping the gleam of sweat gathered there before running a finger around the inside of his collar. He'd already begun to contemplate the return walk to the station when the sun would be higher, the temperature hotter.

He looks in his notebook, checking the details of an address. *Back in the routine.*

His report on the travellers' camp at Lichfield was filed a week ago, and for once James appeared satisfied. Whether it was the contents of the report or the fact that Porter had to all appearances been brought to heel, was hard to tell.

The week allowed for the investigation had been up the at the end of April. With no further sightings of gypsies to be interviewed, no return on the dentistry or medical records, nothing from missing persons, and no member of the public coming forward with knowledge of missing daughters, sisters, wives, or mothers, there had been little else to do other than file the case as *Continuing*. Porter and Willetts had been re-assigned to *more pressing* cases. In line with regulations a watching brief had been allocated to *Bella's* case. It meant it was the lowest priority for further police time, a case with little expectation of any imminent breakthrough or the appearance of new evidence. Like other such cases, it would sink into the subterranean swamp of police files, finally disappearing into the dark depths of the system. Never closed; never thought of.

It was not the tidy conclusion James or Williams anticipated, but their abiding assumption that the killing was the work of gypsies was now taken as read.

In its place, the pressing cases assigned to him amounted to the routine follow up of sightings of German aircrew baling out from shot down bombers or scouring the district for missing bicycles and the occasional spiv.

Despite such irritations, the present week had begun well.

Although his investigation was officially suspended, details from their earlier enquiries were still coming through. Best of all is that Webster has undergraduates searching the clearing. For some days now his university classes have laboured under a hot early summer sun in what the Professor of Forensics dubbed *field-work* - part of their course in the brave new world of forensic science. That morning Porter had received news that a severed hand had been found buried close to the tree, much as Margaret Murray had predicted. Webster's view was that although it was early days, the hand appeared to be a match for that taken from the skeleton. His reluctance to commit to a formal declaration of it being Bella's hand before a laboratory investigation was understandable, but just how many buried hands would he expect his students to find in such a small area of woodland?

He'd spent the walk wrestling over sending a telegram to Murray informing her of the discovery, one that that might substantiate her claim regarding the significance of a severed hand.

At present, it added yet more layers of confusion to his map of the enquiry. A week ago, he'd banished Murray's convictions to the margins of the investigation: lucky guesses, nothing more than coincidence or chance. A woman with time on her hands who read widely. An academic putting together unrelated events and twisting them to her own outlandish view of the world. She was neither mad nor correct, merely obsessive. A woman convinced of the singular correctness of her theory. But now, to have found the hand where she said they would, leant substance to her ideas.

It troubles him. It adds weight to her assertion that it wasn't he himself who must believe in the possibility of witches or magic, or that Webster's scientific denial of such things was important. Instead he should account for what the perpetrators, her killers, might believe. Bella might have been part of a coven whose beliefs had been taken to the extreme.

News of the hand would also affirm the popular notion of locals of the crime being the work of gypsies. Whatever Murray might hold otherwise, in the popular mind there was little differentiation between Romany and witchcraft. The hand would fuel ideas of gypsy curses.

He decides to wait. The waters are muddier than ever, and the last thing the investigation needs right now is yet more speculation and rumour and gossip. He needs time to consider what such a discovery means for the way forward, especially now that Webster, Willetts, and himself have begun treading a hazardous path. A path with repercussions for all their careers.

Believing there remained avenues of investigation still to be pursued, he'd persuaded them to the idea he'd evolved: that the three of them continue an unofficial investigation into the killing. His idea had inveigled its way into their consciences, tugging the heartstrings of their good natures. It spoke to their professional sense. Their shared understanding that despite the lack of interest from superiors, there remained useful work to be done on the investigation. It was work that might yet yield the identity of Bella and of her killer.

His plan had been simple. On the evenings when Porter and Willetts were not required for fire-watching duties they would meet at Webster's house, an imposing residence on the road to the Lickey Hills Beacon. There they would discuss the case, following up in their own time the ideas that emerged. They would do so until either the case was solved or all lines of enquiry had been exhausted. That or the war concluded and they would have other matters to deal with in either victory or defeat.

At the first meeting a few days ago Webster had proved a generous host, particularly dispensing the pre-war whiskey he'd the foresight to stockpile. The room they used as the hub of what was effectively a private investigation would originally have been a rear parlour At some point, it had been re-modelled to run the width of the house, its Georgian windows facing out across once lawned gardens now serving as *Dig For Victory* vegetable patches. It operated as Webster's study and was dominated by a large oak table across which they'd spread the documents relevant to their enquiries. They'd agreed their objective was discovering the identity of the woman all three now called 'Bella'. Once this was done, they would be better placed to seek her killer.

The meeting had established an agreed order to their work, and at Webster's insistence had clarified their objectives. They would pursue answers to those matters each found difficult to leave as they were: *Who was this woman? Why was she murdered? Who had killed her? Why had her corpse been left in the tree?* Though none were prepared to articulate them, each had a personal reason for involvement beyond the obvious. For Porter, it was the desire for justice; for Willetts, completing a job left unfinished; for Webster, it offered the opportunity to prove his methods.

They had compiled a chart of the possible circumstances of

the murder – *gypsy ritual, scorned lover, GI pregnancy, betrayed husband/lover, rape and murder by a stranger whilst sheltering in the woods, a prostitute's rendezvous with a murderous client.* Murray's theory of a trial and execution for crimes against a witches' coven made the list, despite Willetts' scorn and Webster's more rationalised rejection. Top of the list for Porter is the espionage link suggested by the letter from the mysterious Anna.

Next to each theory, they had noted the evidence indicating a particular scenario. When that had been done, they had noted the additional evidence necessary to prove each scenario as the one they sought. In every case it amounted to matters of missing physical evidence to be looked for, people yet to be interviewed, agencies still to be contacted, and the lines of enquiry to be followed.

If a logical approach were to be fully employed, all three would take each scenario in turn, pursuing each until it either yielded what they searched for or was exhausted as a possibility. Having discounted it, they would move on to the next. This was the approach Webster wished to follow.

Porter had vehemently disagreed, arguing that such an approach would take months, possibly years, to complete. Their pursuit was to be conducted part-time with no official sanction or support. He'd argued that all lines must be pursued at the same time, with each of them assuming responsibility for one or two of the possibilities and sharing their results. He was adamant that some enquiries would necessitate visits to similar sources with similar people being interviewed. He accepted Webster's view that it made each interview complex. Interviews would have to cover the full range of possibilities rather than having a single focus. However, Porter held such an approach would prove far more successful in allowing the inter-connection of the evidence. Only in one scenario would all the pieces fit, locking together to solve the case. It was a jigsaw; a puzzle for which they more than likely already held many of the pieces in their hands. All they lacked was the design they were to construct.

Webster conceded, Willetts simply happy to fall into line.

Porter took the espionage scenario and the coven; Webster the gypsy ritual and betrayed husband/lover; Willetts the GI and stranger rape. The allocation felt logical. Porter had good links with Professor Murray and was the one most keen on finding the mysterious Claverley; Webster had the contacts to follow-up on the wide-ranging issues related to the dental and health records and missing persons; Willetts had a link to the secretary at Wolverley as well as personal contacts to the Specials with their knowledge of local prostitutes and sex offenders.

They would meet as often as necessary to share the developing evidence. As they were able to eliminate a line of investigation, that person would switch to support those lines still showing promise. If things went as Porter planned, by the end all three of them would be pursuing the one remaining line of investigation, the only scenario where all of the pieces fitted. There they would find their killer.

He stops next to a small cottage, checking his notepad once more. He looks at the gatepost of the house he's paused in front of. *Glebe Cottage*. He spends a moment fumbling with the wooden gate before finding the latch. It is corroded and takes some pressure to lever open, followed by an equal amount of fiddling and lifting of the gate to get in back into place. A gravelled path ran to the front door. He follows it as it winds around dishevelled borders of poppies, rhododendrons, and tulips. England in late spring.

He knocks the door, extracting his warrant card whilst waiting the moment or two before it opens. When it does, the woman who stands there is an imposing figure, stout in build, somewhere in her late fifties. She wears a grey cardigan, white blouse, tweed skirt, and brogues. Her eyes screw up as she attempts to focus on the figure standing before her, accentuating what is an already pinched face.

Porter holds up his warrant card, presenting it closer to the woman's face. 'Mrs Riley? I'm Detect-'

The woman squints. 'Miss. Miss Riley.' The voice firm, authoritative, irritated. 'And I'm not blind, young man.' She waves the warrant card away. 'You're standing against the sun, officer,' she explains.

He withdraws the card, stepping to the side so he's shaded from the glare. 'I'm terribly sorry. I'm Detective Constable Porter. I've come about your recent sighting of parachutes.'

'Recent?' Her irritation increases a notch. 'Two days ago! They could be anywhere by now! Anywhere!'

He shuffles his warrant card back inside a jacket pocket. 'Again, I'm sorry. I was only given the information by my sergeant this morning. I came straight round.'

'Sergeant!' she says scathingly. 'The man's a fool, like his predecessor! All of them, fools!' She is indignant. 'He thinks I'm seeing things, more like.' She pauses, considering the scale of incompetence of the local station before sighing loudly and stepping aside. 'Oh well, better late than never, I suppose. You'd better come in.'

The room was surprisingly bright, the morning sun spearing it with shafts of light broken by the diamond pattern of leaded windows. It is tidy, compact; functional rather than decorative; sofa, two armchairs, a bureau. A small cast iron range stood next to the ingle-nook fireplace, a black kettle hangs from a bar to the side. Miss Riley swings the bar and kettle over the fire, 'Tea? It's not long boiled.'

'No, thank you. But a glass of water would be welcome.'

'I have some lemonade in the pantry. My own. Very refreshing.'

'That would be lovely.' She disappears for a few moments, returning with a glass. He spends a moment scrutinising the grey / green liquid before lifting the glass to his mouth.

'Oh, do go on, young man,' she urges. 'It won't kill you.'

He drinks, tentatively at first. The lemonade is good,

surprisingly so. He gulps half the glass before remembering his manners. 'It's delicious,' he judges.

'Of course it is,' she says. 'Recipes been in the family for years. My mother, her mother, and so on. The local Women's Institute members would quite literally kill for my secret.'

She indicates they should sit in the two armchairs facing each other that are either side of the fireplace. White lace antimacassars drape the back of each chair and its arm rests. Placing his glass on the floor, he extracts his notepad. Miss Riley sits forward, satisfied that her information is at last being taken seriously.

'So, Miss. Riley, exactly what was it you saw that night?'

'Parachutes. Two of them. Floating down in the direction of the woods.' Her tone is clipped, a woman rarely suffering fools or wasting time in aimless gossip.

'Hagley Woods?'

'Of course. What other woods could be seen from here?' she scoffs.

'And what time was this?'

'About two in the morning.'

He raises an eyebrow. 'That's quite late. I can't help wondering-'

'Why a woman of my years would be up so late? How I can be so certain of the time?' Before he can respond, she plunges on. 'Detective, I have cats. Creatures of habit. I'm afraid that my Copernicus arrives home from his nightly hunt at roughly the same time each night during spring. It's the field mice, you see.'

'*Copernicus.*' Porter writes.

'My cat. Well one of three. Leonardo and Galileo are the others. But they're not as bothered about the field mice as Copernicus.'

He looks up. 'Cats of learning,' he comments, picking up the glass, sipping the lemonade. He finds himself inadvertently smiling at the effect of the drink.

Miss Riley watches approvingly, face softening somewhat but

eyes remaining sharp. She considers him. 'I'm a teacher. At the girls' school in Worcester,' she states.

'Ah,' Porter responds. It went some way to explaining a great deal about her - the exactitude, the slight air of intolerance, the somewhat unfortunate manner.

'And you, Detective?'

'Me?'

'What is so obviously a robust young man like yourself doing here rather than being at the front?'

He sips more lemonade before placing the glass on the floor. 'I'm unfit.'

'Unfit?' She peers at him. 'You look a fine fit young man to me.'

He picks up his notepad. 'Appearances can be deceptive.'

'Well, if you say so.' She took a moment. 'I lost my Trevor. Ypres. The flower of a generation. *A citizen of death's grey land.*'

'Sassoon.'

'Yes, Sassoon.' She examines his face more closely, 'What a surprising young man you are, Detective.'

'These parachutes. Was there anything else?'

'Well, there were men at the end of them. Figures. Not bombs or canisters of supplies or anything like that. Men, most definitely men. They disappeared below the tree line and that was about it.'

Porter notes the details, at the same time scanning the bullet points he's made. 'Well, that appears to be everything.' He ticks off the list. '*Date, time, location*. There's not much else for the report. I just need to take a look from the spot you saw them from. It helps plot the direction they were going in.'

'That would be by the front door. I'd heard Copernicus meowing. I opened the door, and was looking down the path. That's when I saw them, over to my right. It was a full moon. Very bright. Very clear.'

Porter nods. 'Once I've filed this, I'll get straight on to the ARP and to the Ministry of Defence. See if their spotters saw anything. See if any planes were shot down in the area whose crew might have bailed out around here.' He tucks the notebook into a pocket and stands. 'And thank you for the lemonade.' He drains the glass. She stands and takes it off him.

'Not at all. So nice to have a visitor.' She holds the glass up, inspects the dregs of pith at the bottom, grateful at his enjoyment. 'I believe you'll find there was a raid that night. Longbridge I'd say. There were a great deal of aircraft overhead earlier in the evening.'

She walks him to the door, stepping across the threshold onto the gravelled path. 'Here. I stood just here.' She points in the direction of the gate. 'And that's where I saw them. Drifting down over there.' She points towards the woods. 'They disappeared behind the tree-line.'

He makes a sketch in his notebook of approximate location and direction. 'That's excellent,' he says. 'Thank you. Thank you very much.'

She waves a hand dismissively. 'Just doing one's bit. We all do what we can. I must say it's reassuring to have one's information taken seriously. Not like that time a few summers ago.'

'I'm sorry to hear that.'

'Yes. Your Sergeants, again. It was just the same. I went into the station. Told him. Two parachutists landed towards Hagley Wood. He said there'd been no air raids that night, so I was mistaken. Couldn't possibly have been a bomber crew bailing out. Spies I told him. What about spies? Longbridge is only over the other side of the Lickeys. They make munitions, and tanks, and planes. What spy wouldn't be interested in something like that?'

Porter pauses. 'A couple of years ago? When exactly?'

'Summer 1941. Copernicus-'

'Yes, Copernicus and the field mice. Early summer 1941, you say? Can you be certain?'

She tuts, turning, and going back into the cottage and the

writing bureau tucked against the wall. He watches from the doorway as she rummages through a stack of similarly bound books before pulling out a slim volume. 'My journals. I've kept one since I was a little girl. Habit, you see.' She turns to the relevant page. 'Here.' She rotates the book so he can read it. 'See. There. The tenth of August 1941. That would be the day when I saw it, and then here's my interchanges over the following days with your sergeant... Let's see...' She runs a finger over the handwriting before stopping and tapping a word. 'James. Yes, Detective-Sergeant Harry James. Like the bandleader.'

MAY 3RD, 1943: NIGHT

'So, what you're saying is there were unconfirmed reports of two parachutists landing in the area of the woods early in the summer of forty-one,' Webster clarifies, summarising what Porter has spent the previous ten minutes telling them of his interview with Miss Riley.

Porter nods. 'She had the dates in her journal. It's only unconfirmed because Harry James is a lazy sod who couldn't be bothered to take the trouble of filling out the paperwork. If he'd followed it up – as I did – he'd have discovered there were reports of a plane thought to be a Heinkel or Dornier, over the area that night. I put in a call and checked the ARP records. All bombs dropped are recorded by ARP fire-watchers. Those that land and explode and the damage they cause, and those that don't explode so bomb disposal can get to them. No bombs were dropped locally that night, so James didn't check further. There was however a raid further north over Brum. ARP spotters made a sighting of a single plane over the Lickeys but put it down to a stray aircraft having lost their bearings or having engine problems that had cut them off from the main force. Perfect cover for slipping an aircraft in and dropping a couple of spies.'

'So, you're saying that because James failed to record Riley's sighting, there was nothing for the MoD authorities to follow-up,' Willetts puts in, underlining the significance of what Porter is suggesting.

'Exactly.'

'And you believe this supports your Anna theory? The suggestion that this man she talks of was part of a ring of enemy agents operating in the area?' Webster asks.

'One hundred percent. Miss Riley was clear in what she saw. She's bright and lively – a teacher, active in the local guides and WI. She's no crank or lonely old woman craving attention.'

'Well, it's certainly more than I've found.' Webster admits, picking up a sheaf of papers from the table and adjusting his monocle. He taps the papers. 'This is the result of my request to regional police forces for details on missing persons. Sixty-five women in the age bracket of thirty to forty were reported missing in the period we're interested in. July to December 1941.' He looks up. 'As we agreed at the start of our venture, I extended the search to cover the period of twenty to fifteen months prior to the discovery of the body as a precaution to the precise dating of the murder.'

'Sixty-five!' Porter exclaims. 'That's an awful lot of young women.'

'And those are just the ones still logged as missing. There were others who later turned up in other towns, sometimes they were shacked up with some chap, or working elsewhere. Some who... erhm... How shall I put it? Had found less salubrious employment.'

'Is there any way at all to narrow that number down?' Porter wonders.

Webster looks at the sheaf of papers as if an answer might make itself known, like a magician with a *pick a card* trick. 'Well, if we knew more clearly what we were looking for, then perhaps. However, given that we've little idea as to whether or not she's local or had come here from some other part of the country, then it's difficult. As we know our Bella had at least one birth, so I can prioritise those with children, but that's of no help if she kept the birth secret or gave the child up for adoption.'

'So, you have to work your way through all of them.'

'At present, yes. One by one, finding out what I can, adding the details to the basics of the initial missing person report, then seeing if anything fits. Though how I'll know if it does... Well it's what our American friends call a long shot.'

'Intuition.'

'Sorry?'

'That's how we'll know. Intuition. Gut feeling,' Porter clarifies.

Webster shakes his head. 'There we differ, I'm afraid. I would much prefer we rely on facts in these matters. Details. Evidence. If we don't do that...Well, we're back to Professor Murray and her fancies.'

Porter decides not to argue the point. After all, he'd called Webster in for the very reason of adding scientific discipline to the investigation. He sought scientific validity, so he could hardly dismiss Webster's approach, but feels there are aspects in the investigation of a crime that come down to nothing more than *'instinct'*, a sixth sense of what was right. Such things went beyond the narrowing objective reasoning of Webster's science.

'Can we now exclude witchcraft trials from our enquiries?' The Professor pleads, continuing his point.

Porter shrugs. 'I think it's always been on the fringe of possible explanations. But your people did find the hand, a hand that you yourself matched to that of the victim. A hand that had been severed then buried. Whatever our personal views, the fact remains, that much of the physical evidence has striking similarities to what Professor Murray told us would be the expectations of such trials. And I know how keen you are to put store in the physical evidence, Professor.'

Webster snorts. 'Only as the basis for logical thinking. In such a matter as this...well, it appears to be coincidence. Either that or someone's playing a joke on us. And why would anyone do such a thing?'

'Until it can be thoroughly discounted, it has to remain a possibility. It's the approach we agreed to take. As Murray herself said, it's not what we believe, but what her killer or killers might believe that's the issue here. We can't discount it.'

Webster frowns a response.

Porter turns to Willetts. 'How about your Albert. Anything?'

Willetts rubs his chin, furrowing his brow in a show of gravitas he feels suits such matters. He opens a battered notebook, tapping at a page with his pencil. 'Nothing of real use. More a matter of what you might call elimination,' he says. He scratches behind an ear with the pencil, lips tightening as if surveying a list of runners and riders at the racetrack. 'I've spoken to most of the Specials on attachment around here. Got a list of known or suspected sex offenders.' He shakes his head as he scans the page. 'Nothing really. More flashers and fiddlers than any strong stuff like rape. Couple of wife-beaters or blokes who've slapped women around.' He continues his scanning of two more pages. 'Nothing. The lads discounted them as not being the sort – flashers tend to run away once they've shown what they've got to the ladies, hardly the type to attack a woman,' he explains. 'The peeping-toms are the same, not their style, if you like. A couple of the ones done for assault might be worth following up, but most of this was stuff that happened a couple of years or so ago, and they're all off, been conscripted. Might take a while to track them down.'

Webster adjusts his monocle. 'If we're to take this further,' he puts in, 'then we need to consider the fact that sooner or later we will have to approach the military for help with access to some of our *suspects*. If we can't do so, well I fear we either end up wasting our time or having to wait for the end of the war and them being demobbed back into civvy street where we can finally get at them.'

'No, we can't afford to wait for that.' Porter is adamant. 'If our man is in the military he could be killed before we get a chance to speak with him. Too many eventualities.'

Webster speaks the unspoken. 'For all that matter he could already be dead.'

Porter looks at him, turning his head to take in Willetts and the Special's own look of concern. It was a truth they carried with them. 'I know,' he concedes. 'I know. And if that turns out to be the case, then we'll have to prove guilt without the benefit of a confession. Prove it without any shadow of a doubt remaining.'

Webster removes his monocle. He takes in Willetts, nodding agreement with Porter. Willetts is a man who followed. The case is important to him only in that it offered purpose. Willets wanted the job done, a sense of professional satisfaction. He was interested, committed even, but could easily walk away. Porter is different, obsessed with the pursuit of whatever passed for the truth, demanding in finding closure.

'Agreed, Webster states. 'But it strikes me that if we can't do this, as you say, *beyond any shadow of doubt*, then you, Porter, of all of us, will find it hard to walk away. To concede. Her killer might be dead. We may never find him. We may never be sure who killed her. We may never discover who Bella was, or why she was killed. More than that, if things go wrong, this case will blight your career in the police. I'd hate for it to blight your life too.'

'I understand,' Porter says. 'I don't think that will happen.'

'You maybe need to bear in mind Rachel and her boy.' Webster persists. 'Find time for them. Keep part of you safe, kept away from all this. Remember, Bella's dead. She's beyond help.'

Porter sighs. 'I know.'

Studying him, Webster is concerned he will lose that reality.

MAY 10TH, 1943: MORNING

Porter lies staring at the ceiling. Yellow-brown stain, a fingered smear of colour, yellowed lampshade, thick brown twined cord, blistered plaster. Downstairs, a drone of voices punctuated with high-pitched peals of laughter. Rachel, Tommy, Arthur.

He turns to the clock. Seven. He'd finished fire watch duty at 4am. He had an afternoon duty roster at the station from two till ten. Arthur was on shift work at the factory, today was his day off.

He sinks back into the warm sheets, running hands through his hair, awaiting the twinge from his back, the sweet pull of pain. Altering his position, he feels the dampness of the flat sheet underneath him.

He'd had the dream again. The orchard. The sweet fragrance of oranges. The sound of engines, the siren screech of bombs. Warm blood red rain, him lying pressed into the solid white rock, the warm swell of urine on groin. When he'd lifted his head, he'd found himself not in the hot sun of Spain but lying in a dark shadow. He'd looked up, craning his head higher and higher, back straining, sinews screaming against the effort. He knew what would be there. Knew what it was even before he saw it, even before he'd focused his eyes. A gnarled tree. The wych-elm. Bella's tree.

He sits up, swivelling his legs off the bed, grabbing a cigarette from a packet on the bedside table. Lighting it, he draws the smoke in deep.

Through the floorboards he hears the soft trill of Rachel's voice. She was singing, humming some nursery song for Tommy who murmured, joining in, singing along in childish approval. *Normal. Solid. Real.*

He is a ghost in that world.

He shuffles on his clothes; pausing in between each garment to take long, deep drags on the cigarette.

He'd finally been persuaded to Webster's argument that the moment had arrived for utilising official channels, forced to admit there was no other recourse in pursuit of the classified information required to progress the investigation. His telegram signal requesting assistance from the War Office in identifying the current posting of an officer called Claverley had been sent more than a week ago. So far, there'd been no response, not even the obligatory bureaucratic knee-jerk lamenting of an inability to provide such information. Instead, silence. A big black hole of a silence.

And that troubled him more than he could say.

There could be no meeting with Webster or Willetts for the next few days, a combination of his own duty roster and Webster being required in London for a meeting with His Masters at the Home Office. It meant he was currently forced deeper into his own thoughts; and that troubled him too. Of late his thoughts had been... darker. Shadows skittering just out of sight, just out of reach. Thoughts... indefinable. Like his visions of the tree.

He stands looking at himself in the dressing table mirror. Rachel said he looked tired, and that irritated him too. He steps forward, peering closer. *Yes, there were shadows. Yes, he needed a rest. Who didn't?* They were in a war. Sacrifices had to be made, especially by those not at the front. Those who were safe, secure.

He leans forward, studying his image in the triptych mirror of the dresser, a reflection split three ways. By day, Detective; by night Fire-watcher. And, in what down time was left, a comic book caricature of a sleuth engaged in some private crusade. And, in the gaps, Rachel, Tommy – part-time lover; part-time father.

Who was he? What was he? What made him so certain he could resolve all of this – not just Bella, but all of it – Rachel, Tommy, himself?

He stubs the cigarette out in the ashtray on the dresser, finding himself staring into his own eyes in the mirror, eyes black with tiredness of it all. *Windows to the soul* his mother used to say.

A thought passes through his mind, a shape under the surface, dimly made out. Where was Bella's soul? When might it rest?

14

MAY 10TH, 1943: EVENING

Webster's Whitehall meeting had been arranged for the Professor of Forensics to report on the progress of his pioneering work on scientific approaches to the solving of crime.

Home Office funding was the result of months of his pressing the case for adopting the model deployed in America in Hoover's Scientific Crime Detection Laboratory. He'd bombarded officials with letters, research papers, and testimonials from scientists and police authorities alike. There had been meetings and pamphlets followed by lengthy reports of the FBI's achievements over the previous decade. It was early days, but the idea of a major university teaching laboratory turning out those specialised in the use of scientific methods to solve crime was coming to be seen as the future for law enforcement. When the war was over such ideas would be relied upon by police forces everywhere.

'Damned fine work, James. Damned fine,' the cherub-faced Junior Minister concludes.

Webster sits back, the warmth of a very good French brandy easing through him, the soothing contentment of having just eaten one of the best meals of his life in the dining room of the Minister's club. 'Very kind, Minister. Very kind,' he coos.

'Ground-breaking stuff. Ground-breaking.' The Minister's penchant for repetition was part of the ritual of his conversation, a verbal tick both in the aftermath of Webster's presentation and over dinner. Much to his own annoyance, Webster found it a mannerism that was catching.

'Hardly, Minister. Hardly,' he finds himself saying. 'Much of it is of course based on the work of Hoover's Department of Justice.'

'Ah, the FBI,' the minister clucks. 'G-Men!'

'Precisely. G-Men. All very glamorous. Al Capone and Tommy guns and such like, stories for the masses and the cinema. But much of what they do, the really vital stuff, is the humdrum sifting of evidence undertaken by police officers everywhere. It's simply that Hoover's men apply proven scientific methods to it. It's what we're implementing in Birmingham. *Forensics*. From the Greek. *Before the forum.*'

'Yes, yes. All very interesting. Your talk and that. Very interesting, I must say.' The Minister smooths a finger across his top lip, checking the narrow black line of his moustache remains slickly in place. Such a pencil line on his full, round face with its rose red cheeks makes it look as if someone has defaced a renaissance painting of a heavenly child. He sits in a winged back leather armchair, a man at ease in the oak-panelled splendour of his surroundings: deep carpets and upholstery, leather Chesterfields, wine-red armchairs. He belonged.

Webster shifts in his chair, hazily aware of the dulling effects of the meal and the excellent wines accompanying it. 'Well, it's still early days, Minister, but I feel we can confidently say that we are going in the right direction.'

A waiter arrives holding a wooden box of cigars on a silver tray. The Minister scans the contents before selecting one, sliding it back and forth under his nose. A wave of the hand, and Webster is encouraged to follow suit. He willingly obliges. 'The same as Winnie,' the Minister informs him. The waiter snips the ends, lighting both cigars before sliding away to service other members. 'Well, I must say, that's all very encouraging to hear, Professor, very encouraging,' the Minister murmurs. 'I don't need to tell a man like yourself that there are those higher up the chain keeping an eye on all this. Right at the top, mind. The very top.' He sits back, cigar in hand, swirling a crystal goblet in the other, allowing the implication of his words to sink in.

Webster nods, puffing at his own cigar, glancing around at the opulence of their surroundings. The private members club is busy, but they'd managed to find two armchairs in a prime location close to the fire in one of three lounge areas. Aside from an occasional nod by the Minister to a member passing through, they were left undisturbed. Despite rationing and the ever-present threat from air-raids, the club appeared to function much as Webster assumed it ever did - though the Minister had explained over the meal that *these days* there were more uniforms in evidence amongst members.

The Minister watches Webster, the appreciation of fine things evident in the professor's eyes. 'You know, Professor, you may not realise just how valued your work is here in Whitehall. It's talked about in high places. Focused as we are on winning this war - and we shall, we shall - we know the war *will* end. That when it does, we must be ready to build the peace. Work like yours - the tracking down of villainy - will prove essential to such ends. Essential.' He points a finger skywards. 'They know that.'

Webster nods once more. Polite, deferential. The cigar smoke billowing, a hazy dragon tail cocooning them.

'Men coming home trained to fight.' The Minister continues, swirling his brandy. 'Good at it, too.' His tone is serious, focused. 'Winnie saw that. After *the Great War.* Years of fighting, years of working for one goal, one objective. Well, that changes, changes very much, changes very quickly. It means there will once again be elements with differing objectives, differing ideas of what Britain should be like. We must be certain that we have at our disposal the means by which to forge a new society, a lawful, law-abiding society. None of this socialism or communist malarkey. Not here. Not in Great Britain.' He puffs at his cigar. 'Our party have always been the party of law and order. We see your work as a great building block in that aim. We don't want any repeat of the problems of violence and civil unrest we had in the years after *the Great War.*'

'I'm afraid that politics isn't my... erhm, field,' Webster smiles.

'It's all politics, Professor. All of it,' the Minister contradicts. 'Law. Order. Wars. Politics. All the same. All part of it. There will be significant reward for the work that men like yourself are doing, the work you will do. Honours. Acclaim. Gratitude.'

'I assure you, Minister, I seek no reward or honour. I simply wish to serve.'

'Ah yes. Serve. Very good, very noble.' The Minister puffs on his cigar, face full of understanding. 'To serve,' he repeats before allowing a lengthy silence to fall between them. He swirls his glass. Webster, reverential, sits quietly observing the unspoken rules of politeness and civility. Savouring the brandy, the cigar, the moment.

Eventually the Minister speaks. 'What about this case of yours that I read about? This body in the tree. How's that been going?'

Webster stirring, sits forward, glad to speak of something other than politics. 'To be honest, not as well as we'd hoped. That is, not as well as the Detective on the case and I'd hoped. It's all got a little...side-tracked. The official view is that it's all linked to gypsies. The official report some weeks ago, if not fully supporting that position, at least doesn't officially contradict it.'

'Gypsies, eh? A rum do.'

'Quite. The Detective Constable investigating it - the one who called on me to apply my ideas - has a dissenting view. He feels there may be alternative explanations for her death, not to say the unusual manner of her internment. Explanations that ought to be properly followed up.'

'What was his name again?'

'Porter. Detective Alec Porter.'

'Ah yes, Porter. Good man?'

Webster nods. 'I'd say so.'

'And that would be because...?' The Minister arches his brow quizzically.

'Bright. Capable. Decent. Hungry for truth. For justice,' Webster offers.

'Ah, hunger, eh?' the Minister grunts. 'Justice. Fine intentions. Just fine.'

'As it should be,' Webster concurs.

'Indeed. As it should be. But no progress in discovering her identity or the killer, you say?' the Minister pushes.

'Well, Porter has his theories. But no evidence'

'What sort of theories?' the Minister asks.

Webster chuckles. 'Spies.'

'Spies?'

'Spies, real John Buchan *39 Steps* stuff. That or witches.'

'Witches, you say. My, my.' The Minister shakes his head. 'That's a pretty leap, a pretty leap indeed. Tell me, why is it he suspects espionage?'

Webster undulates his shoulders, mind sinking into the moment. 'I think it rather began as a wild idea - labels removed from the victim's clothing. There's no papers. No identity card. No ration book, or the like.'

'Rather tendentious, I'm sure you'd agree?' the Minister suggests.

Webster puffs on the cigar. His words follow the smoke, drifting up and out of his mouth. 'Yes, quite so. But he's also had reports of parachutists being seen in the area in the period shortly before we believe she was more than likely killed and put in the tree. There are local rumours of a spy ring too.'

'Aren't there everywhere?' the Minister chuckles in return.

'Quite. He also received a rather enigmatic letter from a woman about someone she knew, someone she claims was up to no good. A man, so she said, who'd confessed both to his own espionage and to involvement in the killing of a woman he'd interred in a tree.'

'And have you found anything of substance to support such claims?'

Webster blows smoke from his cigar, shakes his head. 'Nothing. Apart from the missing labels and documents, that is.'

'Which any murderer might have done to delay identification of the body and so aid his escape,' the Minister states with some certainty. 'They're not all so stupid these days. Get their ideas from Agatha Christie and the films. That's why we value your work. Keep us ahead of the buggers.'

'Indeed,' Webster concedes.

'But isn't the matter officially closed? You say he's submitted his report. I assume he's given up on such folly?'

'The case remains unsolved, so technically open, but you're correct that without any new evidence coming to light the official investigation has been closed. But Porter? Give up? Oh no, Minister. He's as determined as ever.' He cocks his head in deliberation. 'I must admit that I'm somewhat concerned. Porter's a troubled soul. I feel the matter has become something of an obsession for him. We all want to find the truth, but Porter,' he shakes his head, 'It's like he's on a crusade. Something much deeper.'

The Minister allowing a pause, examines the embers of his cigar whilst rolling it in his fingers. 'He fought in Spain, I hear.'

Webster is surprised at the Minister's somewhat deeper knowledge of a junior police officer whom only a few moments ago whose name he'd been unable to recall. 'Yes, he did. Wounded. That's why he's unfit for duty.'

'Socialist, then?' The Minister observes.

'I'm not sure.'

'Communist?'

171

'No, not a communist, at least...'

'But you don't know,' the Minister states.

'No. Not for certain, that is.'

'But he seems to know a great deal about the business of espionage. The missing labels and so on,' the Minister presses.

'I think that... I think it was one of the other police officers who first suggested that possibility.'

'But Porter is the one running with it. A *crusade*, didn't you say?'

Webster back-tracks, aware he's been somewhat indiscreet about, a man who, if not a friend, was someone he'd warmed to over the weeks he'd known him. 'I've heard of many policemen becoming obsessed with providing justice for murder victims. It's almost natural. That sense of injustice, of wanting to speak up for them. Makes them good policemen.'

'We all want justice,' the Minister states flatly. 'We all want to make the world a better place. Maybe this Porter has specific ideas about what that entails. Maybe his time in Spain filled his head with ideas about re-shaping the world.' He smiles. It is thin, humourless, twitching even straighter the ends of his pencil line moustache. 'I have to state, Professor, that in my own view – and I would imagine that of most of my colleagues at the Home Office - that a man who gave up a university education, putting his life at risk to follow a political ideology, is not a man to be entirely trusted. A zealot.'

'I'd hardly call Porter a zealot,' Webster says. 'A man of strong morals, yes.'

'Nonetheless, you said so yourself that his *obsession* with this case is unhealthy, if not grounds for suspicion as to his motives.'

'Unhealthy? Possibly. For him. But suspicion? Suspicion of what, precisely?'

The Minister sits forward; brandy glass held in both hands like a challis. 'Professor, you must realise by now that this case is part of the reason I wanted to have a talk with you. Your Detective Porter stirred things up with the War Office and the intelligence boys at SIS with accusations about the Yanks at Wolverley. I'm reliably informed the man has now requested information about the location of serving British officers. One name in particular has got the Joint Intelligence chaps jumping.' He taps a short length of ash from the end of his cigar into the pedestal ashtray before looking directly at Webster. 'I don't know all the ins and outs of it, but these intelligence boys are concerned as to why he should be so interested in such matters. I don't have to tell you, Professor, that these are dangerous times. Sensitive times. I don't know what this Porter's interest is in this man, or why it's got everyone over there so stirred up, but he needs to back off.' He examines his cigar, the glowing embers. 'I shouldn't need to remind you that a man like yourself, a man whose work is dependent on Government patronage, has to be careful what he allows himself to get involved in. Whom he gets involved with. I say again, don't know what it's all about – truth be told, I don't want to. Those intelligence boys… Rum lot. But it would be better for all concerned if you were to direct this Porter's attention back to what ought to be his real work – stolen bicycles, black marketeers, and such like. If not… well, it could prove rather damaging for all those caught up in it.' He fixes Webster with a direct stare. 'In my experience, such things have a habit of getting out of hand. I'd hate to see all you've worked so hard for tainted. Your reputation swept away by the tide of affairs overwhelming your Detective Porter.'

Webster opens his mouth to speak. Hesitates. After a pause he shakes his head. 'I'm not certain what it is you want me to say, Minister.'

'I don't want you to say anything, Professor.' The Minister waves his cigar in a gesture taking in the room. 'We are simply two colleagues discussing our work, our shared interests. We're both of us intelligent men. Men who need to think of the future, particularly a future working relationship as colleagues well placed to be able to do each other's careers some good. As such, if asked, I would offer but a simple word of advice on this matter of Porter and his fanciful theories. Steer him clear of all this, Professor. For everyone's good. Steer him clear.'

MAY 12TH, 1943: EARLY MORNING

Porter stares at the rain. The sky is dark, what little wind there is suggesting the storm clouds passing overhead might be there for some time. He tosses his pencil to the side, hunkering down, nestling himself closer into the battlements of the monument. He doubts there will be a raid now. The rain and the low dark clouds offered the bombers cover from anti-aircraft fire, but this was outweighed by the lack of precision in navigation and targeting. The inaction offered not so much a respite but time to dwell on his current dark mood, a mood that had begun with an earlier telephone conversation with Webster. Nothing in the twelve hours since had appeased the sense of frustration and anger building inside him. The first indications something was wrong had been Webster's less than effusive salutation, compounded by his reluctance to discuss the case. Porter had pushed; Webster had become exasperated.

'Alec, have you stopped to think that this whole thing might be getting out of hand?'

'Out of hand? It's a murder enquiry, Professor. Can things get out of hand?'

'You know what I mean. All this cloak and dagger stuff. Don't you think it's a little… melodramatic?'

'You read the Claverley letter.'

'Yes. Yes, I did.'

'And?'

'There's nothing to suggest it has any validity. It might just be the ravings of some lonely soul who's seen the newspaper reports.'

'Professor, you read it. She knows things that weren't in the newspapers, more than that, it was *how* she said it. This is a

174

woman with real anxieties over this man. Whatever else she might be, she's no crank.'

'And this gut-feeling leads you into asking questions about the whereabouts and deployment of British officers in war-time?'

'What are you saying?'

Webster's tone had stiffened, his voice tight. 'I'm saying we're straying into dubious areas. And it's all based on nothing more than a gut feeling - this damned intuition of yours that you keep using as a means of justifying actions that are in any rational terms debatable. Where's the evidence for such irrational certainty? I've not seen it. None of us have.'

'It's a murder enquiry - everything by its nature is uncertain. We're dealing with people who have an interest in lying - gypsies, petty crooks, black marketeers, spivs, pimps, prostitutes. Maybe spies and infiltrators. Possible Nazi sympathisers. Not to mention the murderer themselves.'

'Alec, there are limits-'

'Are there?'

'Of course there are!'

'Such as?'

'Such as pushing into military operations. National security.'

'The issue with Claverley is the man, not his role in the army. If the man's a murderer, his rank or anything else is immaterial.'

'That is so naïve! There's a war on. What if the army don't see it that way?'

'I've no idea how the army sees it. There's been nothing.'

'They're concerned.'

'Concerned? What... How do you know?'

There was a pause. Webster exhaling. 'Alec, let it go.'

'London. Your trip to London. That's it, isn't it? Who did you see there?' he'd demanded.

Webster had paused, considering his approach. 'Look, it wasn't anything like you think. I was given... advice about the case, how some in Whitehall are seeing it. You can't go prodding these people and not expect them to react.'

'And they've said what?'

'That you need to be careful. Seems there's SIS interest in this Claverley. Significant interest.'

'I need to be careful? Professor, why would I need to be careful? I'm a Detective Constable in the Worcestershire CID pursuing a murder investigation.'

'An unofficial investigation.'

'The case is unsolved, not closed. If legitimate leads appear they need to be pursued.'

'And who decides that? You?'

'Why not?'

'There's some questions being asked about your motives,' Webster had conceded.

'My motives?'

'Your time in Spain is a cause for… anxiety, amongst some.'

'What? They think I'm a communist?'

'That political sympathies might be driving your line of investigation.'

'Jesus! What about you? What have they said to you?'

Webster had paused. 'Nothing directly. A reminder of the need for willingness to co-operate, to work for the greater good.'

'But surely this is what your work is all about? Finding answers when there appear to be none. Logic applied to crime. The use of science. The rational application of forensic evidence.'

'Look, Alec, let me assure you that I was clear in putting forward your motives in pursuing this investigation. But doubts remain and will do so for as long as you keep pushing this military angle. This focus on spies and espionage.' He'd heard Webster breath heavily down the line. 'You have to understand that it makes those in Whitehall jumpy.'

'Only if they've something to hide.'

'For goodness' sake, Alec, they're Military Intelligence! Of course they've got something to hide! That's what they do!'

'But what's threatening to SIS about the murder of a young woman in Hagley eighteen months ago?'

'Alec, these people keep secrets for a living. They don't like giving out information, let alone answering questions about the location of military staff like this Claverley. For all we know, we might compromise an operation, provide succour to the enemy - *walls have ears. Carless talk costs lives* - that sort of thing. You've seen the posters. The propaganda. Whatever their reasons, this Claverley is not going to be given up for questioning about a murder. For all we know, he might be in the middle of an operation abroad. He could be a spy himself. He might, at this very moment, be in training for espionage abroad. We're not going to get to him.'

'So, you're saying it's a dead end.'

'I'm saying it seems that way.' Webster had then paused, relenting. 'Look, it's all based on supposition, anyway. You have no definitive proof of what you're saying. It's a hypothesis. After all, Alec, there are other equally valid options we can still follow up on. The gypsies, the angry lover. Even your Margaret Murray's witches' coven idea is still in play.' Silence had echoed back down the telephone line. 'Alec, you have to face up to this,' he'd told him. 'Without the help of the military there's little that can be done about this Claverley. Maybe after the war. You gave it your best, old man. Time to let go.'

15

The rain beat down, a pulsating, incessant rhythm drumming on the stretched fabric of the umbrella, a pitter-patter pummelling its way inside Porter's head. The hand of Father O'Connor clenches the handle of the umbrella, bone-white knuckles locked tight as he and Porter inch forward, side by side, along the graveyard path. As the taller of the two, Porter is forced to hunch under the canopy's meagre shelter. For much of their slow progress from the church he's walked shoulders bent, eyes looking downwards to the gravel.

The vicar suddenly steps forward, pointing out a feature of possible significance, in the process inadvertently tilting the umbrella to an angle that slops the gathered rain onto Porter's shoulders. It oozes through the already sodden material of his coat; a cold hand lain on his flesh.

'There we are, that's her,' the vicar calls above the patter of rain on canvas.

Porter raises his face from its downward angle, the rain splattering against his now exposed forehead. He looks in the direction of the vicar's extended arm, the man's emaciated finger indicating a granite headstone a few feet away. The words on the headstone are etched in gothic font: *Anna Claverley.*

'I knew it!' the vicar calls out, moving closer, reading the inscription aloud as if the act itself makes it more so, more real. *'Anna Claverley. Born May 1893 died December 1933. Wonderful wife and blessed mother.'* He turns to Porter, 'Is this who you were looking for, Inspector?'

Porter continues staring at the headstone. 'Yes. Yes, it is.' He pulls his eyes from the headstone to face the now animated O'Connor. 'And it's Detective Constable.'

'Detective,' the vicar nods. He is thin, pale, skin like bible parchment. With his receding hair and high forehead Porter imagines him in stained glass, crook in hand, halo hovering over pointed features. *A Man of The Book* rather than a man of the people.

'Do you know anything about her?' Porter asks.

The vicar turns from the headstone to Porter and back again. 'I came to the parish three years ago. As you can imagine it's been a busy time. The bombings, the deaths of our boys at the front. I've spent what little time I have comforting the living rather than concerning myself with those already dead.'

'What about the vicar before you? Would he have conducted the burial? Would he have known the family.'

'Ah, yes, Father Brian. Father Brian was here for over twenty-seven years, and you're right, he would have known all of his flock - even those that had slipped from attendance at church. I'm afraid Father Brian passed away shortly after his move to London. The Blitz, God rest his soul.' The Father shakes his head, signing the cross.

'Did she have a son?'

'A son?'

'He'd be in his late twenties or early thirties I think,' Porter suggests.

The Father shakes his head, finger and thumb rubbing his chin in thought. 'I don't know of anyone called Claverley living locally. Not in my time. It was only the Sergeant from the local police station, mentioning it at the last parish meeting, that triggered my recollection of the headstone. I tend to walk here whilst seeking inspiration for my sermons.'

Porter nods aimlessly whilst staring at the headstone, the rain-soaked granite. Mock gothic font, grassed over grave, the urn of daffodils. Nothing. *He'd come all this way to look at a grave. What had he expected? To find Anna Claverley miraculously risen. Her son standing by the grave, seeking the salvation of a dead mother for his murderous actions?* And how could the dead Anna have sent him a letter, let alone one concerning events that happened years after her own death? He was back to Murray. Back to gypsy curses. Magic.

The call from the vicar had come out of the blue. Well, not strictly so. It had come as the result of Porter's insistent campaign of letters to local police stations across the region. He wasn't certain at what point the idea had come to him, but a few days after his argument with Webster he'd had the realisation that although the military were shutting down access to finding Claverley they would find it harder to block Porter's attempts to locate the writer of the letter - possibly Claverley's wife or girlfriend, maybe a mother or sister.

For the past two weeks he'd scanned phone books, contacting local Postmasters for addresses of anyone with the surname Claverley. Then, one by one he'd worked through the list searching for Anna Claverley. Of course there was always the fact that the writer of the letter, the mysterious Anna, may not actually be a Claverley. She might be a girlfriend. A neighbour or close friend. But the fact the letter had been written at all coupled with the compassion and concern so clearly evident in its intent, told him she had to be a Claverley. A woman in some way related to the man he sought.

There had been three promising leads. The first two had led nowhere. Same name, no connection. Now he stood at number three. Literally a dead-end. A letter from a dead woman. He thought of Webster and Willetts. Their reactions. Another blank. Maybe they were right. Maybe it was a cruel hoax, some poor emotionally unstable wretch's fantasy reaching out and pulling him in, pulling him away from whatever the real line of their investigation should be – though God knows what that was. *A jealous or wronged lover? A prostitute and her violent client? A maniac pouncing on some poor innocent caught by a raid in the woods?*

Maybe Webster was right. They'd taken a wrong turn at the start of the investigation. Porter, unwilling to acknowledge it, had plunged on regardless, losing their way.

He reaches a hand round his back. His wound ached. Muscles throbbed. He undulates his spine trying to evade the wave of nausea he knew to be coming. Too much cold air, too much rain, too many wasted trips. Too little medication.

'Are you alright, Detective?' the vicar asks.

'Fine. A twinge. A wound.'

'Oh, I'm sorry. I didn't realise. I didn't like to ask.'

'You mean why I'm not at the frontline?'

The vicar looks to the floor. 'Well, yes. Yes, I suppose that was it.'

'Don't worry. Most people think that too.'

'That's very… Christian of you.'

'Christianity has very little to with it, Father.'

Porter turns from the grave.

The small churchyard is shrouded by the branches of untended trees, boughs reaching across the gravestones. They hang low, arms waiting to scoop up those interred there. The grass between the graves is high. Like most things, even here amongst the dead, the war created its own sense of priorities; the pressing, the urgent, the *does it really matter*. Parklands, flowerbeds, cemeteries - all the things that had seemed so important, so much a part of what was necessary for civilised living before the war, now left untended. Would the dead really be offended if the needs of the living took precedent over the niceties of the deceased? Most of the headstones were dirty, moss and rain working their intentions, plots overwhelmed by weeds and grass. Upturned urns, dead flowers.

He stops, turning back to look at Anna Claverley's resting place. Fresh flowers. 'Someone cares for Anna,' he says out loud.

'What?' The vicar takes a moment in understanding what Porter is talking about. He turns, following the detective's line of sight. The urn full of fresh flowers. The well-kept grave. 'Oh, I see what you mean. That'll probably be one of our ladies. We have some elderly ladies in the village who undertake such work in return for a small retainer. Some donate it to the church, which we're very grateful for. Others do it to help make ends meet. The war.'

'But someone pays for the work.'

'Oh, yes. Often it's the family themselves who do the work on their own departed, but as I say, we have a few well-wishers in the village with charitable intentions who help keep the cemetery at its best. They take on the plots of those who can't get here or have moved away.'

'Would you happen to know who looks after Anna Claverley's grave?'

'That would most likely be Mrs. Mossop.'

'Mossop?'

'Yes. Mossop.' By way of explanation the vicar points in the direction of the church. 'When I looked up the records of where the grave would be there were details of who registered the plot. A woman. Mossop. I assume it's she who sees to the maintenance of the grave.'

'Do you know what her relationship is to Anna Claverley or the Claverley family?'

'Well, as its *Mrs* Mossop, I assume that's a married name. As I said, I don't know all of the parishioners or their stories. I believe she used to live in the village, but I think she now lives some distance away. Leamington seems to ring a bell,' he says tapping at his temple. 'At least she did when the plot was registered.'

'So, she comes here every week to do this work?'

'Oh, dear me no. As I said, much of this is done by our local ladies.' He looks at the grave, tilting his head in consideration of the well-maintained headstone, the urn of clean water, the neatly clipped flowers. 'This is Martha Bainbridge's work. She takes a great pride in her work, does Martha. This is one of Martha's graves, alright.'

'Where can I find this Martha Bainbridge?'

The vicar looks up at the church clock. 'Well, if I'm not mistaken, right now she'll be in the church cleaning the brass work as she does every week at around this time.'

MAY 25TH, 1943: LATE AFTERNOON

Martha Bainbridge was indeed charged with maintaining the grave of Anna Claverley. She'd told Porter of the arrangement. How Mrs Mossop appeared every few months at her door, paying the money owed before disappearing. Kenilworth, she believed.

Kenilworth. 38 Morvina Drive. To be precise. This house.

He stands in the rain in front of a three-storey red-brick house in the centre of a terrace of five such houses. Three storey. Attic windows, Victorian. Sturdy properties reflecting the nature of the town. Solid. Civic pride. The heart of a nation.

Rain pours down, worn black cast-iron drainpipes gushing under the effort of coping with the deluge. A split guttering joint meant water fell across the doorway of the house. Avoiding the stream, Porter knocks. Brass lion head knocker, black painted door. The door half-opens, a small child stands in the gap. 'Yes?' she asks.

'Is your mother in? Mrs. Mossop?'

'Who are you?' the young girl responds.

He bends forward and lowers his face towards her. 'I'm a police officer. Can you tell your mommy I need to speak with her?'

'Who is it, Elizabeth?' a woman's voice calls from the passage beyond the girl.

The little girl half-turns her head. 'It's a policeman!' she shouts as the gap between door and wall widens.

A woman appears at the rear of the passageway; white apron, hair tied back, wiping floured hands on a tea towel. She approaches the door.

'Mrs Mossop?'

'Yes.'

'I'm Detective Constable Porter. I'm here about-'

'Yes,' she says. 'I know what you're here about.' She finishes wiping her hands and folds the tea towel. She stands aside, opening the door wide, an arm draped down, wrapping around the little girl. 'You'd better come in.'

Porter, collapsing his umbrella, shakes off the raindrops and enters. The hall is Minton tiled. An umbrella stand, part of a dark-oak coat rack, stands alongside a matching console table and its surmounted oval mirror.

'Would you like some tea, Detective?' she asks, closing the door behind them.

'And scones. We've made scones,' the little girl interjects excitedly, looking from her mother to Porter and back again.

'Tea would be lovely.'

He places his umbrella in the stand. Takes off his mackintosh. Mrs Mossop hangs it carefully on the coatrack before indicating a door to the right. 'The front parlour. I'll be just a moment. The kettle's only this minute boiled.'

The room is bright, airy, high ceilinged. A large sash bay window looks out across the road towards the crumbling wall of Kenilworth castle. Beyond the wall a decaying keep-tower flies the Union flag. Sandbags, black with the rain, fill gaps in the battlements.

He is still standing, gazing out, when the parlour door opens and Mrs Mossop reappears carrying a tea-tray which she places on a lamp table at the side of the sofa. Porter sits in an armchair opposite, back to the window. 'You have a lovely home,' he says.

She nods. 'We try our best.'

'And a lovely little girl. Elizabeth, is it?'

'Yes. Milk?'

'Yes, thank you.'

She passes a China cup and saucer, at the same time turning the milk jug so its handle faces him. He pours the milk, before lifting two lumps of sugar with the silver tongs and swirling his tea with a matching spoon.

He sips the brew. 'Lovely. And such fine China.' The pattern was apples. Evesham fruit, bone-white China with a gold rim.

'A wedding gift.'

'It's beautiful. Worcester?'

She smiles. 'It was my mother's.'

'Anna. Anna Claverley.'

She smiles again. 'Yes. Anna's.'

He places the cup onto the saucer. 'I'm right in assuming that the letter was from you. That you were…you are *Anna Claverley*.'

'My maiden name. Anne. Una Anne Claverley. After my mother.'

'Why use Anna? Why use the name of your dead mother? You must have known we'd find you?'

'It's the name he took.'

'He?'

'Jack. My husband, Jack Mossop. The man you're looking for. He's assumed my family name. He needed a new one. Part of his cover.'

'Cover?'

Una Mossop sits back on the sofa. She gazes towards the window. She looks out beyond where Porter sits, out beyond the crumbling castle walls. After a moment she sighs, pulling herself back into the room. 'My husband is a dreamer, Inspector.'

Porter takes out his notebook. 'It's Detective. Detective Constable.'

She shrugs and continues. 'When I first met James Mossop, he was…different. Different from all the men I knew. Different from any of the men I'd ever known. He swept me off my feet.' She turns to Porter, a trace of a smile. 'Have you ever been in love, Detective Porter?'

'Of course.'

She regards him quizzically before deciding to accept what he says. 'Then you're a lucky man. A blessed man. You'll know what I mean when I say I fell head over heels.' She sighs, smiling at the recollection, the re-connection to that part of her. 'Jack Mossop was a whirlwind - bright as the sun with a head full of dreams. Jack was going to change the world. Change our world. And I believed him. Everyone did. Jack has this way of making everyone believe whatever he says.' She looks back out of the window across to the castle walls. 'We married a few weeks after we'd met. Lots of people did then. We were on the verge of war; no-one really knew what was happening, what would happen.' She blushes, a still hint of shame. 'We had our daughter just before we moved to be close to his work. By the time I'd caught my breath, before I'd even really got to know him, the war cut into our life. He went away, despite the fact he was reserved occupation. Something to do with aircraft production so he said. It meant he had to travel to different sites all over the country. All very secret. That was autumn of '40.'

She gazes into the distance, finding the spirit of that time. Wanting to be clear. Separate real from fantasy. 'We wrote to each other, but it was difficult. He was always guarded about his whereabouts. I knew it was Birmingham, I guessed Longbridge and the big factories over there. He came back in the summer of 1941 with money, lots of it. More than I thought you could earn working in an aircraft factory. He wore expensive clothes too. And he took me dancing every night.' She smiles before her expression becomes serious, troubled. 'He'd been back a week, when then this man came. I heard them talking. Loud, like an argument. The man left, but I could see whatever they'd argued about had upset Jack. He went all quiet. Worried. The next day he left. He got up saying he'd been recalled, but I knew it was the visitor he'd had.'

She pauses, sipping her tea, refreshing Porter's own from the teapot. 'Anyway, a few months later he came back. This time he was in uniform - really crisp, like the Yanks wore. He said he'd been made an officer. Said he couldn't talk about what he was doing. Said it was top secret. I just accepted it. Like I say, Jack has this way about him. You just believe whatever he told you. But he was drinking a lot. Not like him.' She pauses in recollection of the man she'd known; a man she'd lost. 'After a few days, he went away again, and for months after I heard nothing more from him. Then, in December that year, he turns up again. Unexpected. It was just before Christmas. No word from him for months and then Christmas Eve 1941, he's just there on my doorstep. I was angry, I wanted to have it out with him, but I could tell he was worried. Scared. More than that. He was terrified. Haunted. He said he needed somewhere to stay, somewhere he could think and clear his head. I was sure he'd found someone else, that he was playing me for the fool. I said I couldn't take much more, the lies, the not knowing. That we had to sort things out one way or the other. That night, we slept in separate rooms. I said he wasn't having his cake and eating it.' She shakes her head. Eyes burning. 'I heard him screaming. I went to him, to his room. He sat there, bolt upright in bed, trembling. He said he'd had the most terrifying dream. Said he was haunted by it every night. Said he kept seeing the body of a woman in a tree. He was drenched in sweat. Soaked. I held him. Comforted him. That's when he told me. It just came tumbling out. He said he'd been with a Dutchman. Someone he'd got to know in his work. That a woman had been killed. A Dutchwoman. He said they'd hidden her body in the woods. He kept seeing her in his dreams, calling to him.'

She shakes herself loose of the moment. 'I didn't know what to believe - but I know that he was terrified. And he swore he'd

187

no part in killing her, that he'd just helped hide her body. He said he'd had to do it, that it was top secret, his duty... part of what he'd been doing, what he'd been told to do. Things he couldn't tell me about. Couldn't tell anyone, especially not the police. He told me that one day I'd understand. That one day it would all come out.'

She sighs, exhales long and slow. A tremor. 'So, despite everything, I stayed with him. I held him all the rest of the night whilst he slept. Next morning, when we woke up, he was distant. Cold. We were sat at the table eating breakfast and he just came out and said he'd give me a divorce. Told me he was sorry for all he'd done. Said it was safer not to have any contact at all. That if I was asked, I'd to say he'd not been here. I was to tell anyone who asked that I'd not seen him for months, not since he'd been home that Autumn. After breakfast, he packed his bag and left.'

She closes her eyes. Takes a moment. 'And I've not seen him since, Detective. Not a letter. Not a word. Funny thing, before he left he said I shouldn't think anything of what he'd said. Told me he'd been tired, mixed up. That he'd spoken crazy stuff. It was just a bad nightmare. It happened because he was stressed. It was the war, the pressure on him because of his work. That if I said anything about him having been here or what he'd said it could go badly for him. For us.'

Porter stops writing. sips his tea. There was much to take in. In its way Una Mossop's tale was as bizarre as Murray's witches. A Hitchcock plot of a story. 'You said he assumed your mother's name?' he asks.

'When he was home that last time. I was hanging his clothes. His wallet was in a pocket.' She looks down. 'I took it out. I was worried, concerned about him. Wondered how he had all that money. His ID card was in it. All of the details were right, his details - the date of birth and everything. But not the name. The name was Claverley. Jack Claverley.'

'Did you ask him why?'

'There was no time. I didn't know what was going on. Didn't want him to think badly of me for going through his stuff.'

Porter looks at his notes. 'Did Jack say anything about what it was that he was involved in? Anything else about this Dutchman or the woman?'

'Nothing. When he'd first come home, it was all about the money. Like I said, Jack's ambitious. Later he was all about the secrecy, the importance of what he was doing. He made it all seem very glamorous. Heroic even. He always did. The last time, he was too scared to tell me anything other than the story of the woman in the tree.'

'You say he's involved in the aircraft industry?'

'That's right. Something to do with production. He's not a pilot or anything. Nothing technical.'

'But vital to the war effort?'

'To hear Jack tell it, he *was* the war effort. Essential. He said it was the reason he'd been moved. Why he'd been assigned his new post. It was military. Top secret, all very *hush-hush*. Saving lives. Thousands of lives, he said. That's why he'd come back in uniform. But, like I say, Jack was always full of stories. Mysteries.'

'And that's the last you saw of him?'

'Yes.'

'And you say you've heard nothing since?'

'Nothing. You can imagine when I read the story of the body in that tree...Well, I didn't know what to think. what to do. Not after what he'd told me about secrecy. But I had to find out what happened. If what he'd told me was true.'

'Have you tried contacting him since then?'

She looks to the floor, hands twisting together. 'There seemed no point. Not after what he'd said. After he'd left, papers came through about the divorce. Solicitors. He'd admitted adultery, though I don't believe that of him. Not Jack.'

'Did you write back?'

'I didn't know how to. I mean, was he calling himself Mossop or Claverley? For all I knew he could be calling himself something entirely different. I wrote to the military asking if they could give me the details of the posting of Jack Mossop. Said he was my husband. They were no help. Said they'd nothing about him even enlisting. But he'd told me he had. So, I tried Claverley, but they just ignored me. I mean, God knows what they thought I was trying to do, asking for details of two different men, saying they were both my husband.'

'Have you any idea where he might be now?'

She shakes her head. 'No. None at all. He said it was better I didn't know. Told me not to worry about him. That if there was real danger, he said he'd got something that would ensure his safety and ours. A secret he could use.'

'A secret? Did he give you any idea what it was?'

'Nothing. All he told me was that it was a secret people had died for. Not just one or two. Hundreds he said. Maybe thousands. But that's Jack. He exaggerates. A dreamer.'

Porter puts the notebook in his pocket, rises to leave. 'Thank you. You've been most helpful. It can't have been easy.'

She rises, reaching out a hand which she places on his arm. 'Detective. Whatever it is Jack's mixed up in, whatever else he's done, he's not a killer. It's just not in him.'

'You yourself said you barely knew him. That he'd changed.'

Letting go, she walks him to the door, passing him his raincoat from the coat rack. 'I know what I said. And it's true, something about him had changed. But a thing like that, like killing someone, that doesn't change does it? No matter what. He's not your killer, Detective. Your killer's still out there.'

He turns to face her, catching the concern in her face. 'It's Jack I'm worried for,' she continues. 'Worried that whoever killed that woman might want Jack dead too. Now you've found this body, maybe they'll be looking for Jack to silence him. I'm worried. Worried sick for him. That's why I wrote to you. Not to betray him. I want you to find him, keep him safe.'

She opens the door, and they stand on the step. The rain still gushed from the split guttering. The flag on the castle Keep still sags in the beat of the torrential rain.

Porter extends his umbrella, checking the sky. 'Thank you again. Thank you for the tea.' He hesitates. 'I understand what you're saying about Jack. But this war. Men have had to learn how to kill. Good men. Decent men. All I can promise you is that I won't give up. I'll find him. I promise.'

She looks into his eyes, tears forming in her own. 'Whoever the killer is, he knows you're looking for him. If he knows you're looking for Jack too, he'll know that Jack could lead you to him. That Jack can tell you who they are. Tell you what they did and why. I'm scared for Jack because of what he said they'd do to stop anyone finding them. No matter what he said about bad dreams, he told me they'd killed a woman. I believed him then and I still do. And I'm certain that men who could do a thing like that won't hesitate to kill again.'

16

Solomon threads his way through the throng of uniforms gathered on the platform. It's slow going. Clusters of passengers assembling, breaking apart. Each wave checking him, blocking passage; the dark blue of the navy, the mud brown of the infantry, the blue-grey of the RAF. At their feet, littering the ground like fallen leaves, are rucksacks; white, grey, brown. Here and there, a scattering of women; urgent voices and sausage-roll curls.

He walks scanning the carriages. He is tall and muscular, but in this crowd, dressed in a pale gabardine army mackintosh, he fails to stand out from any of those around him. It takes a few moments to find his carriage and his reserved compartment.

Inside, he tosses his slim leather briefcase onto the seat next to him and slips off his coat. He lowers the blind facing the platform, shutting out the parade of sad farewells that line its length.

Sitting, he takes out a cigarette and lights it, at the same time propping the tan briefcase onto its side. With a series of quick motions, he thumbs in the lock code and slides out the topmost folder. Slipping off the band holding the contents in place, he opens the file and examines the top sheet.

Alec Porter

He looks at the photograph clipped to it. High cheekbones, dark hair, deep-seated eyes. He skims the outline of the his life - scholarship place at Cambridge, volunteering for Spain, the International Brigade, the wounding in an air attack, the hospitalisation, the police-force. He checks personal details - Rachel, Tommy, the domestic arrangement that involves Rachel's dead husband's father.

Reading, he feels justified at the chosen course of action. This Porter is an idealist. Maybe worse, a dreamer. A man of convictions clearly able to articulate them. His volunteering for Spain indicates he is also a man with the capacity to fight for them, to make sacrifices for them. Such a man would not easily let go. The Minister's warning, delivered via Webster, had been a poorly judged intervention. It might even be responsible for stoking the very fire it intended to put out.

Threats were not the answer. A man like Porter had to be convinced, better yet, must convince himself of the futility of his manhunt. It was the only outcome sealing the dead woman's story and its terrible secret.

Porter had proved ingenious in discovering the Mossop woman. Of course SIS knew of her existence, her link to Claverley that might at some point prove a difficulty. But not knowing what Claverley might have told her had always made dealing with her problematic. Besides, she was a woman and she had a child. No one wanted that on their conscience. But what Claverley knew might yet make such niceties irrelevant. Thousands had died to preserve this particular secret. What matter a few more? Two bodies, a mother and her child found in the aftermath of yet another air-raid.

This way was better. This way those whom Porter had drawn into his private investigation would be left with no grounds to dig deeper. There would be no lasting suspicion, no lingering doubt. Convince Porter and the rest would follow. Webster, Willetts, Porter's superiors, Una Mossop - all of them would fall into line.

To make that happen, DC Alec Porter must be given something. Something to follow. It was like feeding a bone to a ravenous dog. It mattered little there was no real meat to the bone, the hound would simply satisfy itself with gnawing away. He would be occupied. Out of the game. It was a solution they'd all agreed to.

There was a shrill whistle followed by an initial tug as the locomotive took up the slack of the carriages and pulled slowly out of the station on its long journey to Birmingham.

Porter needed a truth he could believe. Fed the right truths, he would find for himself the path they wanted him on. Gnaw on the bone he was about to give him. Reach the conclusions that made them all safe.

MAY 27TH, 1943: LATE MORNING

Sat at his desk, hands clenched, DS Harry James stares at the far wall of his office, mind in turmoil, struggling to come to terms with what he'd just learned. He rose, storming down the corridor and into the temporary CID office of Alec Porter.

Porter looks up at the intrusion. 'You want to see me, sir?'

'Just what the sodding hell's going on?'

'I'm not certain what you mean,' Porter responds, abashed by his DSs' manner.

'You can drop the fancy stuff. What have you been nosing into?'

'I seriously haven't a clue what you're talking about, sir.'

'Seriously? Seriously? I'll give you seriously. I've just got off the phone with Birmingham. They've had London on to them. The Ministry of Defence. Seems they're anxious to meet with you. So anxious that they're sending someone up. Seems you've been asking questions about matters of great concern to those in Whitehall. They're very interested to speak to you.'

Porter's face assumes an expression of deep thought rather than the contrition expected. James blusters forward. 'Given that as far as I'm aware the only thing on your agenda has been missing bicycles, black market spivs in Bromsgrove, and sightings of parachutes, I'm going to take a wild guess that it's nowt to do with the bikes. So that leaves the spivs and the parachutes. And I can't see Whitehall being interested in some bugger selling silk knickers down the Bull Ring market. So, it's your body in the tree again. Or am I wrong?'

Porter sits silent.

'What exactly have you been prying into?'

Porter thought of what to say. He's aware of the rumours concerning James' connection with spivs like Morrison. He's little desire for anything concerning Claverley or the link to Una Mossop becoming wider knowledge. The woman was terrified as it was without James turning up at her door. So, he shrugs, wrinkling his face. 'It is, after all, sir, an ongoing case. There have been recent developments, hangovers from previous enquiries. I spoke with a woman locally who saw parachutists come down in Hagley Wood. She says she saw others a while ago around the time we believe the body was put in the tree. She reported it, but it seems it wasn't taken seriously. Maybe my enquiry to the ARP monitoring desk about her sighting has prompted something.'

'And Whitehall are sending someone up here to talk to you about it?'

'Apparently so.'

James scratches his chin. 'So why have they asked for the meeting to be at Professor Webster's office?'

'Well...Webster's one of their own. Funded from Whitehall. Maybe they feel he's got useful input. Forensics.'

'So why not ask for me? Technically I'm the senior officer in charge of the case.'

'I put that report in weeks ago, sir. You yourself signed it off.

You were very clear in your instructions on that point. You told us to stop our investigation. You told us to close the case. Maybe the MoD has found something. If it links to the sighting of the parachutes, then I was the officer who put in the ARP request. They'd have my name on that form and on the final report.'

'Where was this sighting?'

'The Lickeys.'

'When?'

'Summer of 1941.'

'That long ago?'

'But just a few months prior to the murder of our woman in the tree. I closed the investigation as you requested, but maybe they think this old sighting I reported might link into something they've been investigating themselves.'

James dabs his forehead with his handkerchief. 'I'd better go with you into Brum. Seeing as it might be a matter of security.'

'Oh, I'm certain they'll want to speak with you at some point, sir.'

James stops his dabbing. 'Oh? And why is that?'

Porter frowns. 'According to our witness, a Miss Riley, you're the officer who failed to follow-up her sighting.'

James's mouth opens, but it takes a moment for any words or sound to emerge. He looks to the floor. 'Forty-one, you say? Those were busy times. We were under a lot of pressure back then. We had to make instant judgements about reports of parachutes and bombs dropping. We were flooded with them. Flooded. And short staffed.'

'This witness, she's very credible, sir. Very clear. I'm surprised you dismissed her so easily. I followed it up over a year later, and the ARP records were clear. They back up her claim.'

James rubs his chin. Sweeps a finger around the inside of his shirt collar. 'Look,' he begins, mind whirling. 'On second thoughts, I'm very busy this afternoon. Perhaps it's best you go after all. You seem to have this in hand. Best you be the contact. No need for me to get involved. Complicate matters.'

'Thank you, sir.' Porter replies. 'I'll need a car. And a driver.'

MAY 27TH, 1943: AFTERNOON

Webster's office is as ramshackle as ever. A filing system that owes as much to a document's proximity to his desk and the reach of his arms as it does to ideas of alphabetical order or case file numbers. Webster himself sits back, filling his pipe, monocle hanging from a lapel and swinging pendulously at each tamping of the tobacco. Next to him, separated by a pile of manila folders, sits Porter. Over by the wall, Willetts is ensconced on a straight back chair he has once more salvaged from one of the rooms close by. Opposite sits Solomon. His military mackintosh lies on the desk next to his briefcase. The flap of the case is open and two manila folders poke out. Across each 'MOST SECRET' is branded in red-stencilled letters. A third folder lies loosely in his hands. Solomon, weighing it, considered his options.

'What I'm about to tell you is highly sensitive,' he begins. 'I must remind you that you are all already subject to the Official Secrets Act. Should word of any of these matters emerge outside this meeting, you will face summary trial. Imprisonment. Given the gravity of its contents, quite possibly the death penalty.'

Webster nods understanding as does Porter. Willetts sits up straight, hands on knees, still as a rock. Solomon scours the three men's faces, satisfying himself they were suitably appraised.

He flicks open the folder, removing several sheets of paper, even though he has no intention to read directly from any of them. Rather, they serve as props in a moment of drama, a performance. 'I don't need to tell any of you that this investigation you've been pursuing so... relentlessly, has come to the attention of the War Office, specifically to my department. SIS. *Special Intelligence Service*.' He pauses, glancing at each in turn, seeking confirmation that this statement of his role further underlines the gravity of the matter. 'You no doubt have some idea as to the nature of our work, our sphere of operations. In such matters your investigation has caused concern.' He pauses, this time purely for dramatic impact. 'News of the discovery of your body in a tree created ripples in Whitehall. Ripples requiring we keep matters here under observation. Your request to the MoD seeking to locate one Jack Claverley in connection with this case has heightened our concerns regarding your discovery. The man you seek is well known to us. Jack Claverley is a spy. An agent providing high quality military intelligence to Berlin.'

'Good grief,' Webster utters.

'I knew it!' Willetts offers, slapping his knee.

Porter sits still; mouth firmly closed.

Solomon taps the file. 'We became aware of this man some years ago handing out leaflets at political rallies. Leaflets supporting the International Brigade's fight against fascism in Spain.' Webster glances at Porter whose face remains a mask. Solomon looks at Porter too. 'I should tell you, Detective Porter, that not all such volunteers attract our attention or our suspicion, but he was later identified as Jack Mossop, a civilian worker in aircraft production, a man occupying a sensitive role in the defence of our nation. As such, he was placed on a watch list and kept under observation. As were his close family. Some, like his wife, still are, hence how we learned of your discovery of the connection to Claverley.'

'Why just watch him and his family?' Webster asks, monocle twitching in his fingers. 'Why not simply remove him? Arrest him?'

Solomon pauses, raises his hands in acknowledgement of a decision that has come back to bite. 'The simple answer is spy craft. We'd long ago learned a hard lesson: sometimes it is better to merely know who the enemy spies or sympathisers are. In that way we are able to control the intelligence they have access to. If we arrest them, the likelihood is them being replaced with other agents whom we would be unaware of.' He shrugs. 'There was also the fact that at the time it was clear there was going to be a war. We had more pressing matters to concern ourselves with beyond that of a communist sympathiser's misguided thinking, irrespective of the potential sensitivity of his occupation.'

He scans the room, satisfied the drama he is about to unfold has their attention. 'However, when Stalin and Hitler signed their military pact we learned that Mossop had been tasked to work in a more active way. He was part of cell, German agents operating a highly effective route enabling intelligence regarding aircraft construction to be smuggled out of the country. We knew he was a spy, and we knew he was in indirect contact with a German cell, but we were clueless as to who these agents were or how the material was getting out of the country, other than the fact we knew it was ending up in Berlin

The three men sit in silence, absorbing what they are hearing. Willetts in particular is wrapped in attention. *Alfred Hitchcock. John Buchan. Saboteur. Thirty-Nine Steps.* 'We believed the route was linked to two German spies, agents whom we knew to have parachuted into the area in the summer of 1941. Agents who'd eluded our best efforts to find them.' He turned to Porter. 'Possibly the ones seen by your witness, Mrs Riley.' Other than the merest nod, Porter offers little in the way of reaction so Solomon returns to his tale. 'We had intelligence that one of them was a woman. Clarabella Dronkers, the ex-wife of a Dutchman, Johannes Dronkers. Living locally before the war, she knew the area well. We believe these agents were key in ensuring Mossop's intelligence reached Berlin. Some at SIS grew impatient, there was pressure to arrest Mossop, to squeeze him for what he knew of the whereabouts of cell. Then in December 1941, the network fell silent. Disappeared.'

'What happened?' Webster asks.

Solomon exhales. 'We don't know. We knew Mossop had been passing material to the network. We'd discovered there was

Black Market involvement, possibly managing one of the routes out paid for by Berlin. Of course, at that point we'd ensured anything Mossop had access to was low level, items we were aware of. We wanted to reel them all in, make certain we'd identified every single agent and collaborator before nabbing the lot in one go. But then the silence. We suspect *Operation Barbarossa* played a part. Hitler's invasion of Russia in late forty-one ended the axis alliance. Disrupted the cell's work. German agents and a communist sympathiser.'

'Meaning Mossop had to choose sides,' Porter observes.

'Exactly. It would have taken a while for him to get new orders from Moscow. Maybe he was ordered to break contact. Maybe he was told to eliminate the Germans. Maybe it was personal, and he took his own revenge. Maybe they'd killed him.' He pauses, raising his shoulders and furrowing his brow. 'All we knew was that he'd disappeared. If your body is that of Clarabella Dronkers, then it might be he was involved in killing her. A murder committed to cover his tracks or theirs.'

Porter looks to Webster and Willetts who look back. Webster offers a shrug. Willets simply makes do with a shake of his head. 'Clearly there's more,' Porter states.

'Very much so. We had nothing until last year. Then, during a routine security check a sharp-eyed SIS operative discovered a man fitting Mossop's description had popped up working at Castle Bromwich aerodrome at around the time Mossop disappeared. A man calling himself Claverley. Our operative performed discreet checks that appeared to confirm him to be Mossop. That he'd changed identity, got himself some damned good papers, and was now involved in aircraft distribution as well as manufacture. He had access to blueprints. Knew what was made, when it was made, and where. When it was to be dispersed. Critical stuff. Vital.'

'Mossop's wife told me she'd found papers for him using her maiden name. Claverley.'

Solomon nods. 'Spy-craft. Using an identity where he'd have

some background if anyone asked personal questions. The fact of the matter is his re-appearance meant we were faced with a number of scenarios. Despite the fact we're now allies, we had to assume that a committed communist like Mossop might be sending intelligence to Moscow. That it was Moscow that had furnished him with his new identity. Then again, maybe his loyalties had shifted. The possibility that he continued sending material to Berlin, but now did so for money.'

He exhales. To Porter he appears a man lost in the conundrums he'd laid out for them. 'Either he'd killed those Nazi agents or he was still in contact with them. Agents who themselves had gone deeper.'

Solomon opens his hands. An admission of the position they'd found themselves in. 'We were in the dark, and it was worrying. You have to understand that we'd looked for any sign of these agents for months. There were no bodies, or at least none we were aware of. But with the raids it would have been easy to conceal their deaths, pass them off as unidentified civilian casualties. We had no idea what had happened. If they'd disappeared or were dead. What level the threat might be to our plans for invasion.'

Solomon sits back, eyes travelling to the glass bricks of the light-box above Webster's desk. 'We had to know what we were dealing with.'

He shuffles in his chair. 'The decision was to give the man now calling himself Claverley access to higher grade intelligence. Intelligence of a level we hoped would tempt the rest of them out of whatever hole they'd run to. Baiting the line, so to speak. Within a month or so we found it ending up in Berlin. The highest level. It was only then that we knew for certain that Claverley was continuing to work for the Germans. It meant there was every chance that the other members of the cell remained active, but we had no idea as to where or how the intelligence was getting to Berlin.'

'So what did you do?' Webster asks.

Solomon snorts. 'The game hadn't changed. We watched. We waited. Plying Claverley with ever juicier intelligence. Nothing. It was high risk. It got to the point where we were once more thinking of next steps. Pulling Claverley in. Pressuring him. It was then that you found your body in the tree.' He shakes his head. 'Well, it stopped us in our tracks. We had to consider it might be Clarabella Dronkers. That maybe we'd been wrong in our thinking. That the rest of the cell were dead. That Claverley had some new route to Berlin. If the body in the tree is that of Dronkers, it shifts our understanding of what we're dealing with. Once news of your discovery broke, we thought to maintain an even closer watching brief. Thinking Claverley might contact the other members of that original cell. The man we really wanted was their analyst, their leader. The man who knew the whole chain.'

He smiles. It is without humour. 'But Claverley disappeared.' He leans forward. 'It can't be mere coincidence. Claverley's network remains out there, operating in secret, hooked into our planning and intelligence in ways we know nothing about. Maybe they were concerned that Claverley was about to be arrested as a suspect in Dronkers' murder. They killed him, knowing he was the one person who might lead us to them. Or maybe Claverley, thinking the same, ran before his comrades could get to him. Whatever the reason, he's gone.'

'So why the secrecy? The non-co-operation. The cease-and-desist messages from Whitehall?' Webster asks.

'This is an SIS operation, professor. Details of our work or of the existence of enemy espionage rings in this country is of necessity secret: a matter of need to know. We don't want to alert them that we're on their trail. And, of course, there's the small matter that your body may not even be her.'

'But when Professor Webster sent out his circular?' Porter puts in. 'The details of her appearance. Things the professor told us are highly likely to produce a match. Surely you must have known who she was?'

'We don't have her dental records or anything like that. Clarabella Dronkers was Dutch. We know little of her beyond a few basic facts.' Solomon closes the folder, placing it on top of the briefcase. 'To be frank, we're left with egg on our faces. An SIS operation that didn't work as planned. Claverley, the only hope of finding out what happened to these agents - where they are, whether they remain active in a capacity unknown to us and thus doubly dangerous to the war effort, or if all of them are long dead or returned to Berlin - has disappeared.'

Porter grimaces. 'If he's alive, there are a deal of questions I'd like to ask that man.'

'As would SIS.'

'Why are you telling us this now? What's changed other than you've lost him?' Porter asks.

Solomon sits with hands folded in his lap. He appears to take a moment in selecting the appropriate response. He looks from Webster to Willetts and finally to Porter. 'We needed time to check on you, Detective. The matter of your politics. Your motives.'

'Sorry?'

'Detective, you fought in Spain. Sacrificed yourself for the same cause as your fellow-traveller Jack Mossop. We had to be sure of you.'

'Well, I must say, I admire your honesty,' Webster states. He looks at his colleagues, measuring what he finds there. He sits forward; arms spread wide. 'So, Captain. Can we assume you've not travelled all the way up from London to tell us this and then ask us to leave it be?'

Solomon smiles. 'A few days ago I convinced my superiors that it's time for us to work together. Police and SIS. Share what we have. Utilise our differing expertise.' He nods to Porter. 'Your local knowledge with our access to sensitive information.' He turns to Webster. 'Your forensic investigative techniques with our ability to open official channels that would otherwise be closed to you. We want to work with you. We want to find the man calling himself Claverley as much as you do. More so. If we were to pool our resources, we might yet both get what we want. We get our spy and the chance to interrogate him about the rest of his cell; you get the man you believe to be a murderer.'

Webster looks to Willetts and Porter. Willetts shrugs.

Solomon scribbles another note. 'I suggest the first order of things is for you, Porter, to search through records. We need to find out exactly where this man was between disappearing as Mossop in late 41 and reappearing as Claverley in early summer 42. Somewhere in those documents might be a paper trail leading us to who he had contact with in that period.'

'Paperwork?' Porter asks.

'It might furnish ideas as to where he may now have gone to ground. He's accomplished. A man who's fooled both SIS and the military at the highest level. A man with the means of changing identity. An agent good enough to infiltrate highly sensitive operations. For all we know Mossop might be as false an identity as that of Claverley. He may even already have shed Claverley to become someone else. But each disappearance means that for a short time he'd have needed to rely on those contacts made as Mossop or Claverley. Filling in the gaps brings us closer to catching him. Closer to finding the answers we're anxious to have.'

A grim silence lies across the room. Realities bedding down.

Solomon closes his pad. 'And that brings me to my final point. Before agreeing to this joint investigation there's a matter we have to be clear on, one you may not like. It is non-negotiable. If we succeed in finding this man, it may be necessary to see to it that he is never tried for this murder of yours. We may find better uses for him, uses that trump murder.'

Porter opens his mouth to speak, but Solomon holds up a hand. 'Spy craft. It is imperative to the war effort that we keep any capture of this spy-ring secret both from our enemies and even our allies in Moscow. It could prove politically embarrassing for it to be revealed in a trial that our Russian allies have been spying on us. At one point actively assisting our enemies at what was a perilous stage of the war.'

'I promised justice for the woman in the tree,' Porter states. 'Whoever she might have been. Gypsy. Agent. Enemy. She deserved better.'

Solomon slid the folder into his briefcase. 'As I say, you may have to accept that simply discovering the truth of what happened to her will have to suffice as your justice.'

'Isn't that enough?' Webster jumps in, coming to terms with the world they'd suddenly found themselves in. He turns to Porter. 'After all, isn't it what we said we wanted at the start of all this? To find the truth. Surely you can be satisfied with that.'

Porter inclines his head as he considers these new realities. 'If that's all we can have, then I suppose it will have to do.' He sits forward. 'So, Captain Solomon, where do we begin?'

MAY 27TH, 1943: NIGHT

John Avery flicks on the desk-lamp, the blackout curtains closed tight ensure no stray light can betray them. Pouring a large whiskey for himself and one for the man opposite, both sit for a moment, sipping their drinks.

'One of the few good things about this fucking place,' Avery's companion observes.

Avery smiles. Politics and diplomacy did not figure high on the list of reasons for using the man. Maybe it was his Texas upbringing; maybe it was just his nature. Whatever, the muscular Texan possessed a skill set very different to his own.

Offering his companion a cigarette that the Texan takes with a nod of gratitude, he produces a Zippo lighter and lights both men's cigarettes. 'You say he got on the Liverpool train?' Avery finally asks.

The tall Texan exhales a cloud of smoke, nodding. 'Yes, it was him.'

'And the only stop between Euston and Liverpool is Birmingham?'

'Yeah.'

'And our man at Lime Street says he didn't get off at Liverpool?'

'No. He travelled to Birmingham, as we thought.'

'And there's no doubt why he's gone there?'

The tall Texan shakes his head. 'None.'

Lacing fingers together, placing them behind his neck as a cradle, Avery leans back, the cigarette hanging from his bottom lip. 'So, he's digging into this police investigation, which means they've found something unnerving to our good buddies at SIS, got them all stirred up and worried.' He shakes his head. 'They'd sure as hell never have pulled this kind of stunt if not.'

Slipping his hands free, he removes the cigarette from his lips to sit forward, all business. 'So, what have we got?'

The Texan sips his whiskey, a beat allowing his mind to pace around the information he's so diligently gleaned over the past days. 'Ever since this Detective Porter turned up at Wolverley asking questions about a dead woman in a tree over in Hagley you've had me keep an eye on what he's been doing. It appears something he found in Kenilworth has triggered a response from SIS.'

Avery nods. Ever since the call from Wolverley his suspicions had been aroused. He'd been waiting a long time for some explanation of the bizarre, unsettling events of late forty-one, and the recent sudden SIS activity around this police investigation suggested it might be close at hand. As a first step, he'd ensured that both the Embassy and US Europe military command had made the right noises about Porter's enquiry, the hostile diplomatic reaction expected. More pertinently, in doing so, he'd allayed SIS suspicions of any continuing American interest in the victim's identification. As head of OSS and all espionage agents in the country, he'd then assigned the Texan to shadow the investigation. He'd also made use of grateful contacts in the police and local business that OSS had so assiduously cultivated over the year he's been here. But until the last few days, he'd begun to see it as a dead-end. A ghost of their earlier suspicions about what had really happened to the woman they knew only as Bella.

He stubs his cigarette in the ashtray. 'Are we certain it's her?'

The Texan shrugs, stubbing out his own in quick succession. 'From what you've told me of what happened, who else could it be to get SIS so spooked?'

Avery grimaces. 'There's nothing concrete. SIS can't be sure, or they wouldn't have waited weeks before charging off to Birmingham or shutting them down.'

'But it does fit what we know,' the Texan points out. 'The timing of the disappearance, the location. It's sure got SIS rattled. Our information is one hundred percent reliable. Straight from one of the senior officers in the local station.'

'So why have SIS waited until now?'

'Maybe they've kept their distance, hoping for it to all go away.'

'Say that's true. Do you think the police know what it is they've got?'

The Texan shrugs languidly, 'Doubtful. Our contact in the area has reached out to his man, a Detective Sergeant. He's said nothing about who she is or why she might have been killed, other than he tells our guy it's a gypsy thing. He says the meeting between SIS and Porter is to do with an old report of parachutists in the area. If he knew anything he'd have said. Seems he's a greedy fat fuck according to our guy. He wouldn't pass up a chance to sell us something tasty. There's been an official report. They've put it on the back burner. If this Porter knows anything at all then surely this DS would know too?'

'But we know what your DS guy doesn't, that this DC Porter's gone off the reservation on this. This whole *secret enquiry in their own time Sherlock Holmes* shit he's been pulling. What does that tell us?'

'That he's a stubborn *son-of-a-bitch.*'

'Without a doubt.' Avery takes a swig of whiskey. 'What we do know is that SIS will lead them a dance. They've kept this under wraps for almost two years. If it is her, the timing suggests that whatever she had is what got her killed. We have to find out what that was. What did she have that was so important that it got her killed? That now has SIS so wound up?'

The Texan puts his glass on the table. 'What about Washington?'

Avery shrugs acceptance of the point. 'Washington's interested but not overly so. Too many other operations on their minds.'

'Will they back you?'

'Depends on what we find. What about this police contact? Any way your man can push him harder?'

'From what our guy said, I don't think he's in the circle with access to what SIS knows. He's useful for simple intelligence, but he's no thinker. Our other boy's the better contact. Black market guy, you know the type, kept sweet by trade deals, the promise of a brighter tomorrow, a place in the sun courtesy of his Uncle Sam. He knows DC Porter personally, but he's not yet in any position to find out much other than where he is or what he might generally be thinking. He's not an operative, he's just a source.'

Avery nods. 'The less people who know about this the better. As far as he's concerned, we're just interested in anything that might link to Wolverley. We're looking out for our own.

'I know him. He's got no interest beyond his wallet.'

'So, we watch. Watch and wait. See where this takes us. If the body in that tree turns out to be who we think she is, that'll be the time to get more hands on with Detective Porter.'

17

MAY 29TH, 1943: MORNING

Porter stares at the boxes. Pile after pile, row after row. Inside each box are files, bundles of them, each of varying thickness with somewhere between thirty and forty files per box. Manila files tied with string, each containing on average fifty to sixty pages of forms, travel warrants, postings, personnel documents, and billeting arrangements. He knows exactly what each box contains because it had been that way for each of the six boxes he's been through. Each stack five boxes high. Each row twelve stacks in length. There are five rows.

Andrea Floode smiles. Though she'd anticipated the look on his face, she is still unable to restrain herself. 'Happy?'

Porter shakes his head. 'I didn't realise…'

She hops up, perching herself on the nearest stack, crossing her legs to reveal sheer silk stockings clearly not of army issue. 'An army marches on paper. Every soldier's movement has to be logged in triplicate.' She holds up a hand, flicks fingers upright as she enumerates her points, aware his eyes are on her legs rather than her hands. 'Orders typed, travel warrants cut; copies for receiving officer, copies for departing officer, copies for the MOD.'

Solomon had been good as his word. Every document Porter could require in a search for Claverley has been made available to him, along with the services of Floode as liaison and driver. 'That's a lot of paper,' he states.

'If it's of any consolation, from what I've been told by the adjutant in charge of things, this is just the tip of the iceberg.' She spreads an arm to take in the cellar.

He stands back, contemplating the lines of boxes. A veritable mountain of paper. More than he'd imagined. *The tip of the iceberg.*

They'd driven to Compton Verney, an old country estate well away from the bombing and the possibility of destruction. The location made it ideal as an archive. A series of temporary storage bins had been created in the barns, garage, and outbuildings of the old house along with this more secure area deep in the cellars. It was cavernous. From floor to ceiling wood and wrought iron wine racks line the curvature of the walls He estimates there were thousands of bottles, wines no doubt laid down over what must have been decades of collecting.

It possesses a distinctive gloominess, along with a muskiness that caught in the throat. Temporary lighting had been set up. Lamps in protective cages hanging like luminous fruit, drooping vine-like from cables held by metal fixings hammered into the ceiling.

Solomon had been insistent that knowledge of SIS involvement and Floode's role within it be limited to Porter and Webster alone. For all others, those such as Williams and James and even Willetts, she was designated admin support. An officer assigned to facilitate a joint investigation into the sighting of parachutists in the area. She would be Porter's driver. That she was an active agent with experience of operations in France and Belgium was not to be revealed. 'It may be nothing at all, this body of yours and its link to Claverley. If she's not Dronkers, there's little point in more people than necessary being made aware of SIS involvement. If she is, then secrecy becomes even more of an imperative if we're to avoid a leak frightening off the remnants of the cell before we can lay a hand on them.'

There was uncertainty in Porter's dealings with Floode. Was he an equal or a junior partner? She would be under orders to report anything he said or did to SIS, an understanding tainting any conversation between them.

Porter exhales loudly. 'Any ideas?' he asks.

She shakes her head before leaning back on the boxes, arms extending behind her, elbows supporting her pose. 'You're the Detective. I'm just the help. What exactly is it we're looking for?' she asks.

'To be honest, I'm not sure. Transfers taking place around December to January 1941 in the Bromsgrove and wider Birmingham area. Details of postings of military personnel at the time Mossop disappears and Claverley seems to have sprung up in his place. The MoD told Mossop's wife they have no record of Jack Mossop enlisting, nor anyone of that name being deployed to work on military projects. We know from SIS that a man called Claverley was doing just that. Somewhere in here are documents proving they are one in the same. That the Jack Mossop who poured out his confession to Una Mossop is the man SIS have been tracking. The man who knows who murdered Bella.'

'Not to mention serving as proof if you can get him to trial.'

'It's something I've not given up on. Maybe you should pass that on to Solomon.'

She smiles, sinking further back onto the stack of boxes.

'In addition to that,' he continues, 'Claverley now disappears too. So we're looking for details of Claverley's postings, hoping to find some idea of the contacts he might have made, the places where he might feel safe. He's avoided his old family, the Mossop connection, so where has he been during the past few years where he might have forged new connections? People whose paths he's crossed or links that might offer ideas as to what happened to him.

Where he might go if he was in trouble. Maybe even where he might obtain yet another identity. Maybe that new identity is in here, too.'

'It could take weeks, months.' She waves a hand expansively in front of her. 'Needles and haystacks.'

'Worse. One needle, but God only knows which haystack.'

'And just the two of us to do it.'

'Pretty much.'

She sighs and begins unbuttoning her jacket. Slipping it off, she reveals a tight-fitting tan military blouse. She tosses the jacket onto one of the piles and begins fastening her hair back. Hair in place, she proceeds to opening the nearest box. 'Well, best get started then.' She looks around. Her eyes rest on the racks of vintage claret and burgundy. 'All this wine…'

'Find what we're looking for and I'll buy you a case.'

'I might just hold you to that, Detective,' she purrs.

MAY 29TH, 1943: EVENING

They worked all day. Clearing 10 boxes, leaving just 290 to go. A month. Only then would they know if they contained anything of use in tracing the whereabouts of Jack Mossop or his alter ego Jack Claverley.

They drove back to Birmingham, the cross slits of headlights picking out the twists and turns of unlit country roads. Soon it would be summer with much less need to worry about blackout restrictions.

A few miles from home Floode pulls the car to a halt in the car park of a pub. *The Gypsy's Tent.*

'What's this?' Porter asks gazing out through the side windows of the Riley.

She switches off the ignition, the engine dying. 'Well, as we didn't find anything today, I feel it's me who owes you that drink you talked about,' she says, turning to him and smiling. Her mouth is wide, lips plump and full even without lipstick.

'Besides, I wanted to see where it all began. Too dark for the woods. This seemed the next best thing.'

Before he can reply, she's jumped out of the car to stand looking across to the Woods. He gets out but remains by the car. His back aches from the drive, pains shooting up and down the base of his spine. Spending the day bent double going through files hadn't helped. He was finding it hard to snap into the upright position, something he's reluctant for her to see. He leans; forearms folded on top of the car roof. Stretching his back, he takes in the silhouette of his companion.

She was slim, '*boyish*' his mother would have said. Slender where Rachel was full-figured. Even with the heavy material of the uniform, it's clear her body is firm, athletic. During the course of the day he'd learned very little of her other beyond the fact that she was intelligent; quick to pick up on ideas he'd suggest. Quick to suggest ideas of her own. Her manner told him she was Home Counties, grammar school educated. A woman disconcertingly sure of herself.

'It has a certain fascination, doesn't it? The woods. I feel a pull, something gently tugging me,' she murmurs.

'The locals say it's haunted. A place of magic. They say witches hold it special. A mythical place for their ceremonies. Gypsies too.'

She gazes out. A shaft of moonlight – the bombers' moon – silvered the tops of the trees. She whispers agreement, 'I can understand that. You can feel it. Can't you?'

He shakes his head. 'No.'

She turns to face him, holding out a hand, beckoning, 'Come here. Stand next to me.'

He does as he's bid.

Standing next to her, he feels her hand against his back, guiding him closer. 'Here,' she says. He moves closer, feels the growing warmth of her hand through his coat. 'Close your eyes. Go on, close them,' she urges. He does. 'Breathe,' she whispers, leaning nearer, her breath close enough to warm his ear. 'Breathe deep. Can't you feel it?'

He breathes the cool evening air. Breathes deep, aware only of her hand against his back, her hair brushing his cheek. Her perfume. *Air. Her breath. Hand. Air. Her breath. Hand.*

'Well?' she asks.

He opens his eyes. 'Not a thing.'

'You, Detective, have no soul,' she chides, leaning away from him.

'That's a distinct possibility.'

'And there I was expecting a real life Romantic.' She turns away, continuing to gaze towards the moonlit woods. 'What happened to the boy who gave up everything for Spain?'

He shuffles awkwardly. 'If you've read my file – as I suspect you have – then you know what happened to him. He was lost in an orange grove outside a Catalonian village.'

She turns to face him. 'I don't believe that.'

'Why so?'

'Because if that were the case you wouldn't be here now, pursuing the killer of this woman. What's this if not idealism?'

'Stubbornness?'

'That too,' she smiles. 'But that only gets you so far. Stubbornness would have given up. Given up some time ago. This, Detective Porter, is something deeper, much deeper. This is passion. Idealism. Romantic.'

'What about you?'

'Me?'

'What drives you? Why this?'

She looks up at him. 'Maybe I'm an idealist too.' She sees his half-smile, 'What's so funny about that?' she playfully reprimands, turning back to the view.

He shakes his head. 'I've met very few women like you.'

'But you have met some.'

He nods, reminding himself. 'University. Spain.'

They stand side by side, staring out at the tree-line. 'What was it like? Spain.'

'Wonderful. Terrifying.'

'A heady mix,' she says.

'Yes. Yes, it was.'

'You miss it, don't you?'

'What? Being blown up?'

She half-turns towards him. 'The sense of living. Being totally alive.'

He looks at her. A cloud passes across the moon; the deepening blue-grey darkness blurring the details of her face. 'I'm not sure what you mean,' he says.

'I think you do. I had it each time I was dropped into France. Scared, knowing at any moment I might be revealed for who I was. Torture. The firing squads. Yet, I felt...alive. Every glass of wine, every piece of bread, every breath. So...full. Aware each might be the last. The last drink, my last sunrise. My last lover. It had power... feelings I'd never had before. Never had since.' She breathes in, exhaling slowly, almost a sigh. 'I miss it. So, I know you must too.'

'I think you've got me wrong.'

'I don't think so.'

'Maybe once. Not anymore. Not now.'

'Then why this?' she asks.

'Sorry?'

'This case. This single-minded pursuit of your killer.'

'It's... the job.'

She snorts, shaking her head and laughing. 'Now I know you're lying.'

MAY 31ST, 1943: MORNING

'You were late last night'

Porter looks up from the shoe he's cleaning. Rachel stands by the sink sorting washing for the line. The rain had eased, and the

215

morning promised summer sun. Porter, sitting the other side of the kitchen table, picks up his left shoe, brushing it with a wide circular motion. 'Yes. Yes, suppose it was.'

Rachel wipes a hand across her brow. 'This case. Seems we get to see less of you than when you were working day shifts and putting in the fire-watching.'

'Hadn't thought of it like that. There's a lot to do. I'm so busy I don't always realise how late it is. Lot of long drives, too.'

She places a shirt into the wicker basket. 'That's another thing. Stuff like that's no good for your back.'

'I'm fine.'

She turns, plucking a vest from the sink. She rotates the garment over before wringing the water from it. 'You tell Willetts that he needs to look out for you.'

'He's not driving me any longer. They've given me someone from the military. New car too. Lot more comfortable. A Riley'

'At least they're taking you seriously now.'

'Seems so. At least for the moment.'

She lays the damp vest onto the draining board, pulling another from the suds of the sink. 'So where did you get to yesterday? Or is it Top Secret?'

He swops brushes, examining the shoe for scuffs. He shrugs, uncertain. 'Not exactly. It's sensitive, I suppose. We're not sure what we're dealing with.'

'Spies?'

'Who knows. It's possible.'

She lays the vest into the laundry basket, returns her hands to the sink full of washing. 'So, what have you found out?'

'Nothing concrete. Maybe a local connection. The name Dronkers mean anything?'

Rachel gazes out of the window in thought before continuing her swilling of a shirt. 'Dronkers? Sounds German.'

'Dutch.'

'Same difference,' she shrugs again. Hands wet, she wipes a forearm across her brow. 'I thought you said she might be local.'

'Local connection. She may have lived around here under that name.'

'Gosh, how exciting. A spy, living round here.'

He puts the shoe on the floor, compares left with right. 'I may be late tonight.'

'Oh, okay. Shepherd's pie. I'll keep some in the oven for when you get in.'

'We'll more than likely eat out.'

She lifts the shirt to the light. 'Where are they staying?'

'Staying?'

'This driver.'

'Not sure. A B&B somewhere I expect.'

'They're more than welcome to a home cooked meal.'

'I don't think-'

She swivels to face him; shirt held over the sink. 'Not good enough?'

'No, no. It's not that. It's…' he looks at her.

'It's what?'

'I don't think Andrea-'

'Andrea?'

'Andrea. My driver.'

'She's a woman?'

He nods. 'Of course.'

'Of course? What do you mean, *of course*?' she states, a snap to her tone.

'Most military drivers are women these days,' he offers as clarification.

'Oh. I hadn't realised.' She turns back to the sink, busying herself with a stubborn spot on one of the garments. 'What's she like?'

'Like? She's… nice.'

'Nice?'

'Pleasant. Good at her job. A decent driver.' He snaps the lid back on the tin of polish. He picks up the brushes and places them into the wooden boot box Arthur had made as a wedding gift for his son.

She rubs harder at the mark on the shirt, plunging it into the suds. 'How old is she?'

'Erhm, not sure.'

'But she's young?'

He pauses, hesitates. 'In her twenties, I suppose.'

'Has she got a boyfriend or husband?'

'I don't know. Hasn't really come up.'

'No ring, then?'

'Not that I noticed.' He screws up the newspaper, checking for shards of polish that may have slipped onto the raddled floor tiles.

'Some Detective.'

He stops. 'Rachel. She's a driver. She works for Military Intelligence. She's admin and support. Her job is to take me where I need to go. To liaise with the MoD and her superiors. That's it. That's all I know, and frankly it's all I need to know.'

'How long will she be attached here? To you?'

'Till we're done or till there's no point her being here any longer.'

She picks up the basket of washing from the draining board. She turns to face him as he stands, polished shoes in hands. 'You'd best get a move on, then,' she advises.

18

The drive was long, onerous. Bombing raids that had left yet more piles of rubble blocking already battered roads. ARPs, windmill armed, divert what is for the most part military traffic around the deeper potholes and bomb craters. Water pipes spray fountains of water high in the air, damage awaiting overworked repair teams straining to keep pace with the thousands of such fractures.

'This'll take hours,' Porter observes, the Riley snaking slowly round the remains of yet another building crumbled across the road. He passes the time scanning the road ahead that is lined with rows of factory units. Here and there the pummelling of the raids have forced jagged gaps in their walls like the stumps of shattered teeth.

'Looks like it,' Andrea responds, fingers tapping frustration on the steering wheel. 'Light me a ciggie,' she says.

He fishes in her bag on the back seat, extracting a pack of cigarettes. He puts one in his mouth, lights it, and offers it to her. She twists in her seat, leaning closer, beckoning him to place it between her lips, which he does. She turns to the front, drawing

219

deeply on the cigarette before removing it with her left hand and exhaling. 'Thanks.'

'You're welcome.'

'You don't want one?' she asks.

'You may not have noticed, but I don't smoke.'

'Oh, I noticed. I just wondered if I could tempt you.'

He snorts, changes the subject. 'How long have you been doing this?'

'Smoking or tempting?'

'Spying.'

'Let me see. I joined up in early Forty-one.'

'Before that?'

'University. A blue-stocking, no less,' she smiles at her once self. Her once life.

'How did your parents react?'

'They didn't. They died in one of the first raids in Forty.'

'I'm sorry.'

'Four hundred died that night.' She inhales deeply on the cigarette. 'I was tucked up safe in my boyfriend's bed thirty miles away. I found out days later. A telegram. Two weeks later, I joined up. Basic training. Someone there decided that with my education they'd better uses for me than digging ditches or filling sandbags. Turns out I had a penchant for the work, the languages. So, they trained me for France. A few months after enlisting I was in Paris. Back and forth since then.'

'So why this? Aren't those talents under used driving?'

'A rest. A chance to catch up. Charge the batteries.'

'Is that all?'

'Well, if we find Claverley and the rest of the spy ring, what better person to advise on spy-catching than a spy?'

An ARP warden appears in the road directly in front of them, waving them on. The car jolts forward, Andrea avoiding the maze of potholes before finding clear tarmac and accelerating away. Through the side window Porter makes out groups of fire fighters and civilian workers squatting on what remains of the brickwork. They are hollow-eyed with exhaustion, faces blurred by layers of dust. The relief teams now take their turn in hauling at shattered timbers and wooden joists. The beams are scattered across the rubble as if smote by the hand of an angry child.

'Any idea how much further?' she asks.

Porter looks down, consults the map folded across his knees. 'Hard to say. If we're able to keep to the route, maybe eight... ten miles. If we have to divert it could be fifteen.'

'At this speed it'll be getting on for evening before we reach them.'

After a week of trawling through boxes of paperwork, they'd found little beyond what SIS had already managed to gather. Nothing suggesting where Claverley - if he were still alive - might have sought refuge from SIS pursuers or fellow saboteurs. He was a ghost. Mossop ended and Claverley began. And now Claverley was gone too.

The orders assigning him to Castle Bromwich were real, covered with official stamps and War Ministry approval. That in itself created questions for Porter. How had Mossop been able to fool the authorities into believing he was Claverley, assuming an identity enabling access to some of the most sensitive materials of the allied war effort? As far as they could find, he had no existence beyond those few sheets of paper.

Porter was frustrated with the lack of progress. He knew the mantra of policing, that investigating was sifting detail, but he needed to know more about the man they were hunting. It was why they were travelling to Castle Bromwich.

He checked his watch. He didn't know what for. They had little choice in the matter. They needed to get to Castle Bromwich, he needed to talk to those who'd worked with Claverley. Needed to discover what they thought had happened to him.

They had an address for his billeting close to the north Birmingham airstrip where he'd most recently worked. From what they knew, his work involved the despatch of bombers manufactured at Longbridge that had their final wing assembly at CastleBromwich. The airstrip there made it the only place in the region capable of flying such huge aircraft out from. It gave access to blueprints and production lines.

At some point that morning, during yet one more trawl through the endless piles of documents, he'd broken, announcing to Floode he had to get out from the cellar and do what he thought of as *real* police-work.

This is what I do, he'd told her. *Those are the skills SIS say they want. Sitting in this cellar is waste of all that*. At first she'd been reluctant, almost to the point of hostility. She'd argued the need to complete the task at Compton Verney. It was only his telling her she could stay and do that, that he'd get Willetts to drive him to Castle Bromwich, that had swayed her into making the trip.

'Whatever happens, there'll be someone there we can interview,' he'd assured. 'If they're not on duty, they'll no doubt be billeted at the airfield, same as Claverley. Might even be easier to talk to them there. Less pressure.'

Floode focused her attention on the road ahead; she was putting her foot down on the accelerator, trying to make up lost time. 'Any ideas as to how you're planning to go about this?'

Porter shrugs, 'Commanding officer. Then the ranks below: adjutant's office, civilian contractors. Then the men he worked alongside.'

'Any details as to who it is we're dealing with?'

He flicks through his notebook. Grimaces, 'Not really. The CO's a chap called Nicholson. The civil contractor is from Rolls Royce. Not sure of his name.'

She turns her head towards him. 'And you're hoping to discover?'

'Something. Anything. Where he went. What he talked about whilst he was there. Friends that might have helped him.'

She stubs her cigarette out in the ashtray protruding from the dashboard, tossing the stub out the window. 'You do realise that we're chasing a man who never really existed? Jack Claverley is a fiction. He doesn't have to hide; he can just literally cease to be. How do we find a shadow?'

He stares ahead at the fast unwinding of the road. 'Claverley is an invention, a fiction. But Jack Mossop isn't. Jack Mossop has to hide; Jack Mossop can be found. And that's what I intend to do. Find him. He's going to tell me what happened that night in Hagley Woods. He's going to tell me who Bella was. What it was that made her continued existence a threat to Mossop or to his associates.'

He fixes his mind on the road speeding him ever closer to the answers he feels lie ahead. It felt good to find purpose, a focus for action. When he speaks, it's a declaration as much as a response to her question. She'd thrown a snowball and an avalanche came back. 'I'm going to find him,' he states. 'And, if he's not the one I want, then I'll find the rest of them. I'm going to keep going, one after the other, until I find Bella's murderers. All of them. Wherever they are.'

JUNE 3RD, 1943: NIGHT

A waste of time. That was how Nicholson had put their search. *A waste of time and effort* at a time when the country needed all of its energies in fighting *Jerry. The Hun. The Bosch.* That was how he'd described the enemy. Fly boy language. *Boy's Own* stuff. Porter had taken an instant dislike to the man, something that had been returned with interest.

Wing Commander Patrick 'Paddy' Nicholson was six two, trim moustache, pomaded hair, and, as his moustache indicated, a man fancying himself as Clarke Gable. Dashing. Heroic. He was smooth, slick as the oil he used on his hair. The fact he'd been openly sceptical of Porter's wounds and non-combatant status hadn't helped. Nor the fact that from the moment they'd walked into his office he'd had obvious designs on Floode.

Porter slams his drink down onto the table, slopping beer.

'Steady tiger,' Andrea comments.

They'd stopped at *The Crown and Cushion* public house for a meal - if cheese sandwiches and stale pork pie could be classed as such. It was late. He'd refused Nicholson's offer of food in the officer's mess mostly out of an unwillingness to spend any more time in the man's domain than necessary. They'd left with the address of the civilian contractor Claverley reported to, but on arrival at his digs discovered that he was fire-watching. It meant they'd have to await his return to his billet, a large house close to the airfield. A return that would be close to midnight. Porter had managed to ring Willetts at the station, and Willetts had agreed to call in to let Rachel know he'd not be back until the early hours. God alone knew what she'd be thinking.

'Bloody idiot!' he snarls, wiping the slops of spilt beer with a paper coaster.

Floode raised an eyebrow. 'I'm assuming you're referring to Nicholson.'

'Who else? Christ, men like him! Think they're so superior!'

'Ah, would this be your much vaunted socialism seeping out?'

'My much-vaunted intolerance of pricks like Nicholson!'

She screwed up her face. 'Seemed OK to me. A little stuffy.'

'Maybe you're used to men like him.'

'Men like him?' She scrutinises the remark. 'I'm not certain what that's supposed to mean about *men like him* or a woman like me.'

'Men who think they own everything. Think that everything is just laid out for them, awaiting their pleasure.' He sweeps a hand in a grand gesture. 'Like a giant buffet, there for the taking.'

'Wait right there!' She puts her drink on the table, turning to him with a fearsome flaring of her eyes. 'Let me get this clear. You're saying I'm *lying* there awaiting his pleasure? What? You see me spread out and waiting for the first man - any man - who comes along?'

'No, Christ, no. Not at all. I meant…'

'Alec, I don't think you have the first idea about me,' she snarls, turning away, taking out her cigarettes.

'Listen, Andrea. I'm sorry. Really sorry. I didn't mean to slight you, to insult you. It's just that Nicholson reminds me of the world before the war. Class. Privilege.' He holds a hand up, palm out, fingers spread wide, outlining a sign that might be hanging there suspended in the air. '*Outsiders not welcome.* Maybe the way the world will still be after the war.'

'If you mean that men of power and position fight to hold on to what they have, you're absolutely right.' She lights her cigarette, inhaling deeply before blowing the smoke into the fug of the room. 'The war's not going to change any of that. You're an educated man, Alec, you must know that.'

He fiddles with the coaster. 'Maybe that's the issue.' He flicks the edge of the coaster up and down. 'It's when it comes along and confronts you. Reminds you of what it is you're actually fighting for. Conservatism. The status quo.' He picks up his glass, swilling the remaining half of it down. 'Fancy another?'

'I'll get them.' She stands, holding out a restraining hand as Porter begins to get up. She leans towards him, 'See, maybe things are changing.' She stubs out her cigarette.

He watches her walk to the bar - jacket off, army blouse tight across her shoulders, tight at the waist. A group of men are seated close to the bar. He watches their eyes follow her, devour her. She turns, glancing at the men, who look away. She smiles at Porter. Aware.

He takes out his notebook, opening it to scan the last few pages. Claverley had been assigned to operations at Castle Bromwich for almost fifteen months. He'd arrived from Longbridge to serve as logistics officer overseeing the movement of fuselages and wings from the Longbridge production plant to Castle Bromwich aerodrome. The aircraft arrived as a fuselage, wings separate, the electrics and pneumatics already in place. There they were assembled: engines, wings and guns. Then they were flown out. Claverley made frequent trips to and from

Longbridge sorting production issues. The man had power, access to all aspects of bomber construction; the schedules, the numbers, and their destinations. On top of that, the freedom to travel unhindered. A few months ago, April, around the time Bella had been found, he'd disappeared. He'd left in a car on one of his many journeys across the region and not been seen again.

Nicholson had been dismissive. They'd lost several men like that. Caught in a raid. Bodies mangled beyond recognition. He'd assumed it was what had happened to Claverley. He'd informed the Ministry, who'd quickly sorted a replacement, and they'd got on with the business of winning the war. The Ministry seemed happy with that scenario. Porter assumed it was why Una's enquiries had been rebuffed. As Una Mossop, ex-wife of Jack Mossop, she had no connection with the man calling himself Claverley. It meant there'd been no word to her of his *Missing-in-Action* status. There was a war on. People were stretched.

The idea Claverley had used false papers had been news to Nicholson. He had no idea as to why - maybe he'd wanted to lose a wife whom Porter himself had just told him he'd married in haste. Pregnant. In fact, Nicholson had appeared unperturbed by it all. It was, so he said, not his responsibility. The Ministry had issued the orders for Claverley's assignment to Castle Bromwich and Nicholson assumed knew what they were doing. It was the Ministry who would have checked his papers. After all, he'd added, *he couldn't just spring from nowhere without someone in the Ministry having issued his documents.* Besides which, Nicholson had been quite certain: Claverley was *clearly no spy.* In the fifteen months Claverley had worked there, there hadn't been a single incidence of sabotage. There were no missing plans or blueprints. *Nothing out of the ordinary.* In fact Nicholson boasted that production had increased. *What kind of saboteur increased the capability of his supposed enemy*?

Floode returned with the drinks. 'Anything?'

Porter shakes his head. Closes his notebook. 'Nothing new.'

'No startling insights? No hunches?'

He exhales. 'Sherlock Holmes, like Claverley, is fiction. *Today's Detective is all about the science of crime.*'

'Webster.'

'Webster,' Porter nods. 'That's the future. Hard evidence. Fingerprints and residues. Things you can't hide or cover up. Unlike people, they don't miraculously appear or equally miraculously vanish from the face of the earth.'

'But this Mossop fooled everyone.'

'I suppose he did,' he agrees.

'You don't sound so sure.'

He sighs. 'We know he fooled those at the aerodrome - then again, Nicholson is hardly the most insightful of men. But that was because of his papers from the Ministry.'

'So?'

'So who gave him those papers?' He turns, looking directly in her eyes, scrutinising her for a reaction.

'What?'

'What if Mossop had friends in the Ministry. Colleagues. Supporters.'

'A conspiracy?' she asks.

'What if the spying went up as well as down? SIS are looking for his cell, assuming they're all men like him. But what if it goes higher?'

'You're suggesting there's someone at the Ministry heading this cell?'

'Maybe. Not necessarily heading the cell, but someone well placed to help others. I mean, why did it take so long for us to learn about Claverley? Nicholson informed the Ministry weeks ago that he was missing, possibly dead.'

He watches her face, her eyes, detecting a sudden reticence, like the shapes moving behind the frosted glass screen of the snug. She sips her drink. 'Not everything adds up to a conspiracy. There's a war on. People die. People go missing like this every day. Why would anyone make a link to your investigation? You were looking for Bella, a dead woman. Your

Claverley search was off the records. Unofficial.' She tightens her lips, conclusion reached. 'Claverley is just another missing person. Killed or missing in action. It was your visit to this ex-wife that provided you with a link. By that time Claverley was old news. Long gone, presumed KIA. Why would anyone beyond SIS make the connection? It is the *Secret* Intelligence Service.' She takes another drink, placing her glass on the table. 'To be honest, I think you're getting a little carried away. You need to let go. Take your mind off the case for a while.'

'Maybe.' He ponders the point. 'You're not the first to tell me that.'

'Rachel?'

'Rachel.'

She takes another cigarette from the pack on the table, lights it. Through the cloud of smoke, she's aware of Porter staring at the pack. She nudges it towards him. He thinks for a moment, hesitating, then takes one, holding it in his hand, reaching across for her lighter.

She moves fast, grasping his hand, drawing him close. Removing the cigarette from his hand, she slides it gently between his lips. Placing her hand around the back of his head, holding him steady, she draws him in, lighting his cigarette from her own held in her lips. He inhales, gazing into her eyes as the cigarette catches flame. She loosens her grip, allowing him to sit back, smoke drifting between them. Her hand stays where it is, soft on the back of his neck. 'See? I knew you could be tempted,' she smiles.

JUNE 4TH, 1943: EARLY MORNING

He closes the bedroom door as quietly as he can, allowing his eyes to focus on the room. Allowing him to separate shadows from solid, bed from floor, Rachel from eiderdown. With studied deliberation, he slips out of his trousers and shirt having already discarded his shoes at the foot of the stairs. Easing back the sheets, he slides into bed, lies silent, still. Rachel stirs, altering her position, her breathing shallow. He lies expectant, waiting for her to wake.

He finds it hard to settle. His mind racing. Floode. All he can see is Floode. The car, the sheltered lay-by. Her hands, cool, healing where they clutched at his back. Fingernails digging deep. Her breath, hot. Her words, insistent.

How could he lie here next to Rachel now?

He stares at a ceiling etched with the grey of the coming dawn, pushing his mind to deal with what he'd done. The lies he'd told.

The meeting with Harold Heskey had proven brief and frustrating. 'H', as he liked to be known, had worked with Claverley for six months, living with him for the same period. He had nothing to add to their sum of knowledge of the man. By his own admission, Heskey was a workaholic, but he'd told them that even he couldn't keep pace with Claverley - *a man possessed*. Always working, shift after shift. Even when back at their billet, Claverley would spend most of the time sitting in his room, working at the small gate-leg table he'd found in a second-hand furniture shop in nearby Erdington.

Porter had asked to see the room. Another contractor was in there now, Claverley's replacement at the base - *an altogether more sociable chap*. Floode asked what had happened to Claverley's belongings - his clothes, his personal possessions. Porter was more interested in the whereabouts of any papers or notebooks he might have been working on during those spells in his room. 'H' had shown them to a cupboard under the stairs from which he'd retrieved a pre-war suitcase. It was dark brown leather. Two broad straps, battered around the edges, with a trim of lighter leather piping around its rim. Floode had opened it; shirts, underwear, a few pairs of socks. No letters, no photographs. Nothing of Claverley, because there was no Claverley.

Floode had spoken with H, led him aside. Like Nicholson, he was taken with her. Like the men in the pub he'd been flattered at the attention she gave him. Porter had scanned the contents of the case, overhearing H chattering away in the kitchen, '*Some chaps from the Ministry came up a few days after he went missing. They went through his stuff. Can't say as they found anything or not. Not my business. They put everything from his room in that case. They told us to hang on to it in case he turned up. If he did, I was to let them know straight away. Same for any letters or phone calls.*'

'Did you see their papers, their identification?' Porter had asked over his shoulder.

'Well, not as such. They said they were from the Ministry of Defence. Needed to check his room, see if there was anything might explain what had happened to him.'

'So, you didn't actually see any proof of who they were?' Porter had clarified.

'Well, no,' Heskey had faltered, sensing some veiled accusation. 'But they said who they were. Why would they lie? How would they know so much about him?'

Floode made suitably reassuring murmurs. Heskey offered tea. Something stronger.

Porter had shut the lid of the case.

On impulse, he'd run his hands along the side. In Catalonia, when a man wanted to keep things to himself - private things, treasured things - they'd learned to use the piping to gain access to the lining. Solomon had told them that Claverley had contacts in Catalonia. Maybe he knew too. Porter had carefully examined the piping of the case. Almost at once he'd found a thread of a different colour and width, hard to notice unless you were looking for it. He'd tugged, and it had come away in his hand.

He'd pulled the outer covering back, slipping the tips of his fingers inside to feel under the skin of the backing. There had been something there. Thin. *A sheet of paper*? *Too thick*. Card? *Glossy*. A photograph. He'd slid it out from its hiding place.

He'd held it up. It was out of focus, somewhat blurred, but he recognised the woman straight away - Una Mossop, smiling. The light coming from the top of the image was bright. A warm day. Trees in leaf. A riverbank. A time before the war. An eternity ago.

He'd slipped his fingers back under, retrieving another glossy sheet. A second picture, a group of men. Three of them, unsmiling, straight-faced. Civilian clothes, well dressed. They stood outside a tent. To the fore sat a woman. He looked closer, focusing on her face, her eyes. They were shadowed, dark hollows. He'd moved the image further away, the better to look at the whole figure. She was small, petite, a half-smile frozen across her face, an expression suggesting she was self-conscious of her smile. She wore a taffeta scarf. A scarf like the one on the skeleton he'd helped pull from the wych-elm.

He'd stared at the photograph. Bella.

19

Porter stands poised in the doorway. Can't resist the urge to turn round, the compulsion to check his surroundings for anything unusual, anyone out of the ordinary. Misplaced.

Christ, was he going crazy? Paranoia, that's what his doctors called it. After the bombing in the orange grove, he'd been taken to Barcelona for treatment. Despite the issues with his spine, the embedded shrapnel threatening his mobility, the doctors there had been pleased with his progress. His physical wounds were healing, soon it was only the sudden movement, the unexpected sharp twist or turn catching him off guard with a jolt of pain. But the mind? Different story. *Emotional wounds*, they'd told him, *psychological scars, scars that would take longer to heal - months, years, maybe never fully restored*. They'd learnt from *the Great War*. *Shell-shock*. The mind's response to trauma. Emotional collapse. Hallucinations. Flashbacks. Fears. Paranoia. The sense there was an evil out to get him. *Was that what this was?* This hollow fear he felt. Stomach churning over, metallic taste in his mouth, bile rising. The shaking. The palpitations. *Paranoia: suspicion, mistrust, fear. The sense that people are conspiring against you.*

232

He clutches at his jacket, feels the photograph in the inside pocket, lets his hand run down its edge. Real. The photograph was real. Claverley was real. A fiction captured in the frame. He stood with Bella and another. From Una Mossop's description it was possible he might might be her mysterious Dutchman. Another man, quite possibly, Johannes Dronkers, made up the group It was no fantasy. No paranoia.

He turns, entering the portico of the University and makes his way along the main corridor, footsteps echoing off the tiles. He pauses, placing a note in one of the pigeon-holes for lecturers' post before making his way to the stone staircase he knows leads to the lecture rooms. At the top of the stairs, he stops, looking out over the gallery rails to the hallway and the main doors beyond.

The question was *why hadn't he told Floode?*

He turns it over in his mind whilst moving to stand out of sight, framed in the doorway to the lecture theatre. *Was it because of what happened between them*? The guilt, the betrayal of Rachel? Had it frozen him, fixed him? The sense of inadequacy - of having been tested and found wanting. Coming up short where he ought to be at his strongest. Feelings he knew only too well. Feelings now simply old friends, a familiar part of himself.

Then what?

Did he mistrust her? She'd done nothing to deserve that. She'd ploughed energetically through the papers at Compton Verney, enthusiastic about his commitment. Again and again she'd acknowledged the justice he sought. She'd pursued the questioning of Nicholson and Heskey with determination. And she knew things about him, secret things that meant he needed to trust her.

So why hadn't he told her?

Shame.

She was SIS. One of them. Part of... *what? What was it he couldn't see?* What was it he felt was out there just beyond his reach? Lying next to Rachel, unable to sleep, he'd gone over everything. The subtle impediments set in the path of the investigation.

Why would that be?

Paranoia?

Lying next to Rachel he'd realised to his own eternal discredit that it wasn't shame, but selfishness that drove him. He wanted to pursue this enquiry to its end. To not have it taken away, given to those higher in the chain of command if it showed signs of actually going somewhere. He had no appetite for James, Williams, or anyone else muscling him out. Floode worked for Solomon. She was obliged to tell him of the discovery of any evidence linking Claverley to Bella. Should it be found, SIS would take over the search for those responsible for her murder. Not to provide justice for her killers, but to catch them for their own ends. *Spies. Official Secrets.* It would take precedence over murder. Solomon had told them that.

Williams and James would go along with it. He could not.

He checks his watch. Webster was a creature of habit. On cue, the professor of forensics arrives in the university hallway. Having checked his pigeonhole, he begins making his way to a ground-floor office, flicking through the items he'd collected whilst he walks. He pauses at a folded piece of paper, Porter's note, and reads it. He stops dead, looking around. After a moment, he folds the note before placing it in his jacket pocket and continuing to his office.

Porter continues watching. A man in a military style raincoat appears in the main doorway. Once Webster is in his office the man turns back and walks outside.

Porter waited.

Five minutes after entering his office, Webster emerges and makes his way to the staircase, eyes occupied in watching the main doors of the building. As he reaches the gallery, Porter steps out from the shadows of the lecture theatre doorway. Despite the note, Webster is shocked. 'Porter, what on earth-'

'Wait,' Porter interrupts. He holds up a restraining hand,

indicating for Webster to follow him into the nearby lecture theatre. Entering, Porter checks the room, the raked seating, the raised lectern, before sitting on one of the tiered student benches. He stares at Webster who hesitates before following suit. The two sit side by side. Porter leans forward, removing the envelope containing the photograph from his pocket.

'Alec,' Webster begins. 'What on earth is going on? What are you playing at? All this cloak and dagger stuff. Secret messages to *go to your room and wait five minutes before coming to meet* you. What are you doing?'

'Precautions.'

'Precautions? Precautions about what?'

'You're being watched.'

'What?'

'You're being watched. I saw him. Man in a raincoat. He's outside, no doubt waiting somewhere he can observe the entrance without drawing too much attention to himself. Probably one of the benches.'

'I – are you certain? Why?'

'I'm guessing the same reason I've got Floode as my driver rather than Willetts. To keep tabs on what we're doing.'

'Solomon?'

'Solomon. His superiors. Makes little difference. SIS.'

'But why?'

'This.' Porter hands Webster the photograph.

Webster looks at it, then back to Porter. 'I don't understand.'

Porter leans across, pointing to the figures in the picture. 'James Mossop - Claverley - the man next to him is a fit for the man Una Mossop saw. The other figure I don't know. The woman is Bella.'

Webster takes out his monocle, placing it in position. 'Bella? Are you sure?'

'You were the one who gave us the description as to what she would have looked like.'

Webster looks at the photograph. 'Good God!'

Porter nods. Relieved he wasn't seeing things.

'Where did you get this?' Webster asks.

'Claverley's suitcase. His billet near Castle Bromwich. Hidden in the lining, like we were taught in Catalonia.'

'So, Floode has seen it.'

Porter slowly shakes his head.

'But…why not?'

'She was busy when I found it. And then…I just thought it prudent not to.'

'*Prudent*?' Webster asks, eyebrow arching, monocle loosening in the socket.

'She'll tell Solomon. Chain of command. I'd be off the case.'

Webster removes the monocle. 'But isn't that natural? You know, in the order of things. The circumstance. I thought the whole idea was for it to be a joint investigation, a sharing of resources and skills. They're looking for a spy and you a killer. If this is what you claim it to be, then…' He lowers his voice, softening the tone. 'Look, Porter, I don't want to offend you, but isn't it only to be expected that they'd want a more senior officer, someone more experienced in charge?'

'Yes, you're right. It would be a logical action.'

'Then, I don't understand. Why haven't you given it to them? You'd still surely be kept on the case in some role.'

'I doubt it.'

'Vanity?'

'No. No, it's not that.' He pauses, looks Webster directly in the eye, aware of the implication of what he is about to say. 'Professor, I don't think they want us to find Claverley. I don't think they want us to find Bella's killers.'

'What? Why on earth not?'

Porter furrows his brow, lips tight. 'That's the bit I'm trying to work out. This photograph is the only tangible evidence we have of Bella's life. That she existed. That she knew Mossop. Beyond this photograph, …We have a rotting corpse and the story of a woman whose husband ran off. A woman who tells us that before he ran away, he'd taken the identity of a man working for the military. Claverley. A man who subsequently disappears. A fantasist. A man who, beyond his appearance at Castle Bromwich, seems never to have existed other than on paper.'

Webster examines the photograph, gathering a response to his friend's concerns. 'Porter, think about it. If they didn't want you to find Mossop or Claverley or whoever he's calling himself, then why would they have told you about him? Why take you to places where there were those who knew him, people who might help find him? Why have they given you access to every piece of official paperwork you asked for? Why give you Floode to help with the work? Why provide us with access to military officials who'd previously rejected all overtures for help?'

'Are they helping? I mean, just what have they given us? A cellar full of so much paper that it's probably even harder to discover what is useful or relevant - not to mention it removing me from the real investigating. We knew about Claverley from Una Mossop - they didn't bring us that. As for the access, a bunch of military types who know nothing more of Claverley than we do. Less, in fact, as they have no idea who he was or where he sprang from. And that's another matter. How did he get such documents? How did he manage to spring forth fully formed without someone higher up the chain helping him? Someone close to the top. Why's Solomon not investigating that? Why's Floode not asking those questions? She's just another of Solomon's distractions.' He stops short, stares at the floor. All he had were questions. Everything he found led to more and more questions. One had an answer he hoped Webster wouldn't ask of him. Floode.

'So, what are you proposing? You're obviously here because you want something more than a *confidante* to share your theory with.'

'You have contacts. Scientific, technical types.'

'Just what are you asking?'

Porter slides closer, sitting side by side to better indicate what he wants to show Webster in the photograph. 'Take a closer look. What do you see?'

Webster re-positions his monocle, holds the photograph closer. He examines the image. 'A woman, three men.'

'Other than that?'

'Trees.'

'Anything else?'

'A bright day. Autumn, judging by the angle of the light.'

'But not summer.'

Webster looks at the image. 'No. The leaves on the trees are too bare for that. Autumn.'

'Exactly.'

'Exactly?'

Porter takes the photograph, holding it so both can see. He points with a free finger. 'This photo was taken in the autumn. Solomon told us the German agents arrived in the early summer of forty-one so, by elimination, we know this must have been taken in Autumn of forty-one. Barbarossa was June 22nd of 1941. If, as Solomon told us, SIS believed the break-up of the group was caused by German military action fracturing the alliance with Russia, then what are they all doing camping together months later? At a time when Solomon thought Bella was dead and stuffed in the tree. That the rest had fled or were dead?'

Webster took a moment. 'As you recall, Solomon's briefing covered that very point. He speculated Claverley might have been waiting for orders. Those may have come through later. It would fit my parameters of the probability that she was killed in late forty-one. Your image would also support that timeline.'

'Four or five months? He waited from June to November or December for orders? If the organisation running Claverley were that poorly run, he'd never have obtained the quality of forged documents he uses.'

Webster shrugs. 'Possibly. Anyway, the fact that we know that later as Claverley he was still passing intelligence to Berlin tells us the whole proposition of a fall-out among agents is redundant. That Claverley didn't kill Bella because he was a loyal communist and she a fascist. It would seem to support the idea that the rest of the cell are still active. Information like this is just what Solomon is looking for. Another reason why you ought to be passing it on.'

He ignores Webster's point. He instead points at the image. 'In the background, to the left-hand side. Canvas. A tent. From what you can see of it and of the peg ropes, it's a large one. Huge.'

'So?'

'There are markings on the tent.'

Webster squints, peering more closely at the blurred shapes in the image. 'Yes. There's something there. Not sure what it is, though.'

'Possibly a manufacturer's mark. What look like numbers.'

'And that tells us?'

'It doesn't look like a regular camping tent. It could be military, industrial. You've got contacts with the boffins in the RAF. They analyse pictures of bombing raids. They plan the raids. Identify potential targets from photographs taken thousands of feet up. You once told me that as an experiment they'd enlarged crime scene photographs for you. They're experts, experienced in reading enlarged images, even if those images are blurred.' He proffers the photograph to Webster. 'These manufacturer's marks could tell us who made this tent. The manufacturers would know who they sold it to. From that, we might discover who these men are. What they and Bella were doing there.'

Webster takes the photograph, holding it thoughtfully in one hand. 'Let us be clear, Porter. I do not for one moment buy into this developing theory of yours of a conspiracy, or of your questioning the motives of Solomon and SIS. We're in a war. It messes up everyone's lives. It blurs our thinking, clouds our judgement.' He sits back, fixing Porter with a stare, a curl of the lip. 'Your…involvement with Floode is your own affair, a matter for your own conscience.' Porter opens his mouth to speak, but Webster holds up a restraining hand. 'As I say, it is none of my concern. However, I remain concerned for you, Porter. Your well-being. I'm more than concerned for the state of your mental health. Because of that, and only because of that, I'll go along with your request. See what I can do.' He flaps the photograph up and down to emphasise the point. 'But it comes with a condition. If it gets you no further in the matter, you give it up. You walk away.'

Porter stares ahead, thoughtful. Words sinking in. An imperceptible nod of the head.

Webster shakes his head. 'For my part, I'll be honest in telling you that my personal feeling is the sooner you give up on this enquiry, the quicker you'll be forced to see you've let your imagination run away with you. Get back to your senses. Get you back to thinking about your family. About Rachel. About Tommy. This whole thing's more than a little speculative, Porter. What I believe our American allies call a long shot.'

'What else have I got?' Porter responds. 'What else have we ever had?'

———

The Texan watches with a certain relish the figure in a raincoat sitting on the bench close to the entrance of the University. There's no doubt as to who he is, what he is. *Christ these Limeys are so fucking amateurish.* He can't help but wonder why Avery was so certain such a bunch of fuckups could have harboured any secret for more than a few minutes, let alone the eighteen months or more this operation necessitated them to have done.

Sitting in the seat of the car, he watches the watchers. Spying on the spies. He'd been following Porter for some time now. The supposed visit to the hospital a half-mile or so away across the campus had turned into a visit to Webster. He'd recognised the

Professor the moment he'd appeared and had instantaneously picked out his surveillance. Avery would be pleased to hear of it. If the Brits were spying on their own it indicated they had something to hide, either that or had something they themselves want answers to.

He watches Porter emerge from the university. Watches Webster's tail wrestle with recognition of the identity of the man coming from the building where his subject is, wrestle with what to do - follow Porter or stay put? There was no phone box nearby. He would have to enter the University, plead to use one of the administrator's phones, reveal whom he was, seek instructions from his superiors at SIS, lose sight of Porter.

The Texan watches Porter walk along the drive, a car driven by the older Special Constable sweeps up from where it has been parked out of sight of the building and catches up with him.

He watches Porter limp to the vehicle. Maybe not so much a limp, but a manner of walking that suggests some caution in the way he approaches each step. He knew about his action in Spain, his wounds. Spain meant the man had convictions, sympathies, ideas about the world the Texan himself finds abhorrent. He watches as he gets in the car, his back clearly a problem, a hindrance. Such knowledge is useful, filed away, at hand if needed.

He watches the car move off down the drive to disappear around a clump of oak trees. He starts his own engine, easing off the handbrake, pulling slowly away, wondering if Porter's minder, the good-looking dark-haired woman, knows of this clandestine visit. He thinks not, wondering why he's gone to such lengths to keep it so. Could it be Porter has a role beyond that of the stooge Avery thinks him to be? Might he have an agenda of his own linked into his politics, politics that had taken him to Spain where those of similar persuasion had been more than prepared to kill for such ideas.

Following the vehicle, he mentally trips a switch redefining Alec Porter as possibly hostile, a potential target.

20

Webster considered his options. He was not by nature a man prone to rush into things. He thought through options, considering every possibility and permutation prior to any certainty. Problems identified. Difficulties considered. Obstacles isolated and contained.

This was strange territory for him. The man of certainty reduced to the apprehensive.

Porter's request disturbed that balance. He knew he ought to have rejected any demand to make use of RAF technicians. He knew the logic: *there's a war on; time is essential; skills such as theirs are in short supply.* But he hadn't. Something in him had failed to trigger the *right* response, and to his surprise had found himself acquiescing.

He sat in his University office, dark oak panels oozing the truths of all those who'd sat there in the decades before him. The Men of Science. Men of vision. Questers of knowledge. Men of precision, veracity. Seekers of truth. Looking up, he takes in the portraits, the ochre tinted faces gazing down, demeanours patinated with age. Bright eyed men fixed in portraits befitting their status, libraries of books or scientific apparatus framed alongside them.

These were men pushing at the old certainties of their time, resisting the naysayers. Men who had strived, sacrificed, and finally proved their beliefs, vindicating their stubborn natures. Visionaries once labelled fools, some even as mad men and heretics.

He was obliged - directed - to report Porter's request. It was the right thing to do. It would have meant handing over the photograph to SIS, but that too would have been the right thing to do.

But he hadn't.

Now he faced a dilemma. The boffins had done their work, performed their magic. On his desk lay blow-ups of the original image Porter had given him. Eight by six glossies, each a more detailed image of the one preceding it. A section of canvas. A set of stencilled letters and numbers. A manufacturer's code. The tentmaker had been identified, they in turn pinpointing not only when the tent had been made but who it had been sold to.

Barrett Brothers of Feckenham had made the tent in 1938. It was a specialist tent, made to order, one of three made that winter for a circus wintering in the area. A circus for whom they had provided tents going back beyond *the Great War*. A circus every year wintering close to Hagley and the woods.

He picks up the final image, the sharpest, weighing its truth. Evidence. Forensic evidence. All that he preached. All that he worked towards. What would Porter do with such a truth? Could it finally give him his answers, persuade him to stop? Would he share these findings with Solomon and SIS? He doubted it. It was where they differed. Webster sought facts, evidence, the indisputable fragments of events that when pieced together gave a whole. For him, evidence was an end in itself. But Porter sought the great intangibles: *guilt, innocence, justice*. Were there such things? Were there those of whom it could be said they were truly innocent, truly guilty? He found many truths, running them down under a microscope or inside a test tube. Truths that were measurable. Truths that were fixed. Certain. Porter's truths were always just out of reach - blurred, hazy, and ungraspable.

He picks up a pen, unscrewing the top and pulling a notepad closer.

He'd made his decision. Porter would have what he wanted, one more path to rush headlong down. But in doing so, he had to protect him, protect his own work, the work he so passionately believes in: the future of criminal investigation. Whatever Porter's paranoia, someone had to be trusted.

He begins writing. It is the letter forming in his mind since the moment the photographs had arrived from Malvern. No matter what Porter might believe, Floode had to know what was happening. She was the only one he knew of in a position to protect Porter. Protect it all. Porter, Webster, the work.

She was SIS, an educated woman. A blue-stocking. What would her motive be in all this if not to discover the truth? She had to be trusted.

JUNE 10TH, 1943: EVENING

Porter turns the door-handle, closes the door, takes off his hat and coat. It was hot. All day the sun had been high in a sky with precious little covering cloud. He notices the dark line of sweat round the inside brim of his hat. He grimaces, wiping it with his handkerchief before placing it on the coat stand in the hall. 'Rachel!' he calls.

'We're in the parlour,' she calls back.

He wrinkles his face in surprise. The front parlour is only used for special occasions or visitors. Opening the door, he walks in. 'We? The parlour? Have we guests-'. He stops mid-sentence. Andrea Floode sits in one of the armchairs, cup and saucer in her hand. She is smiling. Opposite sits a stern-faced Rachel, Tommy playing at her feet.

'Alec,' Floode says in greeting. 'You didn't tell me what a delightful home you have. You and Rachel.'

'I…No… Haven't I?'

'No, you haven't. Rachel and I were just saying; you're like so many men, taking everything for granted. Never taking the time to appreciate what you have. You really do need to think about how wonderful all this is. How lucky you are.'

He stands, transfixed. After a moment he realises a reply is required. 'No. I mean, yes. Yes, I do.'

Rachel rises, leaning closer to him. He kisses her proffered cheek. 'You should have told me Andrea was coming round to drop off papers for you. I would have been a little more prepared. Could have baked.' Her voice is light, but her eyes bore into him.

'I didn't want to cause any trouble for you. This is lovely. Very homely,' Floode interjects before he can speak. 'Alec was unaware I'd be dropping by, weren't you, Alec?'

Rachel walks past him. 'I'll fetch you a cup, freshen the pot,' she says reaching for the China teapot on the silver tray. The best tea service.

'I'm fine,' Floode states. 'This is lovely. I'll be off in a few minutes. Leave you both to your evening.' She reaches into her bag, 'Just these papers you need to have a look at. Urgent.'

Rachel fixes her lips into a smile. 'I'll just get one for Alec, then.' She glares at Porter and leaves the room.

Porter moves rapidly, crossing the distance between them to confront Floode. He stands over her as she places her cup and saucer on the side table. 'What the-' he begins.

'Hush,' she says, standing and putting a hand to his mouth, fingers resting warm on his lips. She inclines her head towards Tommy, 'Your boy.'

Porter considers Tommy who remains playing with his wooden car. He lowers his voice, but the tone remains hard. 'What are you doing, why have you come here?'

'To see.'

'See?'

'I'm curious.'

'Curious?'

'I wanted to discover a little more about you, Alec. See what it is makes you tick.'

'Tick?'

'What it is that's driving you. Some in Whitehall have their doubts about you, you see. Your motives. Your loyalties. They sent me to see what it is you hold most precious.' She picks up a photograph of Rachel and Tommy from the sideboard, holding it for a moment. 'What you're prepared to risk. How far you'll go. How far you can be relied on.'

Porter takes the frame from her, placing it back on the sideboard. 'This isn't some game.'

'No. No it isn't. It's no game at all. It's real. Very real. People get hurt. Badly.'

'Are you threatening me?'

'Why would I do that?'

He stares at her, mind racing over ideas half-formed. 'What do you want?'

'The truth.' Her voice is flat. Monotone.

'The truth?'

'The truth. I want you to tell me the truth, Alec. About everything, all of the time; the truth. No secrets. None.'

He frowns. 'I don't understand.'

'Oh, come on, Alec! The photograph.'

'How do-?' he halts, letting it go. He exhales. 'I wasn't sure what it was. I wanted to be certain.'

This time it's Floode's turn to shake her head. 'That's a pretty poor lie, Alec. I hope for your sake your Rachel finds you a more convincing liar than I do.'

He flares, teeth gritted. 'Leave her out of this!'

'You were the one brought her in.' She smiles, leaning close, her lips almost brushing his as she speaks. 'Secrets have a habit of getting out. I'd hate to see Rachel hurt, or your boy.'

'He's not my boy!'

Rachel enters the room, halting in the doorway. Floode steps back, her face its mask.

Porter turns to Rachel. 'Rachel. I...'

Rachel gathers her composure. 'Your tea,' she says, indicating the pot in her hand. She places it on the tray along with the fresh cup and saucer she's brought from the kitchen. She bends over, beginning to pour. 'Better drink it whilst it's hot.' She stands, eyes full.

He stands helpless in his awkwardness.

Brushing past him, Rachel thrusts a beckoning arm in the direction of Tommy who is still playing on the carpet, 'Tommy, come on. We'd better leave Alec and Andrea to their business.'

'Rachel. I...'

She scoops the young child in her arms. He submits, holds a toy close to his chest and studies it intently. She rocks him reassuringly. 'Tea will be ready in about half-an-hour,' she states as she leaves room.

Porter stands staring at the closed door.

'Maybe now you'll understand,' Floode remarks as if a demonstration had been concluded.

He turns to her. 'I'll never understand people like you!' he spits.

'I think you need to take a much closer look at yourself, Alec. This is your doing. All of it. I told you there were prices to be paid.'

'Rachel's done nothing wrong.'

'I know.'

'Then what purpose is there in any of this?'

'See it as a reminder. We have an agreement, one you need to stick to. If you don't, then you have to be shown there are consequences. The Official Secrets Act for one. There would be investigations. Not just you. Webster and Willetts, maybe even Rachel - you know a little espionage pillow talk. Trials can be so... messy.'

'What do I get from this reminder?'

'You get to keep your life. Rachel, Tommy, whatever it is you want it to be.'

He stares at the floor. 'And the investigation?'

'You get to see that through.'

He looks up. 'But on your terms.'

She sighs. 'Alec, my love. It's always been like that. But we want to find these people as much as you do. Maybe more.'

'I find that hard to believe.'

'Why is that?'

'I don't see you or Solomon as crusaders for the truth.'

'Is that how you see yourself? A crusader?'

'I'm not sure how I see myself.'

She smiles. 'Has it not occurred to you that there's a higher calling at the moment. The war. Maybe the rest of us consider that a threat to the nation requiring a little more of our energies than a quest for gypsy justice. That it's a threat deserving a little more of the zeal you have so much of for your Bella. People are dying, Alec. Thousands of them, day after day.' She sighs. 'In the circumstance, don't you feel it's somewhat, oh, I don't know… self-indulgent, this crusade of yours?'

She stands by the fireplace, tweaking the ornaments lined across the mantelpiece. 'After all, there's still the very real possibility she may turn out to be nothing more than a dead gypsy. Either that or some tart, a woman finding herself in the wrong place at the wrong time with the wrong man. Claverley may be nothing more than a fantasist who span a tale to delude a wife he no longer loved or cared for. Weaved a story of local legends, of gypsies and witchcraft that you're threading your own narrative around. It's coincidence, not magic. Not true.'

He looks to the floor. Wonders at the thin line between real and imagined. Life and nightmare.

She turns to him. 'The Clarabella Dronkers SIS are looking for may not be your Bella, ours might still be out there, still very much alive. She may have escaped back to Germany. All you have is a dead body. Claverley is Mossop - a fake, a fraud. You said so yourself. So did his wife. He's Walter Mitty. Delusional.'

'I'm not so sure of that,' he still finds himself saying.

She ceases moving the ornament. 'What would you say if I told you there was proof.'

'Proof?'

'That your James Mossop or Claverley is delusional.'

'What proof?'

She reaches into her shoulder bag, removing an envelope. She holds it out to him. 'It's why I'm here.' She hands him the envelope. 'We've found him.'

He takes the envelope, withdrawing a single sheet of paper. 'What?'

'Claverley. We've found him. In Yorkshire.'

'Yorkshire?'

'Harrogate to be precise.'

He scans the letter. 'When?'

'He's been there for weeks. We learned of his whereabouts a day or so ago. Solomon's been checking the details. It's him.'

'Can I see him?'

'That's the idea'

'When can we go?'

'He'll be in Birmingham tomorrow.'

'Birmingham?'

'Yes. St. Margaret's.'

'St. Margaret's? That's a hospital. Is he injured?'

'Have you not read the letter? Look at the masthead.' He looks at the headed paper, the institution where it originated. An asylum. As he stares at it, Floode continues, 'You see, Alec, it turns out that Jack Claverley is insane. Quite mad.'

21

Foreboding. Wasn't that the word? *Premonition. A bad omen.* Gazing out of the windscreen of the Riley, Porter shudders, the hair on the back of his neck stands erect. He feels an icy chill just looking at the outline of the building they are approaching.

'Welcoming,' Floode remarks, as the car traces the slow curve of the gravel drive.

The secure unit of St. Margaret's was a recent addition from the 1930s. It appears as if tacked onto the main house with little thought given of the impact on its eighteenth century Strawberry Hill gothic design. It sits squat, ugly, topped with pointless crenelations. A central buttress thrusts unappealingly from the rest of the frontage. The whole amounts to two storeys of dull grey stone blemished with dark blotches where the ash from surrounding chimneys and smokestacks has been rain-washed into it.

'A children's nightmare,' Floode observes, stopping the car close to the main building. 'Ironic,' she says, switching off the engine. 'After the family sold it to the parish council it was used as a children's home.' Leaning forward, she cranes her neck to

250

take in the full frontage of the house. 'Imagine being sent here. The nightmares you'd have.'

Porter, opening his door, gets out. It was close to lunchtime and staff - the crisp white tunics of orderlies, the blue and white uniform of nurses - criss-crosses the grassed area that separates the old hall from a cluster of newer buildings. He turns to find Floode standing on the other side of the car, arms folded on its roof, watching him. 'Penny for them,' she offers, smiling.

Porter shakes his head. 'You really wouldn't want to know.'

'We have an agreement. Remember? All of it. All of the truth, all of the time,' she says, maintaining her smile. Since the visit to his home and her meeting with Rachel, she'd reverted to her previous persona. It was as if what had passed between them there was trifling, inconsequential. Something so mundane it could be repeated at will with no thought to its consequences.

'Barcelona. The hospital in the small enclave on the outskirts. The beach. The sound of the sea,' he states for the record.

'This reminds you of there?' she asks incredulously.

He shrugs. 'I'm crazy, damaged goods, remember?'

This time it is her turn to shake her head. She turns, waiting for him to make his way around the car, before they walk to the main entrance where she presents her SIS identification. A few moments later a nurse appears and escorts them through the wards.

The place was a maze of corridors, some bright but most dark and foreboding. They linked the series of extensions added to the building over the two hundred years of its existence. They emerge into a large glass conservatory, at the end of which an imposing staircase - oak, wide and curving - leads them to the first floor office of Doctor Woodbridge.

Woodbridge is tall and thin, spindly arms and legs like an insect. He sits behind a desk, his movements sharp and jerky as if conducting an orchestra who can only play staccato. Next to him sits a man he introduces as Doctor Morgan. Morgan is shorter, an older man, white haired, with a bushy moustache that caps his top lip like a ledge of snow. His eyes are large, round and to Porter's mind somewhat out of place on a face that is otherwise high cheek-boned, aristocratic. Both men wear white medical coats; pockets adorned with identification tags. The unit is, after all, a secure one.

The introductions dealt with, they sit. Floode immediately pressing for details of the man thought to be Claverley.

The younger doctor opens a file but makes little reference to it. Like his lab coat and stethoscope, Porter felt it served more as reminder of Woodbridge's position rather than being of any practical use in what he has to say. 'Interesting. Most interesting,' he begins, adjusting spectacles more securely on the bridge of his nose. 'He arrived at Harrogate some weeks ago. No recollection as to his name, family, or anything. My colleagues there tell me they tried to identify him, but to no avail. He was initially diagnosed as a victim of trauma - more than likely a bombing raid so they thought. We've seen many like him.' He directs his comments to Floode, a man explaining the intricacies of a matter he feels a woman might not comprehend. 'Men coming home, finding their family wiped out. They can't handle it. They disappear. Neighbours sometimes returning to their properties when it's safe have no idea what's happened to those around them. Most simply think they were killed in the blast or that the survivors have been relocated.' He shrugs. 'The war,' he offers in summary.

Floode nods. *The war*.

'Whatever, in a stroke of good fortune, it seems one of their staff was back here visiting family and he meets up with an old friend - a school pal who's serving as a Special in Birmingham. He meets him at one of the police stations, and he sees the poster on the wall, the flyer sent out with the photo on it. He immediately recognises the man as a patient at Harrogate. But by then this patient is calling himself Mossop. Says it's the one thing he's sure of. To cut a long story short, the orderly tells his policeman friend of his suspicion, they tell us, and the rest you know.'

Floode turns to Porter. 'It explains why we couldn't find him. No conspiracy, Alec. He was just too far outside the areas we distributed the flyers to. And the confusion of identity is why they couldn't find him against the missing persons list.'

Woodbridge nods, acknowledging those facts. 'It would appear so.'

'So how is he?' she asks.

Woodbridge glances to his colleague before proceeding. 'Physically? He's well. No obvious injuries - which is why the air-raid explanation was always a little...tenuous.'

'And mentally?' she pursues.

'Mentally? There's no apparent physical damage to the brain. No head wounds or physical trauma. Yet he has no memory beyond his name. Nothing as to family, and little if any of his life prior to his admission. He says he isn't married - at least has no recollection of being married. The admissions form didn't list a wedding ring among his possessions.'

'What does he remember?' Porter asks.

'He says that he thinks he was an officer in the army. He wasn't wearing a uniform when admitted, so there were no badges. None of the local bases listed anyone missing. If he is a serving officer, we have no idea where or with which regiment. Beyond that... very little. I myself have had only the briefest of examinations, but from Harrogate's assessment I fear you may have made a wasted journey. Whatever it is you need to ask him about is now more than likely lost, buried somewhere deep in the depths of his mind.'

'But you say there's no physical injury or damage?' Porter clarifies.

Woodbridge taps the file. 'None.'

'So how?' Floode asks.

'You mean why has he lost the ability to recall the events of his life?'

She nods.

Woodbridge settles into his chair, an act delaying any response sufficient for him to assemble lay answers to complex medical questions. 'There can be a number of reasons. It could be a blow to the head, such as in a fall. Something physical but healing quickly and so leaving no sign of the injury.' The doctor shrugs, 'But I very much doubt it. Usually it's a psychological event, an emotional trauma. An experience so devastating that the patient represses it. Hides it away. Doing so necessitates them having to bury the rest of their life up to that point along with it. To recall one past event might trigger the patient into recalling the traumatic event itself.' He taps the side of his head. His temple. 'Everything is linked, you see. You have to repress it all.'

'Is this permanent?' she asks.

He wrestles with an answer. 'As its not physical in origin, the strict answer must be no. But, as to if or when...'

'There's no prognosis beyond each day,' Porter says out loud.

Woodbridge turns to face him. 'Exactly so.' Woodbridge and Morgan fix Porter with appraising looks. 'I gather that you know something of trauma, Detective?' the elder man asks.

'Something,' Porter concedes.

'Detective Porter saw action in Spain,' Floode explains.

Morgan sits forward, 'Ah. You saw others in such states.'

Porter nods imperceptibly. 'Something like that.'

Woodbridge shakes his head, 'Dreadful, the impact of violent action on men. I'd read about it before the war. but seeing it in the flesh... The reality of it is almost beyond comprehension.'

The elder doctor shakes his own head disdainfully. 'We saw it during *the Great War*, you know. I served as a medical officer in the trenches. We had a name for it - *lacking moral fibre*'.

Woodbridge breaks across his intervention. 'Doctor Morgan is, of course, correct. In those early days we knew little of such things. It was seen mainly in the infantry, young men locked in a time of great emotional shock. Something so dreadful that it created a complete blanking of the human mind. It's an illness, a condition barely understood. Nowadays we are a little more… compassionate in our treatment of such a condition.'

'Dreadful,' Porter half-whispers.

'It can change a man forever,' Woodbridge summarises.

'Yes, it can,' Porter whispers.

Woodbridge nods. 'Like this man you call Claverley. A mind in turmoil.'

'What does he talk of?' Floode asks.

Removing his spectacles, Woodbridge begins polishing the lenses on his lab coat. 'Fear. Horror. Blood.'

'Ravings?'

Woodbridge snorts. 'Well, to the layman, possibly.' He holds up the spectacles, examining the sheen of each lens. 'But he's lucid. As if he's…fighting against whatever it is he's repressed. Like he's in battle with it. He keeps talking of entombment. Talks about being trapped. Imprisoned. Apart from that, most of the time he sits and draws. We've had him here less than twenty-four hours, but I see a most fascinating patient. Of course, we'll do everything we can in finding a way through. Try to lead him out of whatever hell he's trapped himself in.'

'So we can see him? Speak to him?' Porter asks.

Woodbridge exchanges looks with his colleague. The elder man shrugs. Woodbridge, nodding, turns to Floode. 'I don't see any reason why not. But I must insist you are circumspect in your questioning. His mind is delicate. He can be lucid, rational even, but deep down he remains vulnerable. I won't risk triggering a memory that might damage his mind more than it already is. Repression, psychosis, is a delicate state. Wherever his mind is, for the moment it is at least in some sort of balance. I won't risk that being disrupted by insensitive questioning.'

Floode rises to her feet. 'I appreciate what you're saying. This man may turn out to be nothing other than a traumatised civilian. But we suspect that not only is he a murderer, but that he may be a traitor, an agent embedded in a spy ring sabotaging the war effort. We may not have time for the…niceties you require. We have to be certain he isn't faking illness in order to conceal himself from the authorities. If he genuinely suffers with this trauma, we have to push him to remember what he's done. We have to know precisely what he's been involved in if we are to have any chance of minimising the damage he has inflicted to this nation's security. I hope we're clear on this.'

This time there is no consultation with his fellow doctor before Woodbridge replies. 'I would stake my reputation that this man is no fake.' He turns to Porter. 'Detective, you need to be aware of precisely just what it is you're dealing with. The memories of men suffering this sort of trauma are not like yours or mine. They are frozen and mute. They have neither narrative nor verbal context. They are automatic, triggered and disconnected from ordinary life. They are coded in emotions and vivid images. In such cases, portions of traumatic experience are stored as isolated fragments. The intense emotional arousal at the time of an event, the trauma, disrupts the normal process of the storage of information and memory. It leaves only fragments of the traumatic memory, fragments that are not integrated with other memories.' He fixes Porter with a hard stare, a man intent on making his point. 'It's like… a shattered piece of glass. Everything is disjointed, separated. The isolated images may be intense - as we might recall a nightmare once we've woken. But just as then, though we cannot recall the narrative, the images can be fierce, dreadful. We call this *the dissociative process*. It protects the sufferer from the intense pain of the experience they went through. You need to understand that this is a man in trauma. Severe psychosis. He is somewhere deep in a world he's created to protect himself.'

Porter remains seated. 'The man we're looking for calls himself Claverley, but we believe he's also this man Mossop. Jack Mossop is a known fantasiser. A man who throughout his life appears to have created for himself personas of importance. That he's been playing these out in his assumed identity of

Claverley. Being a spy gave him the life he fantasised of having. Would that be a factor in his condition? Will he present as Claverley or Mossop?'

'An interesting idea,' Woodbridge replies. The two medical men share a moment of thought. It is Woodbridge who speaks. 'If what you say is the case, that he's this fantasist, Mossop, then it's possible that through the trauma he might now be both with each persona completely unaware of the other. In short, if he responds as Mossop he will be being completely honest if he tells you he has no idea who Claverley is.'

'So you're saying he can be either man, at any time?' Floode asks.

'Well, in a crude way, yes,' Woodbridge reluctantly agrees. 'He may be locked in as Claverley or have reverted to his birth identity of this Mossop.'

'And is each unaware of the other?'

The doctors exchange glances. 'Hard to tell. But yes, that could be the case,' Woodbridge responds.

'Is that possible? Two men inhabiting one body, one mind?' she asks.

'One body, yes, but one mind, no. In such cases the mind - if you will - separates. Two completely different individuals. Multiple personality disorder is the term we use. If that is the case, then it's a most fascinating one. Remarkable. The sort of thing one reads about but rarely gets to see.'

'And their memories?' she presses again.

Woodbridge inclines his head, lips pursed. It is Morgan who speaks. 'Those may well be shared. At least some of them. Childhood, possibly. But Claverley's life, Claverley's memories would be unknown to Mossop. They're attached to his trauma. He'd have to bury those along with the event lest they trigger a recall of what had happened. What he'd done. If he killed or betrayed as Claverley he'd have to wipe everything to do with that life. That existence. Mossop's memory of the time he was Claverley would be blank. Nothing. As if he was sleeping.'

'So let me be clear. You're telling us that it's possible to talk to Mossop and he would have nothing to tell us of his life as Claverley,' she asks the younger doctor.

Woodbridge murmurs agreement. 'Absolutely. It would be like asking me what I knew of another man's life, another man's secrets.'

'So it's Claverley we need,' Andrea states in the manner of a summary.

'Yes.'

'And it's Claverley's trauma that is the reason for the separation.'

'It would seem so. More likely that Claverley's actions caused Mossop to reject him,' Woodbridge answers, finessing his diagnosis.

'In that case, we need to see him right away. We have to know whatever it is that's locked in that man's head.'

JUNE 11TH, 1943: EARLY AFTERNOON

The room was bare, stripped of anything that might give it definition or a sense of difference from the other boxes in the institution; painted walls, a dull livid colour suggesting illness, morbidity. A wooden table fixed in the centre of the space what Porter in fact estimates to be the very mathematical if not geographical centre. Either side are chairs. A single chair on one side and three on the other. The single chair is secured to the floor by bolted metal plates. Natural light comes from a window high on the farthest wall from the door, at the point where wall meets ceiling. The window is barred on the outside.

The man who sits at the table is hunched over, intent on an activity only becoming clear as Porter, Floode, Morgan, and Woodbridge draw nearer to the table. It is a drawing, a drawing he works on with meticulous attention to detail using a set of charcoals that lie on the table next to him.

Morgan leans towards Porter. 'We encourage all our patients

to draw or to paint. There's evidence they may communicate with their trauma through the language of shapes. Of colour and sensation.'

Porter nods.

'Jack,' Woodbridge spoke quietly, approaching the table.

'Eh?' the man grunts by way of reply, not looking up from his drawing.

Woodbridge lays a hand on the man's back, pointing his other hand in the direction of Porter, Floode, and Morgan. 'Jack, you need to stop drawing for a moment. You know who I am don't you? And Doctor Morgan here. These others are the people I told you about. The ones who would be coming to visit you. They need to ask you a few questions.'

The man looks up. Smiling, he sets the drawing aside, laying it on the table, the image covered by the flap of the notebook that falls across it. He stands, extends a hand towards them. 'Hello,' he says. 'Pleased to meet you. My name's Jack.' The man looks to Woodbridge as if seeking confirmation that it was okay to say this. Woodbridge nods approval. 'At least, that's what they tell me. I struggle with it. They think I was injured.'

He was tall, though not sufficient to make him stand out. Maybe just under six feet Porter estimates. He is clean shaven, black hair cut short, fringe swept back in the style of Clark Gable, an effect added to by the slight moustache. The face is tapered, more oval than round, cheekbones less prominent than in the photographs. Above them, his eyes are narrow, appearing from where Porter stands as slits slashed into the face. There are dark shadows underneath, a sense of tiredness, sleepless nights - though these days it was a look common to most people you met. Work, air-raids, the worry. What sets him apart is that the eyes were dead, pupils shuttered like the lens of a camera. It is as if whatever light once burned there had been snuffed out, scorching all around it.

Porter leans forward, taking the outstretched hand. 'So glad to meet you, Jack. My name's Alec. Alec Porter. This is Miss Floode.'

Floode take his hand and shakes it.

'Alec is a police officer, Jack. He wants to talk to you about some things he thinks you can help him with,' Woodbridge enlightens.

Jack smiles, 'I hope so. My memory though.' He shakes his head, 'It's not so good. It's why I'm here. I have trouble remembering.'

Porter and Floode sit. Woodbridge takes the seat next to them, Morgan standing to the side, observing. Jack returns to scribbling in the notebook. 'Do you mind, if I doodle whilst we talk? It helps keep me calm. Helps me remember things.'

'That's fine, Jack' Woodbridge replies. 'You carry on.' Woodbridge turns to Porter and Floode, 'We find it helps relax our patients. As I've already said, sometimes the act of drawing helps bring out things from the subconscious we can talk about.'

Jack returns to the pad, hand aimlessly scratching away with a charcoal stick.

Porter clears his throat. 'It's about what happened to you, Jack,' he begins. 'Something that happened a couple of years ago. In Hagley. The woods there.'

'I'm not… I… I can't seem to remember much at all. Have I been there then?'

'We think so. It's what we need to find out. What do you remember?'

'Growing up. My mom, my dad. I can't remember any brothers or sisters, but I don't know if that's right or that I just can't recall them,' he responds, scribbling in the pad. 'A few things, like when I was at school. The rest…. Nothing.'

'Your work?'

Jack shakes his head, the charcoal moving up and down on the notebook.

'Girlfriends?'

Another shake.

'Claverley?' Floode asks.

'Claverley? Is that a place?' Jack asks.

'No. A man.'

Jack pauses. 'You think I knew him, this man, Claverley?'

'Yes.'

Jack screws his eyes in recollection, searching the pathways of his mind. The charcoal scratches once more. Finally he shakes his head. 'No. Nothing. Did I know him well? Was he a friend?'

'He worked for the military. He's missing. He looked after important contracts and details for the war effort. Secrets. That's what we believe you did,' she prompts.

Jack considers this information. 'I work for the military?' He ponders it a moment longer. 'That's important work, isn't it? Secrets? He's important, then? Claverley.'

Floode nods. 'Very. We need to find him.'

'And you think I can help?'

'Yes,' she presses.

Jack shakes his head, sighing. 'I'm sorry. There's just... nothing. A blank.' He indicates the book in which he's been scribbling. 'I try to write things down,... here, in the book. Things I might remember. I try to do it when I wake up. Things from my dreams. Drawings, too. But they could just be dreams, not real. I can't tell. I can't tell dreams from what's real. Do you understand?'

Porter nods. 'Yes, Jack. I do.'

Floode stares at Jack. Shaking her head, she turns to Porter.

Porter watches Jack scribble on the pad. He raises his voice to a more direct tone, less soft, less giving. He'd once sat in whilst Gosling had delivered to an elderly woman news of the death in an air-raid of a relative. He strove to match that tone. Sincere, concerned. Simple words that might cut through the confusion. 'Jack, this may be hard for you to take in. We don't just believe that you knew Claverley. We believe you are Claverley.' Jack stops drawing. He turns from Porter, to Floode, to the doctors, his eyes widening, face full of confusion. Porter presses forward.

261

'Jack Claverley works at Longbridge and Castle Bromwich aerodrome. He oversees the production of bombers. He knew about fighters, tanks, and munitions - all of them things that are a vital part of this country's defence. Claverley disappeared some weeks ago. He disappeared around the time you were admitted to Harrogate.'

'But… I'm Mossop. Jack Mossop.'

'Yes. Yes, we believe that's who you are,' Porter nods.

'So… I don't follow what you're saying.'

'You're Jack Mossop, but you're also Claverley.' Porter states as calmly as he can.

'I'm Mossop and Claverley?'

'Yes.' Decisive. No room for misunderstanding.

'Detective-' Woodbridge begins before Porter's raised hand halts him.

Jack stares ahead. 'I don't understand. How…?'

'Jack, that's not important at the moment. In time the doctor's here will help you answer all of those questions. For now, trust us, it is possible. It is true. You are Jack Mossop, and you are Jack Claverley. But we need to know why. We need to know why you adopted this other identity. What it was that you were doing at Longbridge and Castle Bromwich. You have secrets, Jack. Important secrets. You know names, names we need to have. Names of the people you worked for, the men you helped. We need to know where they might now be. We need to know what happened. Everything. We need to know about Hagley. The woods. We need to know about Bella.'

'Bella? Who's Bella? I don't know any Bella. I don't know any of this, any of what you're saying.' The charcoal scratches unconsciously in his hand.

'Were you spying?' Floode asks.

'What?' the charcoal jumps on the page.

'Were you spying for our enemies?'

'Spying? No!'

262

'How can you be certain? You've just told us everything's a blank,' she persists.

'Yes. I mean… I can't be. No.'

Woodbridge leans forward, 'Detective, Miss Floode, I must insist. This line of questioning is very distressing for Jack. These accusations.'

'Doctor, please, keep out of this,' Floode puts in. 'I have to insist that you either keep quiet or leave. We have to know.'

Jack looking up from the notebook, stops scribbling. 'It's not true. It can't be.' He looks to Woodbridge, then Morgan. He turns to face Porter. 'I'm Mossop. Jack Mossop.'

'But you say you can't remember anything. How do you know you're not Claverley?'

He shakes his head. 'I…'

Porter reaches inside his jacket, takes out the photograph he'd found at Castle Bromwich. He places it on the table, holding it there, pinned under spread-eagled fingers before thrusting it across to Jack. 'Look.'

Jack reaches out, takes the picture, turns it to face him. He runs a hand across the surface. He looks up. 'It's…me.'

'Yes.'

Jack pushes the photograph back towards his inquisitor. 'So you know I'm Mossop.'

'Yes.' Porter taps the image. 'But this is Claverley.'

Jack's eyes widen. He stares at the photograph.

Woodbridge sits forward, turning to Porter. 'Detective this really is too much. You're putting a great deal of pressure on this man. He's not ready.'

Jack looks up from his study of the photograph. 'Who are the rest?' he whispers. 'These others?'

'They're enemy agents. That's why we need you to remember,' Floode tells him. 'We need their names. What happened to them. What you told them.'

Jack stares at the photograph, eyes searching back and forth for clues, some detail he could latch on to. He shakes his head, pushing it further away. 'I don't know.'

'What happened at Hagley?' Porter asks.

'Hagley?'

'The woods at Hagley,' Porter pushes.

Jack shakes his head, agitated. 'I don't know.'

Suddenly Porter springs from his chair. He reaches across, grasping Jack's shoulders as Jack stares up wide-eyed with fear. 'What happened at Hagley?' Porter demands. 'Did you kill her?'

'Kill?' Jack cries out in alarm.

'Kill. Murder. Strangle. A woman. Bella. You're Jack Claverley. You killed a woman in Hagley Woods. Who was she?' Porter intensifies his grip on Mossop's shoulders, dragging him part way across the table, shaking him like a rag doll. 'Why did you kill her?'

Reacting first, Woodbridge stands, grabbing hold of Porter's arms in an attempt to break his grip on Jack. 'Detective, I must insist.'

Wracked across the table, Jack struggles, face overwhelmed by panic and fear. When he speaks it is shrill, beseeching, 'Killed who? Who do you think I killed? Why do you think that?'

'That's enough, Detective!' Woodbridge shouts, struggling for purchase on Porter's arms.

'Who was she?' Porter demands, tightening his grip. 'Who was she?'

Jack tries to turn from the eyes of the man holding him. 'I don't know! I don't know!'

'Orderlies!' Woodbridge shouts. 'Orderlies!'

Morgan and Floode, now standing beside Woodbridge, grasp at Porter's arms and shoulders, wrestling him clear of a flailing Jack who falls back into his chair, weeping. 'This interview is terminated!' Morgan declares, 'I don't care who you are or what intelligence you're after! This is stopping. Now!'

Woodbridge leaves Morgan standing in front of the now

deflated Porter and moves round the table to cradle the weeping Jack in his arms.

Floode takes hold of Porter's arm, 'Come on, Alec.' She tugs, edging him towards the door. 'We'll get nothing for now.'

Two burly orderlies appear from the corridor. At a nod from Morgan they stand in the doorway forming an escort that ensures Porter is led away.

Moving out of the room, Porter glances back at the group around the table. For the first time he catches sight of the drawing clasped tight in Jack's hand. The drawing he'd been working on throughout the interview.

Scrawled in blackest charcoal, etched hard into the paper, is a tree.

A blackened tree; a devil's tree, a wych elm.

22

Floode and Solomon sit in a room at the rear of the police station. It is late, and apart from themselves the station is empty. With rumours of a heavy raid, uniformed officers have been deployed on fire watch, most of the detectives too. It is war, and in areas like Bromsgrove and its surrounding villages crime now keeps office hours. In a time of man-power crisis, much police work is now deemed petty enough to await a more convenient time to be investigated.

The light in the room comes from a small desk lamp, its green shade casting a narrow pool of pale-yellow light. Solomon had listened intently to Floode's report. She'd begun with her visit to Porter's house and ended with the interrogation of Claverley at St Margaret's. Now he sat, arms folded, mulling over the implications. He shifts forward, resting his elbow on the desk, chin balanced on his hand. 'So the question is where this leaves us,' he says.

Having anticipated a judgment, Floode instead has to ponder a question. After a moment, she finds herself shaking her head. The only answer she has. 'I don't know.'

Solomon grimaces. 'Unfortunately, that remains a privilege we're not afforded. We have to know. We need certainty.'

She undulates her shoulders, inclines her head. Her remit was the field, operations. Analysis was Solomon's. 'Maybe he's simply a good actor, she offers. 'Surely, if anyone knows his capabilities…'

Solomon snorts, 'If he were that good we wouldn't be in this mess in the first place.' He sits forward; arms folded across his chest. 'Tell me again,' he commands.

She gathers her thoughts, retraces her previous words. 'He says he recalls nothing of any real consequence. Dim recollections of his childhood and faces he assumes were parents and wider family. He says he has no awareness of anything of the period of time we're interested in. Not a thing about Claverley or any of the things Claverley was involved in. It's a blank to him. It would appear Jack Mossop knows nothing of Claverley, of that life or of those deeds. He claims he knows nothing of his role in any of it.'

'And you believe him?'

She considers the question that has been plaguing her ever since the meeting. 'It's hard to say. If he's pretending, then he's good. I watched him very closely. Not a flicker to any of Porter's questions. He's plausible. Believable. If it is an act, it means he would know why we were there. Why I was there. Maybe he's sending a message to SIS. To you.'

Solomon accepts her response as the best he could get. Plausibility was an agent's greatest attribute. Floode had it in abundance. Mossop too. It was one of the reasons he'd risen so high as an operative. That he could now be using it to escape trial, to escape execution, was a distinct possibility. 'And the doctors?'

'They're convinced. Textbook according to the medical head of the unit, Woodbridge. I'm told he's renowned in that field. It's his research speciality.'

Solomon looks down, eventually returning his gaze to Floode. 'That concerns me,' he admits.

'How so?'

He taps his fingers on the desk. 'Textbook is too good. An act steeped in research. That was the Mossop I knew, the man I recruited. And, even if it's true - that he has lost his memory in this split personality traumatic state you've explained to me - it makes him too much of a juicy case for those quacks looking after him. They'll never leave him alone. This doctor-' he waves a hand in the air grasping for the name.

'Woodbridge,' she prompts.

'Woodbridge. What if Mossop's condition is genuine? How secure is his mind, how certain can we be of his continuing amnesia?'

Floode shrugs.

'From what you tell me,' he continues, 'this Woodbridge already seems to see it as a potential medical paper, something to make his name with. Pushing, prompting, poking around in Mossop's head.' He raps his fingers on the desk once more. 'You say it's possible for it all to come back.'

'So the doctors say,' she confirms.

He exhales loudly. 'That can't happen.' He drums his fingers ever more rapidly on the desktop. 'And this drawing you saw.'

'The tree?'

'The tree. If nothing else, it shows he has some recall, however vague at present. Some sense of the things he did as Claverley. Was Porter aware of it? Did he see it?'

She hesitates. 'I'm not certain. He could have. Must have.'

'Then why didn't he mention it?' he challenges.

She half-smiles. 'Porter has grown a little less trusting of me. Of us. The business with the photograph showed that.'

Solomon snorts, adding it as a factor to his calculation. 'No matter. At the end of it, it's irrelevant what he saw or didn't see. The purpose of the visit has been served. Porter's found his suspect. He's seen the man's a lunatic. Porter losing his temper like that, the frustration, shows how much he wants to believe Claverley as his killer. We just need to provide the final closure of this narrative. Give Porter his happy ending.'

He gazes into the distance. By nature a decision maker, he is not a man bedevilled by remorse or the fear of consequences. Situations like this required resolution. It was uncertainty, lack of clarity, that disturbed him, not his conscience. It was why he'd been given this task. His superiors, those men like Pidgeon, were uninterested in the *hows* and *whys* of it. Just *get it done. And quickly.*

'You're sure?' she asks.

He sits back, half-smiling. 'In this work, Floode, if I've learned anything at all, it's that it's just at the very moment you're sure of something that it turns around to bite you.' He tuts. 'For his own sake, your Detective Porter for once needs to accept something to be what it seems. If he continues to worry at this particular bone of his then a lot more people will suffer. A lot more. We have to end it. End it now.'

JUNE 13TH, 1943: EARLY MORNING

'What do you mean, dead?'

'As I say, he's dead,' Woodbridge's voice crackles down the line. Hollow, metallic, unable to find words that might clarify a simple statement of fact. 'Dead.' The voice repeats.

'Dead? How?'

'Suicide. Hung himself. Sometime last night. We're not sure when. He was seen on ward rounds at eleven. The body was discovered around seven this morning during the handover to day staff who were just coming on.'

'He hung himself?'

'Yes. Dreadful business.'

Porter tries processing what he's hearing. 'How is that possible?'

He hears a scrunching of paper from the other end of the line, a shuffle across the desk for some hastily noted detail. 'The bed sheets,' Woodbridge eventually responds. 'He linked them together. Formed a noose. He used the bars of the window high up on the wall.'

'I mean; how can that happen? Aren't you aware of such possibilities? Alert to them?' Porter challenges.

'Of course we are. Absolutely.' Woodbridge's voice prickles, his manner cooler. 'This is a model establishment, Detective. A model establishment. We have clear rules and practices around such things. But you have to understand that even at the best of times our resources are stretched, and these are not the best of times. Mossop was not considered at risk. There was no evidence suggesting such a possibility. Nothing.'

'So why?'

'*Why*?'

'Why would he kill himself? Why kill himself now? Why now, after everything he's been through? It makes no sense.'

'That may actually be the point, Detective. *After all he's been through*. In some cases there's a cumulative effect. It all becomes too much. Straw that breaks the camel's back so to speak.'

'So why now?'

There was a moment's silence on the line, a hesitation. 'Perhaps you ought to ask that question of yourself, Detective.'

'What do you mean?'

'To be frank, until your little outburst yesterday, Jack Mossop was fine. Settled.'

Porter grips the receiver tighter. 'You think it's my fault?'

'All I'm saying, Detective, is that until yesterday James Mossop was no more of a suicide risk than you or I. I don't see any conclusion other than that he took his own life whilst the balance of his mind was disturbed. My report to the authorities, and to your superiors, will detail my views as to why that was so. He was distressed, Detective Porter. Upset by your questioning, your insinuations... your accusations. It was too much for him to handle. It took him over the edge.'

Porter's mind raced, skimming possibilities. *Shock.* He had questions. *So many questions.* 'Did he say anything? Anything at all after we left? About Hagley, about the dead woman?'

'Detective, I really must protest! Your attitude. Your behaviour.' His tone was unmistakably terse, clipped, and direct. 'The man is dead. Whatever he might or might not have done, whatever it was you sought from him, he's taken to the grave. All I can say, if it is of any help at all, is that he was a sick man, quite sick. In such a state, men like Mossop are capable of anything. Schizoid personality disorder - dual selves. From the evidence you presented, it is likely Mossop was your Claverley. If so, it is also more than likely that he is the killer you sought. He was a haunted man, Detective. A haunted man. You saw it for yourself with our own eyes. This was a man who at some time had been involved in something so terrible that it forced his mind to shut down. Can you imagine the extent of the act this man must have committed to cause such a thing? In my opinion, Jack Mossop hanged himself because he was brought face to face with what his alter ego Claverley had done. James Mossop could not endure it. *Jekyll and Hyde*, Detective. Mossop and Claverley. Look to your fiction, your Robert Louis Stevenson. A fictional horror that in truth is not so very far removed from reality. You have your answer.'

'Wait. One last question.'

'Very well. What is it?'

'When we spoke he had a pad, a book he was drawing in.'

'To help with recall. The unconscious mind often represents deep truths or events that the conscious mind is ignorant of.'

'Yes, yes, I understand the purpose. He was drawing in it during the interview. I wondered if I could have it.'

'A souvenir?' Woodbridge couldn't keep the distaste from his voice. 'A little ghoulish and, I might add, in somewhat bad taste in the light of what's happened. Anyway, you're too late, it's been destroyed.'

'Destroyed?'

'It was found torn up in his room when we recovered the body.'

'Torn up?'

'Pretty much. It's here on my desk. What's left of it. There's just one image left, the last one he was drawing.'

'A tree.'

'That's correct. I suppose the image took hold in his mind after your interview. It was the last image he drew, the only page left whole. The tree and some word scribbled across the bottom of the page.'

'A word?'

'Yes. Just one.'

'What word?'

'Well, we think it's a word. Was he a scholar at all, do you know?'

'Not that I know of. Why?'

'Someone here thinks the word may be Latin.'

'Latin?'

'Yes. *Tarpeia.*'

'*Tarpeia?*' Porter scribbles the word in his notebook.

'Does it mean anything to you, Detective?'

'No. nothing.'

'Nor to anyone of us. One of the chaps here remembered a little of his Latin history,' Woodbridge sniggers, 'A Scholarship boy. He says it's a legend about a woman's betrayal. Just an odd thing to have written.' He pauses, his analytical mind changing gear. 'I think it's most likely that as with the drawing it's a word that for some reason had got itself stuck somewhere deep in his mind. A sound, a pattern, a rhythm. Maybe a schoolboy piece of learning, but seemingly one with no connection to anything. A leftover fragment of who he once was.'

'Whoever that was.'

'Indeed. Seemingly a murderer and a fantasist. A man clearly delusional even before he found his way to St. Margaret's. I'm afraid it will have to serve as the epitaph to this whole business. Good day, detective.'

The line went dead.

Porter sat in his chair held in the moment. He lowers the receiver into the cradle. *Was that it? Was it over?*

He sits staring at the folder that holds the details he's gleaned about Mossop and his seeming alter-ego of Claverley.

Woodbridge was right. Everything pointed to him as the killer. He'd been in the area at the time of the murder and knew it well. Solomon had provided a link to Bella. *Clarabella Dronkers. A Dutch spy.* A woman. A sometime German agent once part of a group who may have used him and then betrayed him. Irrespective of his later work for the Nazis, Solomon was clear he'd been a committed socialist. An idealist. He'd betrayed all he once believed in, led to that betrayal by those like Bella. Had that been sufficient for her murder?

Why wouldn't such a man in his rage strike out, punish her, entomb her corpse in a tree? A tree that stood in woods he knew well. He would have known the legends. The myths. Seeing it, as the stories suggested, as the just fate of witches and gypsies who betrayed their code. The man was a fantasist, deeply psychologically ill - a split personality. Porter more than most knew the power the psyche exerted over the real. *Demons, devils, angels - what did it matter the origin of such creations of the mind or their intention?* Visions that could drive a man to acts beyond rational comprehension. Una Mossop when describing the last time she'd seen her husband had been clear that he was a man beset by nightmares, haunted by visions that terrified him. A tree, he'd told her. A dreadful act he could never speak of.

Mossop was Claverley. And Claverley was surely a killer.

Wasn't that enough?

Jekyll and Hyde.

Yesterday, hadn't he seen with his own eyes a man desperately unbalanced? What else could send a man into so deep a traumatic state but the murder of a young woman, throttling the life from her. Sealing her body in a tree in a wood of foreboding for any who'd ever been there? *Everyone knew the legends, the myths.*

Wasn't it enough?

A man capable of taking his own life was surely capable of taking another's.

Was this it? Had he reached the end?

He stares at the stack of folders on his desk.

What had Webster said to him? *You might find the killer and be no closer as to how or why.* It gnawed at him.

He pushes the folder to one side. After all this, after all the investigating and chasing across the country, it stubbornly remains as it was? *Speculation. Conjecture.*

It was not witchcraft or the magic Margaret Murray suggested. Nor was it the judgement of a gypsy court, the answer favoured by James and Williams. It was not the murderous happenstance of misfortune suggested by Willetts. The man had known the victim. They had the photograph.

Claverley knew Bella. Bella knew Claverley.

So what was it? What was it gnawing at him? What was missing from this equation of human grief and despair?

Motive.

Why had Mossop murdered this woman, a woman he undoubtedly knew? A woman, so Solomon told them, he'd worked closely with. A woman, given the perilous nature of their enterprise, he'd once trusted with his life? What was his motive, the reason? *Betrayal? Lust? Desire? Greed? The unfathomable workings of lunacy? A full moon?*

He faced the distinct possibility that he'd come all this way only to find he was simply exchanging one *Penny Dreadful* fiction for another. *Jekyll and Hyde* rather than witches and spells, gypsies and magic.

There remained unanswered questions that he might yet comprehend. *Why was she killed? And was it only her?* Mossop became Claverley and Claverley continued his life as a German agent. There remained the possibility that the rest of the cell were still alive, still here in England. If so, there could still be answers. They would know why among them it was Bella alone who'd been selected for death.

Questions piled on questions.

He picks up his jacket from the back of the chair.

He had to see Webster. The photograph. He could find them. There was nothing left to cling to other than his unwillingness to let go.

He no longer knows if this is healthy or not. Maybe Webster is right, Rachel and Willetts too. All he knows is that he could no more let go than he could stop breathing. Bella was deep in him. She demanded more of him than this. She was not satisfied, and until he had all of the answers, neither could he be.

He picks up his notebook, stares at what he's written. *Tarpeia*.

JUNE 13TH, 1943: AFTERNOON

The Texan was in unfamiliar terrain. Certainties disappearing like the early morning mist. He'd learned of Porter and Floode's visit to St. Margaret's soon after it occurred. A little more cash in the right hands, and he'd discovered the identity of the man they'd travelled to meet - Claverley, or, as he'd now learned, Mossop. The news from his man in the police station had arrived shortly after Mossop's suicide.

He draws hard on the cigarette. There's no ashtray. He flicks the butt casually onto the tiled floor, pivoting his foot to extinguish it. The café was dark - gloomy oak furniture, white lace doilies, small leaded windows. *Lyons Corner Café, New Street.* There was one other customer - an elderly lady, grey haired, a fox fur collared coat suggesting both she and it had seen better times. He watches as she sits chewing on a sandwich, masticating three or four minutes for every bite. The waitress -

young, black dress, white apron, bored - stands at the counter, idly flicking through a newspaper.

He writes in his notebook. He would await word from his contact, but whatever any autopsy might decide there was little doubt in his own mind as to the actual cause of Claverley's death: knowledge.

But of what? What was it he'd known that so spooked the Brits? What secrets were they trying so hard to put beyond the reach of Detective Constable Porter and his little investigation? From hard won experience he knew such orders would have had to have been weighed at the highest level. British Intelligence had risked much in extending their hands into St. Margaret's to extinguish Claverley. They were either supremely confident or running scared, making it up as they went along. Something about their actions over the past few weeks told him it was the latter. SIS were improvising. It was a dangerous strategy for an intelligence operation.

He'd had long ago lost belief in coincidence or serendipity. There was plotting, planning, covert actions. *Everything happens for a reason;* so his mother had taught him when he was a youngster on their ranch. In the midst of a wide-open prairie it was an easy creed to believe in, the great guiding principle of religious faith. Much later, he'd learned it wasn't divine intervention, rather the machinations of men and governments that determined who lived and who died. Who fell. Who prospered.

He knows little of Claverley or of the murdered woman whose discovery had prompted his disappearance and subsequent death. All he knows is what his Section Head, Avery, has told him. That eighteen months ago a woman, scared and terrified for her life, had approached the London embassy. A woman who'd spoken of coming into possession of a secret, a secret that would save thousands of American lives; a secret that if others knew she possessed it would have her killed.

Her subsequent disappearance, her failure to attend the second meeting arranged whilst they checked the veracity of her claims, had caused ripples of interest among the Embassy staff but little else. Washington had dismissed her claims as a hoax. Her failure to show up proof of cold feet rather than proof of her fears being realised. But if it were her, the discovery of this corpse and SIS interest in her killer seems to offer that proof. Thus far he'd found nothing to suggest the nature of this secret she'd offered to trade or even if such a secret existed. But what troubled Avery was why SIS appeared so interested in a murder?

He pushes aside the tea he'd ordered. *Jesus why couldn't he get a decent cup of coffee in this lousy country*? Tapping out another cigarette, he fishes for his Zippo and lights it.

Avery's thinking had been clear. The best means of finding an answer was Porter, a policeman whose persistence was forcing SIS to show themselves, something else no intelligence service wished to do. The more Porter pressed; the more SIS revealed of their operation. If that continued, then he backed himself and Avery to be able to discern SIS objectives. At present he had a shape, an outline, a sense of the thing, but one lacking in definition.

He looks to catch the attention of the uninterested waitress who continues with her reading of the paper, stubbornly refusing to meet his gaze. He stands, throwing loose change on the table sufficient for the bill. *Brits*! Back home they were proud to serve. *If you don't like the job, get another. If you take the job, do it better than anyone else.* No wonder this country needed American know-how to get the war won. *Where would they be without Uncle Sam? What would have happened without Pearl Harbour?* Yet so many of them treated regular GIs like shit, resented their being here. *Fuck em! Fuck their lousy country and their notions of hospitality.*

Leaving the gloom of the café, he is ever more certain that this man Porter is the best chance of finding what he seeks, of provoking SIS into hasty actions that would lead to the answers Avery wants to acquire.

He steps into the street, lighting another cigarette. He inhales deeply, smiling to himself. All of this, of course, had one proviso: that Detective Constable Porter lives long enough to do so.

23

Webster withdraws the blow-ups from the foolscap envelope. He makes a point of studying each image whilst he considers their impact on the man who sits opposite. A man he's grown to admire, but one whose actions give cause for concern.

Porter sits upright, expectant. Since arriving at Webster's university office, demanding the professor see him, demanding the results of the blow-ups of the photographs, he's been in high animation. Now he sits almost catatonic, staring at Webster, attention focused on the glossy prints in the Professor's hands.

Webster looks back to the photographs. Another possible thread for Porter to follow down whatever rabbit-hole presented itself.

He places the prints one by one in front of him. They are face down like a dealt hand of cards. He pockets his monocle. 'Alec, don't you think this has gone far enough? I mean, you have to draw a line somewhere. Mossop is dead, but there's more than sufficient evidence to link him to the Bella's murder.' He holds up a hand, enumerating each point in turn on a finger with the other hand. 'He knew her. Knew the area. He had been used,

279

betrayed. He was clearly psychotic – a fantasist – a man who, according to the testimony of his wife, suffered terrible dreams of a dead woman in a tree, a woman he says he'd put in there. Surely you've enough. Good God, it's more than either of us expected when we set out on this!' He looks at Porter who seems to barely have listened to anything of what he'd outlined. 'You're vindicated, Alec. Vindicated! You followed your instincts. You proved everybody wrong.'

Porter eyes Webster coldly. 'Is that what you think this has been about? My ego? My desire to prove everyone wrong? To show others I've a role in this war? A purpose?'

'No. Of course not.' Webster hesitates. 'Not entirely.'

'Not *entirely*?' Porter snorts. 'Hardly a resounding affirmation of my motives.'

'Oh, come now, Alec,' Webster admonishes. 'You have to admit that things have gotten more than a little out of hand these past months. You've become increasingly… well, obsessed with this case, this woman. You had the treatment, the prognosis. You know better than most people the psychology of all this, of what's going on inside your head. The doctors here and in Spain, all counselled you on this, isn't that so?'

'I'm being thorough. It's what you taught me,' Porter states, ignoring the point.

Webster stiffens in astonishment. '*Thorough*? Alec, *thorough* is checking facts, details. *Thorough* is an investigator considering the possible options for an enquiry. What you've done is way beyond thorough. It's obsessive.'

'That's your opinion.'

Webster fights to keep exasperation from his tone. 'Alec, it's the opinion of everyone who's involved in this.' His elbow rests on the desk, but he flicks the hand forward, punching out each name in turn. 'Floode, Solomon, DS James, Inspector Williams. Even Willetts is concerned about your behaviour.'

'I know what I'm doing.'

'Do you? Do you? Are you even capable of making that

determination ?' He holds Porter's gaze, seeking some fissure in his obstinacy. 'What about Rachel?'

'What about her?'

'How does she feel about all this?'

'Rachel understands.'

'Does she?'

'It's the job.'

'No, Alec, it's not. This borders on the psychotic.'

Porter falls silent. 'What are you implying?' he finally manages.

'Alec…' Webster sought the words that might reconcile rather than alienate. 'Your…*history*. Spain. The bombing. Solomon's spoken with your doctors. They told him. It left more than the spinal injury.' He fights to hold Porter's impassive gaze, feels a compulsion to avert his eyes from those of the man making his words seem a betrayal. 'It's understandable that you want to prove things to others, to yourself. I know how it feels, the judgement of others. You told me about Rachel's father, how he sees things – your injury, your apparent physical health, the death of his son. Not everybody thinks like that. You can't blame yourself for what happened. The orange grove. Bella. You survived.'

He holds Webster's gaze, showing no mercy to the man opposite. When he speaks it is with precision, a voice utterly devoid of emotion. 'You think I'm mad.'

'No, of course not.' Webster breaks his eyes from Porter's. 'But you're not well. You're losing track of things. Perspective.'

'So what else does Solomon say? I assume you've been in contact.'

Webster occupies himself in shuffling the prints on the desk. He looks up. 'He believes we're finished with it. In his view you've found your killer. The fact that he's beyond your reach, beyond making the confession, you wanted, is something you'll have to learn to live with. You do know that they found a drawing in his room, a tree, a tree with eyes?

281

That's not a coincidence. As far as Solomon's concerned any link to operational intelligence matters is equally dead. In Solomon's view, their own investigation now suggests that the rest of the cell are either dead or have returned home. Whatever Claverley passed on is time limited, and as such no longer of operational concern. His suicide closes our involvement.'

'He's sure it was suicide?'

Webster pauses in moving the prints, looking across at Porter, puzzled. 'Why wouldn't he be?'

Porter sits forward. 'Don't you think it a remarkable coincidence that the moment we track the man down he conveniently kills himself before we can interrogate him properly?'

Webster struggles to grasp Porter's meaning. '*Conveniently*? Alec, listen to yourself. I spoke with the staff at St Margaret's. I listened to their profile of the man and their opinion as to his state of mind. Woodbridge, Morgan - these men are experts in their field. I hate to say this, but both are convinced that it was your interrogation that prompted his suicide.' He fixes his friend with a firm look. 'He's considering making a formal complaint to the Chief Constable.'

Porter waves away the implied threat. 'Jack Mossop was not suicidal. Yes, he was troubled; yes - his mind was in turmoil. But suicidal? No.'

'Isn't it the case that such turmoil is almost a pre-condition for suicide? The aftermath of a terrible trauma,' Webster ventures.

Porter stares into Webster's eyes, daring a rebuttal. 'No. No, it is not.'

Webster looks down. He exhales. 'Let's assume for one moment that what you say is true. What does that leave? If Mossop didn't kill himself then you're suggesting that someone else killed him. Not only killed him, but had a motive to make it look like suicide. Think about what you're implying. Who killed him? Who would want to kill him? Who would want to make it appear that he took his own life?'

Porter waves his arms in the air once more. 'I don't know.'

Webster sits forward; arms either side of the stack of prints. 'Porter, you must realise that it's one thing to suggest a lack of interest, an unwillingness by your superiors to pursue a line of enquiry. After all, we are at war. There are priorities. Demands on time, resources. It's also one thing to suggest... incompetence on their behalf, maybe a lack of insight or training. But it's a very different matter to suggest conspiracy.' He pauses, letting the words sink in. 'Alec, if you think it wasn't a suicide then it would seem that you ought, at the very least, to have an alternative scenario. If you think that he was murdered, then you must have some idea as to who you believe did it. And why.'

Porter sighs, looks down to his lap. 'It's more a sense of the notion of suicide being wrong. Not fitting. Out of place.'

Webster's tone is conciliatory. 'Alec, old son, before you go around making accusations you need to think very carefully how this comes across. How it will be seen. Your... history.'

A silence settles between them. Webster sits back, waiting whilst Porter considers his position. After a few moments, Porter looks up. 'And there's this word.' He takes a notebook from his pocket, turning to the page he wants. '*Tarpeia*.' He offers the book to Webster who scans it before sliding it back across the desk. 'He wrote that after the interview.' Porter explains. 'I looked it up. It's a Roman legend. The story of a woman's execution for the betrayal of her people. What does that mean?'

'That he was more than likely mad. Out of his mind. It means nothing. A story he remembered about a woman's betrayal. Maybe in his mind it justifies him killing Bella. It's certainly more evidence as to the state of his mind rather than any link in your chain of conspiracy and murder.'

Porter closes the notebook, allowing a silence to settle, a prelude. 'What about the autopsy? That could find something. I've read your papers on such things. Isn't there a difference between a man hanging himself and being hanged forcibly by others? Signs of force, a struggle? Something?'

Webster half-smiles. 'Alec, I doubt very much that the doctors at St. Margaret's will have looked at much beyond the obvious. Hanging - strangulation, bruising, ligatures. There's no reason for them to have looked further.'

'You. You could.'

'Think about it. Everything that's happened. They won't let me within a mile of the body. Why would they?'

'Your reputation.'

'And my reason for doing so? You yourself tell me you don't have a suspect.'

'You won't do it?'

'Porter, I can't do it. There is no reason to do it.'

'So you're saying there's nothing we can do?'

'Maybe it's just that there is nothing. At times acceptance is difficult, but it may be that there is simply nothing else left to do other than accept that it's time to stop. There are no more channels open to us. There is nothing else that can be done, nothing else that could have been done.'

Porter indicates the photographs. 'What about those?'

'These?' Webster spreads his hands across the stack of prints. 'They're the blow-ups of the original group photograph you found. Close ups of those in the picture courtesy of my contacts at photo-reconnaissance.' He holds each up in turn, the image turned towards Porter, jabbing a finger at the figures. Each image is a foolscap sized rendering of the four individual figures isolated from the group picture Porter had found stitched inside the lining of Claverley's suitcase. 'Claverley, or as we now know, Mossop.' *Jab.* 'The woman we presume to be your Bella and our seeming proof that he knew the victim.' *Jab.* 'As for the two other men,' Webster holds up a print in each hand. He waggles the one in his left. 'From the descriptions provided by Mrs Mossop, this one on the left we believe to be her Dutch character.' He discards the print, pushing forward the one in his right hand. 'This other fellow we know little else about other than the fact that his inclusion here suggests him to be an acquaintance of the others.' He slides the print across the desk to Porter who picks it up.

Porter scrutinises the photograph. A tall man, well over six feet. Blonde hair. Face, oval with an elongated nose. The eyebrows are cropped tight, light-coloured and lend an almost effeminate look to the upper face. The eyes beneath are pale, set in deep sockets, a depth undoubtedly exaggerated by an enlargement process that has resulted in the overall grainy quality of each image. The body appears athletic, more than military tautness. The muscles, even beneath the vest, are difficult to disguise. *Who are you? What do you know?*

'Anything?' Webster prompts.

Porter shakes his head. 'What are the rest?'

Webster slides the remaining images across the table. 'Blow ups of different sections of the overall photograph. A blow up of the group as a whole and several of the background.'

'Any ideas as to location?'

'Nothing. A camp somewhere. A hedgerow. Tents in the background. Could be scouts, Hitler youth for all I know.'

'It doesn't look like any sort of tent I've camped in.'

Webster shrugs. 'Does it matter now?'

'Loose ends.'

'Loose ends?'

'If Claverley killed her, there remains the question of motive.'

'Motive? There could be any. Obviously, from what Solomon told us, betrayal. Communist turning on fascists. If the timing of that so long after *Barbarossa* troubles you, then you can take your pick: sex, a quarrel. Who knows?'

'One of these would know.'

'Porter, you're suggesting that you now intend to find the remaining men in this photograph. These are men whose names you do not know. You have no idea of their relationship to your Bella or to Claverley. And they are also men Solomon is convinced have in all likelihood either fled or dead.'

'They'll have answers.'

'What answers?'

'Why Bella was killed.'

Webster toys with the cord of his monocle before tucking it into his top pocket. 'Porter, in so many cases it's not a matter of a killer wanting to kill. It's circumstance. A boiling mixture of emotions - alcohol, primitive sexual urges, that suddenly impel an action. What our friends in France call *Crime Passionnel*. Reasons no-one fully understands, often not even the killer themselves.'

'At least it would be *an* answer.'

'Porter, there may be *no* answers.'

'There are always answers. The gypsy woman was right. We just have to find the right questions to ask. If we accept Claverley was involved in her killing we no longer need to ask who, but why? Why was she killed? More and more I'm coming to believe that it's the most important question of all. It's one we've not pursued because we believed that Solomon told us was why. You must see that. We've come too far to stop without an answer. One of these men knows the truth about Claverley. About Bella. Help me. Please.'

Webster's shoulders slump. He sits exasperated, concerned. Porter was unflinching in his determination. The man wasn't about to stop until he'd exhausted every avenue, maybe not even then.

Webster jags the cord attached to his monocle, fishing it from his top pocket. He waves a hand, pointing a finger to indicate that Porter return one of the photos to him. Webster points at the flap of the tent. 'This,' he begins, indicating a blurred outline of what seems a stencilled number on the canvas, 'is the manufacturer's identification number. You were right.'

Porter stares hard. 'I can barely see it. What is it, a series of letters and numbers? Is that a *P* or an *R*? A *3* or an *8*?'

'Impossible to read. At least, like this. My chaps had it blown up. Like you asked.' Webster pulls out a final eight by eleven glossy print from the envelope, a blow up of the stencilled sequence of letters and numbers. Though still blurred and smudged the serial number is readable.

Porter stares at it. 'I can use this to trace the manufacturer. They might have records of who it was sold to.'

'Barrett Brothers of Feckenham made the tent in 1938. It was a specialist tent, made to order. One of three made that winter for a circus wintering in the area. A circus they'd done work for going back to the twenties.'

'But how…'

'Every year this particular circus winters close to Hagley woods. I'd be surprised if at some time you hadn't seen them there.'

'You know this… How?'

'I traced it days ago. You'd upped and disappeared off to St Margaret's chasing down Claverley. It no longer seemed important. You had your killer.'

'Now?'

Webster removes the monocle. 'Porter, you're not going to stop this madness until you chase it down. I'm not certain I'm actually doing the right thing by telling you this, but you'd only spend even more days and weeks hunting for it. Maybe this just speeds things up. Ends it sooner.'

'Thank you.'

'Don't thank me, Porter.'

Porter rises, scooping up the photograph along with the notepaper with the name of the circus.

Webster tucks his monocle away. 'The other reason I'm telling you this is that I assumed you already knew.'

'Why?'

'Because I told Andrea Floode days ago.'

24

Porter sits on the bench, the day surprisingly chill for the time of year. With little warming sunlight, the paths around the small village pond remain slick from the previous night's rain. He sits slouched forward, elbows on thighs, cigarette gripped in the fingers of his left-hand. With his right hand he absent-mindedly breaks sections of crust from the sandwiches Rachel had made for him that morning, tossing them idly in the direction of the gathered ducks.

The previous day's meeting with Webster had changed things, the professor's revelations confirming his suspicions of Floode and SIS. Something felt wrong. Truth seemed indistinct, a vague shimmering outline of what ought to be clear and defined. He senses there are details missing, key links in the chain. More than this, he's certain they'd been denied him because they contradicted all he'd been told.

He had little to go on. Claverley was dead; the issue as to whether the man had taken his own life or not in some ways, immaterial. The fact was that his only viable suspect was gone.

He had no doubt of the man's involvement in Bella's killing -

either directly or after the fact. The pressing issue was why? *Why had Bella been killed? How was Claverley implicated? Why were Floode and Solomon anxious for his enquiry to stop?* If he found the answer to any of those questions he was sure the whole would unravel, the truth be revealed.

But there was to be no further help from Solomon. No transport, no access to files or records. To some extent that too is of little concern. The files had been used to bury him. He saw that now. All of the SIS support - the access to documents and staff, the appointment of Floode to help him - were nothing more than a distraction. They had weighted him down with irrelevant detail, a barricade of bureaucracy separating him from the truth. Solomon and his superiors more anxious for the enquiry to end more than they wanted it to succeed.

Last night he'd lain awake for some time before succumbing to the inevitable, finally slipping downstairs. He'd sat at the small kitchen table, the grey hours before dawn spent among the twists and turns of the investigation. The more he'd thought about it, the more he'd recognised the interventions of Floode and Solomon led him nowhere other than down blind alleys. More than that, they'd been dead ends designed to give a semblance of assistance, but in reality dissipating his efforts. It was as if they were directing everything, manipulating the enquiry to fit a script of their choosing. From the very start they'd had in mind their ideal conclusion and all of their efforts had been towards securing that end. They sought closure, not solution, and his role had been that of providing the semblance of validity. His determination to find the truth was obvious to everyone. What Webster called his *obsession* made him the perfect verifier of the truth SIS wanted the world to know. He'd not solved the murder of Bella; he'd helped bury it.

He understood the motives of Williams and James for him to stop. For them it was a matter of procedure. A body had been discovered. There was evidence of foul play, a murder. The investigation had been allocated its allotted time and resources, and for them the case had been resolved to the satisfaction of their superiors sufficient for the tying up of the paperwork. *The killing of a person unknown by person or persons unknown.* The sudden death of an itinerant gypsy who had unfortunately for them chosen their patch to get herself killed in. For them, the matter had been dealt with. It was time for Porter to devote himself to current crimes.

Floode on the other hand was Machiavellian. There had been the visit to Rachel's with threats of the damage she was prepared to inflict on Rachel's life. After their visit to St. Margaret's she'd pronounced the enquiry to be over, only for Claverley to be found dead less than twenty-four hours later. And there was the photograph, the connection of Claverley and Bella to two other men. Webster's revelation meant Floode had known of the circus connection whilst interviewing Claverley, but she'd said nothing of it either to Claverley or to Porter. It was a clue, a link in the chain of evidence to the murderer. She had known where the picture had been taken, where they had been; *Hobbs Brothers* circus. *Why had she not taken the chance to have asked Claverley what he'd been doing there? Why had she not pushed him to recall the names of the others in the photo?* It might have ignited a spark. She sought spies, names that Claverley could have given her - why hadn't she asked him?

Bella and Claverley had known each other. She was no prostitute, and he no brutal client whose control had snapped. If he was a spy, Bella was more than likely part of that conspiracy. In that scenario, her murder had a reason, a purpose. The men in the photograph knew that purpose. He had to know what it was.

He brushes off the remaining crumbs, standing and folding the paper bag and placing it into his briefcase. The ducks scuttled back to the pond, the sanctuary of the water. More than his desire for understanding why Bella should have been so brutally murdered and confined in a tree, he is disturbed by something much more sinister: *why it is that Floode, Solomon, and*

their masters are so anxious for him not to pursue the motive for it? If
he is right, Claverley had paid for that question with his life.

JUNE 15TH, 1943: LATE AFTERNOON

Floode read the handwritten letter attached to the police file
containing Porter's report of the visit to St Margaret's and
Claverley's subsequent death. The letter was Porter's private
handwritten note. In it he accepted that with the death of
Claverley all hope of finding further evidence pertaining to the
death of the woman he'd dubbed Bella was unlikely.

She allows herself a smile. Solomon would be satisfied.
They'd closed a damaging breach in what she'd been told was a
matter of national security. The lack of detail as to the specifics of
that threat didn't trouble her. She'd had orders, among them the
requirement to eradicate Porter should he be seen to put that
national security in danger.

She knew it concerned a wider operation set up in the early
years of the war. A time when the threat to the nation's survival
was at its direst. She was trained to follow orders without
question. If ordered to kill him she would comply without
hesitation.

A lifetime ago, she'd imagined herself a teacher. A blue-
stocking. She'd plotted a path to that end - university,
somewhere old and grand, and then teaching in a girls' grammar
or private school somewhere in the southern counties; semi-
rural, yet in close proximity to the theatre, to dancing, and fine
restaurants.

She had been recruited to SIS from university. One of her
tutors with links to the intelligence services telling her they
required young women like herself, ones with a fluent command
of French or German. The training had been tough, her
assignments tougher still. France twice and Belgium. Operations
collecting intelligence of troop deployments. Three of the
resistance had been shot in front of her in the main square of the

town where she'd worked as a hotel maid. In the past eighteen months, five female agents of her own SIS class had been lost on operations in France, two of them brutally tortured before being shot.

In the scheme of things, Porter, Webster, Willetts, and even Rachel and Tommy were expendable. Like Claverley.

She turns the note in her hand. The handwriting is strong, crisp with cursive wide loops. She is surprised he'd succumbed, part of her even a little disappointed he'd done so. His desire to bring to justice his Bella's killers had a certain nobility, a romanticism that had genuinely moved her. It would have been sad to have killed him, but she would have led him to that fate without hesitation

Now he'd return to his humdrum life with Rachel and her boy; a life of stolen bicycles and mortgages; family gatherings shrouded by the bitter resentment of Rachel's father and later maybe even the child and Rachel herself. Would Porter, at some point in the future, locked in the grip of old age and his own sense of mortality, find himself looking back at this moment and wondering? Regretting? Better a bullet?

He'd been close to the truth. Too close. Whatever it was, to her own knowledge the secret they were protecting had cost the lives of at least two people. From what she'd pieced together from fragments of overheard conversations between Solomon and Whitehall, probably more. Whatever it was, the code name she'd heard whispered was one she never wished to hear again. It was a secret protected at the highest level, possibly Churchill himself, a secret Solomon has instructed could never be revealed, no matter the cost.

Tarpeia.

JUNE 15TH, 1943: EVENING

Victor Cavendish-Bentinck pauses in reading the file Pidgeon has passed across the desk. Only a few paragraphs in, he looks up, catching the Major's eye. 'So it's done,' he states.

Pidgeon grunts a response. 'It would seem so.'

Cavendish-Bentinck raises an eyebrow. '*Seems*? Is that the best you can give me, Francis?'

Pidgeon shuffles in his chair. 'It's intelligence, sir. The agents in the field are the ones best placed to make such an appraisal. I can only add that I trust Solomon's judgement.'

The Chief of the Joint Intelligence Committee, current chief of the Service Liaison Office, turns his attention to Solomon who sits next to Pidgeon. The Chief waves the file in the air. 'And you stand by this?'

'Yes, sir. I do,' Solomon affirms.

Cavendish-Bentinck considers the matter. It was his instinct to trust his men. If a man like Pidgeon placed implicit trust in Solomon then it was good enough for the Chief of the JIC.

Satisfied, he places the folder on the desk, tapping its cover. 'What's left to do? The tidying up?'

Pidgeon nods. 'We need to consider the threads our agent picked up regarding Claverley's link to the Dutchman and to this *Hobbs Brothers'* Circus.'

'This photograph mentioned in your report?'

'Yes.' Pidgeon confirms. 'Detective Porter, stumbled across it whilst he was tracking down Claverley. Now he's out of our hair one of our agents is, as we speak, following matters up to a more effective conclusion.'

'You think you've found them?' Cavendish-Bentinck asks.

Pidgeon looks to Solomon whose expression indicates agreement before he takes up the response to the JIC Chief. 'We've had awareness of the wider group Claverley was involved with, the men running the conduit back to Berlin. We know the material is first passed to the Dutchman who'd recruited him.'

'This Van Ralt chap?'

'Yes, Van Ralt.'

'With Claverley on the run we had no access to Van Ralt or his movements. To all intent the Dutchman too had melted away. Claverley's disappearance must have worried them almost as much as it did us. We've built a picture of Van Ralt. Once he resurfaces he should be easier to find. But we'd nothing regarding the bigger prize, the analyst. Porter's discovery of the photograph hidden in Claverley's suitcase might provide the link we've been after for over two years now. We checked surveillance files of Van Ralt. There are several reports of visits to towns across the country, towns where we now know this particular circus was performing. The circus was laid over in Hagley at the time the woman was eliminated.'

'Ah, the mysterious murder this Porter's been investigating.'

'That's correct.' Solomon confirms. 'It was the discovery of her body that set things off again.'

The Chief of the JIC shakes his head ruefully. 'And we've been playing catch-up ever since.'

'To some extent,' Solomon agrees. 'It's been a balancing act. Shutting down a police investigation into her death posed as many threats to the security of *Tarpeia* as allowing it to continue. Instead, we guided it to the conclusion we require.'

'Not always in complete control, however,' the Chief observes.

'Detective Constable Porter proved … determined. It required a little more finesse than was originally anticipated. However, it was his determination that led us to Claverley. A stroke of luck, but one dependent on Porter's persistence in getting his flyers and police support out there. Something our best agents had been unable to do.'

'A lunatic asylum was possibly the last place to look,' the Chief comments.

'Quite.'

Cavendish-Bentinck mulls matters over. 'And this man Mossop or Claverley or whoever he called himself. He had no recollection of any of it?'

'Apparently not,' Solomon replies.

'But his memory may have returned later?'

Solomon looks to Pidgeon, who shrugs before taking up the response to the Chief's interrogations. 'A chance we could not take, sir.'

The Chief nods, furrowing his brow. 'A nasty matter.'

Pidgeon looks down, studying his shoes for a moment, allowing the Chief to have his moment of reflection. 'The decision we made regarding the woman in forty-one left us no option,' he reminds him.

The Chief tuts. 'Still, a nasty business.'

'The war.' Pidgeon offers trenchantly.

'The war.' The Chief re-joins. He gazes across his office to the window and the world outside. Each man considered this justification for much of what they'd done, the things they would no doubt yet have to do before it all ended. 'And now?'

'The rest of the cell must be found and dealt with.'

'Agreed.'

'And the analyst? The leader. What would you have us do?'

Cavendish-Bentinck rubs his chin. 'We've held all along that once this group had served its purpose that we should find him, take him. He'd be quite a catch. A coup.'

Pidgeon inclines his head. 'That being said, there's no telling how he'll react. A *death before dishonour* attitude limits our options. There's also the fact that what he knows about *Tarpeia* remains a threat outweighing any benefit from anything he might tell us of Nazi operations.'

The Chief closes the folder, sliding it away, grimacing. 'Nasty business,' he mutters.

Those on the other side of the desk cannot disagree.

The war.

25

JUNE 20TH, 1943: LATE EVENING

Porter switches the desk lamp off, rising from his desk. *Enough.*

He picks up his jacket from the back of the chair, a sharp twinge in his spine as he hitches it on. He stands back crooked, steadying himself, anticipating the adrenalin that will kick in to mute the surge of discomfort. He needs to keep up with his medication, something he's ignored for weeks. The doctors at the hospital had been clear; it was a regime that had to be followed. A mix of tablets and potions, a dozen or so each day. Some were designed to keep the pain in check, some to keep the nightmare at bay.

The latter he'd discarded some time ago. They made him drowsy, fogged the mind. He needed to be sharp. Focused.

He eases himself upright, warily shrugging shoulders so the fit of the jacket settles into position.

He moves across the room, familiar enough with the disposition of its furniture to negotiate it in the dark of the blackout. He lets himself out into the main waiting room of the station, from there emerging into the eerie moonlight of the world outside.

He looks up at the stars, a Bomber's Moon silvers the trees.

He makes his way down the street, the only sound his own footsteps. No raids tonight, at least none here. Maybe Liverpool. Maybe Sheffield. Maybe London.

He'd seen neither Floode nor Solomon for almost a week. His letter and report appears to have satisfied them, but he can't allow himself to believe they weren't still keeping an eye on him.

As cover, he'd let it be known to James that he was investigating a series of black-market operations in the area, an enquiry necessitating trips to Birmingham and some of the other industrial centres in the surrounding area. James had been satisfied. *Doing some proper police-work at last* he'd observed when passing Porter who'd been deep into a pile of folders at the time. They'd even let him use Willets and a car again. *Necessity. Black marketeers knew no boundaries to their activities.*

Willetts, for his part, had been reticent to say much about the Bella enquiry other than to express a sense of satisfaction that Porter had *got the bugger* when Claverley's suicide had come up during a stop at a pub one lunchtime.

Porter had deliberated ideas for searching for the men in the photograph. The circus and its movement had been easy to trace. Not only did they publicise their shows, but they were required to submit travel details to the authorities as they moved around the country. He knew they had foreign nationals in their ranks but at the outbreak of the war these had all been subject to checks as to their identity and their sympathies. All had been cleared, though he suspected such work had more than likely been conducted at a junior level lacking something in terms of rigour.

Everything he does is now compromised by the necessity for stealth. There's no one he can trust. No-one whom he feels he might in any conscience implicate in his quest. Webster had been clear that he'd gone as far as he was prepared to go in the investigation. Though disappointed, Porter understood why.

And good-hearted as he was, Willetts would find himself out of his depth and susceptible to the pressure of superiors.

Besides, both were family men with wives and dependents. Without letting his imagination get the better of him, he was certain that his further pursuit of the truth surrounding Bella's death was now dangerous, possibly fatal. Leaving aside Rachel, he'd no dependents relying on him. If anything should happen then at least Rachel has her father-in-law, Tommy's grandfather, to look after them both.

If he was correct, those guarding the truth he sought have already killed to preserve it. He couldn't ask anyone else to assume the risks he was undertaking. He sought enemy agents, trained killers and their sympathisers. He was alone. For whatever reason, Floode, Solomon, and their masters were arraigned against him; Williams and James compromised by their duties in the chain of command; Webster sceptical; Willetts unsuitable. The only means of securing the truth lay in finding the men in the photograph - dangerous men, probably spies, possibly murderers - and in persuading them that telling what they knew was their only option. Should SIS find them first that chance would be gone. They would most certainly be executed.

He reaches a hand under his jacket, feeling the cold hard reassurance of the Colt pistol and holster tucked in the rear waistband of his trousers. He'd taken it some days ago from the station armoury where it had lain unused, unthought-of, since the early scares of invasion. Tonight, more than ever, it feels more of a necessity than a precaution.

JUNE 20TH, 1943: NIGHT

They were gone. All of them. *Armstrong, Waelti, Drucke, Jakobs, Richter, Key, Timmermen, Ford, Dronkers*. Most by hanging, Jakobs by firing squad. Now it seemed Claverley had hung himself, if indeed it had been suicide.

Lying in bed, the Dutchman considers his future.

Maybe it was time to leave, disappear. He has money. The Nazis paid well and ideology has never been his motive. The black market was much more to his taste, though the skills honed in it - looking into men's souls, discerning what they valued, what they might be persuaded to trade, were talents suited to the world of espionage. His knowledge of how men might be tempted into illicit activity, find self-justification for betrayal, had proven a commodity profitably traded for Nazi gold.

He knows his worth. He is a businessman, a trader in information, skilled in planning and logistics. What was done with that information, with the fruit of his high-priced endeavours, was of no concern. He has no more loyalty to the Nazis than to his own country.

He reaches across to the bedside table, hands finding his cigarettes and lighter. He lights one, inhaling deeply, greedily. Lying back on the pillows, he cups his head, hands clasped behind his neck, thoughts on the future whilst he puffs on the cigarette.

Where Lehrer dreamed of medals and honour, the glory of the *Fuhrer*, he was satisfied with increasing his Swiss gold. What did the scramble for medals and honour get you apart from killed? Besides, working for a pay-check rather than ideology meant you could resign, taking your talents elsewhere. If the Nazis won the war he would have no problem with his part in it. But now it looked more likely the Allies would triumph or at least engineer a compromise. The arrival of the Americans had seen to that.

He exhales the smoke, watches it drift towards the ceiling. Maybe he should consider America. With its riches and abundance and his new wealth to back him, there were opportunities for a man like himself. He could become respectable. After all, wasn't his story the epitome of the American Dream you heard so much of these days? A self-made man, using what talents he has to enrich himself at the expense of those less committed than himself.

He stubs his cigarette out in the ashtray. Picking up the bottle of whiskey from off the bedside table, unscrewing the cap, he pours a generous glass. He raises the tumbler in mock toast to the gods of good fortune before knocking it back in one gulp, feeling the warm glow fill him. The future. *The New World.*

America.

America. Where their problems had started.

Clarabella. Her husband, Dronkers. Claverley.

He shakes his head. He would learn the lesson from what had happened to them. She'd failed because she'd been weak. Prevaricated. His mind was clear. It was time to cash in.

He twirls the tumbler in his hand, the faint oily slick of whiskey sliding around its sides. Their secret still held much of its value. It's worth might even have increased.

The knowledge Clarabella had discovered would guarantee its bearer a welcome in America. When the story was told, it would change the war. Change the future. Who knows, despite the Americans' fear of the fucking *Ruskie* commies, it might tip the balance of the war back in favour of the Nazis. He snorts. Maybe the *Fuhrer* would give him a fucking medal after all! Send it to him in America.

He puts the now empty tumbler down, lying back against the pillow, arms folded behind his head. He smiles at the thought of a medal from the little Austrian house painter.

What had Clarabella asked for? A passport for her and her bastard child. She'd always thought small! And Claverley? Claverley would have given it away for free, drunk himself to death on cheap whiskey telling the story in bars!

They were fools who had met a fool's end. He was different. He would negotiate a deal that would spin the Americans' heads. Best of all, they would agree to every demand he made, because what he had - what he knew - was worth such a fortune. Maybe more. The idea of selling his silence to the British was no longer on the table – though at one point an auction had appealed to his sense of market forces. SIS had shown with what had happened to Bella and Claverley that they were more likely to kill him than to buy his silence. No, America it was. And soon.

He stretches his legs; a pleasing tremble runs the length of his spine. But before all that, he would fuck this woman from the bar one more time. She was good. Lively. When she returned from the bathroom he would take her from the rear. Show her how a real man fucked, give her a little more of what she so clearly enjoyed.

The door to the bathroom opens; a sliver of light penetrating the blackout of the bedroom. 'About time,' he says. 'You'd better be about show me something special to make up for making me wait.'

She slides into the bed next to him, her naked body chill, cold against his flank. He turns towards her, cupping her breast, her nipple firm from the cold of the bathroom. 'Ah, you're ready,' he murmurs.

'Yes. I am.' She pushes him back, straddling him. He feels his hardness grow stronger as she presses down, the sigh of escaping breath as he readies himself for her.

'I'm going to fuck the life out of you,' he states.

In the darkness of the blackout he feels rather than sees the movement. Feels the sensation of warm liquid seeping across his throat. Senses rather than sees the blade that slides across once more, this time from left to right as she drew back from his embrace.

Instinctively he raises his hands to his throat, the slickness of the blood oozing over them. Unable to speak, unable to make any sound beyond a guttural choking, he stares in shock at the woman dismounting him and slipping out of the bed. He slumps forward, one hand at his throat trying to stem the flow of blood, the other reaching imploringly towards her.

His vision blurs, the massive loss of blood spouts across the sheets and drips to the floor. Dimly, he sees her open the door. Two thickset men he recalls seeing in the bar enter. The woman slips a wrap round herself, muttering a muffled command to the two.

Floode and the two men watch as the prone Dutchman's heart uncomprehendingly beats on, bleeding out the last of his life.

As the darkness encloses his vision he thinks of them.

Dronkers.

Claverley.

Bella.

Her silent curse.

JUNE 24TH, 1943: MORNING

He slams the phone down.

Three days. Three days and not a word.

'Fuck!' he spits at the walls of the phone box. 'Fuck!'

He is not a man to lose control, and even as he curses his mind works to regain its discipline. *Think.* Rationalise.

He presses the button, the coins return to him. He grasps them tight in one hand, their edges biting against the hard cushion of its calloused palm.

Pushing the door open, the spring stiff against his efforts, Lehrer walks out into the early morning sunlight. He stands; hands thrust deep in the pockets of his trousers.

This is the third time today he's attempted to contact the Dutchman. Each time he's used the agreed phone method; a tailor's call to Van Ralt's hotel; the message that his order was ready for collection; a return call by Van Ralt ten minutes later from a phone box. Nothing.

Had he been discovered? Unlikely. The man is careful, cunning.

Dead? A stray bomb? He knew the Dutchman ventured into vulnerable areas, but there'd been no Luftwaffe raid locally for some days.

An accident? He'd scanned the local newspapers but found

nothing suggesting the Dutchman as the victim of a car crash or anything similar.

Had he betrayed them? Fled? Unlikely. There was still a payday left in the work, and the Dutchman was if anything reluctant to let an opportunity for making money pass him by.

Then what? The whole thing was out of character. The only possibility is that he is lying low.

Walking away from the box, Lehrer mulls this over. Things had been difficult over the previous months - the police investigation into Hagley, the persistence of the Detective leading it. The disappearance of Claverley had been a complication they'd been unprepared for. He cursed the sloppiness that had left them so vulnerable, thanking whatever power there was operating in this that Claverley's sudden demise had resolved things. It had rattled him, the Dutchman more so. Maybe he'd suspected the British had discovered something. That they were closing in. It was Van Ralt Claverley had known best of all. The Dutchman who was most vulnerable to any betrayal.

He walks along the narrow lane leading back down to the fields where the circus is encamped. The sun is rising. The day would be clear. Even on such a short walk, dressed only in vest and braces, he feels a glean of perspiration on his back, a dampness across his chest. He forces himself to think of the possibilities, the nature of the Dutchman when under threat.

Whatever his other qualities, the man possessed a strong instinct for self-preservation. That being the case, maybe it was not that the Dutchman feared he was the one being watched, but Lehrer. Maybe the Dutchman was keeping his distance from *The Great Fellaini* because he believes it is the circus that is the subject of surveillance, wary any visit would draw attention to himself.

The Hobbs Brothers had been reduced to one sole surviving brother, the elder being caught up in a bombing raid early in the Blitz whilst liaising with a woman outside a public house in Wolverhampton. The surviving brother is an alcoholic with little interest in anything beyond the rim of a glass or the contents of a bottle, certainly little interest in what went on in the circus bearing his name. As such, Lehrer's comings and goings were subject to little comment, even less concern. His arrival almost two years ago had been readily accepted, his Fellaini paperwork only routinely checked with only the briefest of trials on the high wires. Once accepted, no further questions had been asked. It was a community of outsiders whose desire for contact with the authorities was that it be kept to the minimum.

He enters the grounds, mind fixed on the idea of whether he is now the one under SIS scrutiny. *No.* There was no way he could be. There was nothing linking either himself or their work with anything that had happened. The intelligence supplied to Berlin has no link back to him. The cell was kept in limited groups, and according to the Dutchman's source Claverley died without talking. The British had seen to that. SIS would have had little interest in anything beyond ensuring his silence. It was clear they had panicked. Claverley's sudden resurrection spooking SIS as much as it had himself and Van Ralt. They'd moved him from Harrogate to Birmingham to ensure his silence. SIS concerns were trained on an issue far greater than locating an espionage ring, no matter its impact on the Allied war effort. Claverley's silence was enough for them. With Dronkers gone, Claverley had been SIS's only link to Clarabella and what she knew. They knew a little of Van Ralt's role and his black market dealings, but nothing of Lehrer himself.

Clarabella was dead. Dronkers too. Now Claverley. *There was nothing.*

He shakes his head. *So where was Van Ralt?*

Maybe the Dutchman realised he was a potential liability for Berlin. Maybe he'd reached the same conclusion; he'd outlived his usefulness to the Reich and was expendable. Without Claverley's access to intelligence he had little to offer. It was time for the entire cell to vanish one last time. Maybe Van Ralt had calculated he was a loose end, one Berlin would require eliminated.

Whatever his reasons, he was gone.

He walks deeper into the vast meadow, the sounds and smells of the animals wafting to him, sounds held in the heavy air of a bright summer's morning. Another week and they too would be gone. A season in Liverpool. Another week and he could consider his exit from the role of *The Great Fellaini* and his return to the Fatherland as Thomas Lehrer.

The fact that despite knowing this, that he should be so rattled by the disappearance of Van Ralt concerns him. He prides himself on his ability to remain calm, to see the things that others missed in their emotional entanglements with danger or crisis.

It was panic that had led to the killing of Clarabella. He'd warned them at the time; the Dutchman, Claverley, Dronkers. He'd told them. Told them all. *Had they listened?* Far from it. Instead they'd come up with Dronkers' ludicrous plan, a plan that had got them where they were now. Dead. Claverley murdered by SIS. Dronkers fleeing months ago, paying the price of his rashness. *Taking that fucking boat with those other two cretins. What had they expected? Did they think the British were so stupid?*

He stands at the door to his caravan.

There is no need for panic. He remained secure. He would slip away, the greatest agent the Abwehr had ever known. He smiles, lips set tight. Knowing. Determined. The situation confirms one thing above all others; that wherever he was, whatever hole he'd bolted down, when the Dutchman reappeared he'd have to be dealt with.

JUNE 24TH, 1943: AFTERNOON

Victor Cavendish-Bentinck lay the folder down on his desk, eyeing it with distaste. What Pidgeon referred to somewhat euphemistically as *'tidying up'* was progressing apace.

Cavendish-Bentinck, for one, would be only too glad when it was over and he would no longer be troubled by it. *Tarpeia*

He walks across his imposing office to stand looking down from the second-floor window to Whitehall and Horse Guards. He prides himself that he has a deep understanding of what they are fighting to preserve: *Parliament, Downing Street, St Pauls, Buckingham Palace.* Everything that it meant to be British. Everything the nation stood for. Everything they were fighting for. Dying for.

What price such freedoms?

He was one of only a few to fully comprehend the answer to such a question. At least, one of the few called upon to place the price on such things; decide what must be done to secure the future of the nation and all it stood for. The lines to be crossed. The terrible things to be done. At some point in the future, he knows history will call on him to answer for such things, the choices he's made. Troubled as he was by some of them, on Judgement Day when he stood in front of his God, he would face him strong in the certainty of his actions, willing to be judged.

Everything had a cost. A price. A sacrifice to be made. Freedom is bought with the blood of those prepared to make that payment and those with the strength of purpose to ask them to spill it. He hadn't fought in *the Great War* - his service had been in diplomacy. Others - friends, schoolboy chums, family – had given their lives or, like Ferdinand, his elder brother, returned wounded and broken. Men scarred by all they had witnessed.

Whatever else might be said of him, Victor Cavendish-Bentinck believes he knows the horror wrought by war. It makes him work for the present one to end, and end quickly. Everything he does is to that end. Britain had to win. The Nazis, the evils of fascism, had to be stopped.

Above the city the low clouds are little more than wisps, strands of grey-white stuttering across the deep blue of a summer sky. Below, the pale white of government buildings, their windows criss-crossed with tape, stood as they had for hundreds of years. Mere yards from where he looks down, Charles the First had been beheaded outside Banqueting House, the monarch's bloody end securing Parliament and the future of the nation.

Sacrifice.

Blood.

Nothing changed.

Tarpeia but one more example of doing what had to be done.

He turns back into the room, walks to his desk. Would anyone understand? His commanders, the cabinet? *Winnie*? Did the Prime Minister even truly *wish* to know all that had been done to secure the future of the nation? And if he did, would he approve or, like King Henry cry out for those who would rid him of his troublesome priest and then turn on them, deny those who had taken him at his word, those who carried out what they knew to be his desire?

He stares once more at the folder lying across the blotting pad. The designation TOP SECRET is stamped in red and angled across one corner of it. The letters lie in a beam of sunlight that burnishes their ink a deeper, darker hue. Blood red.

Winnie was a great leader, but there is blood on his hands. *Tarpeia* had seen to that.

He, Victor Cavendish-Bentinck is charged with washing it away.

26

The crowd move slowly. A thin line of two hundred or so funnelled step-by-shuffling-step towards the entrance to the Big Top, a dull grey-white canvas dominating the meadow. Atop the twin peaks of the tent poles, Union Jack flags flutter lazily in a barely shifting breeze. It is said to be the hottest day of the summer. Some talk, others shuffle in silence, mopping brows, simply grateful to be here. A glimpse of a lost world.

The grass is long. In places coarse tufts of couch grass erupt out of what was once lush grazing. The line ripples as men and women stumble, children held tight by hot palms. Now and then it jerks as some step aside avoiding the patches of spiked, uneven ground. Closer to the main tent, progress is easier. A path has been trampled by the narrowing progress of similar lines over the weeks that *Hobbs Brothers' Circus* has been in residence.

From the midst of the line, Porter looks around. Screwing his eyes against the glare of the sun, he looks towards the haphazard collection of smaller tents, caravans, and trailers that litter the remoter edges of the field. He is uncertain what he's looking for other than the face of the unknown man from Claverley's photograph. He's memorised every blown-up inch of it, a face he's convinced holds the answers he seeks. A last chance, the last remaining glimmer of hope.

He feels a tug at his sleeve. 'Will there be tigers?' Tommy asks.

'I don't know,' he answers distractedly. 'Probably not.'

'Of course there will!' Rachel puts in quickly. 'Big ones!' she whispers dramatically. 'With fiery eyes and great big teeth! Huge claws like swords! *Raaghh!*' she exclaims, a hand reaching towards Tommy's face as she mimics the swiping motion of an animal's paw, her expression a facsimile of a roaring tiger.

Tommy jerks his arms across his chest, half-turning away. 'Aagh!' he shrieks, his cry a mixture of childish joy and fear.

Rachel laughs. She turns to Porter, face serious. 'You needn't be so matter of fact all the time. He needs some fun. Some fantasy,' she chastises.

'Sorry,' Porter mumbles, uncertain why.

Looking along the line, he realises it's mainly younger children - chattering excitedly, tugging at sleeves, pointing - who make up the bulk of the matinee audience. Despite the war, most seem to have adapted to their situation, finding adventure in the chaos - like Albert Willetts' boy and his mates, scrumping in the orchards or poaching in farmers' fields. The younger ones, those like Tommy, had known nothing but war. For them the shortages, the bombs, the mounds of rubble, the anxiety of parents, parent's tears, parent's fears, the loss of fathers, uncles, and grandparents is all they'd ever known. The circus was a rare chance for escape. For the older ones it offers a passing appearance of a return to normalcy; for the younger ones, a foray into a world they know nothing of.

'Wonder if they've got candy-floss?' Sheila asks.

'Dunno,' Eric Morrison replies, looking around. 'Might be an opening there if they haven't.' He nods at the queue. 'Lot of trade here, eh Alec? Opportunities for the right sort of man.'

'If you say so,' Porter responds.

Eric and Sheila shuffle along ahead of Porter and Rachel; Sheila's arm knotted possessively into Eric's. Tommy trots back and forth between the two couples.

Rachel, tugging herself closer to Porter, murmurs 'Alec, please.'

'What?'

"Try to be... Try to have a good time... At the very least pretend you are. For Tommy. For me.'

'Rachel...' he begins to protest.

'And be nice to Eric,' she interrupts. 'I know it was your idea to come to the circus - which was lovely - but, if it hadn't been for Sheila, and Eric and his car, well, God alone knows how we'd have got here. Try to show a little gratitude. Please.'

'Gratitude!' Porter snaps.

'I know what you think about Eric. But for me. Try. Please, Alec. Please.'

'Oooh, look, a camel!' Sheila pointed.

'Where?' Tommy implores, turning round, arms held up. 'Lift me up Alec!'

'Tommy, Alec can't, you know that,' Rachel says, reaching down for him.

"I'll do it,' Eric puts in, turning and swooping. 'Can't have our hero, one of our boys in blue, doing his back in,' he smiles. Eric lifts the child easily onto his shoulders. 'There you go soldier,' he says, settling the boys legs around his neck, clasping his feet to his chest. He turns so he's half-facing Porter. 'Sheila told me all about you solving that case. That gypsy girl. Pity they don't pay you extra for a thing like that. You know, a bonus. Maybe you'll get a medal or something. Only seems right.'

'That's not why we do it. It's about duty. Doing what's right.'

Juggling Tommy's legs, Eric fishes a cigarette case from his jacket, offering one to Porter who declines. 'Oh yeah. Duty. The right thing.' He taps a cigarette on the outside of the silver case, lights it. 'That's great stuff, Alec. Great. I understand all that.' He draws in the smoke and exhales. 'It's what Rachel said to Sheila, isn't it?' He waves the hand holding the cigarette around in the air. 'Makes you feel you're doing something... useful.'

Porter's response is lost in the delighted squeal of Tommy's sighting of the camels and Rachel's' tightening grip on his arm.

'There you go, Tommy boy!' Eric shouts, attention firmly focused on Tommy's joyous outburst.

Porter, glaring at Rachel, prises her hand from his arm.

They had reached the box office, a battered old Austin van; bright red paint and overlain images of elephants and clowns flaking away. Eric pulls a bulging wallet from his inside pocket, thrusting a pound note at the young girl dispensing the tickets. 'Four adults and a little 'un, ta, miss.'

Porter reaches for his own wallet. 'I'll get ours,' he objects.

Eric waves him aside. 'Already done. Least we can do.' He leans forward, head almost in the box-office hatch. 'Regular hero, this one, Miss. Regular hero.'

'Ooh, that right?' The young girl looks around Eric the better to take in Porter, her face revealing that her expectations of a hero are somewhat diminished by the figure standing before her, his eyes looking to the ground.

Porter shakes his head. 'No. Not at all.'

'Modest with it, too,' Eric persists. 'He ought to get a discount, don't you think?' he suggests in his best spiv tone, a patina of assumed friendship and presumed like-mindedness.

Before she can reply, Porter has grabbed the proffered tickets from the startled girl's outstretched hand. He bustles past Eric and Sheila. 'Let's get in,' he commands.

————

The steam organ pipes out its tune, a discordant chime of something upbeat and happy. A nursery-rhyme song, familiar yet other-worldly. The Big Top itself is an impressive feat of construction. Over a hundred feet across, at its peak in the pinnacles of the huge main poles, it rises to around sixty feet in height. Above the crowd, a network of ropes hang cobweb like. Trapeze bars and wires tied to massive white poles that form the twin peaks of the tent, supporting the entire structure. From the quarter poles flanking the tent, are banners of local businesses promoting goods and services, additions that draw approving comments from Eric. In the centre, is the main ring, some fifty feet in diameter. Around the perimeter of the ring lies an open area of several feet that is scattered with sawdust, and then the rows of seats. Those beyond the first three rows are raised on wooden platforms similar to the bleachers of American sports stadiums.

The large wooden blocks that prescribe the ring are alternate blues and red, several of which have gold stars painted in their centre. At the far-end, to the left of where they sit, a construction draped in red material protrudes into the Big Top forming a dramatic covered entrance. To its side, a few seats are set in a block with a battered upright piano, a kettle drum and a few other assorted brass instruments lain around; the Hobbs Brothers' Orchestra.

The audience is a good one, almost filling the seats, availing themselves of a rare alternative to the cinema or public house. The war had closed or destroyed most of the variety theatres. Apart from the dancehalls with their limited hours of opening, there is little beyond Hollywood films playing for weeks on end or worthy patriotic Pinewood films.

The audience is a mix of children, parents, and soldiers on leave. The air inside the Big Top is warm; the sour-sweet smell of grass denied the light of the sun hangs heavy. It mixes with the musky smell of animals and the rising temperature of the crowd.

Sheila and Rachel are lost in conversation, gossip about a mutual acquaintance and her philandering boyfriend from what Porter can make out. Tommy sits wide-eyed gazing around the tent, eyes skidding from one object to the next: his young face a study in wonder. Eric has gone in search of snacks. Toffee apples for Sheila, Rachel, and Tommy. Porter abstained. Eric was certain there would be bottles of beer to be found somewhere and that he was just the man to locate them.

Porter leans across Tommy, touching Rachel on the arm. 'I'm off to see where Eric's got too. See if he needs a hand.'

'Oh, he'll be fine,' Sheila replies. 'He's no doubt seeing if he can do a deal on supplying feed for the animals or stockings for the show girls.'

Rachel nods, smiling. 'Okay.'

Leaving the stuffiness of the Big Top, Porter stands in the still rising heat of the afternoon, scanning the layout.

Stringent blackout restrictions meant shows were matinee only. The huge diesel generators accompanying the circus sit idle, now only used for a few hours each day to power the fairground style rides set around the fringe of the Big Top. He knows his chance of finding his mystery man can no longer rely on the authority of his police or SIS credentials, that it might require a stealthier return at night. After a cursory look at his surroundings, he realises that even in summer once it becomes dark and the crowds disperse there is little in the way of lighting to find his way around. Fixing the layout in his head during daylight is essential.

He notes that the deployment of the circus followed the basic arrangements of the military encampments he'd known in Spain. A central core of trucks, tents, and caravans for the running of the business of the circus - the feeding of personnel, communications, records - and an outer horseshoe of caravans for accommodation. For *Hobbs Brothers'* Circus, beyond these lie a wider semi-circle of cages for the lions and tigers, with temporary corrals for the ponies, camels, and elephants.

Satisfied he understands the layout, he begins wandering between the inner ring of caravans and tents in the general direction of what he assumes to be the private quarters of the circus. He takes on the air of someone lost amidst the sensual overload of the circus. An *aficionado*, a fan. A man-child in search of personal wonder.

He passes what appears to be the main office, a red and blue caravan plastered with posters advertising the circus attractions. Images of lions, tigers, and clowns dominate each poster. At the centre, are images of beautiful showgirls clad in gold sequinned costumes, heads adorned with huge white feathers. They pose arms aloft inviting all and sundry to the magic that is *Hobbs Brothers' circus*. Some of the posters feature the major attractions of the Big Top - Hungarian knife throwers, mystical Arabs, Indian snake charmers, Belgian trapeze artists, acrobats from Mongolia and the Russian Steppes.

He is about to move on when something stops him. A poster. A poster featuring two of the major artists of *Hobbs Brothers' Big Top* show. On the left, the Hungarian knife thrower, on the right, the Belgian trapeze artist. It is the Belgian who catches his attention.

He moves closer.

The Belgian stood tall, gazing out at the on-looker; sequinned hosiery, upper body bare. His skin glistens, muscular arms folded across his chest, piercing eyes staring out in steely concentration.

Porter recognises the face, the eyes, that look.

It may have been an illustration, but there is no doubt in his mind that the man on the flying trapeze, the man in this poster - *The Great Fellaini* - is the mystery figure in Claverley's photograph.

He'd found him.

———

'*The Great Fellaini*,' Rachel states reading from the one sheet programme Eric has bought for them – *souvenir for the boy*.

'Wonder who calls them *Great*?' Eric muses.

'Maybe you just decide for yourself,' Sheila states.

'What? Like I could just decide, start calling myself *The Great Eric* or *The Great Morrison*.'

'Don't sound right,' Sheila says. 'Perhaps you need to be foreign for it to work.'

'Promoters, I suppose,' Rachel puts in. 'What do you think, Alec?'

Alec reluctantly turns his attention from the Big Top entrance. More than any of them, he's waiting impatiently for a sighting in the flesh of the man dubbed *Great*. 'What's that?'

'The name. Eric was wondering who calls them *The Great* whatever. How do they get that?'

'Advertising, I suppose.'

'Let's hope he is,' Eric says. 'Great, I mean.'

'Where's he from?' Sheila asks. 'I mean he's foreign, isn't he?'

'Belgium,' Porter says.

Rachel looks quizzically at him. 'How...?'

'The name's Belgian. I met a few. In Spain.'

Spain was a piece of his past never mentioned. Before she can ask anymore a drum roll of tympani and a trilling of the piano mean that Porter, like the rest of the audience, turned his attention to the ring's entrance.

Coming after the previous acts and their disappointingly erratic performances, Fellaini's entrance is all that the crowd anticipated. He is tall. Athletic. Muscular. Despite the trailing powder-blue cloak tied dramatically around his neck, it is obvious that beneath the trappings the Great Fellaini possesses a body toned in the pursuit of his craft. Dedication, Porter thought. Self-will. Belief.

The crowd cheer. Across from them a group of soldiers in uniform shout and begin rowdily stamping feet in unison on the temporary bleachers. One or two whistle, fingers in mouths, whilst the rest roar drunkenly. *The Great Fellaini* glances at them, nodding acceptance of their greeting before returning his face to its fixed mask.

Assistants in the form of two clowns take his cape whilst

close by two others fawn over yet another smaller clown dressed in a parody of the costume of the great man. A few kicks and a comedy chase between them later, the true star of the show begins his ascent to the bars high above the crowd.

The act that follows is everything the crowd wanted. A breath-taking display of athleticism and bravura showmanship. A high-wire act of death-defying leaps, mesmerising swings, spectacular somersaults, astounding double and triple rolls. Each catch, each feat, accompanied and dramatised by tympani rolls and crashes from the band.

Like the rest of the crowd, Porter's attention is fixed on the movement above him, the sweep of the spotlights arcing and spearing *the Great Fellaini* and his almost equally athletic assistants.

The act is drawing towards its climax when Porter becomes aware of Rachel turning her head to fix him with a stare. He looks ahead, upwards, ignoring her steady gaze. After a moment she leans in, half-whispering to him. 'Alec, just why are we here?' she asks.

He turns to her. She is half-turned to face him. He is aware of the look on her face; deeply serious, aware she is fixed on an answer to her question. He furrows his brow. 'Sorry?'

She stares back, dark-brown eyes penetrating his own. 'Why did we come here?'

He shakes his head, a frown of puzzlement on his face. 'I'm not certain what you mean. The circus. Tommy.'

'Don't you dare use Tommy as an excuse!' she snaps.

'What?'

'Where did you go?'

'What are you talking about? When? Where?'

'Earlier. Where did you go earlier?' Her tone is irritation laced with undercurrents of something much more powerful and troubling.

'You know where I went. I went to find Eric.'

'Eric came back by himself shortly after you left. You were gone for another twenty minutes.'

'I was looking for him. I got lost.'

She regards him for a moment, studying his face. Making her mind up, she shakes her head, spitting the word out through clenched teeth, 'Liar!' she curses, turning abruptly away.

The cheers of the crowd drown his reply. All eyes are on *the Great Fellaini*. Porter reaches out, touches her shoulder. 'Rachel, what's this about?'

She shrugs his hand off her shoulder. 'Don't Rachel me. Don't touch me! Do you think I'm stupid? I can see her.'

'See who?'

When she turns toward him, he sees tears forming in her eyes. 'Her. Floode.'

'Floode?'

'She's here. There.' She points.

Porter follows the accusing arm. Sitting in a tan trench coat to the side of the performer's entrance is Floode. Her hair is pulled back from her face, tied in a bun, eyes fixed on the climax of the trapeze act high above her, but it is her. He sits transfixed. Rachel stares at him for a moment before turning away.

His mind races. Floode being here meant one of two things. SIS were either following him, or they were unaware of his presence and were there looking for the same man he was.

The crowd leap to their feet in tumultuous applause at the final act of daring enacted by *The Great Fellaini* and his troupe. The band crash into their closing music, the soldiers whistle and stamp louder than before. The children scream their enthusiasm.

Porter sits, mesmerised, pierced.

The troupe make their way down the ladders followed at the last by *Fellaini* himself. The bows are snapped out, arms raised aloft, waves to the crowd, and he is gone.

The performance over, the crowd begin to exit. Eric and Sheila stand, gathering their things. 'Wow! How bloody amazing was that!' Eric says approvingly. 'He is *the Great Fellaini*. How about some of that, Tommy!'

Tommy chatters away excitedly, arms whirling around.

Rachel stands, checking around the seating, ensuring Tommy has all his things. Porter takes hold of her arm. 'You've got to believe me. I didn't know.'

She stops what she's doing, turning. 'Oh come on, Alec. What is this? Coincidence?'

'No. Yes. It's… complicated.'

'Complicated is what it isn't, Alec. It's all too bloody simple.'

'It's not what you think.'

'Then what is it?'

'I'm not sure… I can't tell you.'

'Then you'd better stay away until you can.' She pulls her arm away, turning from him. Reaching a hand down, she slips Tommy's hand into her own. 'Come on Tommy.'

Tommy turns, looking back confused, pointing. 'What about Alec?'

'He's not coming with us. He's realised he's things to sort out here.'

Behind her, Eric shrugs. 'Duty, eh, Alec? What about getting back? The car. Do you want us to wait?'

'He'll find his own way back, won't you Alec?'

Porter sits transfixed. 'Yes.'

Tommy pulls away from Rachel, running back, reaching up and hugging the still seated Porter around the neck. 'Come on, Tommy,' Rachel calls. Tommy releases his grip and runs to her. She gives Porter one last cold look before turning away, and with that, the two of them follow after Eric and Sheila. Soon they'd merged into the lines of exiting audience and were gone.

He sits staring at their backs. *What was the alternative? Call them back? Tell Rachel he'd lured Tommy and her here because he wanted cover for his investigation?* Tell her how he'd knowingly exposed them to potential danger - the two people he was supposed to love most of all - so that he could find a man he believed had answers to questions that still troubled him? And what kind of a man was he seeking? A dangerous man. A killer. A killer of women. *How did he tell Rachel that?*

How did he explain that Floode was there not because of some lover's fixation, but checking that Porter was keeping an agreement he'd made to stop his investigation, an investigation Rachel herself believed has become an obsession? How could he tell her that Floode was more than a driver, that she too wanted the man Porter so desperately sought? How could he convince her that Floode might be as dangerous a threat to Rachel and Tommy as anyone?

He couldn't.

If he told her the truth it would be the end of them as surely as her believing in his betrayal.

But that wasn't why.

To have her believe him meant he would have to stop.

And he couldn't.

He was close. He could never hurt her. But this, this was different. Webster had labelled it a fixation, a compulsion, a drug. All he knows is that he can only end it with the truth. Without that, it will never stop. He'd had his share of nightmares. The nightmares of Spain, of the orange grove, of his cowardice. Nightmares he would never lose. Nightmares that would pursue him to his grave. Bella was different. Bella's horror had an end. He could remove her from his nightmares, his guilt.

He stops. He has to clear his head. He can no longer afford for any part of him to be thinking about Rachel or anything else beyond what was happening here and now. *Fellaini. Floode.*

The crowd had thinned, the tent almost empty. He looks across. Floode was gone.

If nothing else, he'd learned from what happened to Claverley that he has to act fast. He has to get to *Fellaini* tonight, get to him before Floode, before SIS. He would make the man talk. Whatever else might happen, he was going to get answers.

Reaching around the back of his trouser belt, he lets his hand rest on the reassuring touch of the Colt's grip.

One way or another it ended here. Tonight.

———

Lehrer, thin cotton towel draped loosely around his neck, rubs the sweat from his forehead with the free ends of the cloth. The show had been a good one. The crowd had responded enthusiastically. He in turn had found the elusive inner reserves of adrenalin he needs to ensure each leap and somersault is performed with the élan and panache not always available to the performer. After Liverpool, when this was all over, part of him would miss such moments. To truly be in control of one's own fate.

Reaching for the handle of his caravan, he is suddenly aware of movement close behind him. About to turn to confront the threat, he feels the unmistakable cold barrel of a pistol thrust into the small of his back. 'Get in,' a voice whispers. 'Get in, now.'

27

The tent was dark. A silhouette set against hedges that draw a dark line around the field. The sky was blackening, the fading light casting deep shadows over the washed-out grey of the *Big Top*. Porter uses his sense of touch, hands against canvas, to make his way round the outside of it. Left arm extended, he feels his way forward, ducking under dimly perceived guy-ropes, using whatever light remains to establish a sense of his surroundings.

His hands find a slit in the canvas, part of the large tent flap that serves as a covering of the access point for the audience. Lifting it, he slips inside, crouching low whilst he accustoms his vision to the gloom of the interior.

Blinking, he finds a dim yellow light drawing his attention towards the centre of the space. Over sixty feet away, in the middle of the circus ring, stands Floode and a man he recognises: *The Great Fellaini*. The performer sits on his haunches in the sawdust. Floode stands above and in front of him, bathed in the pool of light provided by a safety lamp powered by the diesel generators that chug in the background. The lamp, one of three Porter knows to be attached to the main poles, enables maintenance work after the shows. The very dimness of the light and the thickness of the canvas ensure blackout is not broken.

He edges closer, each movement preceded by hesitant, tentative checks that there is nothing blocking his path. No object which might be knocked or toppled and reveal his presence. Some inner sense tells him to be wary, to conceal his presence. Nearing the ring, he removes the Colt pistol from his waistband.

Closer, he sees Floode has a gun centred on Fellaini. Whatever they are saying, it is clear she is in charge of the situation. What remains unclear are her intentions. *Why are they stood here? Why wasn't she taking him in?*

His thoughts are broken by the emergence of a figure from the shadows. The man is well-built, muscular, a cheap suit failing to conceal a powerful frame. This was no *Category E* civilian. The man was fit, military fit. He stands with Floode, deferring to her. It meant he too was more than likely Special Services.

'Everything ready?' Floode asks.

The man grunts a reply.

She waves the barrel of her gun in a tight circle. 'It looks as though we can begin,' she says.

'I've told you, I have no idea what you want of me,' Fellaini responds.

From where he stands Porter senses rather than witnesses the smile that spreads across Floode's face. 'That's perfectly okay,' she states, voice light, airy. 'You see, we're not here for you to tell us anything. Quite the contrary.'

Porter edges his way closer, anxious to hear all that is said.

The performer looks up at Floode as if for the first time fully considering his situation. 'Who are you?' he asks.

Floode wags the pistol in his direction. 'Does it really matter? The more pertinent fact is that we know who you are. We know you to be a German agent, part of an espionage cell passing military secrets to the German High Command.'

'Preposterous!' Fellaini exclaims. 'Madness!'

'We have known of the existence of this cell of yours for some time,' she continues. 'You see, we used you, fed you false information. The man you knew as Claverley proved very helpful in that respect.'

Fellaini shakes his head. 'This is madness. I don't know what you are talking about. I don't know any... Claverley. I am no spy.'

'As you like. Your own usefulness, and that of your cell, has long since run its course. Since Claverley's recent disappearance we've spent a deal of time looking for you all, his remaining contacts. Dronkers. The Dutchman, Van Ralt. And of course, you, the hardest of all to find. Claverley knew nothing of the identity of Van Ralt's handler, the man we'd called the analyst. You've proven very elusive Mr Fellaini - or would you rather use your real name? Your German name.'

'This is preposterous. Ludicrous! I am Fellaini, a Belgian citizen. I fled from the Nazis. Why would I be helping them? Why would I do such a thing?'

'You are a German officer. A spy. You parachuted into this country in 1941. You were met by Van Ralt. A mercenary. A man for hire. A collector of sympathisers and contacts. Contacts such as Claverley. Contacts who could be bought. You formed an espionage cell. You Van Ralt and three others - Johannes Dronkers, Dronkers wife Clarabella, and Claverley. We have known this for some time, this and so much more.'

She gazes down at the man who returns her stare unblinking. 'Claverley was Jack Mossop, a petty black-marketeer, a man known to us. A fantasist. A man with communist sympathies who we'd long ago turned as a double-agent. He told us everything about your cell, its members. He fed you the intelligence we wanted you to have. Some of it was real - a sop so you would unquestioningly swallow the bigger lies we fed you. We knew the intelligence was passed to Van Ralt, but the one thing we didn't know was who you were, or how the intelligence was passed to Berlin. Claverley described you, but he had no idea who you were. Had no idea that the circus camp where you'd once met was your cover, the place where you hid in plain sight. After Claverley's disappearance, Van Ralt became even more cautious in his movements. We knew you were still here, active. It was simply a matter of time. Of waiting.'

'This is fantasy. Where is your evidence?'

Floode squats, her face level with that of the man she accuses. 'Evidence?' She stares blankly into his face. 'What makes you think we're required to present evidence? My superior's see you as a threat.' She holds the gun close to his face, stroking it across his cheekbone before pressing the barrel gently against his forehead. Her voice drops, purrs. 'This isn't a court of law. This isn't a trial.'

Though his eyes were unwavering, she is aware he sags.

'My superiors require this matter be ended. Your death ensures that.' She presses the gun harder against his skull.

Porter scrambles to move forward. He has to intervene. He rises from where he'd crouched in the bleachers, begins moving silently towards the light.

Suddenly he feels the sting of pain in his back. It is sharp, hot, the familiar searing burn of hot metal against his spine. He is wracked with pain, desperate not to scream out.

His back spasms, the pain coursing through him, tearing into every synapse and nerve ending it can find. *Too long! He's waited too long!* He bites his lip, gritting his teeth he somehow suppresses the urge to scream out and reveal himself. But now his legs collapse, useless stumps that fail to respond to his command. He crumples, his body slumping to the floor, face down, tasting sawdust and dry hay as he grits his teeth harder trying not to shout out. *Too late. After all this he is too late.*

The sound of the animals and the flapping of the canvas in the gentle summer breeze merge with the chug of the generator. Focused as she is on the man at the end of the barrel of her gun, Floode remains unaware of anything outside the pool of light.

Lehrer closes his eyes.

She holds the pose for a moment before pulling the pistol away.

She rises, nodding to the man in the shadows who moves into position behind Lehrer's back. 'A terrible accident,' she says, looking up at the trapeze suspended high above their heads. 'You were checking the rigging when you fell. A broken neck. Dreadful, but an acknowledged risk in a career such as yours. No one will investigate, particularly not the death of a Belgian national during the war. After the war, well, you'll be remembered as nothing more than what you've pretended to be all these years. A second-rate performer. A side-show. Not an honourable death for an officer of the *Abwehr*, but it serves a purpose.'

Porter presses his arms to the ground, struggles to push his body up. The throbbing is easing, the body's endorphins and adrenaline working to numb the pain. As he rises, he twists his upper body, easing the pressure of the shrapnel against his spine. He has to get up. He has to stop this madness.

Lehrer feels his arms jerked violently back as his hands are held behind him. The SIS agent nods to Floode he is ready. Lehrer feels the man's forearm position itself behind his neck, a knee in the small of his back, the other arm grasping his head.

Porter staggers forward keeping tight hold of the pistol, the pain in his back still flooding through him. Clenching his teeth, sweat flowing down his forehead and into his eyes, he shouts. 'Stop!'

Floode and her accomplice freeze, eyes straining to see into the gloom beyond the centre of the ring.

'Stop or I'll shoot!' Porter forces out as menacingly as he might through the pain.

'Porter?' Floode enquires, squinting into the darkness.

He steps to the hazy edge of the light, gun pointing at Floode. 'Put the gun down, Andrea. Now.'

She takes in the dishevelled figure, clothes covered in

sawdust, face ashen with the pain that is wracking his body. 'Jesus, Alec. What the hell do you think you're doing?'

'I might ask the same.'

'Alec, just go. Leave. You have no idea what you're getting into.'

'Put the gun down, Andrea. I'll shoot if I have to.'

'You won't shoot,' she says. She watches as he holds the Colt tighter, knowing that even as she spoke the sweat is greasing his palm as he strives to hold the weapon as steady as he can. She smiles, nods towards the revolver in his hand. 'Is it the back again?' She sighs. 'As for shooting…It's not in you, Alec.'

Porter flicks the gun up and down, a gesture only partially concealing the trembling in his hand. 'You know nothing about me. What I'm capable of.'

She smiles again. A half-smile. Confident, assured. Everything he is not. She shakes her head. 'I know everything about you, Alec. I know you won't shoot me.'

'People change.'

'No. they don't. Not the deep things.' She fixes him with a penetrating stare, knowing that even at this distance she is capable of holding him. 'You see, I discovered some time ago something very important about killing. It's in you or it's not. It was in me before SIS recruited and trained me. You see, it's not the training that enables you to kill. The training just makes you better at it.'

'The gun, Andrea.'

'You won't shoot. You can't.'

'Whatever you believe you know about me, I will shoot. This man is under arrest. He's wanted in connection with a murder investigation. He's coming with me. If he's guilty, he's going to stand trial. He is going to tell the truth.'

'Truth? What truth?'

'The truth about Bella.'

'And what precisely is that?' she asks.

'He killed Bella. Either that, or he knows who did.'

Lehrer looks from one to the other. A dawning of understanding. 'Clarabella? Me? I did not kill Clarabella. You're the Detective! The one in the papers.'

Porter glances towards him. 'Clarabella?' *She was Bella.*

'The body in the tree? Yes. Yes, she was Clarabella Dronkers. Dutch.'

'She was an agent?'

Lehrer considers his situation. He isn't stupid. He would never betray his country whatever fate that might bring. But this woman's story stunned him. *Claverley a double-agent?* Claverley, the simpleton, the weakling fooling them? Fooling him? If what she said is true, then how far had he betrayed them, their work? The deployment of forces for the invasion, the High Command's plans to repel it, all of it was in part based on the intelligence he'd provided. He had to play for time. Time might allow for word to reach Berlin, time for the chance to redeem their error.

He looks to Porter. 'The woman, Clarabella Dronkers, she worked for us. I am Hauptman Thomas Lehrer of the *Abwher*, German Military Intelligence. She knew the area. She worked here before the war. She helped arrange my acceptance by the circus. I did not kill her. I did not kill your Bella.'

'Then who?'

'Claverley.'

Porter shakes his head. 'No. That's a lie. You're saying that because he's dead and can't answer. Why? Why would he kill her?'

'He was told to.'

'Told to. By who?'

'Dronkers. Johannes Dronkers. Dronkers, Claverley, and another, the Dutchman. Van Ralt. The three of them murdered her. They strangled her with her own scarf and hid her body in a tree.'

'Why? Why kill her?'

'She was about to betray us.' He nods towards Floode. 'If this woman is to be believed, it seems we were duped. That it was

Claverley who was betraying us, not her. Circumstances, Detective. Clarabella gave cause for us to believe she was the one about to betray us.'

'So you killed her.'

'It was Dronkers idea, though Claverley was a willing advocate. Now I understand why. He'd always seemed… squeamish about such things. But it was Claverley who first revealed her betrayal. We believed him. Even before her end, she sought to persuade the others to surrender. They killed her close to the woods. Dronkers knew the area. He said putting her body in the tree would confuse any investigation. He said it put suspicion on the gypsies who camped there. He had the crazy idea of making her killing appear as if it was linked to witchcraft. Clarabella herself had told him all about the place, its mystical connections, the practices of those who worship there. It was his idea to chop her hand off and bury it. His idea to take her wedding ring and shoes.' He snorts at the irony. 'She was a mystic, you see. She told fortunes. She'd done so in the Fatherland before the war. She knew the circus, the circus life. She told us she'd held sessions with Hess and others. She told us the Fuhrer himself feels a deep connection with such things.' he snorts once more. 'Imagine our delight when you found her body and went off looking for gypsies and witches.'

'Imagine,' Floode put in.

Lehrer looks to Floode and back to Porter. 'Of course Dronkers was himself dead by then.'

'Dronkers is dead?' Porter asks.

'Your military shot him.' Lehrer nods in the direction of Floode. 'Ask your lovely friend from SIS about that.'

'Hanged?' Porter looks at her, his expression a question. 'You told me you were still looking for them. Solomon told me SIS were unsure what had happened. That SIS didn't know if they were alive or dead.'

'Picked up in the channel in a boat with two others.' Lehrer continues. 'Don't you read your papers, Detective? Still, I suppose such a story had no connections for you at the time. There was little coverage. Dronkers was machine-gunned on the spot. All over very quickly.'

'Is this true?'

Floode ignores the question. 'This man is a spy, Alec. A German agent. I have my orders.'

'Why kill him?'

'Orders.'

'Andrea, think about this. Why not a trial? None of them. Dronkers, Claverley, and now this man. Why kill them?'

'Alec, this is national security. You don't ask questions. You follow orders.'

'Not orders like these. Shouldn't we question orders that go against all civilised laws?'

'For God's sake, this isn't one of your cosy Cambridge seminars. This is war.'

'So they all die? Bella, Dronkers, Claverley, Lehrer. What about the other man, the Dutchman?'

'He's already taken care of,' she states.

'Dead?' Lehrer looks up, face turning pale.

Floode glances down at her captive. 'Dead. Very dead. You're the last.'

'The last? The last of what?' Porter interrupts. 'What's so damned pressing that all these people have to be eliminated? Aren't you in the least curious?'

'If we don't follow orders people die. Our people.'

'If what you say is true, then one of ours did die. Claverley. What happened to Claverley? To Mossop?'

'He killed himself.' She nods towards the squatting Lehrer, 'Even he said he was weak.'

Porter shakes his head. 'I don't see it.'

'For God's sake! You're not a Detective, Alec. Not a real one. You're a cripple. A coward. You're unfit. You find stolen bicycles.' She shakes her head. 'Walk away. Go back to Rachel. You're out of your depth. Standing there pointing a gun at me like some G-Man. Look at yourself. Your hands are shaking so much you'd never hit us, even if you could find the balls to shoot.'

He involuntarily takes his eyes off her, looks at the gun, heavy in his hand. Seeing his distraction, Floode seizes her moment. She raises her weapon, levels it at his chest. A shot rings out.

Porter staggers, hands automatically searching, scrabbling across his chest, his side, desperate to locate the wound, to stem the flow of blood he knows will follow the shock of impact. His mind races, frantically checking himself for where he's been hit, waiting for the reaction, the pain, the copper smell of blood, the darkness.

Nothing. She missed.

He looks up, staring ahead, frozen, watches as Floode staggers forward before slumping to her knees, torso bending, doubling her up. A second shot rings out. Beyond her, Porter watches the man from SIS crumple, dropping to the ground as he'd scrambled to withdraw his pistol.

Porter stands transfixed.

Watches as on her knees, Andrea somehow raises her pistol and fires.

At point blank range Lehrer topples backwards. Seconds later, from out of the darkness, another shot tears into Floode. A hit dropping her prostrate to the floor.

Porter's mind now grasps the fact that there is another in the tent. The shooter. He spins round, eyes searching the darkness for the source of the shots, gun pointing ahead of him.

'I'd put that down if I were you,' a voice calls from the shadows. 'If I wanted you dead, you'd be dead. Drop the gun.'

Porter drops the gun. After he does so, a tall figure in a pale trench coat steps into the light.

Before Porter can speak, a groan from Lehrer alerts both men to the fact he is alive. Porter moves first, crossing the distance quickly to kneel beside him. A few short paces away, the stranger kneels, checking Floode for a pulse, though her stillness indicates there is little point. Satisfied she is dead, he moves across, similarly checking the body of the SIS man.

Porter examines Lehrer. A broad red stain is spreading down his left side and across the front of his chest. The bullet entered somewhere below his left collar bone. He's bleeding badly, losing blood at a rate suggesting he will not survive.

Porter senses rather than sees the movement of Lehrer's lips. He leans in, trying to catch his words. After a few ragged sounds comes a slow exhale, Lehrer's head slumping to the side. Porter sits back on his haunches. He gazes at the corpses littering the sawdust of the ring, the blood puddling beneath each body.

He senses the Texan moving closer. He stands, turning to take him in, eyes transfixed by the Colt that hangs loosely in one hand at the tall man's side. In the cool of the tent, wafts of blue-white vapour rise from the hot barrel. Quite literally a smoking gun.

The Texan indicates the prone figure of Lehrer. 'What'd he say?'

Porter ignores him. 'Who are you?'

The man looks at Porter, face unrevealing. 'A friend.'

Porter focuses on the accent. 'You're American.'

'Texan,' he corrects.

Porter can't think. 'I don't understand.'

The Texan dips his head towards Floode's body. 'Your friend over there seemed hell bent on shooting you. I couldn't let that happen.'

'What are you? OSS?'

The Texan's voice is level, matter of fact, a man accustomed to violent death. 'We've been watching you for a while. Since your appearance in Malvern.'

'Why?'

Slipping the Colt inside a holster tucked under his coat, the Texan takes a cigarette packet from his pocket, pushes the pack in Porter's direction. Porter declines. The Texan takes one for himself. 'Your visit back then hit a nerve. Seems those who decide these things believe we retain an interest in the answers you might find to your murder.'

'Bella?'

'That the dead woman in the tree?'

'Yes. The dead woman in the tree.'

The Texan lights his cigarette. 'Seems she approached us in late Forty-one. Our embassy in London. Said she had something of great interest to our government. A secret. A big one.'

'But you weren't in the war then.'

'Exactly. She was sent on her way, but her visit was noted in a general intelligence report sent to Washington. Someone there - probably some bored analyst with time on their hands - read it. Seems they were intrigued as to what she might have to say. They asked the Agency to check her out. By then she'd disappeared. Now we know why.'

'She was dead.'

'She was dead. When you found her and started asking your questions at the base, some other smart analyst in DC read the description and put the two things together. Your enquiry became of interest to us. The fact this woman was killed so soon after her approach to the Embassy was of interest. Coincidence? Or was there something to it? What was it she'd had? Had it got her killed? Whatever the case, someone at OSS was intrigued enough to want to find out.'

'Why now? I mean, 1941. What could possibly be of interest to your people now?'

The Texan holds up a hand. 'Hey, not my call. I was tasked to follow you, see what you turned up. You turned up Claverley. Seems we knew him too. SIS involvement tweaked our interest a little further. Especially when they seemed so intent on closing you down.'

'What do you mean?'

The Texan grins. 'I mean that from the get-go SIS have been working their asses off to give you reason after reason to shut down your investigation. You must've had doubts of your own about what's been going on. *Why* was Floode assigned to you? *Why* an SIS operative, an agent trained to kill? Did she really at *any point* actively help, or was she here to keep a closer eye on what you were doing, where *you* were looking? Was she directing you *to* things or *away* from others?'

'They gave me access. Things I'd never have got near to without SIS help.'

'They *buried* you, and you know it. A mountain of paper. *Shit*! If you finally got out from under they figured you'd be tired of it all. Give it up. Sign it off. They needed you to quit. They wanted you to convince yourself there was nothing to be found. What about your superiors? What was their contribution?'

'Williams and James? They wanted it closed. Gypsies they said. But they were just keen to get the paperwork done. They're not conspirators.'

'What about the fact that your professor friend was warned off. Told for his own good to persuade you to close down the investigation.'

'Webster's a good man. Decent.'

'Of that, I've no doubt, but SIS wanted him out of the picture.'

'I…'

'And Claverley. Where did that get you? You found the link to your Bella. That forced their hand. They offered up what they thought you wanted - at least, what they were prepared to let you have. Then… Claverley dies.'

'Suicide.'

'*Really*? *You believe that*? Of course you don't. Then there's the Dutchman, his throat slit. *Why was that*? Why didn't SIS want you talking to him? SIS knows everything - the connection to Claverley, to Dronkers. They're tracking this Van Ralt, and he's suddenly murdered right under their noses? He was last seen in a pub with a woman. A dark-haired woman. A real beauty by all accounts.' He looks towards Floode. 'Or is that coincidence again?'

Porter stares at her corpse. 'It's possible.'

'It's *possible*? All these people dying right under the nose of your security force? That's pretty sloppy work, don't you think?' The Texan tosses the butt of his cigarette away, sparking it into the darkness. 'And Dronkers. The husband.' He indicates Lehrer's corpse, 'You heard that from this guy yourself. Picked up in the channel a year ago, summarily executed. No trial. No statement. And now tonight, this man. Lehrer. Why were SIS so desperate to execute him tonight? And why make it look like an accident?'

Porter shakes his head. The Texan had given voice to his own thoughts, his own conclusions. There was nothing left to say apart from the obvious, the issue haunting him from the start. 'I don't know.'

'Seems to me there's too much you don't know. She was prepared to kill you too.'

Before he can respond the Texan holds up a hand, inclining his head to the side as he listens. Porter hears it too. People. Circus people drawn by the sound of the shots and gathering outside the Big Top deciding what to do. Soon they would enter.

The Texan pulls his trench coat tight around himself. 'No time for this. I can't be seen to have been here. My involvement, my Agency's connection to this, it becomes way too complicated for everyone - my government and yours.' He makes a rapid calculation. 'Once they get inside you'll need to organise a response. You're a police officer. Take charge. Get them to raise the local police. They'll contact your station to confirm who you are. Pretty soon SIS will be all over this, shutting down questions, managing the news. Whatever they ask - your bosses, Solomon, SIS or anyone else - you got here too late. It was over. Lehrer had already killed Floode and her man.'

'But-'

'Listen! You know there's something not right about this.

Claverley, the murder of this Bella woman. Floode, Solomon, SIS, and now this little soiree tonight. Until either of us can work out just what that is, you need to keep things simple. People have died over this. Be clear, Porter. SIS won't have any compunction in killing one more.'

The Texan unties the bonds on Lehrer's hands, takes the gun from his holster and places it in one of them. 'You cornered him. The three of you - Floode, her man, and you. Your back, everyone knows about your problems with your back. Floode had you cover the outside whilst they went in to arrest him. He shot Floode's colleague. Floode shot him, but as he dies he shoots her. You arrived too late to save her.'

'But-'

'There's no time. Tell them that story and make whoever they send believe you. I'll talk to my people in Washington, try to get some kind of handle on whatever it is that's going on here. Porter, I don't know what kind of a rabbit-hole we've fallen into, but one way or another we both need to get to the bottom of what's going on. The lies. The secrets. All of it.'

JUNE 27TH, 1943: DAWN

Porter stretches warily. The twinges from his back progressively more painful, more frequent, and, as last night had proven, increasingly debilitating. He hadn't slept well. Truth be told, he hasn't slept at all. The furore that had broken when he'd called in the shooting had provoked a long night of questioning - first the local CID, then Williams and James. Now he awaits the arrival of Solomon. The instructions was clear; stay there, say nothing.

He sits by himself in the circus caravan commandeered for the enquiry. In the Big Top, the bodies of Floode, the unidentified man from SIS, and Lehrer remained where they'd lain since their deaths. Aside from grey-green tarpaulins lain over them, little had changed.

'It's a bleeding mess,' James had stated in his nasal Brummie upon arrival at the scene. 'A bleeding unholy mess.' Williams had been less severe in his judgement. 'Regrettable,' had been his summation of three dead bodies and Porter's unwillingness to offer anything beyond a brief explanation of how events had unfolded.

Idly, Porter now picks at the loose flakes of wood on the edge of the fold out table the breaking light of dawn casting an unearthly glow through the windows. He looks at walls adorned with posters and flyers from pre-war performances across the lowlands of Holland, Belgium, and France. A circus went wherever it cared. There would be little interest in questioning its intentions or in bothering to interrogate too closely those who adopted its transient way of life. The perfect cover.

The door of the caravan opened. Solomon enters. Behind him, Williams and James attempt to follow, the three of them finishing up crammed into the entrance, James half outside, a step behind and below the other two. Porter rises, a flash of pain immediately making him regret the gesture. Solomon, seeing the flare of pain across Porter's face waves a hand for him to sit. 'Sit down,' he says, Porter obliging. Solomon, Williams, and James crushed together, take up the bench seat opposite.

Solomon tosses his peaked military cap onto the table, a hand sliding back through his hair whilst his eyes study Porter. 'How are you feeling, old chap?'

'Tired.'

Solomon nods.

'Confused,' Porter adds after a beat.

Concerned at overflowing off the edge of the bench, James jumps in. 'He's been asked to write up a statement but insisted we had to wait for yourself to get here.'

Solomon reflects on James' point. 'Is that right?' he asks of Porter.

'I thought you'd want to be the first one to know what happened. To Floode. To your man. It was after all, an organised SIS operation.'

Solomon dips his head. 'Dreadful business. I know the family. They'll take it hard.' He looks out the window. Rain is starting to fall, the wind whisking it against the windows of the caravan, the spattering of the drops the only sound. He turns to Porter and the two detectives. 'Detective Porter's absolutely right. We should go and have a look at the scene. But before I do that, I need to know exactly what happened.'

James dumps his trilby on the table, mopping a handkerchief at his brow in a show of exasperation. 'It's what we've been asking all night. A triple killing. I mean to say, war or no war, we need to know what happened.'

Solomon continues examining Porter's face, gauging his reaction. He turns to Williams. 'Maybe you should both step outside for a while.'

Williams, nodding acceptance, begins to rise. A startled James continues sitting, his frame blocking any exit. Williams finds himself trapped in a contorted half-risen position. 'Sorry?' James says.

'I understand your position Inspector, and yours, Sergeant. But Porter's right. Floode was one of ours. SIS. There may be issues of national security here.'

James looks from Solomon to Williams and back. 'This is a police matter. Three shootings.'

'You can contact Whitehall if you wish, but all you'll succeed in doing is delaying matters further and, in the process - as I'm certain you Inspector realise only too well - you'll be upsetting a group of people that you really don't want to get on the wrong side of. Anything deemed pertinent to any police investigation will be passed on to you.'

Williams nods. 'Come on, Sergeant. He's right.'

Reluctantly, James rises, shuffling uncomfortably away from the bench. He stands to the side, waiting deferentially for his Inspector to extricate himself.

Solomon smiles. 'Perhaps, Inspector in the circumstances your Sergeant can supervise the taking of statements. Perhaps getting the bodies removed from the scene. I know Floode's parents would be grateful for such consideration.'

Williams murmurs agreement, and he and James leave.

With them gone, Solomon stands, dropping his gloves on the table to rest by his cap. He looks around the cramped space. 'I need a tea. How about yourself?'

Porter shakes his head.

Solomon walks to the sink. He lifts the battered kettle, swishing it around, judging the amount of water. Satisfied, he places it on a gas ring and lights it.

'She died instantly if it helps. With the family, I mean.'

Solomon faces Porter, his expression grim. Almost imperceptibly he nods acknowledgement. 'She was one of our best.'

'Strange she should be here. At the circus. That she should be confronting Fellaini.'

'Strange?'

'I thought the link to Bella had been discounted. Floode told me SIS were certain Claverley was the killer. That the operation ended with his suicide. There was nothing to investigate.'

'We did.'

'So why was she here?'

'As I said, we did.' He stands by the sink. He faces Porter, his face set in an expression of one contemplating a confidence. 'Floode was a good agent. The fact that you had your killer didn't mean her work in locating enemy agents was over.'

'Enemy agents? So you knew for certain Bella was a spy?'

'Knew? No. This is espionage, Porter. Often we actually know very little at all. It's instinct. You know that for yourself. Look how far you've come on instinct. Like you, Floode was keen to find a motive for Claverley killing your Bella. Your tenacity infected her. To be frank, she felt bad about how things worked out between the two of you. Felt bad about confronting Rachel in your home. Felt she owed you something. Finding a motive for your murderer, the man Claverley, was doubtless her way of paying that debt. She told me about the photographs Webster sent her. She said he'd tracked down the manufacturer of the tent. She was set on finding the mystery men in the photograph. I told her it was more than likely a wild goose chase – that they'd be long gone - but she was adamant.' He set his expression to grim. 'This wasn't a sanctioned operation, Porter. I can only assume she recruited Simpson - that's the other agent killed tonight - to tag along. She died trying to find your answers, Porter. She died trying to solve your mystery. The tragedy is that with the death of this Fellaini it seems we'll never know.'

Solomon turns to the task of finding a cup.

Porter hesitates, the tall American's words resonate in his head. *Don't trust anyone.* For Porter they were a prod, not a restraint. 'Her name was Bella. Clarabella Dronkers. She was a Dutch national. A spy. One of those you sought.'

Solomon pauses in his search. He turns to Porter. 'You're certain?'

Porter nods. 'Absolutely.'

Solomon, half-smiles. 'We're standing less than a hundred yards from the bodies of two of my people caught up in the madness of your gypsy murder. In the circumstance, you'll understand it if I find your record regarding the matter of proof - other than your own wild speculation - less than convincing. How can you say, *absolutely?*'

'The man calling himself Fellaini was alive when I found him. His name was Lehrer.'

The kettle lets out a high-pitched whistle as it comes to the boil. Solomon stands staring at Porter, ignoring its shrill wail. 'Who?'

'Lehrer, the missing link. The leader of the German espionage ring.'

'Lehrer?'

'The dead circus artist. The man calling himself *The Great Fellaini* was German military intelligence. An *Abwehr* officer called Lehrer. Thomas Lehrer. He recruited Bella and her husband, a man called Johannes Dronkers. His contact here was a Dutchman called Van Ralt, the man we believed to have in turn recruited Claverley.'

'And you believe this?'

'He told me as he died.' Porter returns Solomon's stare. 'I think your kettle's boiled.'

Solomon turns off the kettle but remains standing by the gas ring. 'What else did he tell you?'

'Much of what you yourself told me when we first met. But he filled in the details, details that might have saved us a deal of time and several deaths.'

Solomon returns to making his tea, pouring hot water into the pot and scooping in a tea-spoon of dark leaves.

Porter presses on with his narrative. 'He parachuted into the country in 1941. As you know, there were reports at the time of parachutists in the area, but nothing concrete was found so it was never really followed up. The ring focused on gathering intelligence regarding weapons manufacture and deployment which they fed back to Berlin. They believed they were effective. But they weren't. You told me you controlled the flow of intelligence Mossop had access to.' He gazes out of the window. The rain had gathered pace, battering against the glass with greater urgency. 'Sitting here, going over it all - my investigation, what Floode told me, what Lehrer said before he died - I worked something out. Claverley was far from being a communist sympathiser acting on orders from Moscow. He was SIS through and through. A double-agent. A delusional fantasist whose boastings and propensity for play-acting had no doubt got him into all this. He was SIS from the very beginning. First as Mossop and later as Claverley. Claverley was in fact your idea, your creation all along.'

Solomon stood saying nothing.

Porter continues. 'The Luftwaffe raids based on the intelligence you provided bombed abandoned or deserted airfields and factories. Maybe a few cattle grazing in their fields. As Claverley, Mossop's reports to the group, to Berlin, of the damage inflicted on the allied war effort were as fictional as the location of the targets. It means he wasn't the naïve dupe you told us he was. He had to know what was going on in order to sell it to his contacts. No doubt the reports of the damage were written by SIS. Maybe you yourself. But no one in his position couldn't fail at some point to notice the discrepancies. I see that now. I just hadn't stopped to think it through. He had to have been in on it from the start. You recruited him. Either that, or you turned him.'

'Mossop? My man? Preposterous. I told you, he was a Russian agent.'

'Lehrer said the group came to believe there was a traitor amongst them, but they didn't know who.'

'If that was the case, if they suspected a traitor, then why didn't they accuse this man Claverley. If it's all now so obvious, why didn't they kill him? Why wasn't his the body in the tree? He was the outsider. The obvious suspect.'

'Because he fooled them. He knew they thought they had a traitor, a double agent. So he gave them one. Most likely, you gave him one. Claverley was the one who convinced them Bella was the double-agent.'

Solomon stirs the brew in his cup. 'That's quite an imaginative tale. But you're adding it all up into something it isn't. A fantasy. A delusion. The question is, what is it you're trying to do here? Justify your own sorry failures? Absolve your conscience of Floode's death?'

'It's not the whole story. I know that. But it's all Floode knew. The story you told her. There's more to it. I know that. Lehrer knew it too. Before he died, he realised the real reason for Bella's murder. The reason why you had Claverley frame her rather than one of the others. She had a secret. He told me. *Tarpeia*. The same word Claverley scrawled in a notebook.'

Solomon snorts. Shaking his head, he walks to the bench

table. He sits opposite Porter cupping the tea in two hands. He sips the brew, staring at Porter. He considers the man more than his words. He places the mug down, a hand resting either side. 'Porter. Alec, old man. I really don't have the faintest idea what it is you're talking about. For God's sake! Haven't we had enough of you with your Murray woman and her witches and dark magic? What did that all that '*entombed in the tree*' nonsense turn out to be but a bloody stupid fairy story! A story that threw everyone off the track of finding these people by having us hunting for gypsies and wizards instead.' His show of exasperation ended, he sighs. He sits forward. 'Now it's what, spies? Espionage? Mata Hari? Maybe it's the shock. The shootings. Finding your lover shot dead must be hard on anyone. Knowing that it's because of your fixation, this obsession of yours…. Well, that must be even harder to bear.' He exhales, a short plosive escape of breath. 'Even harder on a man like yourself. A man with your medical history. Stress. Nerves. Breakdown. It can happen to anyone. People are much more understanding these days. Not like before.'

Porter fixes him with a glare. 'There's nothing wrong with my thinking.'

'I wouldn't be so sure. Only have to talk to any of your friends and colleagues. Rachel, her father. Webster, Willetts. All of them suggesting they're concerned about your mental state these past few months.' A pause, each subsequent phrase becoming a beat, a rhythm of fact. 'Pushing yourself. Overdoing it. Obsessed. This case. Bella. Morbidly so. Not the actions of a rational man, of a man in control. Quite the opposite. You've woven a fantasy around this Bella. For goodness sake, you even named her! You need a rest.'

'Her name *is* Bella. And I don't need a rest.'

'Afraid you've little choice in the matter, old chap. I'm certain your Inspector Williams will agree. Sergeant James especially so. Home Office will insist. Can't have a man like yourself running around causing problems. There's a war on, Porter. A war we need to win. That's all any of us are concerned with. You've become a distraction. A fatal one for Floode and Simpson.'

Solomon holds his cup, sipping his tea, letting the moment settle. 'You do have a choice, however. Let it go. Accept the fact that, as far as everyone out there is concerned, Detective Constable Alec Porter is a hero.' He raises a hand from the cup, tracing a newspaper headline in the air. *'The man who solved the case of who put Bella in the wych elm.* The rest of it - Lehrer, Van Ralt, Dronkers is finished.' He lowers the cup, both hands clasped around it in absorbing its warmth. 'You must know there will be no trial. This is national security. They're all dead. There will be no enquiry. These were spies, enemy spies conducting operations against us. We've saved the country a trial, a trial that would have had them all shot anyway.'

'Why is everyone so keen to draw a veil over this?'

'What's the point in publicising it? Stirring up fears of spies under beds. Not good for morale, a spy ring operating under our very noses who we'd been unable to find. More than that. Why tell the Nazi high command that they're bombing empty fields and abandoned factories? With luck they'll continue to bomb them rather than the real targets or the centres of population. You'll be helping save lives, Alec. Hundreds of lives. Maybe thousands.'

Porter looks out of the window. The rain battering against the panes, the trees in the distance bowing their branches in the gusts that sweep across the meadow.

Solomon presses on. 'After the war, once we've won, you give Mossop's widow a national hero rather than a mentally disturbed suicide. You give Rachel and her boy a hero to look up to. Who knows, after all this, possibly a husband and step-dad. Think about the boy's own dad's death. Wouldn't Rachel's father-in-law change his views on the man she's with - the man raising his only grandchild - if you were a war hero rather than the cowardly malingerer he sees you as? And Webster. You give Webster a key part in a success that he can build his forensics department on. Think of the use his work will be in protecting the rule of law in the new Britain. Why risk all of that?'

'Because it's not true.'

'Porter. Alec. This is war. This isn't some undergraduate debating society. Christ, man! You of all people should know that. You went to Spain to fight the Nazis.'

'I went to fight in Spain because I didn't want us to end up like them. The lies. The propaganda. The contempt for life. The contempt for truth. The contempt for decency. The disregarding of the rule of law. The abuse of truth and power.'

'Tell me. Just what is it you want? What do you think this truth is that you're looking for? This meaningless *Tarpeia* nonsense.'

'I don't know.'

Solomon waves a hand in the air. 'Then what's the point of all this?'

Finding only silence, Solomon sits back, spreading his arms wide. When he speaks his voice is measured. 'Alec, write the damned report just as you've been told to. Accept the commendation. Go home to Rachel and Tommy and forget all this. You're done.'

28

Porter sits at the kitchen table, the morning newspaper lain out in front of him, pot of tea mashing under a red and white knitted cosy. The cup and saucer - delicate China, Wedgwood, undoubtedly from Rachel's wedding service. A glass sugar bowl and bottle of milk are arrayed around the tea-pot. All are presently pushed aside, creating space for the bright red metal toolbox he rummages through in search of the small can of oil he knows to be there.

Moving aside rust stained pliers and paint tarnished screwdrivers, he lifts clear a smeared red can, swilling the contents gently from side to side in checking the level of the remaining oil. He places the swan like spout against the metal rod held steady in his hand. He begins pressing the flat metal key-like pump attached to the handle of the can, an action forcing a stream of golden lubricant to ooze onto the spindle. Placing the can on a sheet of the newspaper, he rotates the spindle back and forth, ensuring the oil spreads evenly around the shaft. Satisfied, he locates the spindle into the mechanism, locking it in place by its retaining spigot. After a series of gentle rotations, the spindle revolves smoothly. Content, he places the whole back into the chassis of the toy car, snapping it securely into place.

Tommy would be pleased.

He sits back, arm reaching down and round to his spine, relieving the dull ache shadowing his every movement. He stretches his arms out in front, then cautiously to either side. He feels old, tired. Lost.

Lifting the cosy off the pot, he pours the tea. It is pale and insipid. He tastes it; lukewarm and as weak a brew as it looks. *The third mash already today?*

He puts the cup down and begins packing away the tools. The last thing he needs is a simmering row with Rachel over the mess, or with Arthur over the state of his toolbox.

He lifts the oil-can from the newspaper, placing it back into the tool-box, taking care not to create further drip marks down the side. Looking to where it had stood, he curses. Despite his best efforts he finds a thick black ring, the smeared outline of the base seeping into the newsprint of the paper. He picks it up, fearful the stain might seep onto the tabletop. A fragment of headline catches his eye.

HEROINE AGENT SMASHES SPY RING
Brave Female Operative Dies Preventing Nazi Spy Plans.

It was how it had been told.

Returning to Bromsgrove the morning after the shootings, he'd filed a report in line with what Solomon suggested. There'd been little real choice. An asylum for himself, ridicule for Rachel and Webster, or silent acquiescence and his emergence as a hero.

The story had been carefully crafted, Solomon keeping the role of SIS to a minimum so as not to alert the *Abwehr* or the German High Command to all that SIS had done in feeding false intelligence to the Luftwaffe. The demands of intelligence trumped all else, closing the tale and any further enquiry for good.

It had been agreed for the story to be released to the papers via the local force. Understandably, DI Williams and DS James had been more than pleased to share credit for the operation. More than obliging to see the matter ended. What else could they have done knowing so little of the facts? The story was that of the authorities breaking what was described as *a gang of desperate and violent black-marketeers*. The narrative held the gang to be a mix of foreign nationals and British Nazi sympathisers plotting to aid Berlin. It told how a joint operation involving police and British Intelligence had been alerted by the discovery of one of the suspects, a Dutch national and known black marketeer, in a local canal with his throat slit. The discovery had prompted a raid on the nearby *Hobbs Brothers' Circus*. A raid resulting in a shoot-out and the killing of the leader of the gang. The cost had been the lives of Floode and Simpson. Porter's role and that of Webster in locating the hide-out of the criminal mastermind, a Belgian national calling himself *The Great Fellaini*, was reported as having been key in tracking down the gang.

He screws the newspaper up, placing it in the bucket of wood and coal by the open fireplace. He walks out of the backdoor and into the narrow patch of garden, the bloom of flowers replaced by dark green clumps of sprouting potatoes and onions. Rachel was at work, as was her father-in-law. Tommy was in school. It was the third week of Porter's enforced leave. A leave that should he prove obdurate in his conspiracy claims or indicate signs of recanting his report would become instant dismissal and his sectioning into St Margaret's.

He was officially a hero. There was talk of a medal. A return to work.

The doctors had seen him. They'd checked his back. They'd confirmed the shrapnel had moved and that it was still subject to movement. That from time to time it would press against his spine rendering him temporarily paralysed. Like the doctors in

Spain, they'd told him such paralysis might last a few seconds, possibly a few minutes, maybe hours or days. They warned him that a shock to the back like a bad fall could make any paralysis permanent. Beyond the pre-existing condition, they'd found no evident further damage.

Williams, undoubtedly at the behest of SIS, had insisted on a psychiatric evaluation. The official diagnosis, written in a scrawled hand across his medical record, stamped in blocked red across his police file, was *stress and exhaustion*. The psychiatrists were keen to probe further. His case was a cause of fascination - the trauma of Spain triggering an obsessive fixation on Bella. Bella, like his Spanish adventure, was judged to be a romantic lost cause chased to the exclusion of all else. A fixation. A *Don Quixote* complex, one doctor had volunteered shortly before letting slip that Solomon was pressing to have him committed to St Margaret's under the care of Woodbridge and Morgan should he not take the option of extended leave.

He took the leave. Took the medication.

It dulled him.

He was Porter but not Porter. A shell. Hollow.

He spent his days putting back together broken toys, those jobs around the house that had been left to await the end of the war.

Rachel had taken it all in her stride. He'd hurt her. Hurt her badly. He'd offered little by way of explanation, even less in mitigation of her accusations of infidelity. He'd offered nothing of himself. She seemed to accept it, prepared to stoically continue, though both knew that everything had changed, that nothing would be the same. It was not to be spoken of, a shameful lunacy, locked away in some dark place never to be mentioned.

At some point soon he knows he will leave. If not, they would both be trapped forever. A situation offering nothing beyond material security for Rachel and the outward show of a fulfilled life for himself. A sham. Hollow.

It was a lie. Like everything else that had flown from that moment, that tree. It was a madness. Nothing was real, nothing was true. All was hollow.

Yet everyone appeared to accept it. No one prepared to speak the truth, no one prepared to admit to the wild implausibility of so many things in this case. Rachel, her father-in-law, Webster, Solomon, Williams, and - worst of all – he himself. It was a stage set, an elaborate hoax of a life. No matter the skill involved in the intricate recreation of the surface features of the real world, it was at its heart a fake. An ornate and lavish deception. An elaborate and skilfully constructed artifice of invention.

It was a lie. All of it.

And he could lie no more.

Even now, the truth could set him free. Set them all free. But how to do it? How to protect those he cherished whilst tearing the cover off all that was hidden? He had to cast light into that darkness. Had to.

He had a truth. At least, some shape of a truth. He had to know it was real, that something was finally as it seemed. Lehrer's final word, whispered with his dying breath, haunted him. The word engraved on Claverley's drawing of the tree. *Tarpeia.*

He'd travelled to the Birmingham Central Library and its reference works. There, in the Victorian splendour of the Central library, an aged reading desk in a shaft of light from a fading summer sun, he'd read and learned.

The legend tells that while Rome was besieged by the Sabines, *Tarpeia*, daughter of the commander of the citadel, approached the Sabine leader, *Titus Tatius* and offered his army entry to the city in exchange for *"what they bore on their left arms"*. Greedy for wealth, she had meant their heavy gold bracelets, but once successful in their conquest, the Sabines instead threw their shields - these too carried on their left arms - upon her, crushing her to death. Her corpse was hurled from a steep cliff on the southern summit of the Capitoline Hill. The cliff was thenceforth named after its victim. The *Tarpeian Rock*. It became the place of execution for all Rome's traitors.

He'd read and re-read the details of the myth. All of it reduced to one simple story honed to four bullet points in his notebook:

the greed of women.

the betrayal of women.

the penalty for betrayal.

the death of traitors.

What had Lehrer meant? What had Claverley seen?

He'd spent days scribbling ideas in an old notebook. *Had Lehrer been referring to Floode - she was the only woman there that night - or to Bella?* The legend was a story of betrayal, betrayal by a woman. Lehrer had been duped by Claverley's claims of Bella being a traitor. *Had Claverley planted the idea by using the very word? Was that why Lehrer had called it to mind?* All of them - *Claverley; Dronkers; Van Ralt; Lehrer* - had contrived in Bella's murder because of it.

Had the dying man, confronted with the error of his actions, reached out to the spirit of the woman he'd conspired to murder? Then why not call her name? *Why not call out Bella? Why utter an obscure reference to dim legend and mythology? Tarpeia.*

He worried at it. Was it nothing more than the ramblings of a dying man, a dying mind lost in the chaos of its final breath, its final earthly thoughts.? The reference was surely too random for a dying mind to latch on to, too specific to not mean *something.*

It was a puzzle, an enigma. He needed a key, something or someone that would link the reference. Open the door to understanding.

But what or who was that key?

Tarpeia.

He'd said it to Solomon, and he'd reacted, he was certain he had. His bluster, his ignorance, had been feigned. Porter knew a thing or two about deception by now. Solomon had been struck by his using that word. It had meaning. Could he use that? Was the word itself sufficient to gain access to the truth the secret *Tarpeia* concealed?

He goes inside to the small bureau, removes a sheaf of writing paper. He sits at the table and begins to write. Answers more important now than consequence. The Texan was wrong. There are things that have to be pursued, no matter what the cost.

JULY 20TH, 1943: AFTERNOON

He sits opposite Solomon and Pidgeon. The Whitehall office was imposing - high ceilinged, wood panelled, dominated by the great oak desk that Pidgeon sits behind with Solomon to his right. Heavy curtains designed to reduce collateral damage from panes shattered by the still regular bombing, frame the window. The walls are lined with images of military triumph, heroes both conquering and fallen. In each portrait the central figure is defined in reflective heroic repose or as bloodied and torn on a battlefield. All were men of honour. Each one looking down in judgement on those gathered under their watchful glare.

Pidgeon spreads his hands wide, a gesture intended as indicative of the all-encompassing nature of his words. 'Well, Mr Porter,' he begins, 'it appears we just cannot shake you from your... insistence in pursuing a matter that the rest of those involved believe to be long ago concluded. Some might say you are quite a stubborn fellow.' His face is a fixed expression, hard to read - not quite the smile that might lend some deprecating humour to what he says, but neither is it stern, the offering of a warning of the dangerous ground Porter impeded upon.

'I like to think of it as determination. And I believe it's still *Detective Constable* Porter.'

Whatever it had been previously, Pidgeon's expression stiffens. He pauses, considering the appropriate tone. The Head-masterly rage that Porter's admonishment might have been expected to provoke for the moment held in check. Pidgeon has objectives he wishes to take from the meeting, none of them served by a loss of temper. When he speaks his manner is clipped - brusque even - a man deferring to the outward show of civilities but a man intent on making his points in the clearest possible manner. *'Detective.* I've agreed to meet with you today for one very simple reason; to put an end to what most would characterise as your infernal meddling in matters that divert the attention of decent serving officers from the vital task of beating Hitler.' He pauses to study Porter's reaction. Finding nothing beyond a straight face, he presses on. 'Throughout this investigation, the officers of my department have gone out of their way to ensure there has been full co-operation between ourselves and that of yourself and the local police force.' He enumerates on the fingers of his left hand each point as he makes it. 'We have provided bodies on the ground, gave you transport, and of course, access to intelligence data far beyond what we might have been expected to provide.' His expression is a portrait of sadness. 'Not to mention that two of those officers died whilst carrying out operations linked to your own. And to top it all off, Captain Solomon here personally undertook to see to it that you, Detective, received not only fulsome credit for your part in that operation but, so I understand, there is also talk of a medal.' He sits forward, picking up a sheet of paper that Porter immediately recognises. Pidgeon's hands play along the edge of the document as he continues. 'I say this so that you fully comprehend both why I agreed to this meeting, and why it is that I feel more than a little aggrieved at the tone and content of this letter you saw fit to send to Menzies and Cavendish-Bentinck.' Pidgeon waves the sheet of paper in the air, wafting the document like Chamberlain on his return from Munich. 'Frankly, Detective Porter, you've cost this office a great deal of time and trouble with what can only be described as your morbid fixation. And now you see fit to rub salt into those wounds by these malicious accusations of a conspiracy.'

'Fixation? It's my job. Investigating crime.'

'And you believe there's a crime here?'

'I would call murder a crime, wouldn't you?'

Pidgeon settles back, calculating his answer. 'I'm a military man, detective. I haven't the luxury of such moral judgements, such fine distinctions. We're in a war. A war against a great evil. In war we have military objectives, and securing those more often than not necessitates killing the enemy. So, no. No, I cannot see every death, every killing of my fellow man as murder. There are lines. Gradations. Contexts.'

'So war justifies everything?'

'An honourable war. A just war. A just cause, yes. Absolutely. What's the saying – *All's fair in love and war.*'

Porter's violent shake of the head measures his disagreement. 'Forgive me, Colonel, if I say that even in such hazardous times as these, those are dangerous sentiments. There are rules about such things, even for a soldier - the Geneva Convention for one. But, irrespective of that, there's surely simple right and wrong. You talk of contexts and gradations, but there are some lines that can never be crossed. Never. Believing we are right, that we are the good guys, cannot excuse every action we might wish to take in its name. We do so at our own peril and that of all we say we're fighting to preserve.'

'Ah, of course, Detective, you have some experience in such things, have you not?' He smirks. 'Sacrifice. Killing for a cause. Spain. Quite an adventure.'

'Adventure?' Porter's eyes narrow. 'There was little of the *Boys' Own* about it. Men died. Young men. Good men. Women and children too. Innocents. And yes, we thought we were right. Believed it was a cause worth our sacrifice, one even worth our lives. We believed we were fighting for freedom and for justice. But that's what's driven me here. To find out if we're still all truly fighting for the same thing.'

Pidgeon raises his eyebrows. 'I was at *Passchendaele. Ypres.* I know everything about the Slaughter of Innocents,' he chides. 'Is that what you came here for? To give lessons in *the horror of war*?'

He pushes the letter away, an action chasing it across the desk to settle against the edge of the blotter. 'My superiors in this - these men you wrote to - want this to stop.' He scowls, contempt in his voice. 'I can assure you that granting this meeting was not my idea. Pandering to your fantasies, your calumnies! I am here at their behest. Orders.' He curls his top lip. 'I've read your letter many times, and I still have to ask; just what it is you want? What is the real issue here? Is it your politics? Your conscience about death and killing? Your guilt? Can't you sleep at night?'

Porter rubs a hand through his hair. His back aches, his head throbs, a dull buzz of discomfort runs down his spine - muscles reacting to the recent lack of medication. 'I've no abiding interest in politics. Spain finished me with that. And, no, I haven't come here to lecture on the morality of war. As for my sleep… Yes, I have nightmares. Nightmares about death and killing. Don't you? Don't Menzies and Cavendish-Bentinck? Winnie too? You say you've read my letter. My unofficial, off the record report into the murder of the woman I call Bella. I assume that's why I'm here, why I've been granted this interview.'

Pidgeon snorts. 'Interview? You make it sound official.' He turns to glance at Solomon and then back to Porter. 'Am I under police caution, Detective? Should I call for my solicitor?'

Porter smiles. 'We both know your ability to pull down the cloak of national security renders anything you might say here today, or at any other time, inadmissible in court. I've no jurisdiction. I'm not looking to arrest anyone, to put anyone on trial.' He wrinkles his brow. 'The truth is a simple one: I was given the murder of a young woman to investigate. It is an investigation left incomplete. I merely want to submit my final report on that murder.'

Pidgeon allows his hands to rest on the desk. He steeples his fingers, considering the matter. All three men sit allowing the silence to distance them from what has been said. 'And once this has been submitted?'

'I walk away.'

Pidgeon looks to Solomon. Solomon's expression is one of uncertainty, a movement of the head indicating his lack of any offer as how best to proceed. Pidgeon turns back to Porter. 'What is you want to report?'

'I want to discuss *Tarpeia.*'

Pidgeon tenses. 'Detective Porter, this is the War Office. Military Intelligence. Do you think you can just walk in here asking questions about operational matters and get an answer?'

'It's a simple request.'

'With no simple answer.'

'I'm not looking for simple answers. I've been given those throughout this investigation. None of them work.'

At that moment, a door opens behind Porter. He is aware of someone entering the room, of someone sitting in one of the chairs close to the doorway. He doesn't look round. His interest is the two men in front of him.

Pidgeon sits forward, elbows resting on the great oak desk. He looks beyond Porter in the direction of whoever has entered. His gaze lingers for a moment before his head moves faintly, as if in acknowledgement of something unpleasant that has to be done. He gives Porter the impression of a man acting against his own instincts, his own wishes. 'Very well. Let me first ask you a question. Where did you hear that name?'

'It was scrawled on a drawing by Claverley. I gave it no thought at the time. Everyone was convinced he was delusional. Then, later, I heard it on the lips of a dying *Abwehr* officer. A man calling himself *The Great Fellaini,* who was, in fact, a German agent called Lehrer.'

'And that sparked this idea for your latest report?'

'I've spent the past weeks filling in the blanks with what seem to be viable propositions, propositions that fit the few known facts I have. At the end I had a story. A story of a Nazi spy ring established to obtain intelligence of the production and movement of allied weapons. A group initially comprising Lehrer - a young promising *Abwehr* officer - his local contact, a

Dutchman by the name of Van Ralt, and a traveller, a young woman. Together they set about creating a network unlike any other. They'd learned the lessons of those who'd gone before, those who'd been too easily discovered. They recruited others to their operation. Those such as Johannes Dronkers, the woman's ex-husband and a man with an eye for Nazi gold. Knowing the area, the woman we'll call Clarabella was especially useful. She was a mystic, a fortune-teller. A woman who'd travelled across Europe with the Romany. Their plan was simple. Lehrer, a promising gymnast in his youth, would travel with the circus, whilst the woman Clarabella travelled with the Romany. There would be no prying neighbours of either. No one asking questions of these newly arrived individuals. They lived in communities uninterested in the secrets of those who shared their life. Communities closed to those outside them, especially the authorities. Their travel allowed them to roam to ports and other sensitive areas, places where they could more easily find the means to send their intelligence back to Berlin to their masters.'

'Fascinating. Circuses, gypsies. Like a Grimm's fairy-tale. Do go on.' Pidgeon urges.

'They recruited one more to their cause. Claverley. Claverley was important to them, important enough for them to take a risk, to break their plan of only using those already known to them. Those whose loyalty had been bought and were sufficiently bound to the cause for them to be trusted.'

He pauses, eyes closing, recalling his theme. 'And it was a mistake. A fatal one. Claverley was not what he seemed. Claverley was in fact a low-level intelligence recruit by the name of James Mossop, one of hundreds of such SIS informants tasked with watching out for Nazi sympathisers in their workplace or local communities.'

'How do you know this?' Solomon interrupts.

Porter turns in his direction. 'I spoke to a colleague who told me such informants exist. They lull suspected sympathisers into indiscretions, confessions. They tag them for the authorities, and then keep watch for signs of their undermining the war effort or passing on intelligence. In the event of an invasion, they're to help in the round-up of these potential traitors. A select few are also tasked with killing those sympathisers who might provide key tactical or strategic support for an invading German army. Am I wrong in any of this?'

'You've been thorough,' Solomon admits.

Porter turns back to Pidgeon. 'I imagine Mossop somehow met Van Ralt socially. According to his wife, Mossop liked to fantasise about himself, about his importance. He no doubt did so sufficient to impress the Dutchman who recruited the man he knew only as Claverley to their group.'

He warms to the narrative. 'They must have thought they'd hit the gold mine. Claverley reported his meetings to his handlers, a fact very quickly passed up the line to more senior officers here at SIS. Men like Captain Solomon, or even you yourself, colonel. The details are irrelevant. Mossop posing as Claverley fed them every falsehood you gave him. It was the perfect operation. You secure in the knowledge that the work of this ring was contained where it caused little real damage, whilst at the same time occupying swathes of the Luftwaffe in bombing empty fields and dummy factories. Brilliant.'

Pidgeon makes no overt response, but Porter sees the truth arrive in his eyes. Porter sits back. 'But then something went wrong. Something spooked the ring. Whatever it was, they believed they had a traitor. Suspicion would most obviously turn to the outsider, your man, Claverley. You couldn't let that happen. By then he was too important to you. Somehow he was able to convince them that it was Clarabella who was the traitor, and they killed her. Now, not only was your man safe from discovery, but even deeper in the trust of the ring through his action in unveiling the traitor and in helping to get rid of her. So it continued. Continued until we found her body.'

He stops. Takes a beat. 'That was a problem for you. By then

SIS had similar interests with those of the enemy spy ring. Should the body of the woman be identified there was every chance the investigation might lead to Claverley, exposing him, compromising his work. You couldn't tell us to stop. The police is full of part-timers, men who make a little money selling such information to the press or spivs. You couldn't risk word getting out that he was one of your own, especially as by then he was feeding Berlin false information of plans for the Allied invasion. Instead, you saw to it that the police appointed a naïve young officer to the case. A compliant, green Detective. A man ambitious for a case. A man given the clear instruction to tie up the paperwork and seal the matter forever.'

Pidgeon looks to Solomon. 'If your theory were correct, that would seem a sensible move on our part, wouldn't you say so, Solomon?'

Solomon smiles thinly. 'Very sensible, sir.'

'But then things go further awry. The investigation starts to follow a different direction. Webster gets involved and his forensic ideas start to threaten the simple solution you require. That meant SIS had to have a more direct, hands-on approach, keeping things under control. Claverley learned of the investigation and he runs, most likely fearful Lehrer and the others will see police interest in him as a threat to themselves. Maybe he's even more worried that SIS will disown him, allow him to be executed for a murder in order to protect their secret operation. His mental state, already fragile, shatters. For you, everything from that point on is about control, damage limitation. Everything is now geared to diverting the investigation into blind alleys. You offer mountains of paperwork. You offer help, and when that too seems not to be going the way you want, when your threats to the professional careers of the investigators don't work, Floode offers herself up to the Detective and the lever of blackmail is used to stop him.'

'That seems to be a very arcane justification of your infidelity,' Solomon puts in with a grunt. 'Your relationship with

Floode was your choice. I'm told you were a more than a willing accomplice in any betrayal of your lovely and innocent Rachel.'

Porter nods. 'That's true.' He pauses, shaking the distraction of his infidelity away. 'Whatever the matter of it, it too offers little real certainty. Claverley remains loose and a threat. His revelations in any police investigation would alert the Luftwaffe to what's been happening. They would rethink their strategy. Reconsider their plans for repelling the Allied invasion. So, when he reappears, a traumatised amnesiac, you decide you can't take that chance. You eliminate Claverley, at the same time seeing it as a way of ending the police involvement that had become such a complication to your plans.'

'One thing,' Pidgeon interrupts. 'Claverley was a suicide.'

'Yes, the convenient suicide.' He smiles. 'I've not been entirely idle these past weeks. Willetts spoke to the ambulance drivers on duty at St. Margaret's. Seems there's quite a camaraderie and gossip among the drivers of fire-engines, ambulances, and police-cars. Three patients arrived there the afternoon we saw Claverley. All three were shipped off again the following morning. Seems they were big men. Athletic. Fit. They didn't seem to the ambulance drivers to be the usual patients they take there.'

Pidgeon's expression is one of exasperation. 'This conspiracy theory is becoming quite ridiculous! Most of the patients at places like that are military men, each of them physically fit. They're there not as patients from their physical wounds. They're there from the trauma of battle. Frankly, I would find them *not* taking in fit military men unusual. You're grasping at straws if you see this as evidence of conspiracy.'

Porter shifts his position, frustration pushing through the gnawing pain in his back. 'I'm certain you're correct. I have no doubt that the official records will, if called, show those men as exactly that. That's not a detail I would expect SIS to have overlooked.'

'So where does that leave your story? Oh, sorry, your theory?' Solomon asks.

'Where this all began.'

'And that is?'

'Bella. Her murder.'

'How so?'

'The question behind every murder; *why*? Once Claverley told you of his predicament, his potential unmasking by the cell, why select Bella? Why not Van Ralt or Dronkers? Why her? Why was she the one you selected to be framed as the traitor?'

Pidgeon's eyes shift uneasily, his body language one of a man reluctantly relaxing into the pub bores' shaggy dog story. 'For arguments sake, let's assume for a moment your theory to be correct, that Claverley was as you have it *'our man'*. Who would you choose to die to protect your agent? According to your theory, Claverley is a vital asset in national security. We would be foolish not to protect him.'

Porter agrees. 'At that time you had no idea who the leader of this cell was. Lehrer maintained distance, anonymity. You wanted him but you couldn't get to him. Van Ralt was your only link to him - kill the Dutchman and you lose that link, besides which, he was the one most trusted by Lehrer. You'd assume that Lehrer would never consider Van Ralt viable as a traitor. If nothing else, the money was too good. Van Ralt knew Dronkers. Though he too was a mercenary, he was also a committed fascist tied into the cause. He had nothing to gain from betraying them. He would have been an unlikely traitor for them.'

'So, you've answered it yourself. Your logic is impeccable. If things were as you say, the choice would always be this Bella to be the one to be given up.'

'But you still had to convince them. They would have required more than the word of Claverley. Proof. What proof could he give them?'

'Is that of consequence?'

'Yes. Yes it is. That was the thing that most haunted me. She was the least threatening of the group, yet she was the one you chose. Why? Why her? I thought at first it was because you were working in a hurry. But that couldn't be right. As long as Claverley provided what they believed to be good intelligence he remained safe. They might be suspicious of him, but he was the golden goose laying eggs that promised glory and honour. Riches. They wouldn't move against him without hard evidence.'

He sees in their eyes that they know what he knew. Knew what had been done. Why they'd done it. 'You see, it didn't ring true. There was something missing. Something I was supposed to miss - as were they. Lehrer knew it at the end. *Tarpeia*.' He shakes his head. 'It had me puzzled for so long. Then I saw it too. The secret was the word, the legend.'

'How so?'

'It's a codename. An operation. Our operation.'

'I don't follow.'

'He was repeating a word he'd heard, not one he'd originated. *Tarpeia* is the SIS codename for an allied espionage operation, not the German *Abwehr's*. It wasn't about Bella betraying the Germans, it was Bella betraying us.'

'What! You're now telling us that this Bella was another double-agent!'

'Far from it. SIS gave the operation to protect Claverley that codename because it was about her reward for her betrayal. *We* are the Sabine army. She thought she would be getting British gold, instead she received your shields. SIS had her killed because of what she knew. Not just that Claverley was a double agent. She knew more than that. Much more. A secret you couldn't risk her revealing. This whole operation was much more than protecting Claverley or duping a spy ring. *Tarpeia* was only ever about killing Bella. She wasn't killed as a consequence of *Tarpeia*. She was *Tarpeia*. Lehrer, Van Ralt, Dronkers even Claverley - they were collateral deaths. Bella was your target. She was always your target.'

'Why would that be?' Pidgeon asks. 'You yourself have outlined a perfectly sound set of logic as to why she might have been killed by Claverley. She was what our American allies term the *patsy* for a vital operation. She was one of theirs, after all, not one of ours.'

'So why kill all the rest? Dronkers, Claverley, Van Ralt? What did you think they might know that was worth their execution without trial? Why did they have to be denied a platform for their story?'

Solomon spreads his hands at what he sees as the obvious answer. 'According to your own theory, to prevent the knowledge of a double agent operation reaching Berlin. To preserve the duping of Nazi preparations for resisting an Allied invasion. To save more civilian lives. To save our soldiers' lives. To protect the war effort.'

'It's not enough.'

'Not enough? The saving of countless lives? Ending the war more speedily? It's there in the evidence you yourself offered as proof for your theory.'

'But why not interrogate them? I'm no intelligence officer, but every police officer knows that interviewing a suspect is vital. There's the possibility of them possessing intelligence we are unaware of, intelligence that might be of use. Why summary execution? And why Claverley? He was one of our own. If it was about deceiving the *Abwher* back in Berlin, you could have left him in St Margaret's. Anything he might say would be taken to be the ramblings of a lunatic, a fantasist. Why did he have to be silenced? That bothered me too. But once you understand *Tarpeia* it becomes blindingly obvious: he knew the secret Bella possessed. He knew why she was chosen by you as the patsy. You couldn't risk his recalling that, telling someone. Couldn't risk the chance that someone like me might believe him. That some doctor might take him seriously.'

Pidgeon takes a moment to sift what he is hearing. 'That's quite a story. However, if this theory of yours were true, there remains one obvious flaw. This was years ago. Why the need to eliminate the rest of the cell now? Why would it matter anymore? Why kill Claverley and Van Ralt and this Lehrer now?'

'Because it still matters. It had to be something that mattered at the time, really mattered. But mattered not just at the time of her death in nineteen-forty-one. It had to be something that still matters now. More than that, something that even after the war would be of such potential damage that they had to die.'

Pidgeon shifts forward, face screwed in disbelief. 'And in all this theorising and speculating, detective, did you conclude as to what this might be? This dreadful secret which you say your Bella and the rest were killed to protect?'

He did. He knew their dirty secret.

He knew who put Bella in the tree. He knew why.

And it terrified him.

29

It had come to him days ago. Revelation. Scales dropping away.

He was sitting in the Central Library in Birmingham, researching. Over the weeks since the shooting, his trips there had become part of a fixed routine. Each morning catching the train into Snow Hill Station. The long walk along Colmore Row to the library, the exercise helping his physical rehabilitation at the same time as offering seclusion away from prying eyes. In the days following the shooting he'd been watched. Once or twice catching sight of familiar faces on the train, the same faces later in the reading room and outside Lyons corner café. Over the following days and weeks of his new routine the observations had become intermittent, those interested in his movements now seemingly convinced there was nothing to concern them.

The library had been quiet, a place to think as much as a source of research. He'd sat there day after day, by then accustomed to the derogatory stare of elderly librarians wondering why someone of his age and apparently healthy physique wasn't in uniform as the young men in their own families undoubtedly were. His trips had become commonplace, routine. He was to all intents and purposes precisely what

Solomon and Williams and everyone else thought him to be: a recuperating police officer returning to a pre-war love of books and of learning. Nevertheless, he remained circumspect in his selection of reading material. Anyone checking the reading list he submitted to the librarians each day would find nothing raising concern or alarm in a study of Greek and Roman mythology.

Arriving each day at his usual time, he'd made his way to the vast domed reading room to wait patiently at the counter under a high vaulted ceiling as reminiscent of a Victorian Gothic cathedral as it was a civic building. Gazing up, he was always conscious that its purpose was not adornment; it spoke to the values of the Victorian fathers of the city who'd built it. Held true to the Victorian attitude to learning; part veneration, part intimidator of those wishing to access its treasures.

Having submitted his requests, he'd sit at a study desk anticipating the efforts of the librarian trawling up and down the tiers of shelf stacks to find his chosen tomes. For the next few hours he'd read and make notes, reference books scattered around the same desk that as a matter of habit he'd taken to occupying on each visit. It was at the back of one of three rows of tables, six tables in each row, each table with the capacity to seat five people along one side. The chairs were austere, round backed and wooden. The spindles offered precious little respite for his back, but learning was a practice to be taken seriously. There, under the magnificent clerestory and ceiling of the reading room, he'd worked in studied isolation, mind running over all he'd learned from the investigation.

It was whilst taking a break to ease the tensions and cramps of his back, idly leafing through his notebook, that he'd made his breakthrough.

The notebook itself was a hard covered volume of folio size. It was small enough to slip into his briefcase and to sit among the assorted paperwork without arousing any great attention from Rachel, her father, or any other prying eyes. It contained a series of jottings, a collection of random thoughts awaiting a link, a connection. He carried it with him everywhere. Since the shooting, he'd added to it most days. No matter how obscure the thought process, how crazy the idea, he'd jot it down. It was part fact, part speculative story. It contained all he knew of Bella, Claverley, Lehrer, Van Ralt, Dronkers, and Solomon. It detailed all he'd discovered from the Romany, from Webster and Willetts, and the mysterious Texan. All that he knew, or might possibly speculate of everyone involved in this affair.

Ideas. Theories. Hypotheses.

Consulted. Considered. Fantasised.

Day by day, he'd added to the pool of his knowledge: bit-by-bit; piece-by-piece.

Thoughts. Feelings. Possibilities.

He'd recalled as much as he could of what had happened: rumour; hearsay; gossip; fact. He'd taken advantage of his newfound freedom from surveillance to contact those he thought might yet know something more of these events, some minor fact overlooked. He'd returned to the gypsies and to Mossop's wife. He'd spoken with Webster and to Willetts, and through him accessed his unrivalled connections of drivers, porters, clerks and shopkeepers. Those who passed unnoticed in the world but who let nothing pass unobserved. Comings and goings.

In his notebook, pencil lines were drawn around details. Hypotheses written, then scribbled out. Connecting lines drawn, re-drawn again and again until they finally converged, the one place where all connected.

One place. One event. One motive.

It made sense. *Terrifying sense.*

Tarpeia. A betrayal. A woman sacrificed because of her betrayal. Claverley's role making sense, as did his death. Floode, her words sifted: the things she'd said at the end when she thought the truth made no difference. It all made sense.

The Texan. Why Bella sought the Americans. Why she had to die. It all made sense.

It had come together through idle recall. The most transient of thoughts. The night at the cinema with Rachel. *For Whom the Bell Tolls.* The walk home, the talk of Spain. The truth of war shown in Hollywood films. He'd told her than that the newsreels couldn't capture it. *Not even close* he'd said. *Even the lengthy Pathe news features about defining moments of the war. Dunkirk, Pearl Harbour, Tobruk.* They could never show what it was really like, *bad for morale.*

He'd drawn in the last connecting line. Seeing there was nothing to scribble out, nothing left behind, nothing ignored or missed that might cancel the truth he'd found.

It all made sense.

Bella had a child, something they had known from the start. *Was it Dronkers child?* He had no idea, though the timescales might fit. *Maybe it was the reason they stayed close even after their separation.* Whatever, she was a mother, and he'd forgotten that fact, lost sight of it. Never really considered it. Never thinking of what drives a mother. Rachel knew. She'd told him so many times what she herself wanted, what she dreamt of: *Security. Sanctuary from the war for her and her child. A better life.*

What would Bella have done for such a chance?

After separating from Dronkers what options did she have, a young Romany woman with a child, a woman who'd forsaken her community? She was as much an outcast from Romany society as she was to the outside world.

Where would she have gone, what would she have done - *whore herself?* Webster suggested she had a deformity to her jaw and teeth, so perhaps that was a path denied her. Her worth lay elsewhere, lay as Lehrer had told them in her skills as a fortune-teller. Her powers. She'd turned to fortune-telling, to the circus.

A woman in her position, a Romany with a small child in central Europe at a time of chaos, sought the protection of powerful men. Her fortune telling, the promise of foretelling good military fortune had meant it was possible for her to become connected with such men. She'd met Hess for certain, a man known to believe in the paranormal. A man said by some to be as obsessed with arcane mythologies as Hitler.

He wondered how difficult it would have been for her to foretell for Hess that the assembling might of German military force she'd witnessed in her travels across Germany would sweep all before it. Especially when her journeys with the circus across Europe would mean she'd also witnessed the ill-preparedness of other nations to prevent it. She would have predicted triumph after triumph. *And lo, they came to pass!*

She would have advanced. Belief in the good omen of her powers meant she would have been entrusted with the deepest secrets of powerful men seeking confirmation that their battle plans might be auspiciously received. Plans for Poland. Plans for Czechoslovakia. Plans for France. Plans for the conquest of Russia enshrined in *Operation Barbarossa*.

She'd been sent to England because they trusted her. She had proven herself. Trained her, equipped her. She was the link between Claverley's vital intelligence and the route to Berlin. She knew everything they knew. More than they knew. She had told the fortunes of the High command. She had cast runes for their plans. She knew better than anyone the significance of what she transmitted.

In that way, she had come into possession of the biggest secret of all. *Pearl Harbour.*

He could only imagine how she'd learned of it. A confidence? An overheard conversation? A consultation? What she'd known beyond any doubt at all was that the Americans would reward her for such a secret. Money. Citizenship. A new life for her and her child.

Security. Sanctuary from the war for her and for her child. A better life.

Deep in the espionage cell, she'd have waited. At the first opportunity she'd gone to London, contacted the Americans. It

HOLLOW

was where the report the Texan spoke of had originated: a woman with a secret, a report alerting someone in Washington.

It was a hypothesis missing one vital element. The edifice he'd mapped out crumbled in the face of the one fact he'd yet to reconcile.

Why had SIS ordered Claverley to kill her?

Why did SIS want all record her presence and that of the cell erased?

That answer, once inserted it into his hypothesis, was too terrible to contemplate.

It was an answer that horrified him because he knew it to be true.

The only truth making it all fit.

30

'You knew.'

Pidgeon looks him in the eyes offering nothing by way of reply.

Porter presses on. 'She came here first. Not to the Americans. To you. To SIS. Later there no doubt came a point where despite your reassurances, she realised you had no intention of doing anything. That you'd decided to let it happen. That you had no intention of informing the Americans. You knew the where, the when, and the how of the attack. But you wanted *Pearl Harbour*. Wanted it because an attack on America was the one thing guaranteed to bring them into the war. You needed that attack to happen because despite all of his urgings and fine words all *Winnie* had from Roosevelt were the empty promises of a lame-duck President unable to lead his nation into a fight they wanted no part of.'

Pidgeon sits mute. No outrage, no indignant response.

Porter pushes forward. 'She realised that with your silence, her chance for security was ebbing away. There was a deadline beyond which what she had would be worthless, after the fact.' *Sanctuary. Sanctuary from the war for her and her child. A better life.* 'She couldn't let that happen. She was a mother. She contacted

370

the Americans herself, demanding a meeting. You knew it would ruin everything. No shockingly unexpected Japanese attack outraging American sensibilities meant they might remain neutral. There would be no allies. No troops. No aircraft. And all the time the chance of a German invasion here was multiplying. That's why you had Claverley frame her as the traitor. You needed her silenced. Two birds with one stone. *Pearl Harbour* happens and you embed your agent deep in that cell. She was *Tarpeia.*'

Pidgeon smiles. 'Quite a tale. A gypsy girl! A fortune–teller, no less. A young woman possessing the date and place of the Japanese attack on America!' He snorts, spittle forming at the edge of his mouth. 'She must have been a very powerful mystic indeed.' He looks to Solomon before inclining his head in the direction of Porter. 'Perhaps Detective Porter's spent a little too long in the company of his Professor Murray."

Porter points a finger, indicating the file on Pidgeon's desk. 'It's no fairy tale. It's the truth. But you're right, I don't know how she obtained that information, but I know that she did. She had that intelligence, her secret, and she was going to exchange it for a future for herself and her child.'

He's aware of movement behind him. The unknown man, sitting in silence since his entrance, was getting up. Pidgeon sat upright, looking beyond Porter. Porter follows Pidgeon's eyes, tracking there the path of the figure walking across the room to the window.

Porter turns his head.

The man is tall, elegant of movement, dressed in a dark charcoal grey suit. His thick black hair is brilliantined and swept back, a man aware of the impact of detail. He stands at the open window gazing down to the street before turning his attention back to the silent room. He looks from Pidgeon to Solomon and nods; a decision made. There is no doubt who controls the meeting. When he speaks, the tone of his voice is of someone used to others listening when he spoke.

'Thank you Colonel,' he states.

Pidgeon rises, hesitating for a heartbeat, the sense of irritation evident in the manner of his gathering up of his cap and gloves. He stares hard at Porter before turning to the stranger, nodding, and leaving the room.

With Pidgeon gone, the stranger moves across to occupy the desk. 'It would appear you're in the mood for storytelling, Detective. In which case, allow me put another tale to you. One similar to your own, but one told from a very different perspective.' He pauses; seeming to consider the point he wishes to make, assessing the ground, the way forward. He sits in the chair vacated by Pidgeon, an action placing him directly opposite Porter. He extends his arms in front of his chest, palm upwards as a gesture of openness. 'The Wolf's version, if you will, of your own tale of Red Riding Hood.'

'And you're the Wolf, I assume, Mr…?'

'Smith. Call me Smith.'

'Smith. And your part in this?'

'Let's say I represent wider interests. Those who seek closure of this unofficial and frankly unhelpful investigation of yours.'

'Is the intention to silence me, or to act on what I've discovered?'

Smith smiles. 'All in good time, eh? Let's see how we go, shall we? See how you feel about it all after you've listened to my story.'

'Do I have a choice?'

'You've always had a choice, Detective.'

The man called Smith sits upright, hands withdrawn to rest on the edge of the desk. He addresses Porter, but as he speaks his eyes drift beyond the desk, beyond the room. 'The summer of 1940. This country stands alone. We have no allies. The Luftwaffe is bombing the strength out of the nation. We are weak, an invasion seems imminent. However, we have an intelligence service that is the best in the world, one with considerable connection to its sister agencies in America. Connections and influence we hope will persuade the people of that great nation of the necessity of their joining the fight against the great evil of Fascism.' He glances back to Porter. 'We had been making American intelligence, their OSS, aware of the ambitions of the Japanese for some time. By the summer of 1940, with our help, they'd broken the Japanese codes and developed a technology of cypher decryption machinery which meant they could go on breaking them. The highest code broken was designated *Purple*, the code used for the most secret level of Japanese diplomatic and military messages. Despite what OSS discovered, the American top brass refused to take the threat seriously. Call it indifference, isolationism, apathy. Their neutrality laws meant they were staying at home, happy for *Lend Lease* but, beyond that, nothing.'

He pauses to snort at such naivety. A shake of the head. 'But we had friends. Some in OSS were especially helpful. They sent us one of their *Purple* machines, ironically the one intended for the base at Pearl Harbour. We'd also had success of our own. A group of boffins at Bletchley had broken German cyphers and in December 41 they broke something special. The top-secret cypher code use for high-grade Nazi communications. A cryptographic machine called *Enigma*. We'd got our hands on a machine smuggled out by Polish resistance, and the boys at Bletchley broke the cypher. The combined intelligence from *Enigma* and *Purple* provides unprecedented knowledge of German and Japanese intentions.'

He looks out across the room to the darkening sky. He is there, back in the dilemma of Forty-one. 'But we had to be careful how we used it. If we started to act too accurately on the intelligence we gathered we risked Berlin or Tokyo latching on to what we'd done. Even most of our own high-ranking military commanders were kept in the dark,' he grunts. 'And most still are. They're told the intelligence we give them comes from a deep cover asset in Berlin. We dubbed him *Boniface*.' He fixes

Porter with a cold look. 'Talk of this outside this room will see you summarily shot for treason.'

'I don't see where this is leading,' Porter responds.

'Patience, Detective. Patience. How long have you been looking for answers to this little riddle of who put your Bella in that tree?' The man known as Smith smiles, lips a narrow slit like a scar slashed across the face. 'This is a story. A story must be allowed to run its full measure if it is to be appreciated, if it is to be properly understood.'

Porter sits still, listening.

Smith continues. 'You see, we were sitting on an intelligence trove the like of which the world had never known. It was from it that we learned of *Operation Lina*. German agents sent to prepare the way for invasion.' He chuckles. 'Most were so useless we were able to round them up almost as soon as they parachuted in. Appalling accents, lousy local knowledge. They stood out like sore thumbs. But the *Abwehr* ring you stumbled across was different.' He pauses for the words to sink in. 'We knew they were here. We'd captured an agent in August Forty-one in Cambridgeshire. The poor chap had parachuted right into the laps of the local Home Guard! He was more than co-operative. He told us he was to be followed by others. He mentioned a woman, Clarabella. Seemed he knew her very well indeed. Her reputation. He said members of this group were to be high level, well connected. We waited, but there was no further word of any such sighting. It was then that we had a stroke of luck. Mossop, by then calling himself Claverley, has a chance meeting with Van Ralt and is subsequently recruited. As you suggest, Claverley was always one of ours, a watcher tasked with finding Nazi sympathisers and assessing the level of threat they posed. To begin with, we had little idea of the extent of the cell that recruited him, but when in a report he mentions the name Clarabella we knew we were on to something big. We knew that whatever we fed them with would be believed to be credible and acted on. So, we played our long game. We used

Claverley as the conduit for the intelligence we wanted them to have.'

He looks Porter in the eyes, holding him as his story moves to its climax. 'Then, November of forty-one, we began to pick up intelligence about an attack on Pearl Harbour.' He sits forward. 'You have to appreciate that though *Purple* was useful in understanding Yamamoto's intentions, it was only when it was linked to the *Enigma* intelligence that our analysts were able to truly understand the full picture of what was being planned.' he waves a hand. 'But even with just *Purple*, the American's had sufficient warning of an attack on Pearl to have prepared for it. We saw it. The American's didn't.'

'There's seeing and there's knowing,' Porter observes.

'Accepted. We had convincing intelligence that Pearl was the target. That the weekend of 6th - 7th December would be the probable attack date. From *Purple* we knew that the breaking off of negotiations by the Japanese ambassador was to be the trigger for the attack.'

'And Bella knew this.'

Smith steeples his fingers. 'She read the *Enigma* traffic. The only one in the ring outside of their analyst able to do so. Claverley discovered she'd received *Enigma* training in Berlin. She and this Lehrer, because of the unique nature of their locations, were the only two in the group with access to an *Enigma* machine. You see, the *Abwehr Enigma* kit is pretty portable.' Smith gestures, hands forming a squared off shape on the desktop as if patting butter. 'It's a wooden suitcase affair a little bigger than your average typewriter. Even so, it's too big to use easily behind enemy lines. On top of that fact, despite all their layers of impenetrable cyphers and codes, they were afraid of one being captured. But, with Romany caravans the risk of an agent lugging it around from place to place and being stopped and searched disappears.'

Smith sits back, fingers to lips. 'And she was good. She knew there was a mole. No doubt through looking at what she was sending, she'd realised our ruse. Right away she suspected Claverley to be a double-agent. She confronted him and told him what she knew. But rather than expose him to the others, she offered to hand herself over. Said she had valuable intelligence that would make her of great use to us.'

'She told him about the attack on Pearl,' Porter states.

Smith nods. 'There's an *Abwher* agent in America. Dusko Popov. He's one of ours, part of what we call the XX group - XX for double-cross. The branch runs German agents that have been turned. He was sent with the specific intention to gain intelligence to pass to the Japanese about Pearl Harbour. His intelligence was transmitted via Atlantic U-Boat patrols to Bella's machine for transmission on to Berlin. From there it was sent to Tokyo. She had access to Popov's intelligence. On top of that, through Berlin, she had access to JN-25 - the highest level naval code for the Japanese fleet. A code we'd broken a year or so previously.'

Porter interrupts him. 'But this intelligence she wanted to trade, she didn't know SIS was already in possession of it. That what she offered was of no value to you. But her possession of it, what she might do with it, did. You had to deny it to the Americans. You needed them in the war. You had to prevent her going to them and telling them what she had.'

'Deny is strong.' Smith counters. 'It's not as if it wasn't available. They had *Purple* but ignored it. They had their own men in Singapore but didn't think it important enough to train them to decode the traffic. We told Hoover about Popov, and the FBI did nothing.' He spreads his arms wide in wonder. 'But yes, we watched her. We knew that at some point she'd get frustrated with our delaying tactics, so we kept as close an eye on her as we could.' He sighs. 'We lost her. Claverley slipped up. We were too late to stop her contacting the Embassy.' He looks across at Solomon who furrowing his brow, averts his eyes. Porter wonders about the moment of that news being given. How it had been received. The anxiety it would have caused for those in charge of that part of the operation.

Smith continues, the sense he is warming to the telling. After all, how many people could he discuss this with other than the handful of those complicit in its execution. 'On 2nd December, Singapore Station decoded a message from Yamamoto saying: *Climb Mount Niitaka 1208*. It was the signal for the attack. It gave the date – 8th December in Tokyo, which of course, with the datelines, was 7th December in Pearl. The Japanese ambassador was to break off negotiations on the Sixth but to only communicate the declaration of war on the 7th at 13:00 to coincide with the aftermath of the attack. Bella saw that traffic.'

Smith pauses. Porter is uncertain if it's to gather his thoughts or to reflect on the decisions that had flowed from that knowledge. 'She had the date. She knew time was running out, but she still trusted Claverley. She told him she couldn't wait any longer. She told him she'd contacted the Americans. There was to be a meeting. That with what she had they'd give her everything she wanted. She had the target and the date. She asked him to join her, drive her to London. They'd be rich.'

Porter stares ahead. His mind races with it all. 'Five days,' he finally says. "For five days you knew about Pearl.' He sits motionless. Despite already guessing what had occurred, he is stunned at the enormity of the betrayal. '*Tarpeia*. You had her killed. She came expecting your gold, and you gave her your shields.'

Smith shrugs 'Her friends killed her. Her fellow agents. Her ex-husband and Van Ralt.'

'And Claverley.'

Smith turns to Solomon who'd remained in silence, listening to a story he obviously knows well. Taking his cue, when he speaks he states the matter flatly. 'Claverley watched. Claverley wasn't trained for that sort of thing. We'd stressed to him that her body couldn't be found. It would be too suspicious for any curious American from the embassy. He was told to leave it at the site of an air raid, make it seem like a chance happening. Wrong place, wrong time. But Dronkers jumped the gun. He killed her in the car on the way into town. He'd had the idea of the wood and gypsy curses! Maybe he thought it ironic, given her supposed mystic powers. Claverley…he was unprepared. He panicked. He helped dump the body in that damned tree.'

'And then you waited for *Pearl Harbour* to happen.'

Smith frowns. 'The Americans had everything they needed to see it coming. Everything from *Enigma* and *Purple* has to be weighed: the risk that any action might reveal that we've broken their most secure of cyphers. By keeping *Enigma* a secret, we're shortening the war, reducing the loss of life. To reveal what we knew of the attack on Pearl Harbour was deemed too high a risk.'

'And we got what we wanted. America joins the war.' Porter waves a hand at the report on Pidgeon's desk, 'And everything since that day has all been to keep that dirty little secret quiet.'

Smith stares at Porter. 'Let's not underestimate the involvement of America in this war. Pearl Harbour saved our country at a time when we ran the risk of invasion. American intervention means we'll win this war. Defeating a great evil, possibly the greatest evil of our times. The Americans are our allies. We need them.'

'And the reason you carry on with this secrecy is to protect that alliance. Because God forbid they found out, then there's the very real chance they'd pull out of this war.'

Smith shakes his head. 'No. It's too late for that. They're committed. They have too much to lose. But it would sour the post-war. The *New World Order*. The coming dirtier war against the Russians and communism. We'll need them long after this war is over. They'll need us too.'

'*New World Order*? Just how high does this go? Who do you report to, Mr Smith?'

Smith smiles. Solomon shuffles uncomfortably in his chair.

'Menzies? Higher than Menzies? Churchill?' Porter persists.

'They must have known. You wouldn't - you couldn't - make such a decision without their knowledge.'

Smith shrugs. 'The war,' he offers.

Porter took in the man opposite, those he represented: the men not in this room, the wall of complicit silence. They'd sent Smith to tell him what they'd done, expecting what? *Acceptance? Complicity in their crimes?* Porter snorts. 'They won't stop. The Americans, they won't stop. At the circus that night, it was one of their agents who shot Floode. They know there's an SIS operation, they just aren't sure what it is. They won't let this go. It will come out. It's inevitable.'

'Possibly,' Smith nods acceptance. 'But we have friends in Washington.' He sits forward, hands splayed open. 'You asked how high this goes. High enough. Here and in Washington.'

'What if I go to the Americans? The embassy. Gave them everything.'

Smith smiles once more. 'As I say, we have friends there, powerful friends.' He scoffs. 'But even without that, just consider for a moment what you're advocating. One look at your medical history exposes you as what? Delusional? Obsessive? A man of paranoia? A fantasist? What would you do? Show them your report, your *findings*? And what evidence do you actually have? Your witnesses are dead. All you have is an unidentified skeleton removed from a tree. You're the man who chases after witches.'

'Someone will believe me. The press.'

'The press? The press have their story. You gave them the dead gypsy, an official report signed by yourself, remember? You were also the one who gave them the story of the black-market shooting at the circus. Do you think your superiors, having assumed credit for that operation, will support you in any dissenting report? You have nothing. If you did, you'd have taken it to them, you'd be talking to Inspector Williams, not us.' He shakes his head in dismissal. 'And, of course, you have to think of your other record; your politics. You went to Spain and fought alongside the communists. Once this war is over, who do you think the enemy will be then? There will be no power in Germany or France to buttress the West. This conflict will ravage them just as it did after the Great War, worse. It will be us, this tiny island nation of ours and the Americans standing up to the communists. Do you see American newspaper barons publishing your theory once they know who you are? What you did? They're capitalists. They know what suits American interests in the post-war world. A strong Atlantic alliance. They'll publish nothing to disturb that.'

'What now?'

Smith smiles. 'If you're anticipating a bullet in the head, then you really are delusional.'

'Why not? I wouldn't be the first.'

'I've given you a story. And stories have to have an ending. For us, it ends best with you alive. Dead, you become the source of yet more questions - your friend, Professor Webster, for one. We don't need that. We want to focus on the war, the future, not past actions. Whatever the paucity of this evidence you've accrued, the presence of lingering doubt over Bella undermines what we're trying to do. It's a distraction, a sideshow. One that's become a drain on resources and manpower. We have a war to win. We need the trust of our American Allies. We don't need doubts hanging over our special relationship, doubts that your continuing investigation brings.'

'The Americans are suspicious.'

Smith looks to Solomon before continuing. 'An accommodation will be reached, but it would be easier without your hypothesis muddying the waters. You're a hero, Porter. Valuable propaganda. After the war we could find a use for you in the fight against the communists. The man who learned in Spain the evil reality of a brutal ideology. I've given you your truth. You have what you wanted. Let that be enough.'

'And if it's not?'

Smith exhales. 'Detective Porter, it pains me to have to point out to a man of your undoubted intellect that there are bombing raids all the time. Sadly, to convince the doubters, to avert suspicion as to any possible motive for your death, such a fate would of necessity have to include your new family.' He looks to Solomon and back to Porter. 'Rachel. Poor Tommy. Maybe Arthur, too.'

Porter looks into the eyes of the man calling himself Smith, eyes that leave no doubt as to the truth of what he says. Solomon, Floode, Smith; they were cut of the same cloth. All of them. 'I have one question left.' Porter says. 'Who decided? Who decided about Pearl Harbour? About Bella. About Claverley, and all the rest? Who sent you here? Who decided to tell me? Was it *Winnie*?'

The man calling himself Smith smiles one last time. 'If I were to tell you that, Detective Porter, then I really would have to kill you.'

31

The story had been a shock. Not so much a headline, more a by-line. The story of a dreadful explosion. An unexploded device dropped some time previously going off in a relatively uninhabited part of the city.

There had been one death.

An American officer on attachment as military advisor to the American embassy. His fellow officers and friends had no idea why the Texan had been there. A tragic end, the story said. *A waste of a life dedicated to serving his country*. An attaché was quoted in the report. The attaché, Avery, spoke highly of the man. He told reporters *He would go home like many of his fellow, fallen Americans; a hero who had given his life to protect the freedom he so loved*.

The piece was accompanied by a photograph taken outside the gates of the American Embassy, flag fluttering at half-mast in the background. The caption stated the central figure was Captain Avery, describing him as the senior American military attaché and close friend of the dead officer. He was flanked either side by two British officers whom the report stated liaised closely with the American embassy: Captain Solomon and Major Pidgeon.

Smith had been clear: *we trained most of them.* There were those in OSS sympathetic to American involvement in the war, men as keen as Winnie and SIS for America to join the fight. Men knowing it was what Roosevelt wanted but had been powerless to provide.

Where did it end?

For Porter's narrative to be true, the authorisation would have come from the highest level. Menzies. And if Menzies approved it, then his master also, Victor Cavendish-Bentinck. *And beyond him? The cabinet office? Churchill?* Would *Winnie* have endorsed such an operation? He wanted to doubt it. But he'd learned the issue was not always that of actions taken, but often one of inaction. Passivity. To withhold intelligence. And, if revealed, believable deniability that blamed the inefficiency of analysts. The inertia of the chain of command.

Smith had been clear. He had no reason to lie. The intelligence for the attack on Pearl was always there and the Americans had access to it. Had OSS missed it? Was Roosevelt left in the dark, poorly advised by his own intelligence service, a service recruited and trained by the British? If so, could SIS be held to blame for not passing on intelligence they assumed OSS already possessed?

Did OSS know? Did those men, sharing the aims of Churchill and their counterparts in SIS, those who'd recruited and trained them, simply go along with letting Pearl Harbour happen? Was it betrayal, or mere incompetence? A callous knowing act or an error of judgement, the misreading of complex situations?

And wouldn't those in OSS have sought approval from their own masters in Washington, and they, in turn, from theirs? Did Roosevelt know? Wasn't the attack on Pearl the lever he'd sought? The means by which he might prise his fellow Americans to action? Did Roosevelt and *Winnie* conspire together? Was *Tarpeia* their plan.

Porter was exhausted by it all. There was no end, in all likelihood no definitive truth. At least, none he might ever find proof of.

He had a truth of sorts, but it was one he could never reveal. He could not sacrifice Rachel and Tommy, Willetts or Webster in the hope someone might believe him, find someone with the power to do something. Smith was right, he'd no idea where it ended, how high he would have to go to find those untainted by *Tarpeia*. More than that, he sought among those someone who might be willing to risk the future of the war and the post-war alliance for the sake of an unclaimed and long-dead gypsy.

His decision was almost ordained by one final fact; Bella's remains had disappeared.

Webster had written a letter to him some days after the meeting with Smith. The skeleton stored at the university had vanished. Student *high-jinks*, the Dean had judged. *Medical students and their practical jokes – more than likely turn up in one their beds in a week or so.* It hadn't, and he doubted it ever would. The tree too had been chopped down. According to the estate manager it had been ruined when the body had been removed. *Had to take it down or risk it rotting away, falling down and killing any of them ghoulish sightseers.*

There was nothing left. Not a thing to indicate all that had happened. All he could do now was find a way to keep the desire to solve the mystery alive. Keep Bella in the memory.

He looks out from where he squats at the base of a brick obelisk. It is over eighty feet high from plinth to tip and around two hundred years old. From here, on the crest of Wychburn Hill on Lord Cobham's estate, he can look out across much of the county. He can see the hills of Malvern, and somewhere in its lee, the American military base and the SIS radar station. He can see Hagley and the woods where it had all begun.

He prises open the lid of the paint tin. It had been difficult carrying it up here. Willetts stood by the car, parked in the darkness of a nearby lane as close as he could get to the hill.

He'd told Rachel he was lending the paint and brushes to someone he'd met on his walks in the woods, a man with a garden wall to paint. She hadn't enquired further. Their conversations had long since been functional rather than propelled by any interest in what the other was actually doing or thinking.

He picks up the large paintbrush, dipping it into the whitewash.

He swills it around, stirring the watery base to blend with the pigment. With the mix just right, he loads a large paintbrush. Dripping as he paints, he forms the letters on the wall.

who put Bella in the wych-elm?

He would keep painting this question.

Every time it seemed she might be forgotten, he would remind them.

Year after year.

Remind them he was here.

Remind them of what they had done.

Remind them that at some point, even if years from now, justice would catch up with the truth. Until that time he would paint the question wherever he could, whenever he could. He would keep faith.

Someday it would be answered.

Someday Bella would find her rest.

Someday he might too.

AFTERWORD

Though based on the discovery of the skeleton in a tree in Hagley wood in spring of 1943, this book is a work of fiction. Despite access to the police files of the enquiry, for the most part names, characters, places, and incidents are products of the author's imagination or have been used fictitiously. The actions and motives of historic individuals presented in the story are fictitious. Beyond those individuals, resemblance to actual persons, living or dead, events or locales is entirely coincidental

It is a case that has many myths and theories woven around its central core – that at some point in the period of autumn 1941 a young woman was brutally murdered and her still warm corpse interred inside the hollow of a tree.

It is difficult to imagine the problems faced by the detectives involved in the initial police investigation. Surrounded as we are by high-tech devices for carbon dating, digital equipment picking up minute traces of DNA, the prevalence of video cameras on our streets and our ability to cross-reference personal information making the tracing of individuals so easy. It is too easy to feel that the solving of a crime is merely the push of a button away. At the time of the investigation - mid-April 1943 - Britain was in the midst of a ferocious modern war and fighting for survival. The Blitz, the nightly bombing raids on civilian populations, was an almost unheard of development. For the first time civilians were thrust into the front-line with all efforts and energies geared towards survival let alone victory.

Police resources were thin – a force made up of officers brought out of retirement and those too old or unfit for battle. The physical resources at their disposal were if anything even more meagre. All active police intelligence was on unearthing spies, saboteurs and traitors rather than bicycle thieves or even domestic killings. *John Webster's West Midlands Forensic Science Laboratory* was in its infancy. It was the first of its kind in Britain and closely modelled on an FBI approach that itself had existed for less than ten years.

Little wonder that Webster's '*best guess*' of the period of death and internment was somewhere between 20 months to a year prior to the discovery of the body.

War meant the discovery of dead bodies and death had become almost commonplace in areas such as the West Midlands, as was the frequent disappearance of people either literally blown to pieces or families that were quickly dispersed in the wake of the destruction of their homes. People learned the pointlessness of asking questions around comings and goings. Evacuations, land girl armies, civil guard, and conscription meant it had become a society used to transience and movement with little of the data profiling that tracks us and which we now take for granted.

April 1943 was a different world. A world where myth, legend and folk-lore held a strong grip on the mind of the public. A world where violent death was always close at hand.

It was also a world suspicious of Travellers. Many of the police notes at the time refer to attempts to find and interview those they termed 'gypsy'. The contempt and suspicion of these officers is evident in the notes summing up their efforts, as is the frustration of attempts to list the many variations of the name 'Bella' of the women they spoke with, few of whom could supply much detail in the manner of their own birth and identity beyond their immediate family. Some were interviewed more than once because of such confusion, sometimes offering different variations of their name. That they travelled with little respect for the identity papers or passports required of civilians and military alike added to the inherent suspicion investigators had of such communities. The cataloguing of dead ends speaks of their exhaustion and frustration at such a task.

Fuller details of the actual case, the original investigation, and subsequent theories and ideas are available as an e-book *Who Put Bella in the Wych-Elm: A Resume* from my website:

By subscribing to my email list, the download is free.

ACKNOWLEDGMENTS

Grateful thanks to the staff of the Worcester Hive for their help in obtaining my access to the recently released police files.

To my Beta readers:

Jo Pardoe, Nick Rainsford, Al Pardoe, Howard Parr, Huw Morgan, Vikki Allison, Jan Croft and in particular my brother, Derek Rainsford for the assiduous fact checking that kept me accurate and true re locations and technical details of the era and the experience of those who lived through it. Many a good save was made!

To all the readers who bought *All the Dead Men Lie* and offered the reviews that kept me believing and writing.

Grateful thanks to Joseph, Stefan and James at Spiffing for the cover art, the website design and their own words of encouragement that there exists a world of publishing outside the gatekeepers that are the major publishing houses.

ABOUT THE AUTHOR

"For me, crime writing offers the opportunity to create compelling narratives that draw the audience in whilst engaging them with wider ideas beyond just the consideration of 'cops and robbers' or even 'right and wrong'. The crime genre provides the possibility to consider issues I feel strongly about, issues arising from my own inner city roots and personal experience."

Born in Birmingham, a *'child of the sixties'*, part of that generation of working class kids first encouraged to see continuing in education as a real option. Teaching for forty years in deprived areas of a major city shaping a view of lives blighted by social ills. More importantly, offering insight into the lives of those who each day overcome circumstances that would defeat and overwhelm most of us.

Now living in rural North Yorkshire and writing full time my writing interest focuses on untold stories and unheard voices.

Hollow: Who Put Bella in the Which-Elm continues the concerns of 'ordinary' people placed in situations calling upon them to make moral choices that challenge their beliefs and certainties. Bella's story is the most dramatic of unheard voices, a woman silenced not only by her killer or killers but by the continuing failure of mainstream society to ensure the justice that ought to have been expected in the civilised and caring society that the war was fought to protect.

facebook.com/barryrainsfordauthor
x.com/BarryRainsford
instagram.com/barryrainsford

ALSO BY BARRY N RAINSFORD

All the Dead Men Lie

October 1984. After six months the miners' strike is at its fiercest. Everyday brings yet further hostile confrontation between police and pickets at collieries across the country. In the aftermath of one such incident a picket is found brutally beaten to death.

With 600 hundred suspects, hundreds of them fellow officers, the challenge to Detective Inspector Peter Kalus is difficult enough. That the outcome of the investigation is seen as a political cause for both the supporters of the strike and those who oppose it only adds to the pressure for a rapid solution.

Kalus soon discovers that the victim was much more than a simple miner. He was a man with enemies, any one of whom profited from his death. As the plot unfolds Kalus – a man fighting his own personal and professional demons – is lead further and further into a complex nightmare of political conspiracies, betrayals and murder. It becomes evident that others will also die unless Kalus can unravel the truth of the murdered picket; a truth that if revealed could bring down the Thatcher government and change the face of British politics forever.

Printed in Great Britain
by Amazon

60521904R00231